D1624933

Miss Bingley Requests

Also available by Judy McCrosky

Miss Bingley
Requests

A Novel

JUDY MCCROSKY

CROOKED
LANE

NEW YORK

Copyright © 2018 by Judy McCrosky

Published in the United States by Crooked Lane Books, an imprint of The Quick Brown Fox & Company LLC.

Crooked Lane Books and its logo are trademarks of The Quick Brown Fox & Company LLC.

Library of Congress Catalog-in-Publication data available upon request.

ISBN (hardcover): 978-1-68331-837-8
ISBN (ePub): 978-1-68331-838-5
ISBN (ePDF): 978-1-68331-839-2

Cover design by Zoe Foster
Book design by Jennifer Canzone

Printed in the United States.

www.crookedlanebooks.com

Crooked Lane Books
34 West 27th St., 10th Floor
New York, NY 10001

First Hardcover Edition: November 2018
Originally published in trade paperback in Great Britain by Accent Press, November 2016

10 9 8 7 6 5 4 3 2 1

To Jane Austen, who so vividly welcomes us into her world and who created the characters that bring joy to so many. And to all who love Austen's works, and thus experience that joy.

Acknowledgments

〜

Thank you to my sister, Debby Berlyne, and to my friends Sue Churchman, Sandy Cook, and Ken Sailor, who helped me guide Caroline's journey.

Chapter One

London, England, 1811

'Miss Bingley requests the honour of your presence . . .'

No, that would not do. Caroline Bingley crumpled the delicately scented paper in her hand. Asking for an honour implied that the guests were above the hosts, and that was not the situation. Not at all.

'Miss Bingley requests the pleasure of your presence.' She wrote slowly, her long fingers guiding the quill so that it formed each curve, each line, without spattering a single drop of ink. There, that was much better.

'Caroline, who are you writing to?' Louisa Hurst, Caroline's sister, bustled into the morning room, patting her hair into place. Louisa always rose from sleep later than Caroline did, and her maid spent longer on Louisa's reddish tresses than did Genney with Caroline's dark curls.

Caroline slid her hand to cover her paper. 'Is Mr Hurst still abed?'

'Of course.' Louisa bent over Caroline's shoulder. 'What are you up to? I simply must know.'

Caroline sighed, but moved her hand aside. The sisters rarely kept secrets from each other. And Louisa was mistress of a country estate, Staunton, which belonged to Mr Hurst's family. 'Do not think me foolish, but I am thinking ahead to the first ball we hold at Charles' new estate.'

'Estate?' Louisa walked into the breakfast room and Caroline followed her. 'Has Charles made his decision, then?'

Caroline joined her sister at the sideboard and allowed the footman, standing ready, to place a piece of toast on her plate. He did so quietly, and without dropping so much as a crumb on her person. Mr Darcy's servants were always impeccably trained.

'Mr Darcy,' Caroline said, 'rode out with him this morning to visit one he thought might be suitable.'

Louisa sniffed and took her time deciding between baked ham and sausage rounds marinated in rosemary. Caroline felt a moment's irritation. Fashionable breakfasts did not include meat this season, but Mr Hurst expected it at every meal and Mr Darcy, ever the accommodating host, met this need. Louisa finally selected a poached egg instead, sat across from Caroline and held out her cup without looking, knowing the servant would fill it with tea, and add just the amount of cream she liked.

Caroline scraped butter across her toast, giving Louisa a moment, knowing her sister was of two minds about Charles acquiring a country estate. On the one hand, it suited Louisa very well to have been the first in the family to profit from the advantages that came with wealth. Plus, Mr Hurst had inherited his money, while the Bingley family's had come, shamefully, from trade. Still, her brother's estate would be larger than Mr Hurst's.

'So he has decided to take a country estate before he purchases a London townhouse?' Louisa pretended great interest in her tea as she stirred it, but Caroline knew what was important to her sister. She felt a moment's sympathy for Louisa's loss of stature that would come with Charles's estate, but only a moment's. Caroline had no plans at all for her brother to take a house in town. If he did, there would be no reason for Charles, or his sisters, to be guests of Mr Darcy. Once Charles had his estate, it would be no threat to Caroline. She would be his hostess there, but once she married Mr Darcy, she would be the mistress of the largest and finest estate of any one she knew: Pemberley.

Mrs Darcy. Her tongue shaped the words even though she kept them silently inside her head. Mrs Darcy, Mistress of Pemberley. She would take precedence over everyone then.

She fidgeted with her teaspoon, placing it in her cup, on the saucer, back in the cup, trying each time to make as little sound as possible. It would be some time before Charles and Mr Darcy returned. The day stretched endlessly before her.

There were always calls to be returned. Naturally, once Mr Darcy and his guests arrived in London, everyone who was anyone had left their card. Caroline picked up her spoon and held it before her face, examining her image. How very ill she looked. Her eyes were small and beady, her cheeks sunken, her chin huge, spreading over the spoon's tip as if it was ready to drip from the silver along with the last drops of milky tea. No, making calls held no appeal, even after she put the spoon back in the cup and rose, ostensibly to take another piece of toast, but really to check her image in the mirror that hung above the mantel. How silly of her to be concerned about her image in a spoon, when she looked as lovely as always. Her features were the current fashion, classical in their symmetry, with just enough height to her cheekbones and curve to her upper lip to make an observer realise she was a woman who, while being utterly beautiful, was also intriguing, unlike the vapid beauty of so many of today's fashionable young women.

If she wasn't making calls today, did she want to be in? No, definitely not. Being available to receive calls might make her seem too eager to become a part of society; far better to be not at home. There was always needlework to do, and practice on the pianoforte. Or perhaps she could spend time in the library, learning more about Mr Darcy's preferences from his choice of volumes. She might even find something to read herself, or to at least have close at hand once Mr Darcy returned.

Caroline hadn't done much reading since completing her formal education. There was no need for a woman as accomplished as she to learn anything new. To do so would be to gild the lily. She smiled knowingly at her reflection.

She had opened a book, though, just yesterday. Mr Darcy was in the drawing room, reading while the others played at cards. She'd wandered over to sit by him and when he rose to go to his writing table, she'd picked up his book with a show of great interest. It was a collection of poetry by Lord Byron.

Caroline had giggled on seeing this, and Mr Darcy looked up sharply. 'Does my choice of reading material amuse you, Miss Bingley?'

'Not at all.' She opened the book. 'Lord Byron is a great favourite of mine. He is a trifle risqué though, would you not agree, Mr Darcy?'

Mr Darcy only frowned, so she quickly added, 'Of course, anything written by a member of British nobility must be considered to be among the finest writings this country has ever produced.'

'I find it interesting,' Mr Darcy said, and she looked up to smile at their obvious meeting of minds, when he added, 'that you would think so. Who else do you consider to be one of our finest writers?'

'Why, Mr William Shakespeare, of course,' she said.

'Of course,' he said dryly. 'And who among those writers still living do you particularly admire?'

Caroline's mind went blank, and so she quickly looked down at the book in her lap, opened it at random, and pretended to be deeply engrossed in the poem on the page.

Now, at breakfast, she let her gaze drift from her reflection and sat down again across from her sister, her mind still on the poem. It had been about love. Caroline had never thought much about love. It had not been a part of her parents' marriage, or of her grandparents'. Focusing on Louisa now, though, she wondered, and her mouth opened and spoke words before her mind knew what she would say.

'Louisa, are you in love with Mr Hurst?'

Louisa stared at her. 'Caroline, have you gone quite mad?'

Caroline felt mortified, but at the same time a small flame of something, perhaps part of what made her such an intriguing creature, rose up in her head. 'Forgive me if I shock you, but surely such a topic is not inappropriate between two sisters as close as we are. And there is no one else around to hear our conversation.' The servants didn't count, of course.

Louisa still frowned and so Caroline smiled at her, putting as much warmth into her eyes as she could. 'You, Louisa, are married, and so know more than I about the ways of the world between men and women. I seek only knowledge so that I can hope to make as good a match as you.'

Privately, Caroline did not think Mr Hurst a very good match at all. He had an estate, but not a very big one, and his family was unknown within the circles of fashionable London.

The Bingley grandparents had been merchants, and made a great fortune from the buying and selling of ships and the goods they transported, but Caroline preferred not to remember the ignominious origin of the family's wealth. Her parents at least had not worked in the stores and offices, but her father had still overseen all management of the company. Charles would be the first Bingley to be a landed gentleman.

4

Louisa, without looking down, scooped up some egg into her spoon, but as her gaze was still on Caroline, she didn't notice when the runny yolk dripped from the silver onto the tablecloth. She put the mostly empty spoon into her mouth and swallowed. 'Love Mr Hurst? I don't know,' she said finally. 'The question never arose.'

'I understand.' Caroline nodded. 'But I have a confession to make.' She laughed lightly, trying not to look at the yellow spot on the tablecloth.

Louisa's mouth dropped open and she looked even more astonished at this than she had at Caroline's earlier question about love.

'Mr Darcy enjoys poetry,' Caroline said defensively. Louisa placed her elbows on the table, one dangerously close to resting on the still-moist yellow spot. 'The poems said that when one is in love, one experiences shortness of breath and sometimes a pain in the chest.'

'I have not experienced that,' Louisa said faintly.

'Of course not.' Caroline laughed again. 'I would expect no less of you. Why, surely my sister would not stoop so low as to experience anything that could be mistaken for a common cold.'

Louisa laughed also, and suddenly there was a warmth between the two sisters, a shared moment. Caroline reached across the table and gently placed her napkin over the spilled egg so it wouldn't stain the sleeve of Louisa's green silk morning gown. Because of this warmth, she dared ask a question she had long wondered about. Covering her sister's hand with her own, she asked, 'What is it like, Louisa, between a man and a woman?'

Louisa seemed to understand why Caroline would ask such an indelicate question, or maybe she remembered the time before she was married, and had wondered the same thing. She left her hand beneath Caroline's, and sighed, looking away into a distance Caroline had no hope of seeing yet. 'It involves a number of sounds one would be more likely to hear in the vicinity of a pig barn. And Mr Hurst is very heavy, much more so than one would expect from his relatively diminutive size.'

Before Caroline could absorb this rare sharing of hidden information, Louisa pulled her hand back and stood up so quickly the footman barely had time to pull her chair back. Louisa brushed her hands down along her sides, smoothing out any wrinkles the act of sitting might have formed in her gown. 'I hope,' she said, 'that once Mr Hurst is down, he will take us on a carriage ride in the park. Would you like that, Caroline?'

Later, Caroline sat in the morning room, her needlework in her hand. She was making a cushion, with a pattern of delicately embroidered roses, but although she had been sitting long enough for the sun to shift across the room to the point where it glared off a side table, she had yet to sew a single stitch. Louisa's confidence had given her much to consider.

The poems had also mentioned a sparkle in the eyes of one who loved, and a giddy feeling in the head. While Caroline had often practised putting a sparkle in her eyes as she stood before a mirror, she had always believed any giddiness in the head was to be avoided at all costs. She thought about Mr Darcy and tried to remember if being in his presence had ever brought on shortness of breath or a pain in her chest, but could not recall any such experience. No doubt if she had felt anything similar, she would have retired to her bed with a hot water bottle at her feet.

She pictured Mr Darcy standing, as he often did, before the fireplace in the drawing room, one elbow propped on the marble shelf, one leg crossed elegantly across the other so that all his weight was on one foot. She pictured him sitting in the library in his favourite chair of wine-red leather, a book held in one hand, his long fingers gracefully spread across the binding. She pictured him riding his horse in the park, moving slowly alongside the barouche in which she sat. His long spine erect, his fingers on the reins demonstrating an iron control over the beast, but also a gentle touch.

None of these images helped her imagine a circumstance in which oinks and squeals, and a question of his weight, could be imagined. She wished she'd been able to ask Louisa for more detail, but her sister's demeanour after breakfast had been distant, and it was clear Louisa had important things to do that left no time for sisterly confidences.

Caroline tossed her needlework into the wicker basket that sat beside her chair and rose to go to the library. Perhaps further perusal of poetry would provide some illumination.

*   *   *

The gentlemen returned during the evening of the following day, and they looked very pleased with themselves. Or rather, Charles beamed, his smile warming his affable features, and Mr Darcy did not frown. He stood, a little behind his friend, his gaze resting somewhere over Caroline's shoulder. She tried to watch him, without letting him see that she hoped for a smile, or at least a meeting of their gazes, but he stood apart from the others, somehow approving of what was said without being part of the conversation.

'Netherfield Park,' Charles said, 'will do me very well.'

How large an estate is it? Caroline wanted to ask, but she waited as Charles spoke enthusiastically to Mr Hurst about the grand shooting to be found on the property and the very well-situated kennels for his hunting dogs.

How many servants? Caroline wanted to ask, but Charles was talking about the local people. 'I met the squire,' he said, 'name of Sir William Lucas. Lovely fellow, very pleasant indeed.'

Oh, thought Caroline, *there are people of quality there. I should have known. Mr Darcy would never allow Charles to settle in an unsuitable area.*

'Sir William told me about some of the other families,' Charles said. 'There's a gentleman, a Mr Bennet, who lives in a house called Longbourn not more than three miles from Netherfield Park. He has five daughters, and apparently they are all great beauties.'

Caroline allowed her questions to fade away. There would be plenty of time to ask them later, and from what she'd heard from Charles and her understanding of Mr Darcy and his discerning taste, this estate would do very well. Her brother was on his way to becoming one of the fashionable set.

She let her mind drift, as Charles continued to speak, now extolling the advantages of the stables, and pictured herself, her brother's hostess, smiling and holding out a gracious hand for the gentlemen to kiss as she greeted the guests at Netherfield Park's first grand ball. Music filled her head and she saw the ladies in their colourful gowns, the latest fashions, of course, dipping and swaying as they stepped through the dance. She would, of course, be claimed for the first two dances by Sir William, and Mr Darcy would watch as she moved gracefully, swirling past him in her sky blue gown with the skirt that was wide enough to bell out as she turned, but not so wide as to be unfashionable. He'd pretend, of course, that he didn't watch her, that he cared nothing that other men clustered around her, waiting for their chance to dance with her, laughing at her witticisms, competing to bring her the choicest morsels from the supper table. The gentlemen would all be handsome, but none as handsome as Mr Darcy. He would be uninterested in dancing with anyone else, even if Mr Bennet's five daughters were all beautiful. The other women were lovely, with long necks and elegant postures, but she was the most intriguing, the most refined. Mr Darcy would watch her dance with the other men until he could no longer feign indifference. He would approach her to request the next dances; no, he'd haughtily inform the gentleman who had claimed those dances that Caroline would dance with no one but him. He'd take her hand in his, his eyes would rest warmly on her intriguing face, and . . .

Would she then experience the shortness of breath and pain in the chest that showed love? He would, of course, he'd been entranced by her beauty and wit and he'd lean close as they circled one another in the dance and say . . .

But at this point even her vivid imaginings fell short of picturing the taciturn and dignified Mr Darcy speaking words of love. She had no idea, she realised, of what a gentleman in the throes of love would say to the woman who so bewitched him.

Someone was speaking to her now, but the male voice belonged to her brother and he was definitely not speaking of love. 'Caroline, what say you of the cook? There is a woman in Meryton who is very highly spoken of, but perhaps you prefer to select someone from town.'

Caroline gave herself a mental shake. It was difficult to return from the ball and Mr Darcy's ardent attentions, but she moved her gaze to her brother. 'Charles, your little passions are one of your most endearing qualities.' Now Mr Darcy joined Louisa in staring at her in surprise, for her normal efforts in preparing her brother to be a landed gentleman included trying to tone down his enthusiasms so that he'd appear properly dignified and noble. But Mr Darcy was looking at her, and so she didn't mind allowing Charles his excitement this once. 'I will hire a cook here. Mrs Montague has one I think could be tempted to change employers if the right inducements were presented.'

Charles nodded, content as always to bow to her superior knowledge of How Things Were Done. Caroline glanced from under her lashes at Mr Darcy, but he'd moved his attention from her and stood gazing at the ceiling above everyone's heads. She wondered for a moment what he thought about when he wasn't engaged with the present company, but quickly jumped up and clapped her hands. 'I simply must have a game of cards. Mr Darcy, will you assist me in setting them out?'

He nodded and gave her a short sharp bow. 'Of course, I am pleased to offer you any assistance you require.'

Soon, you will offer me much more, she thought, and followed him to the cabinet where the playing cards were kept.

*   *   *

The date for the removal to Netherfield Park was set for three weeks hence, which would provide the time needed to hire servants and for them to prepare the house for its new master, and to purchase new clothing.

'Because, of course,' Louisa said, 'the dressmakers in an area so isolated from London cannot possibly have the understanding nor the ability to meet our needs.'

'Indeed not,' Caroline agreed. 'And we won't be able to return here for fittings. Although, maybe the local ladies in Hertfordshire are in the habit of bringing dressmakers to their area on a regular basis.' She shuddered. 'Surely they must, because how else would they become aware of the latest fashions?'

Louisa nodded, but the sisters decided that it would save much time and bother for them to simply have their new clothes made while they were still in town.

That afternoon Charles suggested an evening at the theatre to celebrate his new estate. The play was the latest thing, filled with many long soliloquies and much swordplay, protestations of love and loyalty, and some small comedic bits that satirised the well-known among London politicians and nobility. It was also overly long, but that didn't matter because everyone came to the theatre to observe who else was there, comment on their clothing and how ill they looked, and gossip about who had attended with whose wife, mistress, or husband. Long plays simply provided more time to see and be seen.

Mr Darcy's box was one of the better ones: close enough to the stage that one could watch the play but, more importantly, situated so it provided a good view into the other better boxes. Immediately across from her, Caroline saw Lady Amesbury, with her current favourite lover, the Duke of E—. Lady Amesbury! Her family was related to royalty, third, or possibly even second, cousins!

With them was someone Caroline hadn't seen before; a youngish man who wore a blue frock coat. Caroline trained her opera glasses on his person, noticing that both cut and fabric of the coat were of the highest quality. He had high cheekbones, a long aquiline nose, and a chin that, if it had only been a trifle shorter, would not have been out of place on a statue of a Greek god. She couldn't quite make out the colour of his eyes, but they were well situated, not set too deep, and shadowed only faintly by a high brow and arresting slashes of black eyebrows that were suitably masculine without being too bristly. His hair, also the dark of midnight, was a trifle overly long, and she suspected that it brushed the high collar of his coat at the back of his neck, but many young men were seeing long hair as fashionably daring, and his was not wild or unkempt.

As she watched, he leaned over to Lady Amesbury and spoke, tilting his head to indicate across the theatre at . . . Caroline. She immediately dropped her glasses into her lap, but kept her spine erect and her chin at its most elegant elevation. She tipped her head to the left, showing her best profile, and pretended to be listening to Charles and Mr Darcy discussing what Charles should do with Netherfield Park's gardens, but she kept her eye on the young man, knowing that of course he was asking Lady Amesbury about the intriguing creature who was the personal friend of Mr Darcy of Pemberley.

Lady Amesbury sent a sharp glance towards the Darcy box, and then nodded, clearly acquiescing to the young man's request. They both stood and left their box.

Caroline continued watching the Duke, now left alone, as he pulled out a voluminous handkerchief, mopped his forehead and then draped it over his face, leaning back to have a rest. On stage someone suddenly screeched and fell dramatically to the floor, but it caught Caroline's attention only for a moment before she moved her interest to another box where a very young lady, her hand clutched by an equally young man, pretended to try to pull it away as he raised it to his lips.

There came a polite cough from behind the curtain that closed off Mr Darcy's box, and Caroline turned to see Lady Amesbury, followed by the young man. His eyes immediately went to her, and so she looked away, pretending intense interest in the play.

'Stephen demanded an introduction,' Lady Amesbury said in her distinctive husky voice.

Caroline risked a glance back, and Lady Amesbury gave her a gracious smile, which surprised Caroline very much, as Lady Amesbury had never been very friendly.

'Of course,' Mr Darcy said to the request for an introduction. 'I would be honoured.'

'Mr Darcy,' Lady Amesbury said, 'may I present a recent but already dear, dear friend, Stephen Tryphon? Stephen, Mr Fitzwilliam Darcy.'

Caroline, curious enough to no longer pretend a lack of interest, turned to see the two men bow, Mr Tryphon's bow, as was correct, deeper and lasting longer than Mr Darcy's. Mr Tryphon's eyes then turned to Caroline. He was older than she'd first thought, about her own age or a little greater, and his eyes were green.

'My friends,' Mr Darcy said. 'Charles Bingley and his sisters Mrs Hurst and Miss Caroline Bingley. Mr Bingley's brother-in-law, Mr Hurst.'

Caroline didn't rise, of course, but she did incline her head as Mr Tryphon made his bow to her.

There was a momentary silence and then Charles asked the visitors how they were enjoying the play.

'Very much,' said Lady Amesbury, and entered into a discussion with Charles about the new settee and dining table she had recently acquired and how she hoped he and Mr Darcy would do her the honour of calling so they could admire them. Mr Tryphon took a step away from them and approached Caroline, pointing to the empty chair beside her. 'May I?' he asked.

She nodded in a distant fashion, and he sat, twisting to face her.

'I have seen you before,' he said, and then apologised when she leaned back and raised her chin. 'I didn't mean to be so forward. I hope you can forgive me.'

She lowered her chin a fraction and, encouraged, he continued. 'It was at Lord C—'s soiree. We sat near each other during supper, and I wanted to ask you for the honour of a dance, but we hadn't been introduced. When I recognised you tonight and learned that Lady Amesbury was acquainted with you and your party, I jumped at the chance of an introduction.'

The man was simply too forward and eager for her taste, but something about his openness flattered her, and the green fire in his eyes promised that there was more beyond this boyish façade. She granted him a smile. 'I am most embarrassed that I do not recall you, Mr Tryphon, but it is a pleasure to meet you now.'

On stage, there was much clashing of metal and the pounding of feet on the wooden floor, as two young men in hose and tunics began to fence. Caroline let her eyes be drawn to the play and as she expected, Mr Tryphon immediately spoke to draw her attention back to him.

'I can see that you appreciate the theatre, Miss Bingley. Do you also care for art?'

'I do.'

'Of course,' he said, his voice warming. 'A woman as accomplished as I can tell you are must be very talented at drawing and painting.'

She lowered her eyes, feeling warm blood add a rosy glow to her cheeks. 'You are too kind.'

'Not at all.'

She raised her eyes to his, and his smile caused her to blush again.

'Perhaps,' he said, 'you can be of assistance to me. Can you recommend a museum where I can see paintings of quality? I am but recently come to London, and do not know my way around. I do truly enjoy visiting scenes of great beauty.'

His eyes were fastened on her face, dropping to linger on her lips before a slow smile grew on his mouth as he again gazed into her eyes. His intensity imbued his words with a rather shocking forwardness, but as the words themselves were innocent, she glanced back at the stage while mentioning one or two of her favourite museums.

He thanked her, and then looked up as Lady Amesbury told him she wished to return to her box so as to enjoy the next act of the play. He stood, but then hesitated even as Lady Amesbury exited the box, clearly expecting him to follow.

'Would you,' he said to Caroline. 'No, it is too much to ask.'

'You can but ask,' she said, smiling. 'And I can but refuse your request. Surely that is too small a danger for you to fear?'

He looked at her full on and laughed. 'You are right. I could never be afraid of anything you might do or say. You are too good to wish harm on anyone.'

Mr Darcy, Caroline noticed, sent a sharp glance at Mr Tryphon.

'I was merely wondering,' he said, 'if you would be willing to show Lady Amesbury and myself around the Broughton museum tomorrow? Beauty is always best appreciated when one is in good company. Wouldn't you agree? And I know no one else who would understand beauty as well as you.'

She was shocked again, but something about his fervour intrigued her. She glanced at Mr Darcy. He was looking at the stage and not at her, but something in the set of his chin suggested he was listening to her conversation. Could he be jealous? She gave Mr Tryphon a smile much wider than she'd normally grant a man to whom she had so recently been introduced, and agreed to join him at the museum the following day.

After he left the box, hurrying after Lady Amesbury, she sat in silence, heedless of the tragic death taking place on the stage. Had she been too forward in agreeing to spend the following afternoon in the company of this stranger? Since Lady Amesbury would accompany them, visiting the museum with him would be entirely proper. It offered great potential, too, since Caroline had as yet been unsuccessful in achieving acceptance in Lady Amesbury's set, which often included members of the royal family who attended soirées and concerts given at her home.

She'd agreed because she knew Mr Darcy did not want her to spend time in the company of other men. But if she was truly honest with herself, there was more to it. It was the young man. She knew she was acting most unlike herself, but doing something unexpected made everything around her different—the colours worn by those around her; her family's murmured conversations; Mr Darcy's deep voice from behind her. She drew in a deep breath and was suddenly overwhelmed with the joy of being alive.

* * *

The following day, when Caroline was driven in Mr Darcy's carriage to the museum, she was accompanied by both of her siblings. Louisa had paid little attention, the previous evening, to the visitors, but now was curious to see this young man who had stirred Caroline's interest, and Charles wanted to spend time with his sisters. Mr Hurst had preferred to remain in the house, and Mr Darcy had pleaded a previous engagement. Caroline suspected that it might be difficult for him to see her in the company of other men, and that was why he preferred not to join the party, but he was often engaged in his study with Pemberley's steward or other important-looking gentlemen, and so he might have truly had a previous engagement.

As the carriage arrived outside the museum and Matcher got down from his box to hand the ladies out, Caroline saw Lady Amesbury and Mr Tryphon sitting on a stone bench that graced the side of the small terrace at the museum's entrance. Mr Tryphon stood to make his bow and Lady Amesbury graciously dropped her chin as Caroline and Louisa curtseyed.

Mr Tryphon, Caroline noticed, was moving forward to walk at her side when Charles stepped between them, saying, 'How good it is to see you again, Mr Tryphon. I hope you enjoyed the rest of the play last night?' Charles spoke, as he so often did, in his loud jovial way, and Caroline knew it would be rude of Mr Tryphon to offer only a short reply. Mr Tryphon would be engaged for some time with her brother, discussing the play, others that Charles had seen, and then probably the conversation would move to shooting or dogs. Caroline tucked her arm through Louisa's.

'Charming day to view beauty of the sort to be found in this building,' she said, making it clear, she hoped, that she had arrived here thinking only of art, and not of any particular person. 'Wouldn't you agree, Lady Amesbury?'

'Any day is charming when spent in the company of art and beauty.' Lady Amesbury rose from the bench, and moved to Caroline's other side. 'But you are correct, Miss Bingley; there is just the right amount of sunshine, not enough to coarsen one's face, and the right amount of wind, not enough to blow off one's bonnet.'

Caroline smiled her appreciation of this witticism. Louisa had once remarked that witticisms were funnier the richer the person saying them. Mr Darcy had lifted his eyebrow at this, and wondered aloud if everything he said was witty. Louisa had been uncertain how to respond to this, but Caroline, understanding Mr Darcy as she did, had remarked that if he wished everything he said to be witty, she would make certain to laugh every time he spoke.

Caroline's smile widened now, remembering this, and she glanced at Lady Amesbury, hoping that lady did not take offence but, to her gratification, noted that the lady nodded approvingly at her.

'I do,' Lady Amesbury said, 'so enjoy conversing with women of education and culture.'

The ladies arrived at the imposing brass-studded double doors that led into the museum. Mr Tryphon took the opportunity to step away from Charles, Caroline noticed, so he could hold open the door for her. She ignored him and swept past, her head held high, her intriguing eyes flashing aside only once, to see if he was looking at her. He was, and so she instantly looked away and spoke to Lady Amesbury.

'What would you most like to view first?'

'How kind of you to inquire,' the lady said. 'But this visit is for Stephen's edification. I've been here so many times I quite confess that I don't need to view anything, because every item in the collection is stored in my memory. Stephen,' she turned to him as he followed the ladies inside and let the door close behind himself and Charles. 'What would delight you most at this moment? Paintings or sculpture?'

He glanced at Caroline and she was sure she saw uncertainty in his eyes. Was he perhaps wondering what would most please her?

'Any and all items of beauty will immeasurably improve me at this moment,' he said. 'I leave myself totally in your experienced hands.'

Lady Amesbury smiled and turned to Caroline. 'And what aspect of art do you most enjoy?'

Caroline rarely visited a museum or gallery, and had not thought much about art since completing her education. She did paint, though, and thought of the pleasure she gained from using flowers as her subject. 'I most delight in colour,' she said. 'The brighter the better. Although,' thinking she perceived a slight frown on Lady Amesbury's countenance, 'any colour palette must blend with its surroundings and enhance the overall tone of the room in which it is displayed.'

'Quite so,' Lady Amesbury said. 'Shall we begin, then, with the Dutch masters?'

Everyone agreed Dutch paintings were the perfect beginning to an afternoon of culture, and they followed Lady Amesbury as she turned right and entered the first gallery.

Some time later, Caroline wondered if she did indeed want to join Lady Amesbury's set, if all her conversations were as dry as her discussion today of every single painting they saw. Mr Tryphon moved to stand beside her as she gazed at yet another seascape.

'You must tell me what it is in this painting that so attracts you,' he said. 'I have much to learn and dare hope that you will share some of your vastly superior knowledge.'

Caroline had been thinking that there was very little difference between one seascape and another, save, perhaps, the number of boats, but she turned to look at him, and said, 'Of all things, I most enjoy the creations of those so much more talented than myself.'

'You do paint, then?' Mr Tryphon asked. 'I am overwhelmed by your apparent bounty of talents.'

Caroline couldn't recall any other talents he would know about, but since she was very accomplished, she laughed and tapped him lightly on his arm. 'You mustn't flatter me so, sir, or I might begin to believe my accomplishments are greater than they deserve.'

'Nonsense,' he said. 'I am quite convinced your talents are very great indeed. Other than painting, what do you enjoy?'

'Music,' she answered. 'A day is not complete unless I have my time at the pianoforte.'

'Of course.' He nodded. 'I very much hope I might have the pleasure of forming an audience for you.'

Uncertain if he meant he would like to be the sole member of an audience, which would be a most impolite suggestion, or form part of an audience, which was perfectly acceptable, she said something about often having the honour of playing during the little soirées Mr Darcy hosted at his house, and changed the subject. 'And what of you, Mr Tryphon? What are your talents?'

He stopped for a moment, gazing intently at a painting that portrayed a meadow with a small child, wearing a charming dress of yellow and white, intently studying a flower. 'I dabble,' he said at last. 'There are so many fascinating endeavours that the modern gentleman can participate in. I find it difficult to settle on just one or two.'

'I understand. Charles, too, has moved from passion to passion, although his current love of shooting and the dogs that accompany him has lasted rather longer than others.' She moved on past the painting and he fell into step beside her.

'You must have many opportunities to visit institutions such as this one,' he said. 'Do you often travel to the continent?'

'Not at present,' she said, her voice a little sharper than she intended.

He seemed to perceive that he had overstepped his bounds. 'Oh no, of course you wouldn't venture out of the country now. England would not wish to risk one of its most beautiful roses.'

Caroline's head whirled. Conversing with this man was so unpredictable. She never knew if he would utter something outlandish or forward. And yet, tired as she was of viewing paintings, she was still engaged by his company. So many of town's young men were very limited in their conversation; they'd speak of carriages and boot boys and tailors, and perhaps the latest scandal. Caroline accepted this, of course. Titled and wealthy young men were permitted their limitations, and the strictures of society affected them, too, although not as much as they did women. Mr Tryphon was not as polished as other wealthy young men, but he had not uttered anything that went beyond good taste, and she realised she was enjoying herself.

He was half a head taller than her, not quite as tall as Mr Darcy, but it was still very agreeable to look up and see the warmth in his eyes as he gazed down at her. His arm brushed very near hers and there was warmth there, too, moving from his body to hers. A blush rose to her cheeks at this daring thought, and she hoped that he thought her colour came from excitement as she turned to the next painting she passed and exclaimed, 'Oh, I always so enjoy this particular work.'

'Do you indeed,' Lady Amesbury, who'd been walking just behind Caroline, with Charles and Louisa, exclaimed. 'How fascinating.'

Caroline, looking at the painting for the first time, noted it was a portrait of a family. The father stood behind his wife who was seated, the two children on either side of her. She'd never witnessed such a poorly executed portrait in all her born days. 'Observe, if you please,' she said, attempting to put a glow of enthusiasm on her countenance. *The father looks as if he suffers from dyspepsia and gout.* 'The father with his hand resting protectively on his wife's shoulder.' *The mother appears to be in agony from such close proximity to her offspring and the children look as if their clothing itches terribly and at any moment they will tear off the restrictive garments.* 'Every detail of the children's clothing is clearly portrayed.' *The father resembled a toad and the mother a pig. Surely such people were not permitted to breed.* 'And the angelic expressions on the little ones' faces; the emotions the family shares almost leap off the canvas to touch the viewer.'

'Indeed.' Lady Amesbury stood still, her eyes making Caroline feel as if they saw right inside her head. She held her breath, wondering if she had just ruined any chance she might have had of moving up in multitiered London society, when the lady added, 'I do so enjoy meeting a person of discerning taste. You must attend one of my little dinners some time. I am sure you would find the conversation most stimulating.' She glanced at Mr Tryphon, then, and Caroline was unable to read the look that passed between them. It didn't matter, though. She was to be invited to one of Lady Amesbury's dinners, among the most sought-out invitations in town.

Savouring her triumph she examined the next painting with renewed interest. Louisa and Charles came to stand beside her. 'Oh, well done,' Louisa said after glancing about to see Lady Amesbury and Mr Tryphon were on the other side of the gallery. 'I have never seen such a hideous painting.'

'Oh,' said Caroline, trying to stifle her laughter. 'I never imagined I could find anything positive to say about it. I declare, if such a work of art hung in my home, I'd never be able to enter the room without suffering from indigestion!'

The two sisters put their heads together and laughed, as Charles said, his voice bewildered, 'I thought it was a very fine artistic attempt, and that your remarks, Caroline, were very apt.'

Caroline and Louisa looked at each other and laughed even harder. Two other patrons of the museum, who stood at a little distance, turned disapproving faces their way. Quickly stifling her mirth, Caroline stepped back and gazed intently at the nearest painting. She lifted her chin and looked down her nose at the disapproving patrons, indicating her belief that it was they, and not she, who had transgressed. But although she returned her gaze to the painting, she saw nothing of it. Instead, inside her head, visions of herself and Mr Darcy becoming regular attendees at Lady Amesbury's home glowed, more detailed and colourful than any work of art this museum contained.

During the carriage ride home, Caroline delighted herself imagining how pleased Mr Darcy would be to learn she had gained him entry into Lady Amesbury's set.

Chapter Two

～

Caroline sailed into Lady Amesbury's apartments on Mr Darcy's arm. She knew she looked her best, in her gold gown with just the correct amount of décolletage. The ruffles about her hips flowed into a liquid stream of satin and lace streaming behind that showed off her tall, slim figure. No insipidity for Caroline Bingley, no, here was an accomplished woman. The emeralds she wore brought out the green flecks in her hazel eyes; emeralds were threaded through her hair, too, which was swept up to the crown of her head, accentuating her long neck and perfect posture.

She turned her head slightly to look about, as her party was announced, and to set her emeralds sparkling. The room glowed from the light of what must be over one hundred candles on the enormous, but infinitely tasteful, chandelier that hung over the centre of the spacious room. Furniture was set out so that there were several smaller areas around the room's perimeter, two or three chairs, a settee or even a loveseat all facing one another, providing a place for an intimate chat with one's acquaintances. Opportunity to make new acquaintances had not been forgotten as, in an open space in the centre of the room, Lady Amesbury moved graciously from person to person, making certain that everyone had someone interesting to speak to, and was introduced to everyone else.

Earlier that day it had appeared that Caroline and Mr Darcy would be the only members of their party who had chosen to attend. Louisa and Mr Hurst were fatigued after a carriage ride in the park, and Charles had a previous engagement to play cards at his club. Mr Darcy had seemed reluctant to accompany Caroline, but she knew this was simply because he was overcome at having received an invitation from Lady Amesbury. Fortunately, when he realised that Caroline would be unable to attend without an escort, his consideration for her had overcome his hesitation. And after his decision, Louisa and Mr Hurst had decided they would attend, after all, after which Charles decided he could play cards another evening.

Music seeped into the room, but Caroline had no opportunity to see how many musicians Lady Amesbury thought appropriate for her soirées, for the lady herself spied Caroline, still standing with Mr Darcy and, both hands held out before her, came to greet her newest guests.

'How lovely to see you,' Lady Amesbury said, taking Caroline's free hand in hers. She wore sky blue, looking like an angel surrounded by heaven's vault, with a shockingly low bodice.

Caroline heard Darcy sniff and glanced up to see him quickly move his gaze away from their hostess and fasten it on the chandelier overhead. Glancing back at Lady Amesbury, she caught a smile and a sidelong look at Caroline as the lady flicked the wisp of lace she wore in her décolletage, somehow managing to lower it even further. *Isn't life a wonderful joke?* The lady seemed to be saying, *One that only women of true understanding, such as you and I, can share.*

That bodice, Caroline decided, sliding her arm out of Darcy's as he moved aside so Louisa and Mr Hurst could properly greet their hostess, is perfect, even at her age. A woman of such beauty and allure can take any fashion and make it appropriate for herself, and when wearing the absolute latest fashion, as Lady Amesbury of course was, the result could only be perfection.

Mr Darcy was looking about the room, and Caroline was happy he was now showing interest in who was here. Even for him, with his wealth and grand estate, there were people above his station in attendance tonight. He had ambitions, he must have, and there were people here who could help.

With Caroline at his side, once they were married, nothing could stand in his way. Politics was the obvious path for a man such as Mr Darcy. If he needed a little coaxing to achieve his full potential, Caroline was there to help. Just as she'd opened the door to his attending a party at the house of the pre-eminent hostess in town, she would open doors to everything she knew was right for Mr and Mrs Darcy of Pemberley.

Louisa took her arm and drew her to one side. 'Mr Darcy,' Caroline exclaimed, 'must be overwhelmed at finally finding himself included in such an august gathering.'

'Do you think so?' Louisa glanced over to where Darcy stood, making his bow to a cabinet minister. Caroline had no idea what the man's actual position was but that was of no account; here was Darcy, conversing with someone in power.

Louisa raised one slim eyebrow. 'I thought, when you first told us about this invitation, that he seemed reluctant . . .'

'Nonsense.' Caroline watched as he made a bow to a lady wearing a hideous pink gown and enough diamonds to outshine the chandelier. 'Look at him. He's smiling.'

Louisa studied the object of their attention for a moment. 'Perhaps you are correct. Perhaps he was simply wondering if he should insert himself into our family party.'

'He is always so thoughtful,' Caroline said. 'Modesty is rare in a man of such standing in society.'

'And yet, here he is, speaking to Lord T—. Perhaps he has been considering going into politics.'

Caroline gripped her sister's hand. 'Louisa, we think alike. Just think, perhaps it will be this invitation and the people he meets here that will set the course of his future life!'

Louisa's fingers squeezed back. 'And who will he be grateful to, when he looks back on how his dazzling career came to be?'

Both sisters laughed. 'Who indeed?' said Caroline, and imagined how he would show his gratitude.

'What is so funny?' Their brother moved closer, his open face hopeful. 'I do need a good laugh, for I have never seen such dreary company.'

'Dreary, Charles?' Caroline's jaw would have fallen, had she not taught herself through hours of practice in front of a mirror not to make facial expressions that might expose her to ridicule. 'I have never been in such exalted company in all my life.'

He shrugged. 'Exalted, maybe. Everyone wants something, though. Look at them. All speaking to one person while their eyes search the room for someone else, someone who can offer a greater benefit for the time spent.'

Caroline's jaw did fall on hearing this speech from her brother, but she quickly corrected it, and placed her face back into its accustomed polite interest.

'I rather agree,' said another male voice, and everyone turned to see Mr Tryphon, smiling as he made his bow to Caroline. She curtseyed automatically and then, catching the laughter in his eyes, exclaimed, 'Mr Tryphon, why do you say such things? You can't possibly mean such a thing, you, a man so recently arrived in London. Are you not pleased to be part of such a gathering?'

'I am pleased to be part of any gathering that includes the Bingleys.' He bowed again, but kept his face half-turned towards her, so she could see the mischief in his smile.

Louisa raised her eyebrow for the second time that evening, and Caroline knew that Mr Tryphon's attitude towards her was perhaps a bit forward, but suddenly she didn't care. Darcy had glanced over at her earlier, no doubt drawn by the sound of her laughter, and nothing mattered other than enjoyment and the attention of two such men as Mr Darcy and Mr Tryphon. Mr Darcy was the only one who mattered, of course, but if Mr Tryphon's attention assisted Mr Darcy in realising Caroline's true worth, then he was most welcome, too.

Lady Amesbury approached the little group. 'My two favourite people,' she exclaimed, slipping one arm through Caroline's, the other through Mr Tryphon's.

'You say that to every man,' he complained, laughing, 'although since you are addressing Miss Bingley, I am sure there is some truth in your utterance.'

'Foolish man.' Lady Amesbury drew the two of them into one of the more secluded seating areas. 'You know I always mean what I say.'

'For that moment at least,' he said, sitting down on a settee. Lady Amesbury sat Caroline down beside him and took a chair across from them.

'How well you know me,' Lady Amesbury said. 'Cannot a woman retain at least a small piece of mystery?' She raised a hand, and instantly a footman appeared. 'Something to drink,' she told him, her gaze never leaving Caroline and Mr Tryphon. The footman bowed and disappeared.

'My dear,' Mr Tryphon said, 'you will always be a mystery to me.' Their eyes locked and Caroline, wanting to take part in this conversation that was unlike any other in her experience, moved forward on her seat.

'And to me. All the most fascinating ladies of my acquaintance are mysterious.' The other two turned to her. 'Great ladies are like onions,' Caroline said, and then paused for a moment when Lady Amesbury looked puzzled. 'So many layers,' she hastily added, wondering why she'd spoken at all and when she could stop. 'Hidden beauty deep inside, to be discovered only by the greatest persistence.'

'Stephen,' Lady Amesbury smiled at Caroline, 'didn't I inform you Miss Bingley is a woman of the greatest intellect? She sees the world in ways usually invisible to the common mind.' She took one of Caroline's hands in hers. 'I've never thought of myself as an onion before, and to tell you the truth, I wouldn't have considered it the most flattering image. But you, my dear, have made me see the beauty that can exist in such a common object. An onion indeed!'

She and Mr Tryphon shared another look, and Caroline wasn't sure what it meant, but breathed a deep sigh of relief that what she'd said had apparently resulted in Lady Amesbury's approval.

Don't speak without thinking, Caroline reminded herself. *A lady's place is to enhance the company in which she finds herself. Lady Amesbury might not adhere to this rule, but she is a person who stands alone, so far above the rest of us mere mortals.* A warm glow rose in her stomach at the thought of how such a personage favoured her, Miss Bingley, soon to be Miss Bingley of Netherfield Park. Why, perhaps Lady Amesbury would enjoy a stay in the country. Before she could voice the invitation though, the footman reappeared, and set silver goblets in front of each of them.

'No, you oaf,' Lady Amesbury hissed at him. 'Not those goblets. These are my special friends. Bring the crystal, and be quick about it if you value your position here.'

The footman's face betrayed no expression as he gathered the offending vessels. 'Of course, my lady. I apologise, my lady.'

'I declare,' Lady Amesbury said. 'Good help is simply impossible to find.'

Here was something Caroline knew about, and it gave her an

opportunity to introduce the subject of Netherfield. Mr Tryphon spoke first though, telling Caroline about the house he had taken in town.

'Small, but perfectly darling,' Lady Amesbury added.

'I,' Caroline said, as the footman reappeared, 'am currently endeavouring to staff our country estate, Netherfield Park.' Lady Amesbury apparently approved of the crystal the footman set out, for she ignored him, her eyes resting on Caroline. 'I am having the greatest of difficulties,' Caroline continued, 'in filling even the least position with someone who inspires even the smallest amount of confidence.'

'You poor thing,' said Lady Amesbury. 'I know well how difficult it can be, needing to hire a full staff for one's latest home. Especially if that home is in the country. It appears that servants all believe they should be allowed to live in the city, if they so choose, without thinking at all about where their service is required. Please, I hope you will allow me to offer you any small assistance I can provide.'

'I am overwhelmed,' Caroline said, 'and immensely grateful. I am certain that any guidance you might provide will be of the utmost assistance.'

'Nonsense.' Lady Amesbury rapped Caroline on the arm with her fan. 'I am always delighted when I can offer any of my friends a good turn.'

'No doubt,' Mr Tryphon said dryly, 'so that they will owe you a good turn in time.'

She narrowed her eyes at him and then laughed. 'My dear Stephen. So cynical at such a young age.'

'How can I be other than thus,' he said, spreading out his hands before him, 'when I am exposed to such beauty and know it remains outside of my grasp?'

Lady Amesbury's eyes went to his, and Caroline was certain she saw surprise and perhaps a touch of pain, but then they both then they turned to her, and there was only laughter on their faces.

'Do we women truly offer such torture to men?' the lady asked Caroline.

Feeling suddenly daring, Caroline replied, 'As much as we can!'

Mr Tryphon groaned. 'I knew it. There exists a conspiracy among women.'

'Some conspiracies, certainly,' Lady Amesbury said. 'And here is one of mine approaching fruition.'

Caroline turned to follow her gaze, and saw two women standing stiffly as a man, who was clearly uncomfortable, introduced them.

'Let us draw a little closer.' Lady Amesbury rose to her feet and the other two followed her. Standing by a table that held a selection of dainties, the lady paused, apparently to peruse the flowers arranged in a bowl beside the platter of petit fours.

'Miss Allen,' the unhappy man was saying, 'may I have the honour of presenting my wife, the Countess of Fairbanks?' The two women curtseyed, each dipping the minimum amount they could without being rude.

'How lovely to meet you at last,' the younger one, Miss Allen, said. 'I have heard so much about you.' Her face, when she stressed the word 'so', contained what Caroline was certain was malice. But why would a young woman be so rude to a noblewoman, and at a party such as this? 'Surely,' she whispered to Lady Amesbury, 'this young woman must be different from what she appears, to have gained a place on your guest list.'

Lady Amesbury had given up all pretence of not listening and was gazing full on at the trio. She licked her lips and ignored Caroline. Mr Tryphon, though, was watching Caroline, a look of unease on his countenance. Caroline turned back to the tableau.

'How odd,' the countess was saying to Miss Allen, while her husband stood at her elbow, looking as if he wished he were anywhere other than here. 'I have heard nothing about you.' She turned to the man, her eyebrows raised. He quickly looked down at his boots.

'Where did you say you and Miss Allen met, my dear?' the countess continued, placing a possessive hand on her husband's arm.

'Oh,' he mumbled, still not looking up, 'I'm afraid I don't recall.'

'I'm indeed sorry to hear that,' Miss Allen said, 'for I recall every circumstance perfectly.'

'Do you indeed?' The countess turned an assessing gaze on the younger woman. 'Pray do enlighten us. I'm afraid my lord is often forgetting events that he considers unimportant.'

He looked up at that, sending a beseeching look at Miss Allen.

A flicker of a smile played on her lips and she returned his gaze, before she spoke again to the countess.

'Why, it was here, in this very room.' She paused to survey the room, her eyes stopping for a moment with shock on Lady Amesbury. Recovering herself, Miss Allen pointed to a corner of the room that the chandelier's light reached only weakly, so that the area was deeply shadowed. 'Right there, in fact. I confess, my lord, I am quite puzzled that you don't recall our first meeting. It appeared at the time to settle deeply on your consciousness. I trust you have not forgotten our other meetings?' Her voice was light, but Caroline was certain she saw the man's face grow pale.

'Beg pardon,' he said, stumbling over the words as he gave a jerky bow. 'I will fetch us all some punch.' He scuttled away, leaving the two women facing each other.

Beside Caroline, Lady Amesbury gave a little sigh of satisfaction. Caroline watched as Miss Allen made a frosty curtsey to the countess, and the two women parted. As the countess passed by, though, Caroline saw that a red patch stood on each of her cheeks, and her eyes were unusually moist.

Uncertain of what she had just witnessed, and why Lady Amesbury seemed so satisfied with the observed encounter, she turned to her two companions, but before she could say anything, a warm presence appeared beside her. 'Miss Bingley,' Mr Darcy said, 'may I escort you to the supper room?'

He did not acknowledge either Lady Amesbury or Mr Tryphon, other than with the briefest of nods. Surprised, Caroline dumbly took his offered arm and they walked away.

Glancing up, she saw that Mr Darcy's jaw was set and his brows were lowered darkly, shading his eyes. 'I declare, Mr Darcy,' she said, 'you must be hungry indeed, to sweep me away so quickly from my companions.'

He stopped at that, and turned to face her. 'I trust, Miss Bingley, that they are not close nor constant companions.'

Whatever can you mean? she wanted to ask, but something in his dark eyes and the haughty thrust of his chin kept her silent. They resumed walking and he led her into the supper room and to a place at the table where her brother and sister sat. Pulling out her chair, he waited until she was comfortably situated, then gave a sharp bow and departed.

'What did you say to Mr Darcy?' Louisa asked, leaning in close so that Charles, speaking to the gentleman on his other side, could not hear. 'He seems most disapproving.'

'Nothing.' Caroline watched as he left the room. 'Louisa, it was the strangest thing. He cut Lady Amesbury, I am certain. Spoke not a word, simply lowered his head in the briefest nod, and swept me away.'

'Cut Lady Amesbury?' Louisa studied her sister. 'Why would he do such a thing? Especially since becoming a part of her set will enhance his political career?'

'I know not. And I was having such a delightful time, conversing with the lady and—' she paused for a moment, 'and Mr Tryphon.'

Louisa's gaze became even more searching. 'Caroline, is that colour I see on your countenance? Could it be that you are forming an attachment for that young man? Is that not unwise? After all, we know nothing of him. And what of Mr Darcy?'

'Hush.' Caroline turned partly away, as if searching the room, but in reality she wanted to hide from her sister's searching eyes. Louisa knew her too well. 'Of course I am not forming an attachment, especially not for a young man who has little to recommend him. Although, I would think that any association with a person so favoured by Lady Amesbury must be completely above board. She is discerning; she would not introduce me to anyone whose background was questionable.'

'I agree.' Louisa nodded, setting the ringlets that hung over her forehead dancing. 'Forgive me. I should not have slighted Mr Tryphon. I simply wished to—'

'My friendship with Mr Darcy is unchanged,' Caroline said, now searching the room for his imposing figure and not finding it. Then, remembering the way Mr Tryphon and Lady Amesbury spoke to each other, a small flame of daring ignited in her breast. 'But if Mr Tryphon's attentions should come to Mr Darcy's notice . . .'

Louisa brought her hand in front of her mouth to hide the surprised 'o' her lips formed, and then something of Caroline's daring leapt to her. 'I do understand. Sometimes, in order to make a horse run his fastest, it is necessary that there be another horse he intends to outrun.'

Caroline laughed. Louisa, after a moment, joined in. Their brother turned away from the person he'd been conversing with and demanded to know what had so caught their fancy. Caroline and Louisa could not answer, of course, and to their surprised brother's further confusion, laughed even harder.

* * *

According to Charles, the removal to Netherfield Park went delightfully smoothly. According to Caroline, it was a nightmare. Even though all the furniture, clothing, and other necessities that had to be purchased in London had already been taken to the estate, there were still countless details that someone had to take care of. The someone, of course, was Caroline.

Louisa's favourite nightdress had gone missing. The cook's spice chest was too large to fit in the trunk assigned to it. Charles' valet had mislaid the only shaving razor that his master was willing to submit to. And on and on it went, one calamity after another, until Caroline was ready to give up on the estate and spend all of her future life right here, in Mr Darcy's townhouse. Here, where everything unfolded exactly according to schedule, where footsteps were always measured and voices never raised; where no one expected her, Caroline, to solve all the ills of the world.

The day though, passed through its requisite number of hours, as days always did, and by the end of it, Caroline and Louisa, in Mr Hurst's carriage, beheld for the first time the family's new home. The sun hovered on the horizon, a necklace of clouds below its chin, leaving just enough light to warm the tan bricks of Netherfield Park. Windows glinted as the sun set, and then glowed with inner light as the servants within lit candles to prepare for the family's arrival. The grand stairways that swept up from the drive on either side of the double-doored entrance shone white, the marble gleaming from frequent scrubbing. As the carriage wheels crunched on gravel that appeared to be properly raked, Caroline, despite her fatigue, felt her heart lift.

The actual arrival passed in a merciful blur of servants' faces, the bumping of trunks unloaded and carried on footmen's backs up the even whiter staircase that led off the grand entry hall, and the chatter of excited voices as Charles, his sisters, Mr Hurst, and Mr Darcy milled about, while orders were given by the housekeeper, and white-capped maids assisted with the removal of outer wear and offered tea and biscuits to tide the weary travellers over until dinner.

Caroline tried to observe it all, to learn if, amid the chaos, the staff were performing their duties to the standard on which she insisted, but all she truly wanted was to be shown to her room where she could unlace her boots and sink into a soft warm bed.

When at last she was escorted to the rooms that were to be hers, Genney had already prepared a soothing bath for her mistress. By the time Caroline emerged, swathed in her own thick bathrobe, Genney had arranged all her toiletries on the dressing table, unpacked the last of her clothes, and was waiting to assist her into her gown for dinner. Revitalised by the bath and her maid's attentions, Caroline checked her appearance in the dressing table's large mirror. She looked, she thought, exactly as the mistress of a country estate ought to look, regal, composed, and yet open to the new experiences that could be found in the country: picnics in a gazebo pleasantly situated in a rustic bower, carriage rides to explore the countryside, and, of course, greeting one's guests as they arrived for a ball. The neighbours would be fashionable and charming, sophisticated and yet not quite so sophisticated that they wouldn't gaze about with envy and exclaim about the taste and fashion sense demonstrated by the owners of the house, knowing this spoke volumes about the superior aspects of the family so newly arrived in the area.

Her head filled with visions of the people she would meet, Caroline left her rooms, ready for her new life to begin.

* * *

There was not time until the second day after they'd arrived for Caroline to arrange for the carriage to drive herself, Louisa, and Mr Hurst around Netherfield's grounds and into the surrounding countryside. The park was beautiful; there were a couple of lovely vistas, and one very charming gazebo. The new staff were actually performing their duties adequately, and the food served in the breakfast room and in the dining parlour was more than adequate, so it wasn't until the carriage rattled into Meryton, the closest town, that the first tingles of concern skittered across Caroline's consciousness.

The town was small. And dirty. There were pigs being driven across the main street, squealing and grunting, while all traffic had to pause and wait as the swineherd, a ratty-looking child, called to the animals and laid his staff across the rumps of the slower among his charges.

Louisa clutched a handkerchief in front of her face. 'That smell! I am hardly able to breathe.'

Caroline, who'd closed the curtains so as not to be splashed by the mud thrown up by vehicles passing the carriage, opened it a twitch to look outside. 'They are nearly past. Surely this cannot be a regular occurrence here? I don't understand why livestock are permitted in this section of town.'

'I think,' said Mr Hurst, 'this is the only section of town.' He closed his eyes and slid down in his seat, as if hoping to avoid seeing anything of what was outside the security of the carriage.

'That swineherd,' said Louisa, 'such a filthy person. I declare, I can hardly distinguish him from his charges.' The mischievous smile that Caroline loved broke out on her face.

Caroline laughed. 'It's a good thing he is slightly less pink than his charges, or no one would know which grunting thing was him and which was a pig.'

'They're not pink,' Mr Hurst complained. 'With all the mud covering them, the pigs are brown and grey.'

What, Caroline wondered, *will Lady Amesbury and Mr Tryphon think of this place?* Caroline had enjoyed another two visits, in town, with them, before the necessity of last-minute packing made her regretfully refuse all invitations. They'd gone to the theatre one evening, for a play much bawdier than Caroline had ever imagined, but when she saw the others in the boxes, lords and ladies with their paramours, she'd laughed as loudly as any of them at the antics on the stage. Mr Tryphon had sat beside her, close enough for the warmth of his body to reach the bare skin on her upper arms. She'd become more aware of him as the play progressed, the moments when he'd catch his breath before respiring regularly again, the dark wave of his hair and the reddish glints it held in the candlelight, his straight nose, and the times he glanced at her. She'd quickly looked away, but somehow she was still aware of his person, and knew without seeing that he smiled, or looked questioningly at her to see if she was fully enjoying herself. His solicitude pleased her.

Later he'd handed her down from Lady Amesbury's carriage, arriving at her side before the coachman had a chance to descend from his box. He walked her to the door of Mr Darcy's house, waving away the footman who'd come outside to escort her in. He took her hand in his as they reached the door and, without lowering his eyes from hers, he bowed low and brought it to his lips. A shiver passed through her; his eyes so intensely holding hers, his lips warm, even through the material of her glove. He straightened, gave her hand a little squeeze, and seemed about to speak, but the footman, still standing impassively by the open door, cleared his throat. Mr Tryphon bowed again and left, returning to the carriage, which moved smoothly away. Caroline looked after it before passing through the door, wondering if for a moment, she'd experienced a shortness of breath and a pain in the chest.

I do hope I'm not catching a cold, she thought, but somehow the sensations were different from when she was ill. Still, she took a hot water bottle to bed that night.

After an eternity, the pigs and the smell moved away and the carriage once again began to move. Caroline risked another glimpse outside and what she perceived made her eyes widen. 'Louisa, you must look and come to my aid. I cannot see a single shop it would be worth our time to enter. Please tell me I am mistaken.' But no, another glance showed her the same shabby row of shops, their windows grimy, their wares displayed with no eye for a pleasing arrangement.

Louisa opened her curtain and spent a careful time perusing the row of shops. 'Look! Is that a milliner's? The lace is hanging in full sun and has faded as a result.'

'I thought so.' Caroline shuddered.

Louisa shut her curtain with a decisive tug. 'This is dreadful. Whatever can Charles have been thinking?'

When the carriage returned to the house, Louisa wasted no time in asking that very question. Charles was sitting in his study, with Darcy and a man holding a wide-brimmed hat in his hands who was introduced as Dawkins, the steward. Louisa ignored the man, and placed both her hands on the desk across from where her brother sat. 'Charles, this is insupportable. There is not a single dressmaker whose establishment I would even notice, never mind enter.'

Charles ignored her, listening as Darcy finished speaking to the steward, before turning to face her. 'You had no intention of having any clothing made here. I distinctly remember you saying you'd use only your town woman if you discovered you needed anything more.'

'And what has that to do with anything?' Louisa demanded.

Charles and Darcy exchanged a glance before Charles turned back to face his irate sister. Seeing Darcy frown, Caroline stepped smoothly in. 'Louisa, it will be fine. The house is lovely, and the grounds are charming. We all knew that moving to the country would require some adaptations on our part.' Out of the corner of her eyes, she saw Darcy give her a somewhat surprised but approving nod. Caroline put her arm around Louisa's shoulders. 'Come, we must allow the gentlemen to proceed with their business. And Louisa, I truly need your assistance as I unpack my *objets d'art*. Only your discerning eye can observe if I am setting them out in the most pleasing arrangement.'

Louisa smoothed her face, no doubt remembering that unpleasant emotions went along with unpleasant lines upon one's countenance. Smiling bravely, she allowed her sister to escort her from the room.

* * *

The callers, of course, wasted little time before presenting themselves at Netherfield Park. Sir William Lucas was the first to be received. He was a pleasant enough man, Caroline supposed, but his conversation was certainly nothing out of the ordinary, not what she would have expected from the premier man of the district. He spoke about the shooting, which Charles was happy to discuss, and then Caroline heard a word, as she was pouring another cup of tea, which made her pay attention.

'A dance,' Sir William said. 'Oh, nothing fancy, but our assemblies are very pleasant all the same. May I hope that you will all honour us with your presence?' His homely face, with its bulbous nose and heavy jowls, lit up with a smile.

At least, Caroline thought, he used the correct word. It would be an honour for this community for the Bingleys and Mr Darcy to attend any of its little entertainments. Although, perhaps she might dare hope that some of the other callers would prove to be more diverting company.

Sir William departed, with an invitation from Charles to return in the future with his family. He apparently had a wife and a couple of daughters still at home. Before he left, though, he inquired whether Mr Bingley had yet had the pleasure of meeting Mr Bennet. When answered with a negative, Sir William clasped his hands together and said, 'Oh, you will so enjoy the Bennet family. I am certain he will call very soon. He is a most well-read man,' and the man looked at Darcy who, appearing startled to be addressed, nodded. Caroline had noticed that Mr Darcy seemed to find this visitor as dull as she did, for he'd spent most of the time staring into the fire or out of the window.

Sir William then bowed to Caroline and Louisa. 'And the Bennet daughters, five of them all told.' He chuckled. 'The elder two are delightful, and will be good friends for you ladies; and the younger, so energetic and with all the good humour of youth. I just know you will all get along capitally.'

He beamed at them all, his jowls shaking, and finally, mercifully, departed.

Mr Bennet appeared the next day. By then Caroline, after her drive into Meryton, and a visit to the milliner's there to find lace to repair a bonnet, was beginning to realise that her images of people of accomplishment in the area were most likely flawed. She'd held on to hope, though, with the Bennet family. The other callers had sung their praises, of the two eldest daughters in particular, but they also mentioned Mr Bennet as one of the most well-read and witty in the whole county.

When this paragon finally made his appearance, the Bingleys, Hursts, and Mr Darcy happened to be sitting by the fire in the largest parlour, the one that faced north. Louisa had set up an easel, claiming that with the light so perfect, how could she do anything but paint? Caroline stood at her side, to offer encouragement and note areas worthy of improvement.

'Mr Bennet, of Longbourn,' Stevens, the cadaverous butler, announced. Both Louisa and Caroline stepped out from behind the easel, to better view this new arrival.

He was a small man, fine-boned, with a full head of white hair and a wispy beard, definitely not in fashion this year, clinging precariously to his pointed chin.

'How very lovely to meet you at last.' Charles leapt out of his chair, from where he'd been observing Mr Darcy at the writing table, penning the latest in a long series of letters to his sister, Georgiana. Charles held out his hand and took hold of the visitor's, shaking it enthusiastically. Mr Bennet, Caroline observed, subjected her brother to a keen searching glance.

'Thank you,' he said. 'And may I add my congratulations to those I am certain you've received from the more effusive of our neighbours, on acquiring this fine estate.'

Charles then introduced Mr Bennet to the others. Caroline noticed that Mr Darcy, when making his usual short sharp bow, spent a little more time observing this new acquaintance than he had any of the other local people they'd met. Maybe, she thought, there were some people worth knowing in this place. Mr Bennet's manners were very good, he'd be out of place in town, of course, but for an area such as this, they did him very well.

He stayed only a short time, as was proper, sitting on the edge of his chair and sipping the tea Caroline handed him, but not taking the time to finish it before he jumped up and begged pardon, but he had matters at home that must be seen to. 'I reside in a household with six females,' he said with a sidelong glance at the gentlemen, as if expecting understanding. Charles and Mr Hurst nodded politely; Darcy observed him but made no response. Darcy, Caroline had noted, seemed little inclined to speak or otherwise interact with their new neighbours. *That does very well for him, no doubt,* she thought with a tinge of exasperation. *He will leave and return to Pemberley. I, however, must reside here and deal with these people every day.*

Charles walked the visitor to the parlour door, and Mr Bennet, just before he left, suggested that his wife and daughters would be delighted if Mr Bingley, and any of his other guests, would grace Longbourn by returning the call.

'I'd be delighted,' Charles exclaimed. 'As would Darcy, I am certain of it.' He glanced at his friend who, observing that a response was expected, gave a small bow.

'Very good,' said Mr Bennet. 'You can have no idea of the benefits your visit will bring to my wife and daughters. No idea at all—and the ways in which the visit will enhance the pleasures of my library.' And ending the visit with this cryptic remark, he departed.

For the next couple of weeks, Caroline was kept very busy. There were so many things that needed doing to properly set up the household, things that simply couldn't be entrusted to the servants. They tried, of course, but how could they possibly know the best section of wall in the morning room on which to hang the portrait of her parents so that the light caught it exactly so, first thing in the morning? Or just how far apart the chairs in the parlour needed to be to ensure a close enough distance for easy conversation while preserving the air of formality that room required?

Menus, provisioning the larder, checking the work of so many servants who were new, examining each room to ensure that during the long months the house had been empty no mould or unpleasant creatures had flourished.

'I declare,' she remarked to Louisa, 'one would think that if the servants hired were capable, the masters should not even notice a removal had taken place.'

'Are you unhappy with your servants?' Louisa asked.

'I took the best of what was available.' Caroline fussed with the folds of her gown as she sank into a chair beside her sister. 'But an artist, as you know, is only as good as his tools. I made do, and I continue to make do.'

Charles and Mr Darcy entered the room. Charles' cheeks were flushed with wind and sun, while Mr Darcy, who always managed to look proper even if he had just been out of doors, looked the same as always: not a hair out of place, his stock perfectly tied. Caroline sent him a polite smile as he bowed to her.

'What a perfectly lovely day it is outside,' Charles said, holding his hands out to the crackling fire. 'Why don't you and Louisa go for a walk? I cannot have you becoming peaky.'

'I am not peaky,' Caroline said sharply. 'I have been far too busy to even think about wasting time walking about in an aimless manner.'

'Then,' said Charles, 'you deserve an evening of entertainment. There is to be an assembly in Meryton, and we simply must attend.'

'No doubt,' Louisa said, 'this will finally provide you with an opportunity to set eyes on the famous Bennet sisters.' She inclined her head towards Caroline and both sisters laughed.

Charles had returned Mr Bennet's call, and Caroline had been most curious to hear his account of these local beauties whose praises were sung far and wide by all, possibly all in the entire county. He'd returned, though, with no additional information.

'I spent my time with Mr Bennet in his library,' he'd reported, sounding surprised to be asked about such a subject as the appearances of young ladies. 'He has an excellent collection of books, and he permitted me to examine several volumes.'

Caroline, recalling how narrow the pursuits of men could be, shooting and dogs and books, sighed. 'You can't possibly expect us to endure an entire evening with these people. I am certain the music will be an affront to my ears. And there will be no one with whom I can dance, except for the members of our own party.'

Her eyes went to Mr Darcy, who said, 'I quite agree. Charles, you cannot expect me to spend an evening with such tedious company.'

Caroline smiled her approval of this meeting of minds, and he returned her a warm glance.

'What utter nonsense,' Charles protested. 'I have met not a single soul I would describe in such terms. They are all such delightful people I feel quite at home here already.'

'I sometimes wish,' Mr Darcy said, 'that I could see the world as you do, where every sky holds the promise of a rainbow, and every person you meet is a source of joy.'

Caroline laughed.

'But then,' Mr Darcy continued, 'I remember that my time on Earth as allotted by God is limited, and I thank Him a thousand fold for providing me with eyes and ears that show me who is worthy of my time and who is not.'

Charles laughed too. 'Fitzwilliam, it is when I hear you speak thus that I thank God you are my friend.'

Darcy appeared gratified, but Charles continued, 'It is because He gave me an opportunity to do good in this world, by helping one as dour as you to experience joy, from time to time. Here, now, you cannot refuse me this moment when I can add to my list of good deeds. My soul requires it! You simply must accompany me to the assembly. I am certain you will have such a good time that you will thank me for all of your limited allotted days.'

Darcy, whom Caroline knew held a genuine affection for her brother, allowed his smile to warm his dark eyes, but Caroline, who knew him well, could see the doubt still there.

'The attire of the locals will be an affront to your eyes,' Louisa, wanting to take part in the game, said, and the sisters laughed again.

'Nonsense.' Charles rubbed the last of the cold out of his hands and threw himself onto the settee across from where his sisters sat. 'The people here are accomplished enough that they don't need to be concerned with the latest fashions.' He sent a mock scathing glance at his sisters. 'The music Sir William's daughter played when I dined with him was very good indeed. We simply must attend. I insist.'

'I wish,' Caroline said, 'your curiosity concerning the Bennet daughters had been answered. I am sorry indeed that you had to cancel your dinner engagement at Longbourn.'

'My curiosity?' Charles laughed. 'If I am curious, it is only because there are so many people here with whom it has been a great pleasure to become acquainted. Every person I meet has much to offer. And I was sorry indeed that business took me to Town and away from Netherfield Park. I now have to make up the lost time, and the assembly will offer the perfect opportunity.'

Caroline glanced at Darcy to see how he took this apparently unavoidable visit to the country assembly. 'As he has stated,' she said, 'Mr Darcy feels no pleasure at the thought of spending an entire evening with such company as this area has to offer, and I am in agreement with him.'

'I do not,' he said, seemingly resigned, 'but we are newly come to this area and it is our duty to participate in such social events as are open to us, and to set an example of proper behaviour. The way we conduct ourselves will be noted and while I cannot claim I will enjoy the experience, the expectations I place upon myself demand that I act as the gentleman I am.'

Charles clapped him on the shoulder. 'Well said. And who knows, perhaps there will be a fair countenance that will tempt even you, sir!'

Mr Darcy, Caroline observed, did not look as if he expected anything at the assembly to tempt him, and especially not the countenance of anyone who lived in this area. 'Mr Darcy,' she said. 'Would you join me in a game of cards before dinner? Come Louisa, let us show Charles how much pleasure and good company we have right here, in our own household.'

Louisa prodded Mr Hurst in the side of his waistcoat for, as often happened when he sat by a fire, he was asleep. 'I agree,' she said. 'Charles, how can you want for further entertainment with all that is on offer here?'

'I can't imagine,' he said, and pulled out a chair to sit at cards.

* * *

Caroline examined her appearance in the mirror, as her maid hovered anxiously behind her, and thought how she couldn't imagine looking forward to anything less than the anticipation she now experienced on the evening of the Meryton assembly.

Only one who knew Mr Darcy as well as she could tell he'd worked himself into a lather about it, although Darcy being Darcy he'd appeared, at luncheon, as calm and fashionable as usual, not a hair out of place, no wrinkles in his coat. Really, it was most unkind of Charles to subject his friend, never mind his own sisters, to such an unpleasant evening.

She sat across from Mr Darcy in the carriage, and examined him from beneath her lashes. As usual he showed no sign of his emotion. His high-brow was unlined, his lips showed no tendency to purse, his cheekbones revealed skin that was clear and uncoloured by the red of displeasure or the paleness of dread. She knew, though, that he was unhappy. She wanted to reach out and touch his hand, so that she might share his burden, but knew he would not welcome the gesture.

He kept his face toward the carriage window, watching as the lights of Meryton approached, and made no response as Charles chattered on about the people who would be present that evening, and those he had not yet met but how much he welcomed the pleasure that doing so would bring him.

Too soon the carriage rolled to a stop, bumping one last time into a pothole, as if to remind Caroline of the discomfort to come. Catching Louisa's eye, she heaved a sigh, and permitted her brother to hand her out.

The assembly room, as she'd expected, was small, overly heated, and stuffy. The faces that turned, and they all turned as her party made its entrance, contained eyes dulled with stupidity and mouths open with wonder as they perceived their betters. The men bowed and the ladies curtseyed, so at least they knew their place. Head high, Caroline followed Charles as Sir William rushed over to greet him.

'Really,' she whispered to Louisa, 'the man looks like a footman, the way he bows and scrapes. And not a very proficient footman, either.'

Now others ventured closer to be introduced. Caroline wore a distant smile and paid no attention as the faces and names were paraded past her. Darcy, she noticed, was beginning to look pained. 'Poor man,' she said to Louisa, 'what he must be suffering.'

After what seemed an eternity, people returned to their conversations, and music began. Caroline winced to hear the squeak of the violin. 'I'd wondered,' Louisa whispered, 'what greater indignities they could heap upon us, and thought that we'd reached the end of the pile. But this music . . .'

'If you can call it that.' Caroline gathered her skirts in her hands, to search for an out-of-the-way place to stand, when she noticed her brother's gaze sharpen as he glanced across the room.

'Who is that?' he asked Sir William, who had not stirred from his side.

'I'm not surprised you honour her with your notice,' the man said. 'That is Miss Bennet. Miss Jane Bennet, the eldest and the loveliest of that fair bevy.' He saw Charles was still staring across the room. 'Would you permit me to introduce you to the Bennet sisters?'

Curious now, since they'd all heard so much about these paragons, Caroline followed Charles as he dodged around the dancers to the other side of the room. Mr Darcy, she noticed, now stood by the front wall, gazing outside into the muddy street, no doubt finding that view more inspirational than the sight of any of these people could be.

Mrs Bennet was a woman who had perhaps once had pretensions of being a beauty. Her voice, though, was overly loud and grated on the ear, as she thanked Sir William for the introductions. The squire, Caroline noted, had made the introductions faultlessly. No doubt much effort had gone into preparing him for his presentation at court, and some of what he'd learned had been retained.

Mrs Bennet now turned to Charles, and in a voice calculated, no doubt, to draw all attention, complimented him on the fine choice he'd made in Netherfield Park. Charles responded enthusiastically, happily listing the many fine features of his new house. His eyes, though, kept moving to the face of Miss Jane Bennet.

She was pretty enough, Caroline supposed, with her light-coloured hair arranged on the top of her head. Something like her own hairstyle, Caroline thought with shock. Miss Bennet's eyes were large and an appealing shade of blue. The girl looked demure, as was fitting, but she lifted her eyes to Charles before turning to Caroline to make her curtsey. Caroline hardly remembered to respond, as she saw the glow on her brother's face, and her concern rose when he asked Miss Bennet to honour him with the next two dances. The girl agreed, of course.

Caroline hadn't paid any attention to the other sisters, but she now looked at them. The one to whom Miss Bennet now spoke was the next eldest. She had dark curly hair, and had permitted her maid to do a slovenly job of arranging it, for curls fell wherever they chose, over her ears, down her back, and there was even a short one bouncing over her forehead. Her eyes were dark, but shone with what could only be seen as mischief, as she darted her glance from person to person in Charles' party. A saucy one, no doubt, who thought herself above her station, but with nothing whatsoever to recommend her. The other sisters were also beneath notice; one actually had her nose in a book, no doubt because she was so plain that she preferred to hide her countenance. The last two were young, giggling together as they watched the young men pass by. To her surprise, a couple of these men asked the young girls to dance. Caroline was certain the mother would put a stop to this inappropriate behaviour, but Mrs Bennet simply waved a languid hand as the men each seized a sister by the hand and pulled them to their position in the dance.

Charles, at least, made a proper bow to Miss Bennet, and she returned it with a curtsey before placing her hand on his arm and allowing him to lead her to their places.

Time passed, but did so only reluctantly. Music played, violins scratching, the flute piercing her ears. People danced, or stood about in groups, talking. Caroline noticed many avid glances sent her way, and towards Mr Darcy, too. At one point he rescued her from boredom and asked her to dance, but his face was so shuttered, his head held so high, she knew he took no pleasure in it. No more than she did, that was evident. He also danced with Louisa, while Caroline danced with Mr Hurst, usually a chore but tonight she was glad because he at least knew how to dance like a gentleman. The locals swung their arms too much; talked too much; smiled too much. Really, it was insupportable.

Someone offered her a glass of a muddy pink liquid, telling her how much she'd like the lemonade. She took a small sip and it took all her self-control not to spit it into the smiling face of the woman who'd given it to her, still standing there staring. Caroline gave her a frosty nod and, sweeping past, deposited the glass on the nearest surface. Spying Darcy standing uncomfortably by a wall, not too far from where several women sat alone, no doubt pining for dance partners, she moved to his side.

Charles joined them, his face flushed from the exertions of the last dance. 'Charles,' she said, 'if you grin any more widely, your teeth will fly out and then you will look silly indeed.' She glanced at Mr Darcy to see if he appreciated her wit, but he was staring off at nothing.

Charles ignored her, as she'd learned brothers often did their sisters. 'Come, Darcy,' he said. 'I must have you dance. I hate to see you standing about by yourself in this stupid manner. You had much better dance.'

'I certainly shall not.' Darcy pulled himself back from whatever thoughts had occupied him. 'You know how I detest it, unless I am particularly acquainted with my partner. At such an assembly as this it would be insupportable. Your sisters are engaged,' he sent a glance towards Caroline who had, in a moment of utter boredom and weakness, agreed to dance with Sir William, 'and there is not another woman in the room whom it would not be a punishment to me to stand up with.'

'I would not be so fastidious as you are,' Charles cried, 'for a kingdom! Upon my honour, I never met with so many pleasant girls in my life as I have this evening, and there are several of them you see uncommonly pretty.'

'*You* are dancing with the only handsome girl in the room,' said Mr Darcy, to Caroline's surprise, as he looked at the eldest Miss Bennet.

'Oh! She is the most beautiful creature I ever beheld! But there is one of her sisters sitting down just behind you, who is very pretty and I dare say very agreeable.'

'Which do you mean?' He turned, and Caroline did, too, and saw the saucy sister, the one with the messy hair. 'She is tolerable,' Mr Darcy said coldly, 'but not handsome enough to tempt *me*; I am in no humour at present to give consequence to young ladies who are slighted by other men. You had better return to your partner and enjoy her smiles, for you are wasting your time with me.'

Charles shrugged and left. Caroline sent a sympathetic smile towards Mr Darcy. He glared at her, although she knew the ire was not for her but for the insupportable assembly and everyone else here. He stalked off and, sighing, she spotted Sir William approaching to claim his dances.

The tedium was somewhat relieved when Charles passed by with Miss Bennet on his arm, and they stopped to converse with his sisters. For their brother's sake, both Caroline and Louisa were civil and indeed, Miss Bennet was a pleasant surprise, for her voice was light and pleasant, and her conversation interesting.

'It is so lovely to meet you both,' she said. 'Dare I hope that you will be remaining with your brother in the neighbourhood?'

Caroline allowed herself a smile. 'I will have that good fortune, as I will be keeping house for my brother.'

'I, alas,' Louisa said, with hardly a trace of sarcasm in her voice, 'will depart later this year, for my husband's estate in Kent.'

'How very fortunate you are,' Miss Bennet said to Louisa, 'to be able to spend time in two such beautiful parts of England.'

'Indeed,' said Louisa. Caroline tried to find something to say about the beauty of Hertfordshire, but failed.

'And your time in London,' Miss Bennet said, 'must be very exciting.'

'Although,' Charles quickly cut in, 'we adore the country. The fresh air, the sunshine—so much beauty.'

Seeing his eyes return to Miss Bennet's face, Caroline said, 'Indeed. Many are the attractions.'

'Oh, I quite agree.' Miss Bennet looked down for a moment, and a gentle blush coloured her cheeks. 'I must confess I would not care to live in London all the time. I would prefer to have your discerning taste, and spend time in the country as well.'

Mr Darcy walked past at this point, chin raised, a look of acute distaste on his haughty features. 'Mr Darcy,' Louisa said, with a meaningful look at her brother, 'appears ready to depart.'

'Oh, we cannot think of retiring at this early hour,' Charles said, his eyes on Miss Bennet. 'It would be very rude.'

Miss Bennet favoured him with a shy smile.

'But perhaps,' Caroline said, 'it would be viewed as a kindness if Mr Darcy is unwell.'

Charles stared after his friend. 'He was in the best of health earlier this afternoon.'

'Perhaps,' Caroline said, leaning forward so that she could speak softly, 'he finds the country air unwholesome.'

'What?' Charles stared at her. 'Darcy loves the country. Consider how he is at his happiest when he is at Pemberley.'

'Then perhaps it is the air here,' Caroline said, wishing, as she often did, that her brother was more adept at understanding the delicate art of conversation.

'The air here is perfect.' Charles, once again, gazed at Miss Bennet.

'Then,' Caroline said, impatiently, 'it must be something particular to this part of the country that causes him distress.'

'Oh,' Miss Bennet said. 'I cannot believe there is anything here that could distress anyone.' She searched the room for Mr Darcy.

Caroline followed her gaze, and saw that Darcy had sat down. Near him was one of the older ladies of Meryton, and every sinew in his body strained to move him away from her vicinity. She sat quite still, sending him puzzled looks from time to time, clearly not understanding the torment the poor man experienced in this place.

'Is he perhaps very shy?' Miss Bennet asked. 'He is sitting near to Mrs Long, who is very agreeable. Perhaps if he made more of an effort to speak to people, he would be happier.'

'Mr Darcy,' Caroline informed her, 'never speaks unless he is with his intimate acquaintances.'

'Oh.' Miss Bennet took a moment to think about this. It appeared to be difficult for her to comprehend. 'If he is thus with people unknown to him, it must be difficult for him to form new acquaintances.'

'You appear to have formed an erroneous impression of him,' Caroline said. 'With us he is remarkably agreeable.'

Miss Bennet looked horrified. 'It appears I have given offence.'

'Nonsense,' Charles said, glaring at Caroline.

'Please forgive me,' Miss Bennet continued. 'It is apparent that I am in the wrong, to judge a person I have so recently met.'

Very nicely put, Caroline thought. Out loud, she said, 'No offence given. We understand how that which is new can often be misunderstood, and first impressions can be misleading.'

Charles smiled at her, and Caroline smiled at Miss Bennet, and Charles and Miss Bennet walked on, leaving both sisters agreeing that they'd been pleasantly surprised by her, and that she was a charming girl.

As the evening grew late and her hopes rose that soon this punishment would come to an end, Caroline noticed that while the stares at her and her party did not grow fewer, those aimed at Mr Darcy showed, not awe, not respect, but a curious sort of disapproval and even anger. Needless to say, this did nothing to improve her opinion of the local people. She continued to speak to those who addressed her, uncaring what she said. At one point she heard the name 'Bennet' and listened long enough to hear a woman whose name she'd long forgotten tell her that Miss Mary Bennet was the most accomplished girl in the neighbourhood, and that a treat was in store the next time Miss Mary played the pianoforte, but she then returned her attention to trying to puzzle out why Mr Darcy was attracting so many sullen faces.

It must be envy, she thought, *for surely they are all too dull to understand and sympathise with the pain he is feeling at having to spend time in their company.* When she had an opportunity to join him she stood at his side. 'How like cattle they all are, would you not agree, Mr Darcy? They can move only in a herd, and stare without comprehension at their betters.'

He smiled slightly at that, and a warmth grew in her chest. It encouraged her to place her hand on his sleeve. 'Oh, how I wish you could now escort me from this room and from all the memories I will retain from this dreadful experience. Why, I am certain I will have dreadful nightmares in which farmyard animals ask me to join them in a dance.'

He didn't place his hand over hers, but neither did he move his arm away. 'I am doing my best,' he said, 'to draw happiness from observing Charles' pleasure, but am realising the limits of friendship.'

'Charles is fortunate to have a man such as you to call his friend,' Caroline said, anxious that Mr Darcy might refuse to associate with the Bingleys after this experience.

'I am fortunate, also,' he said, and his eyes met hers and held them for a moment.

The assembly ended, at last, shortly after this conversation, and Caroline hardly noticed the discomforts of the carriage ride home, so filled was she with thoughts of how Mr Darcy felt fortunate not only to have Charles' friendship, but also for the time he spent with Charles' sister.

Chapter Three

The assembly, tedious though it had been, provided plenty of fodder for conversation the following day.

'Truly,' Louisa said as she scraped marmalade onto a piece of toast. 'When I saw what they were wearing, I didn't know if I was somehow transported to a ball from two years ago!'

'If you could narrow it down to two years ago,' Mr Darcy said, 'you have a more discerning eye than I. I saw no fashion at all, from any year.'

Caroline laughed. 'Why, Mr Darcy, you surprise me. I had no idea you pay such close attention to fashion.'

He turned to her, eyebrows raised. 'If I didn't know you better, Caroline, I would think you were offering me insult.' He patted the neckcloth knot his valet had tied that morning, one that Caroline knew was the very latest rage in London. 'Do I truly appear to have no fashion sense?'

Caroline laughed even harder as he stood up, made a mock bow, and twirled his person about so she could appreciate the cut of his clothing from all angles. 'Mr Darcy, that is a thought that could never be attached to you. Your attire is always the height of fashion. No, I only meant that I was unaware that you pay such attention to women's fashion.'

'Bravo, Darcy,' Bingley cried. 'You show yourself very well, sir!'

'And you are correct,' Darcy said to Caroline, as he regained his place at the table. 'I meant the clothes the gentlemen wore. I noticed nothing at all about any of the women. There was no beauty to be found among them.' He turned to his friend. 'With the exception, of course, of Miss Bennet. Although, she smiled too much.'

'I must protest,' Charles said. 'While I freely accept I enjoyed Miss Bennet's company more than anyone else's, there were many pretty girls there, and they were all lively and very pleasant. And how is it possible for someone to smile too much? Darcy, did you not even trouble yourself to speak to some of the people there? I found them all to be very good company.'

'Good company!' Darcy pretended great surprise. 'I saw not a single countenance that stirred me to any interest at all. Mercifully, they observed my lack of enjoyment, and so while I paid them no attention, they returned the compliment.'

Charles began again to protest, but Caroline cut him off. 'Mr Darcy, I could not agree with you more. While Jane Bennet is a very sweet girl, and I should be happy to know her better, there was no one else there with whom it was worth my time to speak. Now that we have done our duty and appeared at one of their assemblies, surely there is no need for us to do so again.'

'I must protest again,' said Charles, laughing. 'Surely you cannot mean what you say.' He turned to Mr Darcy who, despite his earlier show of good humour, was again scowling. 'Darcy, if only you had made the effort, I am certain you would have enjoyed yourself at least as much as I.'

'Made the effort?' Darcy raised an incredulous brow. 'I could have much better put an effort into reading a book to improve my mind, or ridden Nelson so at least I could have received some exercise.'

'Dancing is superb exercise,' Charles said, holding out his cup so Danvers could pour him more tea. 'And my mind was much improved by the conversations I had. Did you know there is a dog breeder here who has won hunting awards for several of his puppies? Perhaps I should visit his kennel and see if there is a suitable dog for Flossie—'

At this point Mr Darcy coughed loudly and Charles, remembering where he was, flushed a deep red and apologised to his sisters for speaking of a matter unsuitable for feminine ears. Caroline took a sip of tea. Unfortunately, she started to choke, and sputtered helplessly as Charles came around and helpfully pounded her back.

When she could again breathe, she remembered something that had been niggling at her mind. Leaning close to Louisa, she said softly, 'I am concerned that I have made a dreadful mistake in inviting Lady Amesbury and Mr Tryphon to Netherfield Park.'

She had mentioned the invitation shortly before leaving London. Lady Amesbury's response had been less than enthusiastic, but Caroline, once she was settled in to the new house, had decided to make the request formally, and so had written the invitation on her new stationery and sent it off. She missed her friend. Lady Amesbury was always amusing, and she showed Caroline a side of London, and indeed of life, that was until now unknown to her.

She'd learned much already, and some of it required further thought. For example, since gaining entry into Lady Amesbury's set, she'd begun to realise that sometimes people acted in ways that were not usually admired. And, when they did, sometimes the reaction from others was not disapproval, but a sort of respect, even envy. This surprised her. Surely, only proper behaviour should be valued? Lady Amesbury, though, was admirable in every way, and so her actions should be emulated by everyone, especially Caroline, who would be part of the fashionable set once she became wife to Mr Darcy.

But enough thinking. It was too much like work.

She'd mentioned in the invitation to Lady Amesbury that others among her new acquaintances would be most welcome, and had made special mention of Mr Tryphon. She'd not thought of him often since leaving town, but memories of his person entered her mind from time to time.

Yesterday, a reply from Lady Amesbury had arrived, on beautifully embossed paper that was tinted pink and scented with orange and cinnamon, the lady's personal perfume. It said that she and perhaps some other friends would be delighted to spend time at Netherfield Park, and that they would arrive three weeks hence.

Now Louisa looked at her with a puzzled expression. 'I thought you were delighted to renew the acquaintance.' Caroline said nothing, and saw her sister's face change as the realization dawned on her. 'Oh, my. Can you imagine the lady, who has entertained the prince, speaking with Mrs Bennet?'

Caroline groaned. 'Louisa. I had rather hoped that you would console me and make me feel better.'

'Feel better?' Charles demanded. 'Feel better about what? Caroline, are you ill?'

'Not at all,' Caroline said, more sharply than she'd intended. 'I am merely thinking ahead to Lady Amesbury's visit here. I do not think she will find any one here agreeable.'

'Nonsense,' Charles said. 'Look how wide and varied her acquaintances are in town. She will enjoy the opportunity to meet new friends.'

'Lady Amesbury?' Darcy leaned forward, his eyes dark, his brow lowered. 'Is she to join us here?'

'Why, yes,' Caroline said, surprised at his tone of voice. 'Did I not mention it to you? I am quite certain I did.' She hadn't, though. For some reason Mr Darcy seemed less than fond of the lady, even though, through Caroline's friendship with her, he had met many of the most influential men in London.

'You did not,' he said, frowning.

'It is of no matter,' she said, paying attention to her tea cup as she stirred the already cool liquid remaining there. 'Now that we have a country estate, it is only right that we entertain our friends.'

Mr Darcy looked to Charles, but Caroline could not read what passed between them. 'If I did not mention it,' she said, 'it was only to spare you any further distraction. You have seemed pained since we came here, and I didn't want to add to your burden.'

'Burden?' Charles said to his friend. 'Are you displeased by our coming here? Do you think I should not have taken this estate? I thought you seemed most pleased with it, but if—'

'I am completely content,' Mr Darcy said, glaring at Caroline. 'The estate is perfect for you, Charles, and it gives me great pleasure that I could assist in any way your gaining a place in the country. But you must rely more on your own feelings. I can offer only my opinion.'

'I do,' said Charles. 'But you have seen so much more of the world than I, and have had so many more experiences. After all, you have been master of Pemberley these many years. Your advice is invaluable.'

'It appears,' Caroline said, trying to keep the taste of acid out of her voice, 'that everyone present is extremely happy. I am so glad. And the visit of my friend will only enhance my own happiness.'

Charles looked surprised, but Mr Darcy said, his voice calm, 'I cannot say that I approve of Lady Amesbury, neither do I enjoy many of her friends and their forms of entertainment. I will, of course, do all I can to ensure her happiness during her visit. You may find, though, that she will not find pleasure here, with the people she will meet, and in that, to my surprise, I find we have much in common.'

'Darcy,' Charles said, in a tone of reproach.

'You know me,' Mr Darcy said to him. 'I abhor anything that is less than completely honest. I am not unhappy here, the shooting is excellent and the country hereabouts offers much in the way of riding and walks. And I am always happy when I spend time with you.'

Caroline waited to see if he would mention his happiness when spending time with Charles' sisters as well, with one in particular, but he did not so much as glance her way.

'Thank you.' Charles' eyes were suspiciously moist, but he contented himself with shaking Mr Darcy's hand.

Caroline stood, giving up on any pretence of eating more, and went into the music room. A session of practice on the pianoforte was just what was needed to clear her head.

That evening, after the cards had been put away and Mr Hurst had been supported by a footman as he made his way upstairs, Caroline sat in her boudoir and stared into the mirror as her maid unpinned and brushed her dark hair.

What did Mr Darcy see when he gazed at her? The sister of his good friend? An intriguing woman? The future mistress of Pemberley? If not, what could she do to help him see his perfect future?

Unfortunately, she could not devote all her time to this, as there were many demands on her time. The Meryton assembly did not supply an end to socialising. Calls had been made and had to be returned. And those calls in turn would have to be returned and there would never be an end to her having to be polite and pleasant to the insufferable people here.

* * *

'There will have to be cake,' Caroline said with a sigh, surveying the smallest of the three sitting rooms she used for company. It held only one settee, six chairs, and three small tables. The fireplace was small, and tended to smoke and sputter, no matter how carefully the fire was laid.

'Apple tart with powdered sugar?' Louisa asked hopefully.

'No, I think not.' Turning to the footman calmly awaiting his orders, Caroline said, 'Some of that lemon cake we had yesterday. And use the brown-and-green china set, not the blue Delft.'

He nodded and left. Caroline sank into one of the two chairs that were padded. The other chairs were made of wood, with spindly curved legs and while each had a cushion, they were not very comfortable. Caroline had quickly discovered that this was the best room to use when she was visited by people she wished would not stay long. It was small and rather gloomy, especially since Caroline always decided not to light all the lamps, only those by the inner wall. The windows were set rather deeper than in other parts of the house, for the walls here were older and thus thicker than elsewhere. Charles had told Caroline that she was free to purchase new furniture and rearrange any part of the house she wished, but she had kept this room exactly as it was. Today, it would serve her purpose well.

The Bennets arrived for their visit early, but Caroline had discovered this was their usual habit whenever Mrs Bennet was included. Also as usual, all five sisters accompanied their mother, although Miss Mary quickly sought permission, which was granted, to spend time in the library.

Sighing loudly, Mrs Bennet perched herself on the edge of a chair, and looked about with sharp eyes. Spotting some needlework that Caroline had been working on, she snatched it up. Jane, who was seated beside her mother, leaned over to look.

'That is very lovely,' Jane said to Caroline. 'Your work is always so—'

'It will do,' Mrs Bennet said loudly. 'But I know you have seen some of Jane's work, have you not?' Waving the needlework in the air to accentuate her words, she continued, 'I swear I have never seen such exquisite work as Jane's. Her stitches, so tiny, so even. Her colour sense is unrivalled in this county, perhaps in the whole country. And she has such a delicate touch; there is never so much as a tiny wrinkle in the linen.'

Caroline had pasted a politely interested expression onto her face as soon as these visitors were shown in. Her eyes, though, were now glued to her needlework. She'd worked long and hard on that piece, as it was to be fashioned into a pair of slippers for Mr Darcy, to be presented to him when their engagement was announced. He hadn't actually proposed yet, but Caroline was certain this was only a matter of time.

Mrs Bennet continued to flap the delicate piece as she spoke. She'd moved on from Jane's needlework to Jane's skill with ribbon, despite the fact that both her elder daughters were endeavouring to convince her to permit someone else to play a part in the conversation. This little drama played out with unyielding regularity every time the Bingley women were with the Bennets, and there had been several, too many, calls during the two weeks since the assembly. Also as usual, the younger sisters giggled non-stop, even as they stared avariciously at Caroline and Louisa's clothing and jewels.

Mrs Bennet appeared to have run out, for the moment at least, of items to praise about Jane. She flung Caroline's work carelessly onto the table which held the tea things. Fortunately Louisa had not yet poured, and so there were no filled cups or spilled drips to stain the delicate embroidery.

Caroline snatched up her work and examined it anxiously, but fortunately it appeared unaffected by its rude handling. Caroline took out her workbasket and threaded a new length of green silk on to her needle. She knew what would come next, for the order of events was unchanging during these calls. Mrs Bennet sat up even higher, lifted her chin, and looked about the room. 'And will the gentlemen be joining us today?' she asked brightly.

Louisa poured and Caroline put down her work to pass Mrs Bennet a cup of tea. Despite her usual impeccable manners, the cup rattled against its saucer, as she tried to restrain herself from spilling the hot liquid into Mrs Bennet's lap. 'Unfortunately, no,' she said, proud of how cool her voice sounded. 'They have business elsewhere.'

'Such a busy man, your brother.' Mrs Bennet took her cup and gazed hopefully at the table that held the lemon cake. 'Surely this cannot be healthy for him. I thought he looked a little peaked the last time we had the pleasure of seeing him. That was at Lucas Lodge, was it not? Such lovely people they are, and such good friends of ours. We were all so glad that you could join us for that little party. Wasn't the music delightful? And the food? But I noticed, Miss Bingley, you danced only twice. Were you feeling unwell?'

Mrs Bennet paused to draw breath at this point, and Caroline hastened to speak. 'You will be happy to learn, Mrs Bennet, that I am in perfect health, as is my brother.' She tipped her head back and gazed down her nose at Mrs Bennet. Seeing that the woman was about to open her mouth to speak again, she turned to Jane. 'I hope you are in good health, Miss Bennet. And you, also, Miss Elizabeth.'

Miss Elizabeth, for some reason, had a smile in her eyes, but she said in all seriousness, 'We are indeed very well. You are so kind to ask.'

Caroline nodded and resumed her needlework. Before Mrs Bennet could swallow her mouthful of cake and speak again, Elizabeth continued, 'I must congratulate the Bingley family on how well you have adapted to life in the country. I did wonder if you'd find life here a little dull after all the entertainments available in town.'

Caroline met Louisa's eyes. Life here was exceedingly dull. 'I am glad it appears so to you, Miss Elizabeth.'

'Mr Bingley, in particular, appears very happy to be here,' Elizabeth said. 'Whenever I see him in company, he is most effusive during his conversations.'

Jane, Caroline noticed, sent her sister a pleading glance, but Elizabeth ignored it. 'Can it be,' she asked, 'that he finds some of the people of Meryton more interesting than some among his acquaintances in London?'

'Charles,' Caroline said, unable to keep a bit of steel out of her voice, 'enjoys the company of a great many people. And, many of those people are indeed to be found in London.'

Elizabeth nodded, as if Caroline's words were fascinating to hear. 'Mr Darcy, though,' she said, pausing to take a sip of tea, 'does not appear to find country society very much to his liking.'

Caroline frowned, and looked quickly down at her work, to hide the dislike she felt at hearing Miss Elizabeth speak so impertinently. 'Mr Darcy has a great many things on his mind. He is, after all, the master of Pemberley, one of the finest estates in the country.'

'Yes, I have been informed of his status.' Elizabeth paused again, her eyes dancing. 'One would think that residing here for a time, free of all his responsibilities at home, he would be more likely to take advantage of available entertainments. Sadly, he appears quite unhappy whenever I have encountered him.'

Of course he's unhappy, Caroline wanted to say. *How could you possibly expect a man of quality to enjoy spending time with people so decidedly below his rank?* Instead, she smiled politely. 'Will you have some more cake?' she asked Jane. Jane refused, but Mrs Bennet eagerly held out her plate, covered liberally with crumbs, some of which fell to the floor, for another piece. Lydia and Kitty giggled. Why those children were permitted out in polite society was beyond Caroline. If they were her children they'd soon learn the uses of discipline in instilling some manners and decent behaviour.

Louisa busied herself pouring more tea. Elizabeth smiled at Caroline, who realised the snippy miss had not taken the hint that the subject was to be dropped, and was awaiting a response to her comment about Mr Darcy.

'Mr Darcy, and indeed all of our party, will soon have more company with whom we plan to share many enjoyable hours and entertainments,' Caroline said. 'Lady Amesbury, my very dear friend, will soon be joining us.' She couldn't keep herself from stressing the words 'Lady' and 'dear', and as Elizabeth leaned back in her hard chair, Caroline was sure she recognised surprise and envy in those dark eyes. 'I am certain that you will no longer have any reason to think Mr Darcy, or any one of us, unhappy then.'

'I am so glad,' Elizabeth said, smiling. 'It will be most pleasant for the rest of us, also, to benefit from the greater variety of people you are bringing to the area. I am certain that any personage who is your dear friend will be delightful indeed.'

Although Miss Elizabeth's words said nothing one could take offence at, she had stressed the word 'dear', and now Caroline could see only amusement in her eyes. A sense of pique rose inside her, and she said, 'The lady will bring many of our friends with her. Possibly even Lord E—will form part of her party. Oh come, you must have heard of him. He is very high up in the government. Mr Darcy, in fact, will be especially glad to resume the acquaintance, for they have had many discussions about politics and business and other concerns with which Mr Darcy is always happy to involve himself.'

'How delightful for Mr Darcy.' Miss Elizabeth put down her teacup, the liquid inside only half gone. 'But perhaps he would find other concerns equally interesting, if he took the trouble to speak to anyone.' She turned to her mother, who was fussing with Jane's hair, and then looked back at Caroline. 'Thank you for a most delightful afternoon, but I am afraid we must depart now. I trust you will excuse us?'

Once the guests had finally left, after many words of gratitude and invitations to call on them at Longbourn, Caroline and Louisa left the small room, leaving the servants to clear away all signs that the Bennets had been there. Caroline carried her needlework and workbasket to their favourite sitting room, one with an excellent view of the gardens and enough natural light to sew by.

Sitting down, Caroline called for more tea, needing fortification. Too weary to complain when Louisa added her order for apple tart, she picked up her needle and then exclaimed in dismay. 'I shall have to unpick everything I have just completed. Look.' She held out the work to Louisa. 'The stitches are too tight.'

Louisa commiserated and the sisters fell silent, enjoying the silence. Before long, Mr Hurst joined them, looking for his tea. Charles and Mr Darcy, Caroline knew, had been in the billiard room during the call, because somehow Caroline had forgotten to inform her brother that Jane Bennet and members of her family were expected. Dealing with Mrs Bennet's constant praise of her eldest daughter was difficult enough without the fuel added by Charles' obvious admiration. Together, the two of them could sing Jane's praises until both grew weak from hunger and thirst.

'We need,' she said to Louisa, 'to have a little talk with Charles.'

'Speak to Charles about what?' Mr Darcy asked. Unnoticed, he had just entered the room. He flung himself into a chair, his long legs stretched out before him, and examined the tea table. Taking an apple, and not a tart, Caroline observed, he began to pare it with the knife the footman handed him.

'About this foolish infatuation with Miss Jane Bennet,' Caroline said. 'Surely, Mr Darcy, you have observed how often Charles is to be found by her side whenever we are together.'

Mr Darcy sat up straighter and looked at Caroline with obvious admiration. 'I have,' he said slowly, and then paused.

'Come now, Mr Darcy,' Caroline said. 'You are among friends. You must know that anything you have to say on the matter will be welcome.'

He nodded and drank some tea. 'I have observed that he appears to prefer her company to that of any other person. I assumed, though, that this is one of his interests that will swiftly be gone and replaced by something else. I believe that because the lady in question does not appear to be equally enthralled by him.'

Caroline grimaced. 'The lady may not be as interested, but the mother certainly is. Mrs Bennet appears convinced that the match is as good as made.'

Mr Darcy frowned. 'I am not certain that we should take anything seriously that that woman utters. She has too few thoughts in her head, and so she repeats them constantly, over and over.'

Caroline laughed. 'Why, Mr Darcy, you are too cruel!'

He grinned, the sudden flash of humour in his eyes as unexpected as it was rare. Something deep within Caroline's chest did a little flip-flop, and she quickly looked down to her needlework. She'd unpicked each stitch she'd sewn that afternoon and was now endeavouring to repair the damage.

'Do not concern yourselves,' Mr Darcy said, his voice serious once again, 'with speaking to Charles about this matter. I will observe him more carefully and will discover if we need to take action.'

Caroline smiled, enjoying being a conspirator. Lady Amesbury had taught her the joys of observing other people and affecting the flow of their lives. Not that she would do anything cruel, of course, but it was entertaining, and often informative as well, to take careful notice of those who came to one's attention. And, Mr Darcy had said 'we', not that he'd take care of the matter by himself. Caroline moved her eyes to his, and smiled some more. 'Are you not concerned,' she asked, 'that in carrying out your plan, you will find yourself more often in the company of the Bennet family?'

'Bennet family?' The voice was Charles', and Caroline's throat grew tight, but fortunately her brother appeared to have overheard only the last few words she'd uttered.

'Is the Bennet family scheduled to call tomorrow or some time soon?' he asked hopefully.

'No, I regret that we and the Bennets have no set engagements at present.' Caroline kept her eyes on her work, concerned that if she looked up and caught Mr Darcy's eye, she would be unable to contain her laughter.

* * *

Lady Amesbury, when she arrived, did not bring a large party. No lords, no politicians, no government officials came to Netherfield Park. Not even Lord E——, the lady's lover, had accompanied her. Perhaps the affair had ended, as she'd heard they often did, Caroline thought, and felt very daring for thinking of such risqué matters. Lady Amesbury was accompanied by only one person: Stephen Tryphon.

With her visions of dinner parties and musical evenings, of Mr Darcy furthering his political career and being ever-more grateful to her for providing the opportunity, shrivelling inside her head, Caroline curtseyed to her guests. When she rose, Mr Tryphon's warm smile showed her that he was very glad to see her. She put her welcoming smile on her face in response, but her disappointment was too great for her to do anything beyond the necessary courtesies due any guest by a polite host. After asking a servant to show them to their rooms, and telling Lady Amesbury and Mr Tryphon that once they had refreshed themselves they should come to the blue sitting room for tea and cake, she went to the small parlour where no one ever came and, despite its association with the Bennets, she sank into one of the padded chairs, unable for the moment to face anyone.

Why had Lady Amesbury brought not one of the people who usually attended her events in town? Did she think Caroline, and Netherfield Park, too inconsequential to interest them? But if she was concerned about the quality of the accommodations, and the society to be found here, why had she come herself?

She allowed herself only a little time, though, to think about her disappointment. She was mistress here; she had duties to perform. Telling herself that at least her friend had come and the bonds of friendship were strong, she rose to ensure that the servants were preparing the blue sitting room for her guests. And besides, Lady Amesbury would no doubt have interesting news from London.

Lady Amesbury did indeed have interesting news. She talked about fashion, who had attended the theatre with whom, who was seen riding in whose carriage, what Lady So-and-so had said to Lady La-di-da during tea at Lady Amesbury's home, and which gentlemen were hoping to gain the hand, or at least the notice, of which lady.

During the recitation, which Caroline endeavoured to enjoy, even though she couldn't help thinking of how much more gay it would be if this lovely room was now filled with important people from town, all of whom would be impressed by how elegant the furnishings were, how very good the tea was, and what a remarkable hostess Miss Bingley was, Mr Tryphon remained silent. He smiled when Lady Amesbury said something intended to amuse, and nodded once or twice when she looked to him to help her remember a detail of what this lady wore or what that gentleman had said about a horse, but she appeared to need only his support, not his words. When not attending to her, he looked at Caroline, his watchful gaze almost bashful, as if to gain an understanding of whether she was glad to see him.

She tried to appear gay and carefree, as if all she had to think about was the delight of having her dear friends with her after so long, but her disappointment was more difficult to overcome than she'd expected. Apparently her façade was less effective than she'd hoped, for when Lady Amesbury rose at Louisa's invitation to see more of the house, he remained behind, watching Caroline. She sat still, gazing down at her clasped hands on her lap.

'Forgive me,' he said, 'but I cannot help but observe that your spirits are not as animated as I became accustomed to during our time together in town. Are you quite well?'

She looked up at that and smiled. 'I am very well, thank you.'

'Is it the country air, then, which so disagrees with you that it has leached all colour from your cheeks?'

How had she not remembered how rich his voice was, and how his eyes could express the wealth of feeling that his words could not? Sitting up straighter, suddenly realising that while a large number of guests had not come here, Mr Tryphon had, she smiled a true smile and said, 'I thank you for your concern, but all is well since my friends have arrived.'

He smiled, also, and his eyes grew warm. He reached out to her, and she wondered if her words had been too forward, but he merely covered her hand with his own for the briefest moment and then placed his back on his leg. Her eyes followed it, and she noted how beautifully proportioned it was, with his square palm and long fingers. His nails were manicured, but the sinews beneath the skin moved as he shifted the hand's position and they spoke of strength and skill. Her gaze moved from his hand to the grey linen of his trousers and the curve of his thigh muscle hidden beneath the fabric and then, suddenly realising her eyes were close to a part of his body that one did not examine under any circumstances, she turned to the teapot, her face hot with the blood that had rushed there. 'Would you like some more tea?' she asked brightly.

He remained silent for a moment, watching her, and she was unsure of what his expressive eyes held. But then he blinked, and all she could see was polite interest. 'No, I thank you,' he said. 'I did observe, though, a lovely park when we drove through your grounds earlier. Perhaps you would do me the honour of taking a walk with me, so I might better enjoy its beauty.'

Caroline wondered why Mr Tryphon, of all her acquaintances, so often made her feel as if his words said one thing but meant another, but pushing away this thought as she'd pushed away her disappointment, she readily agreed. Taking time for her maid to fetch her a wrap, she led him out the front door.

*　*　*

During the weeks since the family had arrived at Netherfield Park, Charles and the gardeners had made many improvements to the gardens. Now, as Caroline and Mr Tryphon strolled over the manicured grass and along the paths that wound between topiary cut to the shapes of birds, she was proud to show them to him.

'The flowers are particularly lovely,' he said, 'and I am very much enjoying their placement and the array of colours. May I presume that this represents your good taste and eye for beauty?'

Caroline had had nothing to do with the gardens, not caring about the outdoors very much unless it offered an opportunity, as it did in town, to see and be seen. Lowering her eyes modestly, she murmured, 'You are too kind.'

He stopped at that and put a finger beneath her chin, raising her face until he could see her full on. His finger was warm and gentle and his countenance, as he gazed at her, held a sort of hidden joy that was unexpected. Not removing his finger, his eyes turning serious, he said, 'I am not too kind. I can never be kind enough to one who is as generous as you have been to this young person so newly arrived in London.'

Caroline knew not what to say, and she was unable to tear her eyes from his. 'Please,' she whispered, and was uncertain if she wished him to stop touching her and saying such things, or if she wanted to hear more.

'You are so beautiful,' he said, his finger rising to trace the curve of her cheek. 'And so very elegant and accomplished. How can I not take the time and search for the words to tell you how I feel?'

'How you feel?' she asked, a flame of panic rising in her chest. She stepped back so that his hand fell to his side, and even though her cheek felt suddenly cold without his touch, she turned and pointed to the first thing she saw. 'Charles ordered that bird bath especially from Hinton and Sons which is the finest emporium of monuments and statuary in the country. Observe how the carvings beneath the basin show the fine detail of the vines and flowers.'

Mr Tryphon still looked at her, she noticed, and not at the bird bath, lovely though it was. He had a slight smile on his lips, as if he understood exactly what was on her mind and was enjoying her confusion. It was a gentle smile though, not malicious in any way. *I understand,* it seemed to say, *but I stand by my words and soon you will recognise how ardently I mean them.* Her breath caught in her throat and the garden was suddenly very still, no birds singing, no rustle of wind on leaf.

Mustering all her willpower, more confused than ever, she walked on at her usual pace, unheeding of if he followed her or not.

He did, of course, and maybe she had imagined all that had just happened. He strode beside her, slowing his steps to match hers, and made only inconsequential comments about the shrubbery and the view from her favourite gazebo. When they returned to the house, though, and he took his leave, he held her hand for a moment, and then bent low over it. His eyes, when he rose and released her, held such warmth, such hope, such fire, that she was flustered once again, and she hurried away into the house without expressing her polite gratitude for his company during the walk.

*   *   *

'A dinner at Lucas Lodge,' Louisa intoned. 'Of all things, it is what I most despise.'

'You say that no matter where we are to dine in Meryton,' Caroline said, but as she was very much in agreement with her sister's opinion of

Lucas Lodge and its inhabitants, although it was not as bad as the Phillips' home, she reached over and clasped Louisa's hand, where it dangled down the side of her wing-backed chair.

Mr Hurst apparently agreed, also, for he lifted his head from its recumbent position on the back of the settee, and nodded, before again lying back.

Charles and Mr Darcy entered the room, the former rubbing his hands together briskly. 'Are we all set?' Charles asked. 'I just know this will be a most delightful evening.'

Caroline lifted her eyes just enough to look at him, unable to find the energy to refute his assertion. There was no sense in saying anything to her brother that implied she, or any of the others, was not expecting a delightful experience. Charles would simply list all the reasons he was correct, or pretend he had not heard her.

But surely he had winced at one point during Miss Mary Bennet's performance at the pianoforte during the last visit to the Lucases? Had he not noticed the spectacle the younger Bennet sisters had made of themselves, dancing during that same visit? And how could he have not been discomfited when the family had dined with the Longs, and the conversation had turned to the benefits of raising goats?

Unable to repress a shudder, Caroline remembered a discussion, during a call from Mrs Bennet's sister, Mrs Phillips, about her disdain for long sleeves, clearly unaware that they had been all the rage in London.

Lady Amesbury and Mr Tryphon had not yet come downstairs, and Caroline thought that maybe it would be best to convince them to plead headaches so they could avoid the impending visit. She heard the sound of their steps in the hall, though, and unable to come up with a reason why they should avoid the evening's entertainment without putting herself in a bad light for having accepted the invitation, roused herself enough to stand up.

The family party moved into the front hall, where Caroline permitted her maid to wrap a shawl about her. Lady Amesbury moved to take Mr Darcy's arm, leaving Caroline to take Mr Tryphon's. Caroline was a trifle surprised that the lady had shown such preference for Mr Darcy, since he gave her no indication he welcomed her presence, but as Mr Tryphon was always ready to give his arm to her, she decided that Lady Amesbury must be assisting her in making Mr Darcy jealous.

There were several carriages already standing empty on Lucas Lodge's white stone drive, their coachmen huddling together around a fire inside a barrel.

The Lodge was full of light and sound when she entered and handed her wrap to the waiting maid. Candles and lamps glowed throughout the front hall and around the large rooms the Lucases used for entertaining. Voices rose and fell, laughter bubbled, the noise loud enough to grate on her ears. Sir William approached, his lady on his arm, his bloodhound face split wide with his customary smile.

'Welcome, you are most welcome indeed.' He bowed to the ladies. 'And come in good time.' He rubbed his hands together and bobbed on his heels, a habit of his that always made Caroline think of a pigeon that walked towards one, hoping for a dropped crumb. Lady Lucas smiled at Caroline and Louisa and made her curtsey, which they returned. Lady Amesbury and Mr Tryphon moved towards the pianoforte, which Sir William wanted to show them.

Once the pleasantries and introductions were completed, everyone was free to do whatever and go wherever they pleased. The problem, Caroline thought, smiling at Mrs Long as she passed by, was that there was nothing anyone wanted to do and nowhere anyone wanted to go. Except, of course, for Charles, who crossed the room to where Miss Bennet stood with her mother. Caroline watched him go, and then searched for Mr Darcy, to encourage him in his observations of her brother.

He was nowhere close to Charles. Looking about the crowded room, she finally spotted him hovering near the drinks table. Moving closer to him, smiling distantly at those who approached her but not stopping, she assumed he'd sought fortification before he moved to where Charles and Miss Bennet stood. Mrs Bennet had relieved them of her presence, for she was on the other side of the room, laughing at something her youngest daughter said.

As she neared Mr Darcy, Caroline observed that while he held a glass of punch in his hand, his attention was not on it or on Charles and Miss Bennet. Instead, she was astounded to see, he was gazing at Miss Elizabeth, who conversed with Colonel Forster, the highest-ranking officer of the militia company, recently stationed near by.

Whatever could Darcy be thinking, she wondered, but then realised what he was up to. He was listening to Elizabeth so he could recount some foolish thing she'd said, to entertain Caroline and the others after they returned to Netherfield Park.

Colonel Forster bowed to Miss Elizabeth and moved to speak to some of his men. The soldiers added a festive air to the room, in their red coats and white breeches. Several of them, Caroline noticed, were clustered around Mrs Bennet and her two youngest.

Miss Elizabeth's friend, one of the Miss Lucases, joined her friend, who looked over her shoulder at Mr Darcy, and then with a sly smile, asked her friend, 'What does Mr Darcy mean, by listening to my conversation with Colonel Forster?'

Miss Lucas glanced at Mr Darcy, but at least tried to be circumspect about it. 'That is a question which Mr Darcy only can answer.'

Miss Elizabeth, oh, the impudence, turned to face Mr Darcy full on. He, for some unfathomable reason, did not turn on his heel and stalk away.

Miss Elizabeth turned her back on him, and said to Miss Lucas, 'But if he does it any more, I shall certainly let him know that I see what he is about.'

More curious than ever, Caroline moved to the side to where she had a view of Mr Darcy's profile.

'He has a very satirical eye,' Miss Elizabeth continued, 'and if I do not begin by being impertinent myself, I shall grow afraid of him.'

Caroline stifled a gasp. How dare that chit speak so of Mr Darcy? Had she no sense of what was owed to one of his rank? Glancing at him, expecting to see his brow lowered, she gasped again, this time unable to keep quiet. He was looking at Miss Elizabeth full on, and he was smiling!

On hearing her gasp, though, he turned away from the two and moved to Caroline's side. 'Are you quite well, Miss Bingley?'

'I know not,' she said, 'but I must ask the same question of you. How is it that you stand by when one such as she speaks of you with such lack of respect?'

His eyes moved again to Miss Elizabeth, who with Miss Lucas had moved some little distance further and was speaking to a couple of the red-coated officers. 'I am quite well,' he said.

Convinced now that Mr Darcy was suffering from some dreadful ailment, Caroline coaxed him into bringing them both a glass of punch by pretending to feel a little faint. He absently handed her the glass he'd obtained earlier, but she insisted she needed a fresh drink. He then led her to a chair, gazing at her in concern, and stood beside her as she sipped. It was dreadful, much too sweet. 'Thank you,' she said, 'for your kind attentions. Oh, how I long for the entertainments of town. Do you not also, Mr Darcy?'

Mr Tryphon, whom she'd quite forgotten about because she was so taken with observing Mr Darcy observe Miss Elizabeth when he was supposed to be observing Charles and Miss Bennet, appeared and took the chair beside Caroline.

'I saw that you looked a trifle pale,' Mr Tryphon said. 'Even though I knew Mr Darcy would take good care of you, I had to approach to ensure that all is well.'

'Thank you,' Caroline said. 'I was a little dizzy, no doubt from the closeness of the room. So many people in such a small space. Is it not unfortunate that the Lucases think they can entertain everyone in Meryton all at once?'

Mr Tryphon nodded and smiled at her witticism. Mr Darcy, though, said, 'I am much relieved to see that you are recovered, Miss Bingley.' He bowed and moved away. She stood, needing to ascertain if he was finally going to check on Charles. Instead, with a growing sense of unreality, she saw him move towards Miss Elizabeth and Miss Lucas.

Ignoring Mr Tryphon, who protested, 'I am certain, Miss Bingley, that it would be much better if you sat a while longer,' she followed Mr Darcy.

She arrived just in time to hear Miss Lucas say to her friend, 'Here he is again. Why do you not ask him yourself?' She smiled and took Miss Elizabeth's hand in her own. 'Or, are you now afraid?'

Miss Elizabeth's eyes danced with mischief, something better suited to a person much younger than she. *Really*, Caroline thought, *is there no end to the lack of manners one person can display?*

Apparently there was not, for Miss Elizabeth turned to Mr Darcy and, with utmost seriousness, asked, 'Did you not think, Mr Darcy, that I expressed myself uncommonly well just now, when I was teasing Colonel Forster to give us a ball at Meryton?'

He regarded her for a moment, and then replied, 'With great energy; but it is a subject which always makes a lady energetic.'

She nodded, almost as if showing respect, but said, 'You are severe on us.'

'It will be her turn soon to be teased,' said Miss Lucas to Mr Darcy.

Caroline's dizziness became real. Both these girls dared to speak so to him? And he, smiling, seemingly enjoying the conversation?

'I am going to open the instrument, Eliza,' Miss Lucas continued, 'and you know what follows.'

'You are a very strange creature by way of a friend!—always wanting me to play and sing before anybody and everybody!' Miss Elizabeth playfully tapped Miss Lucas on the arm. 'If my vanity had taken a musical turn, you would have been invaluable; but as it is, I would really rather not sit down before those who must be in the habit of hearing the very best performers.'

At least, thought Caroline, *she has that much sense in her head.*

Miss Lucas continued to entreat her friend, and at length Miss Elizabeth gave in, perhaps because Mr Darcy gazed at her with what appeared to be encouragement.

'Very well,' she said, 'if it must be so, it must.'

They made their way to the pianoforte that stood in one corner, and others in the room, observing them, made pleased-sounding noises and moved to take seats from which they could observe the instrument and she who played it.

Caroline stood quite unmoving, unable to stir, until she felt a warm arm about her waist and blinked before recognizing Lady Amesbury. Mr Tryphon stood at a little distance, clearly distressed.

'You over-exert yourself, Miss Bingley,' he said, his voice filled with concern. 'Please allow me to escort you to a seat and bring you some refreshments.'

Caroline turned to face him. She'd thought of him often since their walk together in Netherfield Park's gardens, in fact, she sometimes found it difficult not to think of him. She could not understand why this would be. Why would she spend even a moment thinking of any man other than Mr Darcy? After all, he was the man she would wed. While she always thought about Mr Darcy when she was with him, somehow, when she was elsewhere, there were so many other things to fill her mind. It was the result of being an educated and accomplished woman, no doubt, but she felt a trifle guilty, as if she'd somehow done wrong to Mr Darcy, and resolved to do better in the future.

Now, though, she looked at Mr Tryphon, at his handsome face, not as handsome as Mr Darcy's, of course, but very pleasant all the same. The concern for her in his eyes, and the slight smile that formed on his lips when he saw that she looked at him; surely those were good reasons why, at times, he was in her mind? It would be rude, after all, to treat him as if he did not exist.

So, for his sake, she smiled and protested that she felt in the best of health. 'If I looked distressed at all, it was on Mr Darcy's behalf,' she said. 'He suffers so greatly from having to show himself among people such as those present.'

'He suffers?' Lady Amesbury said, with such surprise in her voice that Caroline hastened to defend him.

'Of course. He is unaccustomed to moving among circles that are so decidedly beneath him. Making conversation with one such as Lady Lucas or, heaven forbid, Mrs Bennet, causes him great grief.'

'I am astonished,' Lady Amesbury said. 'I would have thought that any one with a cultured mind would find great amusement at such a gathering. Am I not right, Stephen?'

He nodded. 'It has indeed been a most interesting evening so far.'

'Now it is I who is astonished,' Caroline said. 'Pray, enlighten me on the amusements to be found.'

'Oh, where to begin?' Lady Amesbury laughed and looked about the room. 'There, that woman, the one in the hideous yellow gown. Does not the sight of her make you laugh? And the conversations! Two ladies were speaking of whether or not to buy a shoat, a baby pig, of all things! Why would anyone even consider bringing such a dirty, smelly thing anywhere near their property? A gentleman and a lady wondered whether they should continue to instruct their daughter in music, or engage a tutor. I can't imagine anyone who has the time to spend instructing their off-spring. And the wiles used by one young woman in particular. How she'd smile, so coyly, and flutter her lashes, and come close enough to several of the young men of the militia so that they moved closer in hopes of encountering the warmth of her touch. And how she'd move away, just before allowing this, and look at the unfortunate men, and laugh so gaily as if together they had just shared the greatest joke in the world. Poor young men, they had not the least chance of resisting her. Why, I could learn a thing or two about flirting from her, and I have been married more than once, so clearly I am well versed in that particular art.' She laughed again at the memories, and then put a hand on Caroline's arm. 'But tell me of this Mrs Bennet and her daughters. I have heard much about them, but have yet to be introduced.'

'You have encountered at least one,' Caroline said dryly. 'The youngest, Miss Lydia. And no doubt her sister, Miss Kitty, was not far away. They are attracted to anything in a red coat as a moth is to a flame.'

'Without the risk of becoming burned, no doubt,' Mr Tryphon said. 'Unlike what might befall those poor young men.'

'Do you,' Caroline asked, 'dislike flirting, Mr Tryphon?'

'Not at all,' he said hastily. 'It is useful in encouraging a certain sort of interaction between men and women.' He smiled, and assumed a scholarly air, ticking off his points as if on a blackboard. 'It enables a young woman to show a young man that she is interested in him in ways that do not overstep the bounds of propriety. It provides amusement, both for those engaged in it and for those who observe. It is one of the social arts, and as such is worthy of study.' He paused, and his face became serious, as if his thoughts had suddenly turned dark. 'However, there is an inherent risk, one that is more likely to strike down the young man.'

Caroline didn't like seeing him appear sombre, and so endeavoured to bring back his former, lighter mood. 'And what risk might that be? Do tell me, I am all ears.'

'Why,' he said, and did not answer her smile with one of his own, 'the risk of a broken heart.'

All three fell silent for a moment. He was looking at Caroline so intently that she wondered if he referred to himself. She thought back and wondered if any of her behaviour or conversation with him could be construed as flirting. She didn't think so. Despite it being a social art, she saw no reason for it. Except, perhaps, with Mr Darcy, but any flirting she did with him was always refined and in good taste. And it wasn't truly flirting, she decided. It was merely the easy interactions between two good friends.

Lady Amesbury, who quickly became bored with any situation that did not involve her speaking, asked, 'On what grounds, dear Stephen, do you assert that men are at greater risk of having their hearts broken? Is not the tender heart of a woman equally, if not more likely, to be so abused?'

Caroline's eyes were still held by his, but when the lady spoke, he appeared to give himself a mental shake, for he turned to her with a wide smile. 'Not having such a tender heart myself, I find myself ill equipped to speak of a lady's heart. But I do believe that men, who are unable to share their innermost thoughts and feelings with one another as women do, find that their emotions run deeper and so are experienced more fully.'

'How charming,' Lady Amesbury said. 'Let me assure you, my dear one, that you should feel free to share any of your innermost thoughts and feelings with me, whenever you like. And I am certain that Caroline will be most happy to offer you the same service.'

Caught off guard, Caroline hastened to nod. 'Of course. For we are friends, are we not?'

'You two are more than that, I think.' Lady Amesbury took Caroline's hand and placed it through Mr Tryphon's arm. 'You are my two most dear friends, and so must be as equally dear to each other.'

Beneath Caroline's touch, his muscle tensed, and she marvelled at how it could feel as hard as stone, and yet have nothing of a stone's harshness or cold.

Lady Amesbury smiled at the two of them, appearing almost maternal in her regard, which surprised Caroline. She realised she did not know if the lady had children. She had mentioned being married more than once, but beyond that, Caroline knew very little about her personal life. 'Tell me,' the lady said, 'which person here is Mrs Bennet? For it is of she that I have heard others speak most often.'

Caroline was aware of Mr Tryphon turning, as his muscles shifted beneath her fingers on his forearm, and his side brushed hers as he moved his upper body. Her skin tingled where contact was made, and she marvelled at how this could happen, even through all the layers of his and her clothing. Clearly, though, both of her friends wished to behold Mrs Bennet, and so despite her own preference to think about that woman as little as possible, she looked around to find her.

'It is never very difficult to locate her,' she said, and indicated with her head the direction they should look. 'One merely has to listen for the loudest and most irritating voice in the room.'

Sure enough, Mrs Bennet sat in the midst of several of the local women, her hands flying as she spoke. She paused, said something else and instantly everyone around her burst into laughter. She laughed, also, her voice rising above all the others.

'I see what you mean.' Lady Amesbury's face showed, not the disgust Caroline expected, but an almost avid look. 'I look forward to speaking to her myself. Just think,' she turned to Mr Tryphon, 'of what might be learned.'

'Mrs Bennet, I can assure you, has very little to teach anyone, let alone a person as cultured as yourself.' Caroline could not understand Lady Amesbury's reaction to Mrs Bennet. In town, the lady surrounded herself with only those of the highest circles.

'And may I assume,' the lady continued, 'that the young woman so often by your brother's side is the eldest Miss Bennet?'

Caroline must have looked surprised that she knew that, for Lady Amesbury quickly explained. 'He has spoken of her to me. I can see that she is truly beautiful, perhaps as beautiful as he thinks she is. There is something of the young naïf in her bearing.'

'Naïve indeed. But that term could be equally applied to Charles. I don't know what he can be thinking in singling her out as he does.'

'Can you not?' Mr Tryphon patted her hand where it still rested on his arm. 'That is one of the things I most admire about you, Miss Bingley. You are unaware of the darker impulses we all carry.'

'Are you implying,' she said, trying to rein in her anger, 'that my brother spends time with Miss Bennet out of some dark, terrible impulse?'

'Oh no, not at all.' He quickly sought to explain himself. 'I merely meant that we cannot always choose, with our reason, who we fall in love with. The heart has its own logic. As I am learning myself, even as we speak.'

His hand still rested on hers, and he tightened his grip, not enough to hurt, but enough that she felt as if he was trying to tell her something through the contact. What that might be, however, she did not know, although a faint idea was beginning to grow in her mind. Before she could think any more about this new and somewhat alarming realisation, Lady Amesbury asked to have the other Miss Bennets pointed out to her.

'Is the young lady currently at the piano one of them?' she asked. 'I think she plays quite delightfully.'

'Yes,' Caroline replied. 'That is Miss Elizabeth. Do you truly find her playing delightful? She puts a great deal of feeling into it, but her technique is very poor.'

Lady Amesbury smiled. 'Certainly she is not half the musician you are, dear Caroline. But among this group, I feel she is more than adequate. Mr Darcy appears to agree with me.'

Caroline whirled, letting go of Mr Tryphon's arm in her haste to locate Mr Darcy. He stood at some little distance from the pianoforte, but from his position he had a good view of the performer. She moved to the side a little, so she could see his face. A small smile rested on his lips, and his eyes were warm.

'I can assure you,' she said to her companions, 'that Mr Darcy finds nothing to admire about that particular person. Why, some of his most amusing utterances owe their existence to his disdain for Miss Elizabeth.'

'Indeed.' Lady Amesbury raised a brow. 'But look, she is leaving the piano. Another young woman, it appears, is about to perform.'

Caroline groaned. 'That is Miss Mary Bennet. I can find little good to say about Miss Elizabeth, for she is impudent and disrespectful to her betters. I am willing to confess, though, that I would rather listen to her perform than Miss Mary.'

'Really?' Lady Amesbury listened for a moment. 'Technically, Miss Mary is the better player.'

'Yes, but she plays only to receive accolades from those who hear her.

Surely you agree, Lady Amesbury, that a true musician plays for herself and the pleasure she can bring others, not for praise.'

'I agree with Miss Caroline,' Mr Tryphon said. 'The purest art is found when the performer allows the music to speak for itself.'

Caroline smiled at him, and his smile leapt to his face in return.

'My goodness,' Lady Amesbury said with a mock pout. 'I had no idea I was in the presence of two such exalted musicians.'

Mr Tryphon laughed. 'Exalted? Not I. I do not perform in any manner. No, I am simply an admirer of beauty in whatever form it chooses to take.'

The trio drifted apart at this point, moving about the room in the aimless manner of people at a party who were happy to be on their own but were willing to find entertainment, should it offer itself.

Mary Bennet had completed her chosen concerto, but Caroline's hope that someone more accomplished might be permitted to perform, herself for example, was disappointed, for Mary began to play some airs and other trifles that were suitable for dancing. Several people immediately moved to the area that had been cleared for dancing including, Caroline was displeased to note, Charles and Miss Bennet.

Caroline wondered if Mr Darcy had remembered at any time during the evening that he had promised to observe them. Searching for his tall form, she was relieved to see him standing alone. She began to wend her way through the crowd, eager to learn what Mr Darcy had surmised about Charles' affections.

As she neared Mr Darcy, Sir William, whom she hadn't noticed standing near by, turned to Mr Darcy and spoke. 'What a charming amusement for young people this is, Mr Darcy! There is nothing like dancing, after all. I consider it as one of the first refinements of polished societies.'

Mr Darcy, appearing surprised to be addressed, said, 'Certainly, sir; and it has the advantage also of being in vogue amongst the less polished societies of the world. Every savage can dance.'

Caroline was much relieved. This was the Mr Darcy she recognised. How foolish she'd been to even consider that he had found something pleasing among the people present at this gathering.

She'd thought Sir William would be subdued by being put so clearly in his place, but the man merely smiled. 'Your friend performs delightfully,' he said, speaking of Charles, 'and I doubt not that you are an adept in the science yourself, Mr Darcy.'

'You saw me dance at the assembly, I believe, sir,' Mr Darcy said.

'Yes, indeed, and received no inconsiderable pleasure from the sight.'

Glancing about the room, no doubt seeking inspiration for something to say that would further irritate Mr Darcy, Sir William's eyes fell on Miss Elizabeth who was moving towards them, but without intention of speaking. Sir William called out to her, 'My dear Miss Eliza, why are you not dancing? Mr Darcy, you must allow me to present this young lady to you as a very desirable partner. You cannot refuse to dance, I am sure, when so much beauty is before you.'

He took her hand meaning, Caroline saw, to give it to Mr Darcy.

'Now,' Caroline said with savage glee to Lady Amesbury, who had materialized at her side, 'you will see Mr Darcy at his best. He despises all the young women of Meryton, but that one in particular.'

'Does he?' the lady asked, and something in her voice made Caroline look back at the little tableau. Mr Darcy, as expected, was clearly taken aback at this offer but, instead of stepping away with distaste, was lifting his hand to take that of Miss Elizabeth. It was she, and not Mr Darcy, who drew back.

'Indeed, sir,' she said to Sir William, 'I have not the least intention of dancing. I entreat you not to suppose that I moved this way in order to beg for a partner.'

'Of course she did,' Caroline whispered, 'but can she be so ignorant that she thinks she has a chance with a man like Mr Darcy?'

'Perhaps she does, my dear,' Lady Amesbury said, and with growing disbelief, Caroline heard Mr Darcy say that he would very much like the honour of dancing with Miss Elizabeth.

A greater surprise awaited Caroline, for Elizabeth was determined not to dance, and withstood Sir William's entreaty. She curtseyed, and turned away.

'Well,' Lady Amesbury said to Caroline, 'perhaps he is not as indifferent as you suppose.'

'Nonsense,' snapped Caroline, forgetting to whom she spoke, and stepping forward, she accosted Mr Darcy.

'I can guess the subject of your reverie.'

'I should imagine not,' said he, still gazing after Miss Elizabeth.

'You are considering,' Caroline said, trying but failing to keep desperation from her voice, 'how insupportable it would be to pass many evenings in this manner—in such society.' *There*, she thought, *now Lady Amesbury will see how completely I understand this man.*

But the night's surprises were not yet over, for though he turned away from Miss Elizabeth and looked at her, he said, 'Your conjecture is totally wrong, I assure you. My mind was much more agreeably engaged. I have been meditating on the very great pleasure which a pair of fine eyes in the face of a pretty woman can bestow.'

Caroline gaped but then, realising he must be speaking of herself, inquired coyly, 'Would you please inform me of the lady who has the credit of inspiring such reflections?'

Mr Darcy replied in all seriousness and without even pausing to think, 'Miss Elizabeth Bennet.'

Caroline stepped back, reeling as if from a blow. 'Miss Elizabeth Bennet! I am all astonishment. How long has she been such a favourite?—and pray, when am I to wish you joy?'

Mr Darcy looked down at her. 'That is exactly the question I expected you to ask.' Was that disapproval she heard in his voice? 'A lady's imagination is very rapid,' he continued, 'it jumps from admiration to love, from love to matrimony, in a moment. I knew you would be wishing me joy.'

He smiled, and suddenly Caroline felt a little better, for it was his usual smile when they spoke to one another, a smile that hinted at a shared meeting of minds. Playfully, she spoke in turn. 'Nay, if you are serious about it, I shall consider the matter is absolutely settled. You shall have a charming mother-in-law, indeed; and, of course, she will be always at Pemberley with you.'

She continued in this vein, speaking in turn of Miss Lydia and Miss Kitty, and how he would have to find husbands for them, so they would not also have to live at Pemberley, but as she spoke, her heart sank, for instead of joining her in this amusement, he listened with complete indifference and indeed, moved off at one point as she was still speaking. Hurt and silenced by astonishment, she watched him go and only after some time became aware of Lady Amesbury standing close beside her.

'And will you seek,' Caroline said bitterly, too upset to care how this affected her friendship with the lady, 'to rub salt in my wounds and mock me for my pretensions about Mr Darcy?'

Lady Amesbury took Caroline's hands in hers and said, 'What nonsense you speak. I could never mock you, for I hold you in too high respect. Are we not friends?'

Caroline blinked back the sudden wetness in her eyes. 'You humble me. I will never forget the condescension you show me. Indeed, I cannot even imagine a better friend than you.'

'I am relieved,' the lady said, 'and I think that the time for formality between us has long passed by. Please call me Eleanor.'

'I am made speechless by this honour,' Caroline gasped, 'and will comply only if you do me the honour of calling me by my given name.'

'Of course.' Eleanor stood on her toes and leaned in to kiss Caroline on the cheek. 'And I hope you are not too disappointed by Mr Darcy's apparent lack of judgement in this matter. Men are so often swayed hither and yon by the flash of a slender ankle or the sight of a pretty face. He is too sensible, I am sure, to continue thus.'

'You give me hope,' Caroline said, but she thought not of Mr Darcy but of her brother. 'And while I am well-acquainted with Mr Darcy, I think of him only as my brother's friend. There is nothing for me to be concerned about.' *I lie*, she thought, *but only as all women do, to preserve their sense of confidence in front of their friends.*

She and Eleanor smiled, and slipping their arms about one another, moved through the room, eager to find a new source of entertainment.

Chapter Four

The next morning Caroline arose somewhat later than usual for she had been so overwhelmed by her experiences during the previous evening she'd been unable to get to sleep for some time. Thoughts had run through her head and she'd been unable to quiet them: Mr Darcy's smile, Mr Tryphon's firm arm, Mr Darcy's haughtiness, Mr Tryphon's eyes, Lady Ames–, no, Eleanor's greatness of character, and always, Miss Elizabeth's eyes. After a prolonged effort that took too much time, Caroline had convinced herself that Mr Darcy had been joking. Sleep had at last found her and if she'd dreamt of anything, she did not recall it on this sunny morning.

She realised that Louisa, Charles, and Mr Darcy would already have breakfasted, but Mr Hurst would not yet have arisen. Knowing that the servants always made certain breakfast was available and the foods and tea were served fresh until the last person had eaten, she did not trouble herself to hurry through her morning ablutions. Once Genney had finally selected a gown Caroline felt would suit her today, and had completed dressing her hair to her satisfaction, she left her room filled with confidence that perhaps today Mr Darcy would declare himself.

Approaching the breakfast room, she heard the murmur of voices, and recognised those of Mr Tryphon and Eleanor. As she was about to enter the room, she distinctly heard the words 'Mr Darcy' in Eleanor's voice and paused, wondering what her friend could have to say about him.

'You have nothing to concern yourself with, Stephen,' Eleanor said. 'He is chasing after someone who is well suited to him.'

'Do you think so?' Stephen sounded surprised.

'When a person has spent a lifetime studying other people, as I have, she learns to recognise the signs.'

Mr Darcy? Chasing someone well suited to him? Who else could it be but herself, Caroline Bingley?

'That leaves you a clean field.' Eleanor's voice broke into Caroline's thoughts.

There was a sound, as of someone pushing the chair back so as to stand up. Caroline wondered if she should hide. *No*, she thought, *this is my home and I am its mistress. I have no reason to hide. If they come out I will be merely about to enter the room.* Such subterfuge was not required, though, for the sounds indicated that the person who had arisen from the table had merely gone in search of more food at the sideboard.

'Do you truly think she will have me?' Stephen's voice sounded casual, but Caroline was certain she heard a touch of wistfulness in it.

'Of course. You have much to offer, as I have discovered myself.' The two laughed then, and Caroline was uncertain how to interpret the sound, for it spoke of shared secrets and something else, a sense of hidden pleasures. But why would they laugh about hidden pleasures? What kind of pleasure would Eleanor need to conceal, she who moved through her world with the confidence of one who knows who she is and can do whatever she desires?

'You are very handsome,' Eleanor continued, 'and exceedingly charming when you exert yourself. And you are rich, did you forget?' She burst into laughter, and he joined her.

Caroline was confused by their laughter, but something else in the conversation held first place in her head. How could anyone forget he was rich? Her family's attaining of wealth was recent enough that Caroline never forgot it, not for a moment. All through her life she had behaved in a manner accepted in those circles where wealth was assumed, spoken of casually, as much a part of a person as was her hair or her feet. Even now, when she was rich, she never forgot the risks of revealing her family's ignominious past, in trade. That knowledge would be enough to cause her downfall, for she would be shunned by all the people she most wanted to impress.

'Yes,' Stephen said. 'And soon I shall be truly rich, shall I not?'

Perhaps he has a business deal about to come to fruition. Or a wealthy relative who is elderly and who, when he or she passes on, will leave everything to this much-beloved descendant.

The clinks of knife and fork placed on plate, and cup on saucer, were suddenly more definitive, and Caroline realised her friends were finishing their meal. Smoothing her gown to ensure that her pause to listen had not wrinkled it, she placed a delighted smile on her face and entered the room, where equally delighted smiles greeted her.

*   *   *

The next several days flowed one into the next, the rhythm of life in the country passing by as a stream gurgles past the trees that grow along its banks, their leaves rustling with the wind but staying attached to their branches, remaining in place. Drives about the countryside, overseeing the servants, receiving callers, making as few calls as possible, hosting a dinner for the Lucases, games of cards during the evenings.

Caroline observed Mr Darcy when she could, for he often was absent from the house or closeted in the library with Charles. She looked for the clues Eleanor had used to know he pursued Caroline, but he seemed much the same as always, polite, reserved, and gentlemanlike.

She went for no more walks with Mr Tryphon, but he often sought out her company, holding a skein of silk when she needed to make it into a neat ball, offering to be her partner at cards, holding out his arm to escort her in to dinner. Mr Darcy, who had been accustomed to being her escort before Eleanor and Mr Tryphon's arrival, was very well-mannered about this, stepping aside each time Mr Tryphon drew near as dinner was announced. Caroline was impressed to see how nobly Mr Darcy treated both her guests, even though she knew he did not respect them. He hadn't said anything, he would never be so rude, but to one who knew him as well as she, the signs were clear. He stood further away when the whole party was assembled after dinner, and spent more time looking out of the window, even though it was dark and so nothing could be seen. He preferred to read or write letters, instead of playing cards, and even when an evening of music was the selected entertainment, he listened but without his usual intensity.

This evening was typical. Louisa and Mr Hurst, Caroline and Mr Tryphon made up a table for cards. Mr Darcy had been reading, sitting in a chair by the fire, but after a time he set his book aside, rose, and moved to the window.

Caroline rose also, suddenly weary of the game. Mr Tryphon leapt to his feet. 'Miss Bingley, please sit. Whatever you desire, I will bring it to you.'

She waved him off. 'Thank you, but there is nothing I require. I merely thought that perhaps Eleanor would like to participate in the game for a time.'

'Then allow me to relinquish my place. Everyone's enjoyment will increase when two such accomplished women take part.'

Caroline looked to where Eleanor sat, reading the letters that had arrived for her earlier that day. Eleanor received many letters, as she'd explained to Caroline, so she could keep up with all the latest news from town. Caroline loved to watch her friend when she read a letter for the first time. Eleanor's features were fluidly expressive as she absorbed the details her friends sent her. Her brow might furrow, her beautifully curved eyebrows lower, she might go so far as to nibble on her lower lip. The next moment she would throw back her head and let out a silvery peal of laughter, before her mood would change again and her fingers would tighten on the paper.

Now, stepping away from the card table enough to prove to Mr Tryphon that she was determined, she caught Eleanor's eye. Surely her friend would recognise Caroline's desire to have an opportunity to speak to Mr Darcy. Caroline had never mentioned her expectations for him and Pemberley, but she knew a woman as observant as her friend could not have helped but notice the attraction between Caroline and Mr Darcy. To her surprise, Eleanor looked from Caroline to Mr Tryphon and back to Caroline, but then returned her attention to her letter. Caroline turned back to Mr Tryphon, astonished to realise that Eleanor had responded to his request, presumably to keep Caroline with him, instead of to Caroline's. When she turned, she saw him looking straight at her, his face solemn, and something in his eyes sent a shiver down her spine. As soon as she moved towards the table, she realised she must have imagined this, for his smile was as broad, his eyes as warm, as they always were.

'I do apologise,' she said to the three still at the table, 'but I am unaccountably weary of cards.' Gaining a sudden insight, she added, 'Louisa, perhaps you would be so kind as to play us some music. I would so love to hear that new concerto you have been practising so beautifully.'

'I would be happy to do so,' her sister said, 'if you truly believe my feeble efforts have reached a point where the music will not harm rather than enchant the present company. But I require a page turner.'

Louisa turned to her husband but Caroline broke in quickly. 'Mr Tryphon, I am certain, would be delighted to perform this service.' She turned her brightest smile on him, took a step closer and rested her hand on his arm. He looked at her hand, moved as if to draw her closer, but then squared his shoulders. 'Of course. I am honoured that I can take part, even in such a small way, in the creation of music as lovely as I know this will be.' He followed Louisa to the pianoforte, leaving Mr Hurst to grumble about the unfinished game of cards.

Caroline moved towards Mr Darcy, but Eleanor called her to sit beside her. Caroline sent a wistful glance towards Mr Darcy, but sat next to her friend, consoling herself that she might learn something amusing that was happening in London. Eleanor was usually very stingy with her letters. She showed them to Mr Tryphon, though. Caroline had once entered a room to see the two of them, heads bent, reading intently. When they'd looked up and seen her, the letter had instantly vanished and both had risen, expressing their joy in seeing their friend.

Eleanor folded away the one she was reading, and asked, 'Were you not enjoying Stephen's company at cards? Was he perhaps not skilled enough? It was my impression that you were ahead in points.'

'Mr Tryphon is an admirable partner,' Caroline said, a little surprised at her friend's query. 'I was simply weary of playing. I am certain spending time with you will be much more amusing.' Putting as much uninterest into her voice as possible, she asked, 'What news from town?'

'Nothing much,' Eleanor said. 'I am distressed, though, to learn that you are weary. Perhaps if Stephen, after he finishes assisting Mrs Hurst, were to take you for a brief turn outside, the fresh air will return to you the gaiety I so adore in you.'

A warmth rose up in Caroline and she clasped Eleanor's hands in hers. 'All I need when I am weary is to hear you speak thusly. No one could have such a dear friend as you.'

The two smiled at each other and then Eleanor disengaged her hands, gently, but she broke the connection. 'Shall I let Stephen know that his service is once again required?'

Caroline sighed. 'I thank you but I have no wish to venture outside. Can you not tell me something of what takes place in London? Even without your presence, which must be difficult indeed to bear for those still there, some of our friends must have encountered something that will amuse we who languish here in the country.'

'I'm afraid town life is very dull.' Eleanor sat up straighter. 'Oh look, Louisa has finished that lovely piece. Stephen will be free to attend us. Whenever I am weary, his presence is the finest tonic in the world.'

Caroline shot to her feet. It had clearly been a mistake to sit with Eleanor instead of moving to where Mr Darcy stood by the window, but she hadn't wanted to be too obvious in her desire for a private moment. 'Louisa,' she said, moving towards the piano, 'please, it would so delight me if you could play the other piece we were practising together. You play it so much better than I, and Mr Tryphon is clearly a very talented page turner, for you didn't miss a single note.'

Louisa looked a little surprised, for usually Caroline preferred to be the one sharing her accomplishments with the company, but she nodded and began to play. Mr Tryphon stared at Caroline a moment, his look unreadable, but she didn't care. Wasting no more time, she moved on, never taking a straight course, but ensuring that she would end up beside Mr Darcy.

At first he seemed not to notice her presence. After a moment, she spoke. 'I wonder, Mr Darcy, what it is that is so engaging outside this window. It must be that you have eyes like a cat, to see so well in the dark.'

He turned at the sound of her voice, and studied her for a moment. 'Sometimes,' he said at length, 'it is those things we cannot see that shine most brightly.'

Nonsense, she wanted to say. Caroline disliked talk of things that made no sense even more than she disliked poetry. She put a playful note into her voice. 'And is there something out there that neither of us can see but which shines brightly?'

He did not answer, but turned once again towards the night.

A frisson of fear sent a chill through Caroline. Mr Darcy, she knew, often preferred to stand alone, even when in the midst of a lively party. And he did seem to prefer looking outside to playing cards. As far as she knew there was nothing outside in the direction this window faced—a lot of muddy fields and meadows, crossed once by a curve of a road. 'Can you share with me what you see?' She truly was curious now, but in case he was joking, she did not want to appear gullible. 'I would so dearly love to know.'

He sighed, and turned towards her, away from the window. Reassured now that she had his full attention, that she had been able to tear him away from whatever it was that drew him to the darkness without, she laughed. 'There is nothing at all shining outside, is there? I knew it! Perhaps it is only your own reflection that draws you to the glass.'

He smiled a bit at that, and she continued. 'I did not know that personal vanity was one of your faults, Mr Darcy.' When he frowned, she rushed on. 'In fact, I did not know you had any faults at all. I have never, until now, seen even one.'

'I am not perfect by any means, Miss Bingley,' he said, but his tone was light.

'Indeed not. I did not expect you to be.' She tilted her head to one side and pretended to study him in great detail. 'Although when you were so determined to gaze out of this window, I did wonder if I observed a most alarming imperfection. For the next habitation this direction from Netherfield Park is Longbourn.' She smiled up at him. 'Tell me true, now, is it thoughts of Mrs Bennet that have you unable to look away from where she is at present? Or of Miss Elizabeth and her fine eyes?'

His transformation was immediate. She didn't see a single muscle in his face move, but even though he still stood before her he suddenly was many miles distant. He offered her a frosty smile, a brief bow, and left the room.

All astonished, she stood without knowing for how long, when a faint warmth appeared at her side, and she blinked and saw Mr Tryphon.

'I think,' he said softly, 'that perhaps country life begins to wear on you. You long for the lights and laughter of the city.'

'I thank you for your concern,' she said, lifting her chin, 'but I am exceedingly content to be exactly where I am.'

He gazed at her, his eyes moving over her face, her eyes, her cheeks, her mouth, back to her eyes. 'You, Caroline Bingley, are a woman created for the light. You deserve to have it shining on you always. I wish I . . .'

'Yes?' she said as he paused. How was it that Mr Tryphon's words could so easily entwine her so that she felt, in his presence, as if a warm shawl had floated down to rest about her shoulders?

'I wish you would allow me . . .' His lips moved, he appeared to be struggling against something held within himself, then he turned abruptly away to gaze, as had Mr Darcy, out of the window, 'It is too soon,' she heard him whisper, and wondered what it was about this window that made men say such strange things.

He shrugged then, and turned back, his countenance again what it always was, smiling, gentle. 'You appear to be slightly chilled,' he said, 'standing so close to this window. I wish you would permit me to at least fetch you a wrap, and, if I may be so bold, allow me to escort you to a seat by the fire and to fetch you a cup of tea.'

She gazed at him, feeling warmed already. He was kind, and always solicitous of her well-being. Even if sometimes his words, his nearness, his touch, suggested images and emotions she could not understand, he was her dear friend, Mr Tryphon. Unlike Mr Darcy, he never walked away from her without speaking. Mr Darcy was the man she would marry—she'd always known that; just as she knew Charles' life was bound to that of Mr Darcy's sister, Georgiana. But that was no reason she could not enjoy a friendship that had begun so easily she'd scarcely noticed when Mr Tryphon became a constant companion. There was no reason not to enjoy a mild flirtation, especially since she was sure Mr Darcy had noticed it and did not approve. They were not engaged yet; she was free to do as she pleased.

She held out her hand to Mr Tryphon. He seized it instantly and held it in his, then raised it to his lips, for his broad shoulders and back shielded the action from the room. The warmth of his lips, the faint whisper of his breath on the back of her hand, and above all, the secrecy, brought a rush of heat to her head, and she swayed, suddenly dizzy. He instantly placed her hand on his arm, and touched her lightly on her back until she was again steady on her feet. Only then did she look out into the room, seeing Louisa now sitting with Eleanor, and Mr Hurst lying back in his chair. Not a one of them was paying any attention to her and Mr Tryphon.

Smiling, she permitted him to escort her to a chair by the fire, find her wrap on the settee, and fetch her a cup of tea. The wrap was unnecessary, as indeed was the fire, for the warmth of his mouth on her hand filled her still.

* * *

The next afternoon Mr Tryphon approached her, and pretending great secrecy, sat beside her and said into her ear: 'I still believe, Miss Bingley, that while country life may not be unpleasant for you, too much time spent indoors is. Would you not permit me to take you for a drive?—Your sister, also, of course. I thought that perhaps we could go into Meryton, so that I might purchase a length of ribbon to complement your beautiful new gown.'

Caroline was surprised, for she was wearing a new gown, one she had not worn since he and Eleanor arrived. 'I am shocked,' she whispered back, enjoying the game of secrecy, 'to learn that a man exists who is so observant about a woman's attire. You do realise, sir, that stating such a thought is shockingly forward.'

He grinned. 'I am only forward with you, Miss Bingley, for with you I feel as if my entire future rests in your hands.' Before she could think about this, or respond, he leaned back and spoke in his normal voice. 'So it is agreed, then? We shall take a trip to Meryton to visit the milliner's and witness the locals going about their business.' He then leaned forward, and said softly, 'Your gown yesterday was a gentle yellow, which flattered your skin tone and warmed the depth of your eyes.' He winked at her, as she sat in stunned shock, and then stood up to arrange for the carriage.

Eleanor and Louisa decided to accompany them. It was a pleasant day, sunny with a gentle breeze that wafted the curtains at the carriage windows and played with the errant lock of hair that fell across Mr Tryphon's brow.

As they crunched through the gravel on the drive and then rolled onto the road that led to Meryton, Eleanor smiled at Caroline and said, 'What a splendid treat this is, to get out among the local people. How much we will learn about life lived in a manner so different from our own!'

Mr Tryphon nodded, but then said, 'While improving one's mind is never a wasted effort, I am not certain that learning about life so rustic as this can offer any improvement.'

'Nonsense.' Eleanor tapped his arm with her fan. 'If nothing else, it will greatly improve your appreciation for all the things your wealth and position in life bring you. Wouldn't you agree, Caroline?'

'Yes. These people can have nothing to offer to us.'

'Except,' Eleanor said, her eyes dancing, 'amusement.'

'I wish,' Caroline said, 'I could find pleasure in what we observe. For me, alas, I can recall only boredom when I look back on the times we have spent in company here.'

'I, also,' Louisa said. 'When I think of having to listen to Mrs Bennet's shrill voice, the only thing I can think of is how pained my ears become.'

Caroline laughed at that, and Eleanor picked up on her humour, leaning forward to where Caroline sat across from her. 'You see, you demonstrate my meaning perfectly, Caroline. Here you are, laughing, and you have Mrs Bennet to thank for your amusement.'

Everyone laughed at that, and Caroline leaned back against the squabs, willing for a moment to forego proper decorum, and proper posture, in order to better enjoy her friend's delightful company. Eleanor's hair, that day, had been brought to the top of her head, but then permitted to fall in gentle ringlets down the sides of her face. Her blue eyes, so large and often so guileless, now shone with the glint of mischief that encouraged all those around her to join her in her amusements.

Eleanor's eyes, Caroline thought, and the way her mouth, the full lips creating a rosebud on her face when she was serious, could widen into an irrepressible smile, were why her parties were always so successful. Eleanor was a brilliant hostess; she knew exactly the correct blend of people to bring together, but it was her vivacity and the way she always shared her pleasure so that others could experience it, too. It was impossible to feel sad when Eleanor was happy.

A memory came to Caroline then, that of the man whose wife and mistress had been at the same party. Caroline hadn't realised at the time why the two women meeting had been so awkward, but Eleanor had explained later, her enjoyment of the situation so great that Caroline had felt amused also. It seemed to her now that none of the three, man, wife, mistress, had appeared to enjoy the party from that moment on. Could Eleanor have brought them together on purpose, solely for her own amusement?

She pushed aside the curtain over the window beside her. 'Here we are in Meryton,' she said gaily. 'All the amusement we could wish for is just outside our carriage.'

Eleanor thrust her head out. 'My dear Caroline, you are right as always. Look at what has been laid out for us—Redcoats aplenty and Bennet sisters galore.'

Caroline looked out, although she wasn't comfortable moving her head out nearly as far as Eleanor was doing. She could see well enough though, to note the festive air the officers gave the little town, the bright red coats dotted about, sometimes singly, sometimes in a group. The local people almost faded into the background, wearing mostly brown or grey homespun, no colourful ribbon or fabric to offer delight to the eye.

The sound of laughter reached her, but instead of the gentle sounds of Eleanor's silver peals, this was overly loud. Looking about, she spotted the two younger Miss Bennets, standing shamefully close to three officers who clearly did not mind such proximity. The youngest, Miss Lydia, reached out to one officer standing across from her and clasped his fore-arm with both hands, the act bringing her close enough to him that, oh could she be seeing correctly, the side of her chest brushed his upper arm. The other sister, Miss Catherine, not to be outdone by her sister, wasted no time in seizing the arm of the officer closest to her, and the two sisters laughed, paused when one officer spoke, then laughed again, even louder.

'Lydia! Kitty!' Caroline heard, and saw Miss Bennet and Miss Eliza-beth hurrying across the street towards their sisters.

'I do pity the two eldest Miss Bennets,' Eleanor said, 'for they are forced to do what their mother should be doing: attempt to demonstrate some manners to their younger sisters.'

'An impossible task, I would think,' Mr Tryphon murmured.

'At least,' Caroline said, 'Mrs Bennet does not appear to have come into town with her daughters. We are spared that much.'

'But we will not be spared tomorrow evening, I fear,' Louisa said, 'for I am certain I heard Miss Lucas tell Miss Elizabeth, when we saw them last, that both the Bennets and the Bingley party are to come to dinner.'

Caroline sighed, suddenly wishing to see no more of Meryton. The carriage was slowing though, and would soon stop by the milliners so everyone could get out and look at ribbon. 'I truly do not dislike spending time with Miss Bennet,' she said, and Louisa nodded her agreement. 'The mother and the three youngest are simply impossible though, and even

Miss Elizabeth, of whom I thought quite highly at first, has revealed herself as being impertinent.'

'Perhaps,' Eleanor suggested, 'we can find a way to avoid the invitation for tomorrow—a touch of a fever perhaps? A cold coming on? Surely that would be excuse enough.'

'I fear we cannot do that,' Caroline said, 'much though I wish we could. Charles does not believe in subterfuge, and Mr Darcy would be horrified to know we even considered such a thing.'

Eleanor laughed and waved a hand. 'Oh, Mr Darcy. His ideas of proper society are out of date now. There is no need to be so disapproving, so unhappy. Perhaps I can persuade him to find at least some pleasure in the foibles of others.'

Mr Tryphon sent Eleanor a look that Caroline couldn't read, but she was more concerned about Mr Darcy. 'He suffers greatly, Eleanor, you mustn't admonish him. For one of his standing to be forced to attend events with the likes of Mrs Bennet is too much to bear. His attendance at these entertainments is noble, for he does so to honour his friendship with Charles.'

'Have you not considered,' Eleanor said acidly, 'that if Mr Bingley was a truer friend, he would not subject Mr Darcy to situations that are clearly painful to him?'

Caroline's jaw dropped. How could her friend speak so unkindly of Caroline's brother, especially since he was Eleanor and Mr Tryphon's host? Before she could gather her wits to say anything, though, the carriage came to a stop and Mr Tryphon leapt outside, reappearing to open the door on the other side and hand out the ladies.

They entered the shop but Caroline had no interest in ribbon, nor in the new bonnet Louisa showed her. She walked about, her booted feet tapping on the rough wooden floor, without seeing anything.

Eleanor came up beside her, looking down at the floor. 'I am so sorry. I simply do not know what came over me. Can you ever forgive me?' She glanced up sideways, her eyes imploring.

Caroline didn't know how to respond. This was Eleanor, Lady Amesbury, her dearest friend. But what she'd said about Charles . . . Caroline had never thought about Mr Darcy's presence before as anything other than something natural. Charles enjoyed his company, as did she and Louisa. She'd never considered how he felt about being here. Surely, if he was unhappy, he would leave? He'd never struck her as being the sort of man who permitted others to dictate to him. And he lived in the country, at Pemberley, so he knew before coming to Netherfield Park the sorts of entertainments a country estate would offer. No, surely there was no truer friend than was Charles to Mr Darcy. Eleanor could have no reason for saying what she had.

Caroline looked now at her friend, still standing meekly beside her in the dingy shop. Eleanor didn't belong here. She was made for bright lights and glistening crystal.

When Eleanor saw Caroline looking at her, she made a little moue with her full lips and opened her eyes comically wide. What could Caroline do but laugh and take her friend's hand?

Seeing the two of them happy together, Mr Tryphon came to them, his fingers streaming with a multitude of coloured ribbons. 'See what a bouquet I have plucked for you, Miss Bingley!'

She smiled and reached to take a ribbon, a bright red one, from his hand. 'This one is lovely, perfect for my hair.'

'Oh no, my lady,' he exclaimed, 'you misunderstand. I do not offer you a single bloom. I have bought you an entire garden.'

Again, she was helpless against the goodness of her friends. She curtseyed, saying, 'Kind sir, I accept this bounty, and can only hope I can use it in such a way as to do justice to your kindness.'

'If my offer can in any small way enhance your happiness and beauty, I will consider myself well repaid.' He bowed deeply, then took her hand in his. 'Well repaid,' he repeated, looking deeply into her eyes.

Louisa came over, her hands full of lace, wanting to know what all the gaiety was about. 'I am happy,' Caroline said, 'that is all. I am happy being here with those who are most dear to me.'

She put her arm around her sister, and smiled, and her happiness did not fade even when they left the shop and encountered Miss Lydia prancing down the street, each of her hands through an officer's arm, her raucous laughter filling the air.

* * *

A few days later, the bubbly happiness had faded to ennui. It had been raining all day and now, in late afternoon, Charles had just told the ladies that he, Mr Darcy, and Mr Hurst, had been invited to dine with the officers in Meryton.

'This is too cruel of you,' Caroline complained. 'How can you in good conscience abandon us on such a dreary day?'

'Yes,' Louisa said. 'This is positively un-brotherly, Charles. I will not have it and would admonish you had I the energy.'

Charles laughed, for indeed Louisa reclined on the sofa in almost the same position usually assumed by her husband. 'You do appear sleepy, dear sister,' he said. 'Perhaps a quiet evening will suit you best, and so, in truth, I am doing you a favour by removing the noise and smoke that gentlemen always impose on the ladies.' With a wave, he took himself off, leaving the ladies more despondent than ever.

After some time during which neither spoke, Caroline bestirred herself enough to move to the window.

'Tell me,' Louisa moaned, 'that you see something to give us hope. A touch of blue, perhaps, in the sky, or, dare I ask, a sunbeam chasing away the rain.'

'Alas, I can offer you no comfort. It is not raining at present but looks likely to do so again very soon.' Caroline returned to her chair and threw herself, in a ladylike way, of course, into it.

To make matters worse, Eleanor and Mr Tryphon had departed as the end of their scheduled visit had arrived. Caroline had entreated her friend to stay a few days longer, but Eleanor had merely given her a hug, and talked about the responsibilities awaiting her in London.

'I would love to stay, of course I would, but I cannot delay my appearance in town any longer.' Eleanor kissed her on both cheeks, and vanished out of the front door, following the footmen bearing her trunks to the carriage.

Mr Tryphon stood before her then, bowing to say goodbye. He took her hand in his and, as he had done so often, kissed it while he still bent low, his eyes burning a path up to hers. 'I will not laugh,' he said as he stood up and released her hand, 'I will not dance, until you are once again with me.'

Mr Darcy stood nearby, next to Charles, as they bid the guests farewell. He had not yet proposed, and Caroline wondered if his silence made Mr Tryphon's words even more seductive. Caroline knew that he watched this encounter, even though she could not see him from where she stood. She smiled warmly at Mr Tryphon, and even reached her hand towards him, as if to caress his cheek. 'I will miss you also, dear friend.'

He leaned forward, as if into her caress, and stopped only a hair's breadth away from her fingers. 'Be well,' he whispered, 'and if you think of me at least half as often as I will think of you, I will be a happy man.'

She smiled again, took her hand away, and he left. She did not go outside to watch the carriage leave, fearing that the dust from the drive would dirty her gown. To her surprise she missed him, missed his smiles and the illicit thrill that came from some of the things he said, so forward but also so lovely to hear.

She missed Eleanor too, of course; her absence was unbearable. 'I do so wish,' she said now to Louisa, 'that Eleanor was still here. She could always add a gaiety to even the dreariest of days.'

'Yes, someone else to converse with would be most agreeable.' Louisa sat up from her recumbent position. 'That gives me an idea. The gentlemen have been invited out this evening, and we have not. But why should we not invite someone to join us? Miss Bennet, perhaps.'

They looked at each other. 'Why not indeed?' Caroline murmured. 'She is the sole creature in this area I can see spending an evening with. Miss Bennet is charming.'

Louisa clapped her hands. 'It is settled, then?'

Caroline nodded and rose to go to the writing desk. 'I will send her a note immediately.'

'My Dear Friend,' she wrote. 'If you are not so compassionate as to dine today with Louisa and me, we shall be in danger of hating each other for the rest of our lives, for a whole day's *tête-à-tête* between two women can never end without a quarrel. Come as

soon as you can upon receipt of this. My brother and the gentlemen are to dine with the officers.

Yours ever,
Caroline Bingley'

The servant she sent to bear the note to Longbourn returned quickly
with a positive response. 'Delightful,' Caroline said. 'I so look forward to
this evening.'

Her hopes, and those of Louisa also, were dashed soon after Miss
Bennet arrived, for Jane had come on horseback and her clothing, even
through her travelling cloak, was very damp from the rain which had
started again, just as Caroline had predicted.

Caroline suggested that Jane might like to change out of her wet clothes,
but Jane, never wanting to be a bother, said she hardly felt the damp. The
three ladies sat together in the parlour, and Caroline made sure that Jane sat
by the fire, even though she was concerned what the damp might do to the
silken cushions on her chair. They chatted as ladies do, about the goings
on of their neighbours, and embroidery and the loveliness of the grounds
surrounding Netherfield. Although she didn't ask, Jane was clearly very
interested in any mention of Charles. Caroline told her about his comings
and goings, but was careful to say nothing of how often Charles spoke
of Jane.

All seemed well, but once they sat down to dine, Jane began to sniffle,
and by the time the soup was cleared away, she developed a most unpleasant
cough. Even though she tried to muffle the sound, by bending her head
down to cough and using her handkerchief to cover her mouth, it became
apparent to Caroline and Louisa that their friend was ill. Against Jane's
protests that she was perfectly well, only a little tickle in her throat, Caroline sent servants to heat water for a bath and prepare a chamber, for it was
clear Jane could not return home that evening.

'Not in the rain,' Caroline said to Louisa, once Jane had been bathed
and put to bed with a warming pan, 'and definitely not on horseback.'

'I cannot imagine what her mother was thinking,' Louisa said, with a
little laugh of incredulity, 'sending her daughter out on a day like today

on horseback. I would never have so much as imagined such a thing could happen.'

Caroline nodded, puzzled. 'I know they have a carriage. Like you, I feel such a thing must be unthinkable, and yet it happened.'

When the gentlemen returned, Caroline told them of the unfortunate events. Charles didn't even take a moment to wonder at Jane coming on horseback; his thoughts were all of her health and comfort. Caroline wondered for a moment if he would so break with propriety as to go up to see her, but was able to reassure him that all that could be done for Jane had indeed occurred.

With all the upheaval, everyone stayed up discussing it until much later than usual. The next morning, Caroline dressed hastily, wanting to check on Jane. She appeared to be fast asleep, lying on her back, her face turned away from the door. Her breathing was audible, but not too loud and so Caroline, reassured that Jane had not worsened during the night, was about to leave when Jane turned her head, her eyes open.

Caroline saw no option but to enter the room. 'My dear one, how do you feel this morning?'

'I am well,' Jane said. 'You have been so thoughtful but I need not trespass on your kindness any longer. I shall send a note to Longbourn and my father shall come for me in the carriage.'

Jane's face was flushed, and for the first time, Caroline felt a small frisson of concern. She heard a step behind her, and turned to see Charles, who was clearly torn between the fact he could not look into a lady's bedchamber and his need to learn if Miss Bennet was better.

He took one look at Caroline's face and said, 'I shall send for Mr Jones at once.'

'Of course,' said Caroline, and walked over to Jane in her bed. 'You poor creature, we cannot even think of you leaving when you are in discomfort. You cannot travel until you are better, so please, give ease to our hearts, and stay at least until the apothecary has seen you and given you leave to rise from your bed.'

Jane protested, but in truth she looked relieved, and asked only for paper to send a note home. Caroline had sent one the previous evening, saying only that Jane would spend the night at Netherfield, and that the

Bennet family should not worry. She brought paper, pen, and a writing desk to the bed, aided Jane in sitting up, and then stepped back to give her some privacy while she wrote. Once the note was complete, Caroline gave it to a servant who bore it to Longbourn at once.

Jane lay back, clearly fatigued by her efforts. Caroline suggested a tray be brought, but Jane refused any food, asking only for a cup of tea.

Caroline returned to her rooms and called Genney to dress her hair. When she went downstairs, the whole family and Mr Darcy were present to breakfast together, a rare occurrence since usually Mr Darcy rose earlier than anyone and Mr Hurst much later. Caroline had barely sipped her first cup of tea, when the door to the breakfast-parlour was opened, and a footman entered and announced the arrival of Miss Elizabeth Bennet.

Miss Elizabeth was close behind him, and when she entered the room Caroline gaped at her, looked at Louisa who appeared equally surprised, and then back at Miss Elizabeth. Was the entire Bennet family mad? Elizabeth had evidently walked, for her stockings and petticoats were filthy with mud, and her face was near as flushed as that of her sister.

'You came by foot?' Caroline asked. 'Three miles?' As soon as she spoke she felt embarrassed. Her question had been impolite, but surely Miss Elizabeth must have known how odd her arrival and appearance would seem to other people.

'I did.' Miss Elizabeth made a hasty curtsey. 'Forgive me for my intrusion, but I must know. How does my sister?'

All three gentlemen had risen to their feet when she entered the room. Mr Hurst now sat back down and bent his head over his plate of eggs and kippers. Charles, ever the gracious host, came forward to Miss Elizabeth. 'There is nothing to forgive. Please, be welcome.'

'I thank you,' she said.

'Miss Elizabeth,' Mr Darcy spoke, and Elizabeth looked up, startled. 'You are to be commended for your concern for your sister.'

'Would you like some tea?' Caroline asked, going into automatic hostess mode.

Elizabeth didn't respond for a moment, staring wide-eyed at Mr Darcy. With an apparent effort, she turned to Caroline. 'Tea? No, I thank you.' She stood awkwardly, looking more like a milkmaid than a lady.

'You must be fatigued after your walk,' Louisa said. 'Would you care to sit down and rest?'

Caroline knew her sister well enough to know that as she'd asked the polite question, she was hoping Elizabeth would refuse. No doubt Louisa was concerned about Miss Elizabeth's muddy clothing getting dirt on the furniture.

'I thank you,' Eliza said, 'but please, can you tell me how does my sister?'

'I saw Jane a few moments ago,' Caroline said, realising that answering Miss Elizabeth's question might be the quickest way to be rid of her. She was unable to sugar-coat the situation, though, even if the knowledge might encourage Miss Elizabeth to stay. Perhaps if Miss Elizabeth knew Jane was truly ill, she would allow the Bingley carriage to take both sisters home to Longbourn.

'I am afraid your sister slept poorly last night, despite the comforts we hastened to offer. She is flushed and I fear she is feverish. She was not well enough, this morning, to leave her room.'

Miss Elizabeth grew pale, and swayed for a moment on her feet. Mr Darcy, Caroline noted out of the corner of her eye, took a step forward, but Miss Elizabeth drew in a deep breath and asked in a quiet but firm voice to be taken up to see Jane.

Caroline escorted her and paused at the doorway as Miss Elizabeth rushed to her sister's bedside. Jane's face lit up at the sight of her sister, and she held out both hands. Eliza took them in her own and sat down on the edge of the bed, disengaging one hand to cup it around her sister's cheek and then to push Jane's damp hair away from her forehead. Both sisters had obviously forgotten Caroline's presence and she, relieved, returned to her breakfast.

After breakfast, and a second cup of tea, Caroline and Louisa returned upstairs to see how Jane did. 'I confess,' Caroline said as they neared Jane's room, 'that I am somewhat concerned about our dear friend. I am happy that Mr Jones will attend her.'

Louisa nodded. 'I too. Jane truly is the sweetest of creatures.'

When they entered the room, Miss Elizabeth was tenderly bathing her sister's face. 'Dear Jane,' Louisa said, 'I cannot bear to see you thus. Do you suffer overly much?'

Jane smiled, without the warmth of her usual expression, but her countenance reflected the joy she felt in seeing her friends. 'I cannot say that I am well, but with you and my sister here, I cannot say that I suffer, either.'

Louisa opened the curtains, just a bit, so that the air in the room was lightened. She then left the room, and returned with a clean bed gown. She and Caroline busied themselves by the window as Miss Elizabeth assisted her sister to change.

'Shall I read to you?' Caroline asked.

'I thank you,' Jane said, sounding surprised, but before Caroline could fetch a book, Mr Jones, the apothecary, arrived, followed by Charles who hovered by the door, looking worried.

The Bingleys left the room while Mr Jones conducted his examination. Outside the closed door, Charles paced up and down the hallway, his hands thrust into his pockets. Mr Darcy came up the stairs and looked inquiringly at him, but Caroline shook her head to show they did not have any news.

After what seemed an eternity, the door opened and Mr Jones and Elizabeth came out. 'As you surmised,' he said to Caroline, no doubt assuming that it would be she who, as mistress of the house, would be in charge of whatever was required. 'Miss Bennet has caught a violent cold. She will recover but it will take time and so you must tend her until she can get the better of it. I have advised her to remain in bed.'

Miss Elizabeth opened her mouth to speak, but he apparently knew what she would say, for he turned to her.

'I will send the draughts as soon as they can be made up, and they will greatly ease her headache, and may aid with the fever.'

Miss Elizabeth nodded, clearly overcome with distress, and she returned to her sister's bedside.

Charles saw the apothecary out, thanking him over and over again. The gentlemen then announced their intention to go out.

The day passed quietly. Since Jane was reluctant to relinquish her sister's hands, Caroline read from a book of poems she found in the library. She assumed Mr Darcy had been reading it. She didn't recognise the poet's name, but knew that if he approved of it, it would suit Jane very well. Louisa sat close by also, working on her embroidery. Jane sometimes dozed, but when she was awake she looked lovingly from face to face of the three women who kept her company, and seemed content.

Her face was still flushed, and the next time she appeared to sleep, Elizabeth said, in a trembling voice, that the fever still raged. The clock rang three shortly after, while Jane still slept, and Eliza rose reluctantly and said she must go, but Caroline could see how much she wished to stay. Caroline, despite her concern for Jane, knew that she and Louisa could look after Jane perfectly well without the added burden of another houseguest. 'Shall I send for the carriage to take you home?' she asked.

Eliza looked at her sister and back at Caroline, and resolutely raised her chin. 'I thank you,' she said softly. 'That would be very kind.'

Jane woke at this point and having heard that her sister was leaving, reached out and clutched Elizabeth's hand. 'Oh no, please, Lizzie, do not leave me. I feel so much better just knowing you are near.'

'Do not be concerned, dear Jane,' Caroline said, putting a smile on her face. 'There is no need for your sister to depart. We have plenty of room, as you know, and it would be no problem at all for her to remain by your side.'

Elizabeth studied Caroline for a moment, almost as if she knew that Caroline did not like having yet another Bennet present, especially not this one with her fine eyes. She clearly wished to stay, though, and so she very prettily offered her thanks. Jane spoke of her gratitude also, and after a glance at Louisa, Caroline left the room to send a servant to Longbourn to acquaint the Bennets with Elizabeth's stay and to bring back clothing and other necessities.

* * *

By the time the clock struck five, Caroline had wearied of reading. She and Louisa left the Bennet sisters alone, and retired to dress for dinner.

'What a tedious afternoon,' Louisa said as they closed the door to Jane's chamber behind them.

'I heartily agree,' Caroline said with a sigh. 'It is enough to make me see a positive light on Eliza's being here.'

'Yes, I can see that, but we still need to have a chamber prepared for her, and we will have to speak to her during meals and any other times she chooses to join the family downstairs.'

'I expect,' Caroline said, 'she'll be happy with a pallet in her sister's room at night. Although, I suppose you are correct, and we'd better find a chamber for her to use.'

They reached the door to Caroline's rooms, and parted.

Caroline sank on to the bench before her dressing table, and examined her reflection. She looked very ill, her skin was wan, and her eyes held no sparkle. Her hair, too, appeared to have lost its usual lustre. *Clearly*, she thought, *it is unhealthy for me to spend time in a sickroom.* Perhaps Eliza's presence here was a blessing, after all.

Thinking of Eliza, though, brought on thoughts of Mr Darcy and his admiration of her fine eyes. She wondered why on earth he had said such a thing. Perhaps he'd briefly taken leave of his senses, although Mr Darcy, of everyone she knew, was the person most in his right mind, with a stern control over his emotions and, most likely, his thoughts as well. Could he have been joking that evening at Sir William's?

During their more recent engagement at the Lucases, Darcy had said nothing about Elizabeth, but he had looked in her direction several times, and Caroline wondered if he was thinking about her eyes and other features. Surely he had no reason to study the countenance of someone so clearly beneath his notice. His earlier comments must have been an attempt at humour, born from his discomfort with the company they were keeping.

His wit was dry, that much she knew, and she was not always able to comprehend when he said something with all seriousness or when he meant it to be taken as a *bon mot*.

Not that he'd ever used sarcasm when speaking of her, of course, but he could show incisive humour when he so chose. She remembered when he'd said that Elizabeth was no more than tolerable, and that he was in no humour to give consequence to young ladies who were slighted by other men. How Caroline had laughed at that, and even he had smiled.

No, he could have had no serious intent when he spoke of fine eyes. Caroline determined to think no more about Miss Elizabeth. She smiled into the mirror and it seemed as if her eyes had regained at least some of their usual vivacity. Ringing for her maid, she started her preparations for dinner.

*   *   *

At six-thirty, as she walked past the chamber in which Jane lay, Caroline sent a servant to summon Elizabeth to join the family for the evening meal. As she did not come downstairs right away, Caroline was reluctant to wait. After all, Eliza might have some little task she felt was necessary to do for her sister, but more likely she was doing her hair or changing her dress, and who knew how long that would take. Her delay in appearing was another sign of the poor manners demonstrated by her family, and Caroline led the others into the dining room without waiting for her inconsiderate guest. They were all seated by the time Elizabeth arrived.

Charles rose to his feet with alacrity as did, Caroline noted with displeasure, Mr Darcy. The latter, she knew, was merely being polite. 'How does your sister?' Charles asked, even before Eliza was properly seated.

'I am sorry to have to report,' Eliza said once the footman had pushed her chair closer to the table as she sat down, 'that she is no better.'

'That is grievous news indeed,' Caroline said before Charles could respond.

'Most grievous,' Louisa added.

'How sad that she should have contracted such a bad cold,' Caroline said.

'Most shocking,' Louisa added.

At this point Charles was able to partake in the conversation. 'Does she suffer much?' he asked. 'Is there anything, anything at all, I can do to alleviate even the smallest portion of her distress?'

'Oh, she must suffer so greatly,' Caroline said.

'Indeed she must,' Louisa said, taking a portion of boiled potatoes from a footman. 'I recall well the last time I was ill. How my head ached. I can still recall every twinge.'

'You poor thing,' Caroline said tenderly. 'I think that I detest being ill more than anything else in all the world.'

'Can I serve you some chicken?' Charles asked Eliza.

'I thank you,' she answered.

Mr Hurst, seated next to Eliza, had ignored her until now, but looked up when she requested her chicken without the rosemary and garlic sauce. 'You prefer your food plain?' he asked with great surprise.

'I do indeed, sir. I find the heavier sauces disguise the taste overly much of what I am eating.'

'You are saying that you prefer a plain dish to a ragout?'

'I do.'

Caroline was shocked to observe Eliza appeared amused by Mr Hurst. He however, did not notice the impertinence, merely grunting and returning his attention to his food, from which it rarely wavered during meals.

Caroline turned to Mr Darcy and noted that he too, had observed the interchange. 'I do apologise,' she whispered to him, 'that my invitation to a friend has resulted in our having to suffer further unpleasant company.'

He stared at her for a moment. 'I am in no way distressed by Miss Bennet's or Miss Elizabeth's presence. You must not fret on my behalf.'

'Your generosity to these people knows no bounds.' She noted that he too had taken no sauce with his chicken and wondered, for a moment, if he had always eaten thus or if this was a new habit he'd formed.

He picked up his fork and commenced eating.

'Do you have any particular plans for this evening?' she asked him.

He put his fork down and turned to her again. 'No,' he said. 'I will read if I can, and I would like to get some letters written.'

Her attention was caught by Charles' laughter, and she looked to see that he and Eliza were apparently enjoying their conversation, for as he laughed, she gave him a pleased smile.

When the last dish was cleared away, Eliza said she hoped they would excuse her, but she wished to return to her sister, and Caroline, of course, said she understood completely and granted her leave to depart. The footman had barely closed the door behind her when Caroline, at last, felt able to speak her thoughts,

'Such manners! If I didn't know better, I would never believe she was related to Jane. Dear Jane, so sweet, and such lovely manners. I declare, I felt for you exceedingly, Mr Hurst, having to sit the entire meal beside such impertinence.'

Mr Hurst opened his mouth to respond but his wife was faster. 'She had no conversation to help you pass the time, my dear,' she said to her husband.

'And such pride,' Caroline added. 'So much pride, and nothing to be proud of.'

'She has nothing, in short,' said Louisa, nodding in agreement, 'to recommend her, but being an excellent walker.' She snickered at this point, and continued, 'I shall never forget her appearance this morning. She really looked almost wild!'

'She did indeed,' Caroline said. 'I could hardly keep my countenance. Very nonsensical to come at all! Why must she be scampering about the country, because her sister had a cold! Her hair, so untidy, so blowsy!'

'Yes, and her petticoat, six inches deep in mud.'

'Your picture may be exact, Louisa,' said Charles, 'but this was all lost upon me. I thought Miss Elizabeth Bennet looked remarkably well when she came into the room this morning. Her dirty petticoat quite escaped my notice.'

'You observed it, Mr Darcy, I am sure,' said Caroline, pleased to observe an expression of distaste upon his countenance, 'and I am inclined to think that you would not wish to see your sister make such an exhibition.'

She was pleased when, as expected, he said, 'Certainly not.'

She smiled at him, knowing they were of one mind. 'To walk three miles, or four miles, or five miles, or whatever it is, above her ankles in dirt, and alone, quite alone! What could she mean by it? It seems to me to show an abominable sort of conceited independence.'

'It shows an affection for her sister that is very pleasing,' said Charles.

Her brother, she knew, found it difficult to think ill of anyone. She turned to Mr Darcy and, lowering her voice as if to impart an important confidence, said, 'I am afraid, Mr Darcy, that this adventure has rather affected your admiration of her fine eyes.'

He paused a moment, regarding her with an expression she could not read. 'Not at all,' he replied, 'they were brightened by the exercise.'

Caroline knew not how to respond to this, so she turned to Louisa.

'Miss Bennet is very sweet and also quite unwell. I long to see her now, to ascertain for myself if she has improved any.'

Louisa was in full agreement with this, and the two left the dining parlour to sit with Jane.

The four women stayed together in silence, Caroline and Louisa sewing, Elizabeth hopping up and down like a rabbit, fetching cool water and clean cloths to bathe her sister's face, tempting her to sip a spoonful of broth, or simply moving between bed and a chair, depending on if her sister slept or, when awake, wanted her hand held.

After a long time, during which Caroline did at least complete a floral motif on one of the slippers she was embroidering for Mr Darcy, a servant knocked at the door and summoned the ladies for coffee. Elizabeth apologised but requested to stay with Jane, who was asleep but sometimes tossed her head from side to side. The other two left only after protestations of how much they wished they could stay with dear Jane, since their presence gave her much comfort, but then left in case Eliza suggested that they do so.

As Caroline poured coffee, Charles begged to know how poor Miss Bennet fared. 'Alas,' she said, 'dear Jane is still feverish, I am afraid.'

Charles jumped up and paced, stating, 'There must be something I can do.'

'Please, Charles,' Caroline said, 'do not distress yourself. You will do Jane and anyone else no good at all if you drive yourself into a sickbed as well.'

Mr Darcy looked up at that, and Caroline realised she had spoken more sharply than she'd intended. 'Besides,' she added, her tone more measured, 'having the company of Louisa and myself provided her much comfort, but now she requires quiet so she can sleep.'

Charles clenched his fists for a moment, staring up as if he could see through the ceiling into the room where Jane lay, but after a moment he heaved a great sigh and sat back down.

Once everyone was served Mr Hurst asked if he should summon a servant to set up the table for cards. Since he asked the same question every evening that no other entertainment was scheduled, Caroline had already arranged the matter, and shortly after, the family sat down to play loo.

A little time later, Eliza entered the room. *She tries to pretend she is shy and demure,* Caroline thought. Charles rose to his feet and waved at her. 'I am very happy to see you,' he said. 'Does your presence here mean your sister is a little better?'

She smiled at him and said, 'She sleeps more quietly now, and so I thought it all right for a time if I join you here.'

'I am delighted to hear it,' Charles said. 'Will you join us at loo?'

She paused, and Caroline saw her eyes go to the table and the piles of coin that rested there. 'I thank you,' she said, 'but as I will be able to remain with you for only a little time, I will amuse myself with a book.'

As they resumed playing, she came over to watch, positioning herself between Mr Bingley and Caroline. Mr Darcy's eyes, Caroline noted, had followed her as she approached.

'Is Miss Darcy much grown since the spring?' Caroline asked him. 'Will she be as tall as I am?'

Mr Darcy pulled his eyes down to his cards. He didn't look at Caroline, but at least he no longer gazed at Eliza. 'I think she will. She is now about Miss Elizabeth Bennet's height.'

'How I long to see her again!' Caroline cried. 'I never met anybody who delighted me so much. Such a countenance, such manners! And so extremely accomplished for her age! Her performance on the pianoforte is exquisite.'

'It is amazing to me,' said Charles, 'how young ladies can have patience to be so very accomplished as they all are.'

'All young ladies accomplished!' Caroline was shocked. 'My dear Charles, what do you mean?'

He turned to her and nodded decisively. 'Yes, all of them, I think. They all paint tables, cover screens, and net purses. I scarcely know any one who cannot do all this, and I am sure I never heard a young lady spoken of for the first time, without being informed that she was very accomplished.'

Oh Charles, Caroline thought, *have you not learned the difference between what is said of a person and what is true about them?* She was about put this in words, when Mr Darcy spoke.

'Your list of the common extent of accomplishments has too much truth. The word is applied to many a woman who deserves it no otherwise than by netting a purse or covering a screen. But I am very far from agreeing with you in your estimation of ladies in general. I cannot boast of knowing more than half-a-dozen, in the whole range of my acquaintance, that are really accomplished.'

Caroline sent Miss Elizabeth a glance of triumph. 'Nor I, I am sure.'

'Then,' observed Miss Eliza, 'you must comprehend a great deal in your idea of an accomplished woman.'

Mr Darcy sat across the table from where Miss Elizabeth stood, and he sent her a small smile. 'Yes, I do comprehend a great deal in it.'

'Oh, certainly,' cried Caroline. What was going on? Why did Mr Darcy address his comments to Eliza? Why did he smile at her, when he never smiled at any one except his intimate friends?

'No one,' Mr Darcy said, 'can be really esteemed accomplished who does not greatly surpass what is usually met with.'

Caroline felt a little better. *This will show Miss Elizabeth Bennet how distant she is from being as accomplished as I am.*

'A woman must have a thorough knowledge of music, singing, drawing, dancing, and the modern languages, to deserve the word; and besides all this, she must possess a certain something in her air and manner of walking, the tone of her voice, her address and expressions, or the word will be but half-deserved.'

Out of the corner of her eye, Caroline observed Miss Eliza, but was disappointed to see not a chastened air but a mischievous smile.

'All this she must possess,' added Mr Darcy, and Caroline knew her triumph would come, but then he continued, 'and to all this she must yet add something more substantial, in the improvement of her mind by extensive reading.'

Caroline's jaw dropped but she hastily rearranged her features into an expression of calm. Inside her head, though, her thoughts reeled.

Miss Eliza's impish smile turned into a laugh. 'I am no longer surprised at your knowing only six accomplished women. I rather wonder now at your knowing any.'

Mr Darcy smiled at her again. 'Are you so severe upon your own sex as to doubt the possibility of all this?'

Instead of accepting his superior understanding of the world, Eliza said, 'I never saw such a woman. I never saw such capacity, and taste, and application, and elegance, as you describe, united.'

'Nonsense!' Caroline said, and at the same moment, Louisa cried, 'You insult those in your presence!'

'I apologise,' Eliza said. 'I meant no insult. Am I to take it, then, that the two of you are among the six of which Mr Darcy spoke?'

'Indeed,' Caroline said, not caring if her displeasure showed. 'And there are many more among our acquaintanceship who are even more accomplished than we. You met one such, in fact, during the last many weeks. Do you not recall my dear friend, Lady Amesbury?'

'I do,' Elizabeth said gravely. 'I remember her very well.'

Something in the tone of her voice made Caroline wonder if Miss Eliza had not thought highly of Eleanor but surely no one, even one with so little knowledge of the fashionable world, could have failed to recognise Eleanor's quality. Before she could say anything, though, Mr Hurst pointed out, in a peevish tone, that all the card players had let their attention stray from the game. As all conversation was then at an end, Miss Elizabeth excused herself to check on her sister.

'Eliza Bennet,' Caroline said, when the door had barely closed behind her, 'is one of those young ladies who seek to recommend themselves to the other sex by undervaluing their own, and with many men, I dare say, it succeeds.' She looked at Mr Darcy. 'But, in my opinion, it is a paltry device, a very mean art.'

'Undoubtedly,' he replied, 'there is meanness in all the arts which ladies sometimes employ. Whatever bears affinity to cunning is despicable.' He gazed directly at Caroline as he said this, his expression sober, and she assumed he shared her opinion of Eliza Bennet. Something in his gaze, though, suggested that she not speak any more on this topic, and so she returned her attention to her cards.

Elizabeth joined them again sometime later, but mercifully her appearance was brief. She told them that Jane was much worse and she could not leave her.

Charles became distraught at this, even though Jane was clearly well enough to be left, since Eliza was here and not upstairs. 'I insist,' he said, 'that Mr Jones be sent for immediately.' Caroline, sorry to see her brother so unhappy, suggested that an express be sent to London at once, for surely no country advice could be matched by that coming from any of the city's eminent physicians.

'Caroline!' Louisa said. 'That is a very good idea. That is what we must do! Dear Jane must have only the best care.'

'No, I thank you,' Eliza said. 'It is too much trouble.'

Again, the lack of manners, Caroline thought. *We offer her the best, and she turns us down.* Then she had another thought. Perhaps, being a Bennet, Eliza was concerned about the cost of such a visit. That, at least, showed a touch of manners, even if her refusal was unbearably rude.

'Then,' Charles pleaded, 'at least permit us to send for Mr Jones.'

Eliza hesitated, clearly torn between wanting something to be decided and her wish to return to Jane as quickly as possible. After more discussion, things were settled; Mr Jones would be sent for early in the morning if Miss Bennet were not decidedly better.

Eliza hurried out of the room to return to her sister. 'I did agree to this,' Charles said miserably, once she had gone, 'but I shall not sleep a wink tonight, out of worry.'

'I understand completely,' Caroline said tenderly. 'Louisa and I are utterly miserable to know our friend suffers so unbearably and we can do nothing to alleviate her pains.' She patted her brother on his shoulder, and then suggested, 'Why do Louisa and I not play duets on the pianoforte? It will give us all much cheer, I am certain.'

'Without completing this hand?' Mr Hurst said, sounding most put out.

'Of course not,' Louisa said. 'We will have music after the game is finished.'

Chapter Five

Caroline heard Charles coming out of his rooms long before she was ready to even summon her first cup of tea, which she always drank before rising from her bed. She heard his voice, calling for a housemaid, who was then sent to Miss Bennet's room to inquire as to her welfare. Caroline refused to be outdone by her brother, and so sent Genney to pursue the same information.

Sometime later she received the news that Miss Jane Bennet was somewhat improved, but that Miss Elizabeth had requested paper and pen, and had written a note taken to Longbourn, asking that their mother come so she could form her own judgement of the situation.

Caroline closed her eyes upon hearing this, and Genney moved a step back, thinking, no doubt, that her mistress wished to sleep some more. Caroline was fully awake; she had closed her eyes in pain at hearing that her home was to be once again assailed by the presence of Mrs Bennet.

When Caroline finished dressing, and Genney had made up her hair for the day, Caroline ventured out to Jane's room. Even before she drew close enough to open the door, her ears were filled with the sounds of Bennets, many of them, and all speaking at once. Squaring her shoulders, she entered the room and saw not only Mrs Bennet, but the two youngest Miss Bennets, also. She closed her eyes for a moment, seeking a moment of peace that she knew might be the last she would experience for some time.

Her moment was cut short by Mrs Bennet's approach. 'Jane wished to return home, but I will not hear of it. She is much too ill to be moved.'

Caroline looked over at Jane, who was sitting up in bed and trying to listen to her youngest sisters as they both spoke at the same time.

Fortunately for Jane, both sisters talked only of officers, and so it wasn't difficult to follow the two verbal streams.

Jane did look somewhat better, Caroline thought. Her face was less flushed, and her eyes were clearer. She still looked very tired, though, and when she attempted to respond to one sister or another's comments, she often was unable due to coughing.

After a few moments, Caroline observed there was another person in the room. Mr Jones, looking a little overwhelmed, was just packing up his bag. Caroline approached him, trailed by Mrs Bennet.

'The apothecary agrees with me,' Mrs Bennet said, raising her voice to a seemingly impossible volume in order to be heard over Miss Lydia and Miss Kitty. 'Jane must not be moved. The risk is too great.'

Caroline glanced at Mr Jones and he, as if understanding her concerns, gave a reluctant nod. 'Miss Bennet is indeed much improved,' he began, but was interrupted by Mrs Bennet.

'How can you say such a thing? Improved indeed! She is so pale and thin, practically wasting away. Just look at her.'

They all turned to survey Jane, who was laughing at something Lydia had just told her.

Mr Jones cleared his throat. 'As I said, she is,' he glanced at Mrs Bennet, 'somewhat improved. A little improved. A very little. I believe, though it would be best to permit her to continue to rest and receive care here. She will then gain strength before she is transported home.'

The revelation that there would continue to be Bennets in the house threatened to bring on a headache, and realising she needed fortification, Caroline suggested the Bennets accompany her to the breakfast parlour. Mrs Bennet and the two youngest accepted with alacrity. Elizabeth, after a brief murmured conversation with Jane, accompanied them.

As soon as they entered that room, Charles, who had apparently been pacing up and down in front of the sideboard without taking any food, and preventing Mr Darcy from taking any either, since he blocked the way, turned to them and said, 'I trust, Mrs Bennet, that you did not find your daughter worse than expected.' He gazed at her, his brown eyes wide and hopeful.

'Indeed I have, sir,' was her answer. 'She is a great deal too ill to be moved. Mr Jones says we must not think of moving her.' She sank down into a chair, fanning herself with her hand, and appearing to suffer a great deal more distress than did Jane. 'We must trespass,' she said in a weak voice, 'a little longer on your kindness.'

Caroline, who was relieved to learn that Mrs Bennet could speak at a lesser volume, looked at her brother and shrugged.

He ignored her; indeed, he appeared to have not noticed her entry into the room. 'Removed!' he cried. 'It must not be thought of. My sister, I am sure, will not hear of her removal.'

Caroline, who'd been making her way towards the sideboard, longing for a piece of toast, turned back and said with cold civility, 'You may depend upon it, madam, that Miss Bennet shall receive every possible attention while she remains with us.'

'Oh, I thank you from the bottom of my heart,' Mrs Bennet cried, her volume once again sufficient that no doubt her husband, back at Long-bourn, could hear every word she spoke.

Caroline smiled, moving her lips as little as possible, and once again faced the sideboard. Her goal was not achieved for Mrs Bennet continued, forcing Caroline to once again turn back politely.

'I am sure,' Mrs Bennet said, 'if it was not for such good friends I do not know what would become of her, for she is very ill indeed, and suffers a vast deal, though with the greatest patience in the world, which is always the way with her, for she has, without exception, the sweetest temper I ever met with.' She paused to draw in a breath, and looked about the parlour. 'You have a sweet room here, Mr Bingley, and a charming prospect over the gravel walk. I do not know a place in the country that is equal to Netherfield.' She stood and approached the sideboard. Before Caroline could so much as request a cup of tea, she had the footman filling her a plate. Sitting down at the table, she cracked open a boiled egg, and asked Charles, 'You will not think of quitting it in a hurry, I hope, though you have but a short lease.'

He now appeared in much better spirits, no doubt because Jane would not be departing. He waved to Caroline to precede him to the sideboard, and she was at last able to gain tea and a plate of food. 'Whatever I do is in a hurry,' he replied to Mrs Bennet, 'and therefore, if I should resolve to quit Netherfield, I should probably be off in five minutes. At present, however, I consider myself as quite fixed here.'

Elizabeth smiled at him. 'That is exactly what I would have supposed of you.'

'You begin to comprehend me, do you?' he said with a laugh.

'Oh! yes, I understand you perfectly.' There was much merriment in her voice, and Caroline observed that Mr Darcy who, as usual when in the presence of Bennets, had withdrawn to the window, turned to look at her.

'I wish I might take this for a compliment,' Charles said, moving to select his breakfast now that everyone else was eating, for the two younger Miss Bennets had been quick to follow their mother and were eagerly downing toast and eggs. 'But to be so easily seen through,' he added, 'I am afraid is pitiful.'

Mr Darcy, Caroline noted, had not eaten yet, but he had also not attempted to gain access to the sideboard.

'That is as it happens,' Elizabeth said. 'It does not necessarily follow that a deep, intricate character is more or less estimable than such a one as yours.'

Caroline was happy to see her brother returned to good spirits, for he had been distraught ever since he learned of Jane's illness. Still, Miss Eliza was once again showing her impertinence.

Her mother apparently thought so also, for she cut in, 'Lizzy, remember where you are, and do not run on in the wild manner that you are suffered to do at home.'

Elizabeth said nothing more, and Mrs Bennet began repeating her thanks to Charles for his kindness to Jane, and apologised for troubling him also with Lizzy.

Charles, as always, was gracious, even to someone like her. 'It is no trouble at all. Please do not think so for a moment. I am delighted to offer any assistance I can. And I know my sister feels the same as I do.' He looked meaningfully at Caroline and she stepped into the role he created for her.

'Of course. Dear Jane is our friend, and you are our neighbours. In the country, I am sure that neighbours look out for one another.' She did the best she could with her smile, and it seemed to satisfy Mrs Bennet, for she beamed at everyone present, and then asked that her carriage be called.

The two younger girls had been busy eating and staring around the room and at all the people within it. Now, realising the visit was about to come to an end, Miss Lydia stood and addressed Charles. 'Thank you for breakfast, it was very good. I hope you have not forgotten that you promised us a ball at Netherfield.' She approached where he was seated, and placed her hand on his shoulder. Leaning over so she could smile into his face, she said in what she probably thought was a whisper, 'You must keep your word, you know, for it will be the most shameful thing in the world if you do not.'

'I am perfectly ready, I assure you, to keep my engagement; and when your sister is recovered, you shall, if you please, name the very day of the ball. But you would not wish to be dancing while she is ill.'

Miss Kitty gasped in pleasure, but Lydia paused a moment, as if Charles' last thought had not occurred to her. Caroline was certain that Lydia would be willing to dance or do anything else she thought would give her pleasure, no matter how many of her relatives were lying in a sick bed. Nonetheless, Lydia stood back and clapped her hands together. 'That is exactly as it should be. I am completely satisfied with your response, Mr Bingley. It would be much better to wait until Jane is well, and by that time, most likely, Captain Carter will be at Meryton again.' Her smile grew wider at this thought, and Caroline raised her eyebrows at Louisa. No wonder the horrible girl was willing to let time pass for her eldest sister to recover. It was not altruism; it had to do with officers.

'And when you have given your ball,' Lydia considered, almost bouncing on her feet in her excitement, 'I shall insist on the officers giving one also. I shall tell Colonel Forster it will be quite a shame if he does not.' She seized Kitty's hands and the two danced around in a circle, causing one of the footmen to step hastily aside, so they didn't tread on his feet. He was quick-witted, Caroline noted with approval, for he also thought to snatch a pink vase of flowers off a side table, just before Lydia bumped the table with her hip.

Finally, Caroline could draw in a deep breath, for Charles escorted the Bennets to their carriage and they all departed, with the exception, of course, of Miss Elizabeth. She returned to her sister, leaving the breakfast parlour mercifully empty of any but the immediate family and Mr Darcy, who was considered family by everyone, since he was as a brother to Charles. Not to Caroline, though, her relationship with him was most definitely not that of siblings.

To emphasise this, Caroline smiled at him when he returned to the table. 'At last, Mr Darcy,' she said, 'you can eat in peace without constant interruptions from that horrible woman and her equally horrible daughters. And no more insults will come your way either. I could hardly believe that such a person exists as that Mrs Bennet. Has she no sense of propriety at all?'

'Clearly not,' Mr Darcy said, scraping jam onto a piece of toast.

'Is that toast cold?' Caroline asked, gesturing to the quick-witted footman. 'John can fetch you a fresh slice.'

'It is no matter.' Mr Darcy rested his hands protectively over his plate, removing them and beginning to eat only when John stepped back to his place beside the sideboard.

* * *

The day passed much as the day before had done. Louisa and Caroline spent much of the morning sitting with Jane, who slept less and had better colour in her face. She was still very weak, and her voice was softer than usual, but clearly she was improved. Caroline passed the time sewing, but she also found her eyes wandering to Elizabeth.

Caroline knew that she and Louisa were as close as sisters could be, but surely neither of them would expect the constant attention and fawning attitude that Elizabeth bestowed on Jane. It seemed that Jane had no more than to think of something than Elizabeth had already fetched or done it. Elizabeth adjusted pillows, smoothed bedclothes, bathed her sister's face, fed her broth with a spoon, exchanged a glass of water for a new one filled with cooler liquid, read poems, chatted about what had occurred during the Bennet visit earlier that day. She was never completely still, and yet she created a space of calm and serenity around all who were present.

Caroline examined Elizabeth's eyes surreptitiously. Try as she might to see why Mr Darcy called them 'fine', she could see nothing that suggested they were anything other than a pair of eyes. The brown colour was nothing out of the ordinary, and while Eliza had dark eyelashes and eyebrows, the lashes were no longer or shorter than those found on other faces, the eyebrows were no longer, thicker, or thinner either. The eyes were nicely shaped, slightly slanted, but that was currently out of fashion, and people much preferred eyes that were round and spaced further apart.

No, it was a mystery. Louisa would probably say Caroline had wasted her time, for certainly no woman could begin to understand why a man said or felt the things he did. Understanding was unnecessary, for all a woman had to do was listen, and smile, and agree. And, after marriage, apparently participating in something that produced sounds more commonly associated with pigs, was added to this list.

As Caroline thought back over the morning, it appeared that Mr Darcy enjoyed Eliza's conversation, even when she disagreed with him. That was all Caroline could think of that was different from her own conversations with him. But why would a man wish to be mocked?—Especially Darcy, always conscious of his bearing and position in society.

No, it was impossible to work out, and so there was no sense in continuing this fruitless inquiry.

Caroline stood up and announced that while she was loath to tear herself away from Jane's company, especially since she knew her presence offered solace to the sick woman, she had duties which simply could not be put off any longer. Jane, sweet thing that she was, was kind enough to point out that although Caroline's presence did afford great comfort, she understood that there were many duties for the mistress of a house such as Netherfield, and she did not in the least take any offence from Caroline's departure. Louisa chose to leave too, at this point, and they left with words of gratitude from both Bennet sisters.

She did not so much as think a single thought about a Bennet during the rest of the day, until later that evening. Indeed, she'd almost managed to forget the visitors' presence until then, for Eliza did not join the family for any meals, presumably preferring to have food brought to Jane's room.

They were not playing loo, for Charles and Mr Hurst had decided to play piquet; Louisa was watching them, and Darcy was writing a letter to his sister. Caroline, still somewhat perturbed by what he'd said about Miss Elizabeth, even though it was clearly just some joke he was having at Caroline's expense, decided she must pay him more attention. Perhaps, in assuming everything was settled between the two of them, she had given him the impression she was no longer interested.

His writing to Georgiana gave her much to share with him, for she loved the girl as if she truly was her own sister. Caroline made sure that her best wishes would be included in the letter, and also made many compliments to Darcy himself, to let him know her esteem of him was high indeed.

Miss Elizabeth came in quietly, without disrupting anyone, and took up some sewing. Caroline, watching Mr Darcy carefully, was pleased to note that he paid no attention whatsoever to this addition to their party.

'You write very well, Mr Darcy,' she said. 'I am all envy, for I cannot write in as beautiful a hand as you.'

He said nothing.

'And,' she continued, 'if Miss Darcy were to judge the extent of your affection for her by the frequency and length of your communications, she would be in no doubt at all as to its depth.'

He looked up at that. 'My sister does not need letters to understand my affection, nor do I to understand hers.'

Caroline paused, then said, 'How delighted she will be to receive such a letter as the one you are now composing.'

He did not respond.

'You write uncommonly fast.'

Without looking up, or even slowing his writing, he said, 'You are mistaken. I write rather slowly.'

'How many letters you must have occasion to write in the course of a year! Letters of business too! How odious I should think them.' *There*, she thought, *that shows him that I am observant and considerate.*

'It is fortunate, then,' he said, 'that they fall to my lot instead of to yours.'

'Pray tell your sister that I long to see her.'

'I have already told her so once, by your desire.'

His tone was somewhat reproving, Caroline thought. Clearly he did not wish her to repeat things when she conversed. 'I am afraid you do not like your pen. Let me mend it for you. I mend pens remarkably well.' *There. That showed concern and that she could be of assistance to him. As mistress of Pemberley, she could ease his burdens.*

'Thank you, but I always mend my own.'

He was considerate also, and did not wish her to distress herself for his sake. Truly, their marriage would be a meeting of equals, each playing their own role in perfect balance with the other.

For the first time, Caroline was distracted by Elizabeth's presence. She had put down her sewing and was making no pretence of not listening to the conversation.

Well, she could listen all she wished, Caroline was unashamed of anything she said to Mr Darcy. 'Tell your sister I am delighted to hear of her improvement on the harp; and pray let her know I am quite in raptures with her beautiful little design for a table.'

He put down his pen at that, and even turned to face her. 'Will you give me leave to defer your raptures till I write again? At present I have not room to do them justice.'

She was pleased to see how important he knew her thoughts would be to his sister. 'Oh! It is of no consequence. I shall see her in January.'

Mr Darcy continued writing his letter.

When he finished it, he turned to Caroline and Elizabeth. 'Would you be so kind as to indulge me with some music?'

Caroline leapt up, eager to entertain him, and to be the focus of his attention, but her manners recalled to her that Eliza was a guest, no matter how unwanted she might be. 'Please,' Caroline said, holding out a hand towards the pianoforte, 'would you grace us with a performance?'

'I thank you,' Elizabeth said, equally politely, 'I am certain my gifts in music are much inferior to yours. I would much prefer to listen at first, so that I may be better inspired later.'

Caroline seated herself on the piano bench, and Louisa joined her, wishing to sing as Caroline played. The songs they used were well known to both sisters, and so Caroline was able to observe her audience, without needing to look every moment at the sheets of music. At times Mr Darcy did indeed regard her, and she was certain he appreciated the pretty picture she made, sitting at the dark wooden instrument, her pale green gown spread out behind her to fall gracefully down the back of the bench. Her sister stood at her shoulder, and with her lighter hair and yellow gown, the two surely presented an image of feminine beauty and superior accomplishment.

Caroline gradually grew tenser, however, for it seemed that at first Mr Darcy looked upon her at least every other time she paid attention to him, but soon he looked at her only one in three times, or even one in four. Her hands faltered on the keys, Louisa sang a line more loudly to permit her to recover, but it was difficult to return her concentration to what she was doing. Why did Mr Darcy gaze upon Elizabeth rather than on her?

Caroline had been playing some of Louisa's favourite Italian songs, but her fingers now felt clumsy. Rather than relinquish the instrument, though, she switched to a Scotch air, which although livelier, was less demanding. She became concerned as she played, for Mr Darcy stood up and approached Miss Elizabeth, bending his head to speak to her. She smiled, but made him no response, and instead of moving away at this incidence of incivility, he leaned even closer to her and apparently repeated his words.

They spoke for some minutes, while Caroline's fingers danced across the piano keys and her mind whirled. The music sped up, reflecting her increasing tension, and Louisa experienced no little difficulty in fitting each line's words into the shorter time allotted her. At last Caroline played the final chords.

She stood, passed Louisa without a word, and made her way towards Mr Darcy and Eliza. 'I am very glad to see, Miss Elizabeth,' she said, 'that your sister does so well that you can leave her entirely alone for an entire evening. You must be content indeed to see such happy effects of your nursing skills.'

As she'd hoped, Eliza instantly showed signs of guilt over having abandoned Jane. 'Indeed, she is much improved, but you are correct, even though she was sleeping well when I left her, she might awaken and want me.' Making a polite excuse to Mr Darcy, she left the room to return upstairs.

Caroline sank into the seat she'd just vacated, suddenly overcome by weariness.

* * *

The next day, Caroline spent only a couple of hours with Jane, who was feeling so much better that Elizabeth suggested she might come downstairs for a while later, to see something different and even spend some time with the others present in the house. Caroline encouraged this, knowing that if Jane were present, Elizabeth would have no opportunity to work her wiles on Mr Darcy. Caroline didn't want to admit how badly frightened she was by the way Mr Darcy paid Eliza so much attention. Caroline hadn't even spoken to Louisa of her thoughts, for she didn't want to appear foolish, like an aging spinster seeing her last chance of a life drifting away.

Still, why on earth would Mr Darcy be interested in Elizabeth? She represented everything he most despised, and even if she had possessed some attributes that won his admiration, her family connections made any attraction he might feel impossible. Why, he himself had said, after they'd first met the Bennets, that the sisters were unlikely to marry well.

Perhaps he was merely toying with Miss Elizabeth for his own amusement. Caroline found the woman amusing, at least whenever she was not attempting to steal Darcy's attention. Darcy's wit was often dry, Caroline knew, and perhaps he enjoyed causing Eliza to say outrageous things. Yes, surely that must be it.

Shortly after the midday meal, she encountered Mr Darcy and he suggested they go for a walk, as it was most pleasant outside. She assented immediately, cheered to discover that he still sought her company.

As they walked through the gardens, she could not get Elizabeth out of her mind, even though the sun was warm on her face and the air sweetly scented by the flowers they passed. Darcy was unusually silent, even for him, and somehow whatever Caroline said, Elizabeth pushed her way into the conversation.

'I thought Miss Elizabeth looked remarkably ill yesterday evening,' she said. 'She cannot be faulted for her devotion to her sister, but surely she should be able to find some time to attend to her person.'

'I thought she appeared remarkably well,' he replied.

Her hand rested on his arm, and now she pressed on it a little to indicate she wished to stop. Bending over a particularly large specimen of a red rose bush, she thought of what to say next. Clearly, pointing out

Eliza's physical defects would not induce him to see that lady in a worse light. The relations, though, never failed.

'I hope,' she said as they resumed walking, 'that you will give your mother-in-law a few hints, when this desirable event takes place, as to the advantage of holding her tongue; and if you can, do cure the younger girls of running after the officers. And, if I may mention so delicate a subject, endeavour to check that little something, bordering on conceit and impertinence, which your lady possesses.'

He smiled at her, and the warmth in his eyes sent a blush into her cheeks. She ducked her head slightly, knowing how alluring a lady could appear thusly, both shy and inviting. 'Have you,' he asked, 'anything else to propose for my domestic felicity?'

'Oh! yes.' She gave him a sidelong glance and then looked up again, trying out the bewitching smile she'd practised in her mirror. 'Do let the portraits of your aunt and uncle Phillips get placed in the gallery at Pemberley. Put them next to your great-uncle the judge. They are in the same profession, you know, only in different lines. As for your Elizabeth's picture, you must not attempt to have it taken, for what painter could do justice to those fine eyes?'

Darcy looked up at that, and following his glance, Caroline saw a bird flitting not far overhead. 'It would not be easy, indeed,' he said slowly, as if musing, 'to catch their expression, but their colour and shape, and the eyelashes, so remarkably fine, might be copied.'

Caroline stopped dead at this, unable in her shock to move, but it took him time to notice. By the time he did observe that her hand was no longer through his arm, he'd walked a full two steps ahead. He immediately came back to her, apologising and asking if she had tripped or had a stone in her shoe. She shook her head no and once again placed her arm though his.

Just as they began to move ahead together, they sighted Louisa and Elizabeth, walking together and coming towards them. They had just come around a corner not six steps ahead, and Caroline felt her face blanch. Could the two women have overheard her conversation with Mr Darcy?

As soon as they took another step closer, she said, 'I did not know that you intended to walk.'

'You used us abominably ill,' Louisa said, but her tone was light, and Caroline sighed in relief, 'running away without telling us that you were coming out.' She then gave Caroline the smallest of winks, and came up on Mr Darcy's other side. Caroline smiled inwardly. How she loved her sister! Louisa took Darcy's other arm so the three could walk abreast. The path was only just wide enough for them, and Eliza had to walk alone behind.

She and Louisa took a step ahead, but Mr Darcy held them back. 'This path is not wide enough for our party. We had better go into the avenue.'

Caroline tightened her fingers on his arm. He was always so considerate, but she had no intention of permitting Elizabeth to continue through the gardens with them.

Fortunately, in one of her few moments of manners, Elizabeth realised she was not welcome. 'No, no; stay where you are. You are charmingly grouped, and appear to uncommon advantage. The picturesque would be spoiled by admitting a fourth. Goodbye.'

Darcy opened his mouth, no doubt to protest, but Caroline pulled on his arm as she stepped forward and before he could say anything, Elizabeth had run off towards the house, while Caroline and Louisa moved further into the garden with Mr Darcy between them.

* * *

That evening after dinner, when the ladies left the gentlemen to their port, Elizabeth quickly excused herself and left the drawing room. Caroline breathed a sigh of relief, and turned to her sister. 'I declare, has the air suddenly become fresher and less stifling? Even with her sister so ill, Eliza is always about where we are, especially when Darcy is around. She can scarcely allow the poor man to breathe, always at him with her impertinence and her "fine eyes".'

'Guests,' Louisa agreed, 'should know when they are welcomed and when they are not. Fortunately, dear Jane is recovering well and should soon be able to return to Longbourn.'

'That moment cannot come too soon for me—' But before Caroline could continue her thought, Elizabeth reappeared, and holding the door open, she offered her arm in support of—Jane!

Caroline and Louisa both leapt to their feet, exclaiming their joy at seeing their friend up and about. Elizabeth made certain Jane was comfortably seated by the fire, a blanket over her knees, before turning to the others. 'As you see, she is much improved.'

Jane smiled and held out her hand to Caroline. 'I thank you for all you and your brother have done for me. And it does me good to discover that you are not yet wearied of my presence.'

'Wearied!' Caroline cried. 'Dear Jane, Louisa and I treasure every moment we can spend in your company. Can I fetch you something, a cup of tea, a bowl of broth?'

'Thank you,' Jane said again, smiling, 'but I have just dined upstairs. Your servants have shown me every courtesy. They are to be commended for their attentions, and you also deserve respect, for you are their mistress.'

Caroline smiled and pulled a chair so she could sit close to Jane. Louisa too, drew nearer, so as better to converse. 'It does me a world of good,' Caroline mused, 'to see you once again restored to us.'

'Restored?' Eliza asked. 'In what way had Jane been removed from you? It seems to me that she has been closer than ever to your presence, since she has resided in your house for some days now.'

Caroline glared at her, but upon seeing Jane smile at her sister's comment, she smoothed her countenance and said, 'Restored to us in both spirit and body, of course. While you, dear Jane, suffered so terribly, I often feared that you were not wholly with us, but on a different plane, fighting against the illness. But now you are the picture of health, and so I am happy.'

Jane smiled and reached out to take Caroline's hands. 'You are so good.'

'I merely attempt to match your goodness.' Caroline squeezed Jane's hands. Out of the corner of her eye, she saw Miss Elizabeth make a wry face; and had she been so rude as to roll her eyes? Caroline turned sharply to see, but Eliza gave her only a gentle and affectionate smile. Removing her hands from Jane's, Caroline sat back and gazed into the fire.

The next hour passed swiftly. Caroline and Louisa spoke of when they and Charles were younger, of his mischievous exploits that had their nurse tearing her hair out in frustration.

'I'll never forget her face,' Louisa said, laughing. 'He came in, absolutely covered in mud, and clutching what must have been the ugliest puppy in all existence. She was ready to take a switch to him, but when he explained that as well as the puppy, he'd brought back a rabbit and a bird with a broken wing, she was so overwhelmed she had to sit down and call for her smelling salts. While she recovered, we helped Charles bring in the animals and hide them in the old nursery.'

Caroline laughed too at the memory. 'We were so proud of ourselves, rescuing these bedraggled creatures. Of course the bird died the next day, the rabbit gave birth to six little rabbits, and the puppy got out of the room and somehow made its way into Father's study, where it piddled on the day's newspaper and chewed up a pile of Very Important Papers.' She glanced around at her engrossed audience. 'Father was most displeased, and he called Nurse on the carpet and spoke to her most sternly.'

'I think, in fact,' Louisa said slowly, trying to recall, 'that she left the house not long after.'

Caroline nodded. 'Yes, that's right. She was replaced with someone much worse, though, which did not please us one bit. It was very difficult to do anything at all that escaped Nurse Edwards' notice.'

From there, she and Louisa moved on to a discussion of their time at finishing school, and then to parties in London, plays they had seen, and carriage rides in the park.

Jane and Elizabeth were enraptured by the world revealed to them. 'We never attended a school,' Jane explained.

'No school?' asked Louisa, looking at Caroline with a glance that clearly said, *This explains much.*

Elizabeth shook her head. 'No, there are few schools for young ladies in these parts. But Father did an excellent job with us, ensuring that we all can read and write very well. He also brought in tutors at various times, to teach us drawing, painting, music, and Mother showed us how to sew and do all the other things that are necessary when running a household.'

Caroline raised her eyebrows. Somehow she doubted the Bennet sisters knew the first thing about being mistress of an estate. No doubt, however, they knew enough to get by in their level of society, and that was all that mattered.

'The most educated and accomplished lady I know,' she said, 'is my dear friend, Lady Eleanor Amesbury. She moves in the highest circles in town, and I myself have seen members of the Royal Family at her entertainments.'

'Oh!' Jane cried, 'how very exciting. Did you dare approach them, even speak?'

Caroline had not, believing that one did not speak to one's betters unless invited to do so, but she chose not to say this. Instead, she spoke of Lady Eleanor's house, the chandeliers, the very many servants, and the style of food, of music, of clothing worn by both the women and the men. Jane was clearly transported to another world, her hands clasped in her lap, her eyes fixed on Caroline's face so as to not miss a single detail of this life so different from her own. Eliza leant back in her chair and glanced about the room, almost as if she was bored. No one could be bored, though, when learning about Lady Amesbury. If someone like Caroline herself had been overwhelmed by becoming part of such society, it was no wonder that country girls like these Bennets were amazed and disbelieving. No doubt Eliza, in another of her subterfuges, was merely trying to hide her admiration.

The gentlemen joined them just as Caroline was talking about how amusing it had been when two gentlemen had almost come to blows over which one of them would escort Lady Amesbury into the dining room. 'It was only thanks to Eleanor's quick thinking that they didn't, but of course she had to do something, for if the gentlemen had fought, they would have done irreparable damage to her lovely room, which held many works of art, including sculptures which could have been knocked down and broken. And she gentled them so cleverly, by suggesting they fight a duel the next morning, instead of fighting now and ruining her party.' Caroline glanced at her audience. Jane looked half horrified and half fascinated, and even Eliza was listening closely, although she had no particular expression on her face. 'When Eleanor said that,' Caroline continued, 'everyone laughed, and at that the gentlemen realised how ridiculous they had been. They shook hands, Lady Amesbury took both their arms, and everyone went in for a well-deserved supper.'

As she finished speaking, the gentlemen approached, and Caroline's gaze went to Mr Darcy. He was looking at her, not at Miss Elizabeth, and so even though his expression was somewhat disapproving, she gave him a triumphant smile. 'You were present at that party, were you not, Mr Darcy?'

He nodded reluctantly. 'I was, but I am afraid that my recollection of that particular event is somewhat different from yours.'

'In what way?' asked Eliza. 'It is always so interesting to learn how different people observe the same event.'

Before he could answer her, before Caroline could find a way to return Mr Darcy's attention to herself, Charles swooped down upon Jane. 'Miss Bennet, I cannot begin to express how delighted I am to see you here, looking so much recovered.'

She smiled and looked down. 'Thank you. It is I, however, who cannot begin to express my gratitude to you,' she looked up at his smiling face, 'for being so generous and kind to one to whom you owe nothing.'

'Owe nothing?' he said, incredulous. 'What nonsense you speak. Say anything more on this and I will become convinced that you are still ill, with a brain fever or something that has completely addled your wits.' He said this in a tone of such affection, that although Jane could have felt affronted, she merely gave him another shy smile.

Mr Darcy approached at that point, and offered Jane a polite congratulation on her recovery. He was followed by Mr Hurst, who bowed and said he was very glad to see her. The two men then left to pursue their own interests in separate parts of the room.

Charles did not stay still for a single instant. He built up the fire so Jane might not be chilled. He suggested she move from one side of the fireplace to the other, which was situated slightly further from the door into the drawing room, and so would prevent her from feeling a draft. He called for tea, and poured it for Jane himself.

'Charles,' Caroline called to him, 'please do sit still, you are making me positively dizzy.' He did not reply, but once he was assured Jane had all the tea and cake she wished, he sat down near her and the two conversed, ignoring everyone else in the room.

Mr Hurst, sitting at a little distance from Caroline, said, to no one in particular, 'I wonder if I should ask for the card table to be set out. A game of cards would fill the rest of the time quite nicely.'

Caroline had recently overheard Mr Darcy speaking to Charles, saying that he had wearied of playing cards so often and hoped that other entertainments might be found. Caroline quite enjoyed the games, but she did not wish Mr Darcy to be unhappy, or even slightly wearied, when she could prevent it.

'I am so sorry, Mr Hurst,' she said, 'but we did not intend to play at this time.'

He looked about at the others, but as no one spoke saying that they did wish to play, he crossed his arms across his chest and pouted. Caroline did not give him another thought for she knew he would soon stretch out on the sofa and fall asleep.

Mr Darcy picked up a book, and so Caroline did also, but instead of giving it her full attention, she kept a wary eye on Miss Elizabeth, who was watching her sister and Charles as they spoke in low tones to one another. Louisa, who sat nearby, gazed into space, fiddling with her bracelets, taking one or two off, then another one off, then putting them back on in a different order. She was probably completely unaware that she did so, and would be mortified when she discovered she'd been fidgeting instead of sitting calmly. Turning her attention once again to Eliza, Caroline saw a small smile on her lips, and it widened when Jane burst into laughter at something Charles said.

Caroline looked more closely at her brother. He was leaning forward, as if his entire body yearned to be closer to Jane. His attention was fully engaged, his face animated. *Could it be*, Caroline wondered, *that this is more than one of his many passing fancies?* But surely that was impossible. Not even Charles, who was always friends with everyone and anyone, would think seriously about an alliance with a family such as the Bennets.

Her mind once again at ease, she glanced back at Mr Darcy, who was still engrossed in his book. 'Mr Darcy,' she called, 'your book appears to interest you very much. Will you tell me the title so that I might read it when you have finished with it?'

He told her the name and author, without so much as lifting his eyes from the page.

She moved over to sit beside him. Looking over his shoulder, she said, 'There is very little conversation in your book. Look at how densely the print covers the page.'

He made no response.

She took out her book, which she'd selected because it was one she'd seen him reading, and opened it at random. She read a few lines, turned to the first page, read it, turned to the last and read it. Then, putting it down, she stifled a yawn. 'How pleasant it is to spend an evening in this way! I declare after all there is no enjoyment like reading! How much sooner one tires of anything than of a book! When I have a house of my own, I shall be miserable if I have not an excellent library.'

No one responded to what she said, Mr Darcy did not so much as nod approvingly, but she was certain he'd heard what she said. Now he would realise that even though she did not spend as much time reading as he did, she would have the proper affection for Pemberley's library.

How very dull the evening was becoming. She glanced again at Mr Darcy, but he appeared to be fascinated by his book. A small pinprick of pique grew inside her. Surely his behaviour would be considered rude, to ignore her when she spoke so directly to him. Since he so often became irritated when interrupted, she determined not to speak to him again for some time.

She looked about the room in search of some amusement and heard Charles, while speaking to Jane, mention a ball. She turned immediately towards him, and said, 'By the by, Charles, are you really serious in meditating a dance at Netherfield? I would advise you, before you determine on it, to consult the wishes of the present party; I am much mistaken if there are not some among us to whom a ball would be rather a punishment than a pleasure.'

'If you mean Darcy,' cried Charles, 'he may go to bed, if he chooses, before it begins—but as for the ball, it is quite a settled thing; and as soon as Miss Bennet is fully recovered, I shall send around my cards.'

Mr Darcy had looked up from his book on hearing Charles say his name. He looked, to Caroline's eye, less than enthused about the upcoming dance.

'I should like balls infinitely better,' she quickly said, 'if they were carried on in a different manner; but there is something insufferably tedious in the usual process of such a meeting. It would surely be much more rational if conversation instead of dancing were made the order of the day.'

'Much more rational, my dear Caroline,' Charles said with a smile, 'but it would not be near so much like a ball.' He turned back to Jane, and Darcy returned to his book.

Caroline tapped her foot, making certain it was hidden beneath her gown, but she simply could not sit still. Darcy continued to ignore her, and she suddenly thought of another way to draw his attention. She stood and walked about the room, knowing that as her figure was fine and her carriage elegant, she looked well, but Darcy still continued to read. At last, the pique tightening her shoulders so that she had to be careful to keep her head high, she thought of one last thing to try. Since he'd spent so much time looking at Eliza, perhaps he'd look up if the two ladies walked together. Surely, in that case, he would realise just how unfashionable Eliza was when compared to a lady of true accomplishment.

'Miss Eliza Bennet,' she said loudly, 'let me persuade you to follow my example and take a turn about the room. I assure you it is very refreshing after sitting so long in one attitude.'

Elizabeth looked surprised but agreed. And, Caroline was delighted to note, Mr Darcy looked up. He gave Elizabeth only a passing glance, but sent a quizzical look at Caroline. Good, she was a woman of mystery. Walking about a room in this manner was unusual, in fact she could think of no other time she had seen anyone do it. Not only was she mysterious, she was also innovative. And, to her further delight, his hands closed the book that rested on his lap. 'Please,' she said to him, 'would you care to join us?'

'I thank you,' he said, 'but no. There can be but two objectives for your choosing to walk up and down the room together, and my presence would interfere with your achieving either of them.'

Caroline turned to Elizabeth, and whispered, 'What can he mean?' Louder, so Mr Darcy could see her delight in this mystery, she said, 'What does he mean? I am dying to know his meaning!' And, turning back to Eliza, 'Can you in any way understand him?'

'Not at all,' was the answer, 'but depend on it, he means to be severe on us, and our surest way of disappointing him will be to ask nothing about it.'

'Oh! there is no reason to disappoint him,' Caroline said. 'And I simply must know his meaning.' She pulled her arm out of Eliza's, and stopped in front of Mr Darcy. 'Sir, I simply must know of these two motives.'

'I have not the smallest objection to explaining them,' he said. 'You either choose this method of passing the evening because you are in each other's confidence, and have secret affairs to discuss, or because you are conscious that your figures appear to the greatest advantage when walking; if the first, I should be completely in your way, and if the second, I can admire you much better from my present location.'

'Oh! Shocking!' Caroline cried. 'I have never heard anything so abominable.' Indeed, she was rather shocked. Not that Mr Darcy expected that she knew her figure appeared to greater advantage when she walked, because she did know this, but because he'd spoken so openly about sitting back and admiring the feminine form. 'Miss Eliza, how shall we punish him for such a speech?'

Elizabeth laughed. 'That will be simple, indeed, if you have the inclination.' At Caroline's inquiring glance, she continued, 'Tease him—laugh at him. Intimate as you are, you must know how it is to be done.'

'Upon my word,' she said coldly, 'I do not.' Darcy still watched them, and as she looked at him now, expecting to see anger growing on his countenance, he merely smiled at Elizabeth and raised his brow. Poor man, to be so spoken of. Brave man, to so masterfully refuse to show his rage.

'Tease calmness of temper and presence of mind!' she continued to Eliza. 'No, no—I feel he may defy us there. And as to laughter, we will not expose ourselves, if you please, by attempting to laugh without a subject.'

'Mr Darcy is not to be laughed at?' Eliza cried while laughing herself. 'That is an uncommon advantage, and uncommon I hope it will continue for it would be a great loss to me to have many such acquaintances. I dearly love a laugh.'

Mr Darcy's smile had grown at Eliza's words. 'Miss Bingley,' he said, 'has given me credit for more than can be. The wisest and the best of men—nay, the wisest and best of their actions may be rendered ridiculous by a person whose first object in life is a joke.'

Before Caroline could say anything at all, Elizabeth faced him full on, and said, 'Certainly there are such people, but I hope I am not one of them. I hope I never ridicule what is wise or good.' An impish smile grew.

'Follies and nonsense, whims and inconsistencies, do divert me, I own, and I laugh at them whenever I can. But these, I suppose, are precisely what you are without.'

Caroline glanced over at Louisa, who was now also listening to this conversation, and whose countenance clearly showed the shock and horror that Caroline felt. How dare this person speak so to Mr Darcy?

He, however, appeared completely unruffled. He responded to Eliza in a calm voice, and there was even still a small smile about his lips. 'Perhaps that is not possible for anyone. But it has been the study of my life,' and now his expression did become sober, 'to avoid those weaknesses which often expose a strong understanding to ridicule.'

'Such as vanity and pride.' Something in the way Elizabeth said those words distracted Caroline from her horror and she observed that Darcy and Elizabeth now spoke to one another as if there was no other person in the room. Their eyes were locked, and they appeared, if not exactly adversaries, two people who disagreed yet enjoyed the act of disagreeing. She had never before seen this expression on Darcy's face, nor seen him so thoroughly engaged in a conversation with a lady that he ignored everything and everyone else.

'Yes,' Mr Darcy said, 'Vanity is a weakness indeed. But pride—where there is a real superiority of mind, pride will always be under good regulation.'

Elizabeth turned away at this point, and Caroline noted she'd turned so Mr Darcy would not see her smile. Offended beyond all limits on his behalf, Caroline asked acidly, 'Your examination of Mr Darcy is over, I presume? And pray what is the result?'

Elizabeth turned to her, the smile still present. 'I am perfectly convinced by it that Mr Darcy has no defect. He owns it himself without disguise.'

'No,' said Darcy, and at last there was an edge to his voice. 'I have made no such pretension. I have faults enough, but they are not, I hope, of understanding. My temper I dare not vouch for. It is, I believe, too little yielding—certainly too little for the convenience of the world. I cannot forget the follies and vices of others so soon as I ought, nor their offences against myself. My temper would perhaps be called resentful. My good opinion, once lost, is lost forever.'

'That is a failing indeed,' Elizabeth said, softly and with what Caroline thought might be a touch of sadness. 'Implacable resentment is a shade in a character. But you have chosen your fault well. I cannot laugh at it.' At this, seemingly unable to remain serious for more that a moment, she laughed and her countenance brightened. 'You are safe from me!'

Darcy, instead of turning away, appeared to consider what she'd said. 'There is, I believe, in every disposition, a tendency to some particular evil—a natural defect, which not even the best education can overcome.'

'And yours,' Elizabeth said, 'is a propensity to hate everybody.'

'While yours,' he replied with a smile, 'is wilfully to misunderstand them.'

They both paused for a moment and Caroline took her chance to change the subject. She needed Mr Darcy to return to the man she knew, for she felt almost afraid of this Darcy who took outright impertinence as valid points in a discussion, and, even more, participated in a conversation like this. Caroline had never heard anyone speak of their own faults. Why would they? Everyone else discussed them, not to their face, but they all knew that this happened. People needed to present themselves to their greatest advantage in the world, and any faults were hidden as deeply as possible. A shiver ran up her spine, and she felt the skin on her arms erupt into goose pimples.

'Do let us have a little music,' she cried. Yes, something cheerful and bright. 'Louisa, you will not mind my waking Mr Hurst?'

Her sister had not the smallest objection, and the pianoforte was opened. As she walked towards the instrument, she glanced at Mr Darcy and saw that his eyes were still on Miss Elizabeth. And in his eyes, Caroline saw fear, but somehow she knew it did not stem from the same source as hers.

* * *

Caroline woke the next morning with the hope that today she would finally see the last of Miss Elizabeth. If this meant that Jane also would be leaving, well, she was able to bear up under the disappointment. Sure enough, both Bennets came down after breakfast, and Jane requested the use of Charles' carriage, for the purpose of bearing her back to Longbourn.

Caroline was exultant, although she did wonder why Jane needed their carriage, when the Bennets had one that was perfectly adequate. Her happiness enabled her to view Charles' dismay with equanimity.

'Surely, Miss Bennet,' he said, 'you are not yet well enough to handle the stress such a removal requires. Much better to wait another day, or two even, before attempting such a thing.'

Jane, however, showed a firmness Caroline had not hitherto suspected.

Since Jane was determined to leave that very morning, Caroline saw no danger in supporting her brother, and she added hers to his voice, and suggested that the day be used for preparation and relaxation, and that the trip to Longbourn could thus be more easily accomplished the next day.

To her surprise and dismay, Jane and Elizabeth conferred, and agreed to that plan. Still, the rest of that day passed quickly. Mr Darcy, she noted, had apparently wearied of Miss Eliza's presence as much as she had, for he said not more than a handful of words to her throughout the entire day.

The next day was Sunday. After morning service, the separation, so vehemently hoped for by seemingly everyone with the exception of Charles, took place. Caroline found that she could smile warmly at Elizabeth, now that she was leaving and her sorrow at losing Jane's steady presence took her by surprise. Still, she was more than happy when at last the Bennet sisters were helped into the carriage, and she could stand on the steps and wave goodbye.

'At last,' she observed to Mr Darcy as they entered the house. 'It is ever so much more pleasant when one is with one's own family and friends without the inconvenience of visitors, especially when those visitors are not of one's choosing.'

'I heartily agree,' he said, and despite Charles' hangdog expression, Caroline's happiness was complete.

Chapter Six

～

Caroline sat down at the breakfast table and contentment washed through her. She took a sip of tea, and sighed happily. Everyone else had come down by this time, and there was conversation; Mr Hurst grumbling about how the weather, somewhat foggy, would interfere with his plan for a day of shooting, Louisa consoling him with a promise of a card game later. Mr Darcy spoke to Charles of a planned meeting that day with Netherfield's steward, and what they needed to consider doing with an area that should perhaps be left fallow over the winter. So many voices, all speaking at once, and yet to Caroline it was the most serene and peaceful breakfast she could imagine, for not a single voice belonged to a Bennet.

Only Charles appeared unhappy. In fact he was uncharacteristically silent, replying to Darcy only in nods or monosyllables. Caroline, however, was so content she found herself empathising with her brother, even though she was glad he no longer had the opportunity to spend so much time with Jane. There was no sense in his continuing down that particular path, and she'd tell him so as soon as an opportunity arose.

Still, she could understand, since she was certain that if she were to be parted from Mr Darcy, she would also no doubt pine away. Charles, of course, couldn't be nearly as attached to Jane as she was to Mr Darcy, but she could still pity her brother, who often experienced emotions and passions to a far greater extent than either of his sisters did.

She thought now about her feelings for Mr Darcy, gazing at him from beneath her lashes, where he sat across the table from her. He was turned sideways to speak to Charles who was beside him. Mr Darcy's profile, Caroline thought, was one of the most noble of any of her acquaintance. His high forehead, the way his hair waved across it so crisply, his straight nose and determined chin all spoke of his superior breeding. Those features, when joined to her classical beauty, would produce children who would be free to travel within the highest circles of society. Why, perhaps one of her offspring would marry into the royal family. Such an event was not beyond the realms of possibility.

Of course, producing a child would mean doing with Mr Darcy the thing that Louisa said involved sounds similar to those found in a pigsty. Looking at Mr Darcy, she could not picture him ever doing anything so undignified. Mr Hurst was much more like a pig in appearance, being short and, while not exactly round, he did have some meat around his middle. Also, the skin on his face was often a reddish colour, much closer to the pink of a pig than Mr Darcy's pleasant paler skin that was lightly tinged with tan from all the time he spent outdoors. Mr Hurst also tended to breathe more audibly, especially when he was asleep, and some of the noises he made then, when stretched out on one of the sofas in the drawing room, did resemble grunts.

Caroline paused, struck by a new thought. Could the act of creating a child take place when both parties were asleep? She knew that it happened in the marital bed. But if Louisa was asleep each time, why would she comment on Mr Hurst's weight? Did that mean she woke up while the act was still underway?

A sudden image of Mr Tryphon, bending over her hand, his lips hot on her skin, his eyes burning up into hers, surged into her mind. Others crowded in, his firm forearm beneath her fingers when he escorted her into dinner; the brush of his hand over her shoulder and sometimes on to the back of her neck when he seated her at the table; his side pressed against hers when he pulled his arm in closer; her arm linked through his when they walked together in the garden.

Caroline stifled a gasp, for a lick of flame surged up from the most private area of her body into her chest. She sat still, every muscle in her body tense and yet somehow alive, all at the same time. She drew in a ragged breath, realising she had not breathed for a long moment, and saw Louisa looking at her oddly.

'Caroline,' she said, 'are you quite all right?'

Everyone else had now turned to her. Mortified, Caroline said, 'Yes, of course, that last mouthful of toast was merely a little dry.' Hastily picking up her teacup, she took a small sip.

The others turned back to whatever they had been doing, and Caroline took advantage of the moment to try to compose herself. What on earth was going on? She focused on slowing her breathing, and picked up her fork, holding it perfectly, as a lady should. She used it to pick up a small, ladylike amount of scrambled eggs, and chewed and swallowed the mouthful in a deliberate, ladylike manner.

Having regained control, she permitted herself to raise her eyes from her plate and once again look at Mr Darcy. To her relief, no strange feelings rose up in any part whatsoever of her body, at the sight of his dark hair, his ash-grey morning coat, or his hands as he pointed to something on the piece of paper he and Charles were perusing.

'It would be best,' she said to Louisa later that morning, 'if Mr Darcy would speak soon, so that things will be quite settled between us.'

Louisa nodded. 'He might,' she said thoughtfully, 'be waiting until his sister is a little older. Charles, of course, could not even think of discussing marriage with Georgiana now, as she is only sixteen.'

'Other girls are married at sixteen.'

'True, but you know how protective Darcy is of his sister. Especially since . . .'

Caroline nodded. Poor Georgiana had been most cruelly used during the incident in question. Even though it had not been in any way his fault, Mr Darcy blamed himself, and so was now determined to watch over his sister so as to ensure her current and future happiness.

'Perhaps,' Caroline mused, 'you are correct, and Mr Darcy is thinking ahead to a double wedding. Oh! Louisa, would not that be splendid, both Charles and I standing up with Mr and Miss Darcy. It would be the wedding of the season!'

'No doubt.' Louisa was focused on her stitchery.

'I am sorry,' Caroline said softly. 'I did not think. Your wedding with Mr Hurst was lovely, and very fashionable.'

Louisa sewed another three stitches, and then looked up. 'It is all right. You need not suffer any pangs on my account. While Mr Hurst's position in society is nowhere near the Darcys', it was a very good match for me. And my wedding was perfectly suited to both Mr Hurst and myself.' She turned and reached for Caroline's hand. 'I am not like you, you know. I have observed how you have thrived since starting your friendship with Lady Amesbury. You grow more lovely and animated when you are in the company of the people she knows. I am content with a quieter life, one spent with one's friends of long acquaintance and known habits.'

'How well we know each other,' Caroline said fondly.

Louisa grinned. 'Fortunate indeed, when you consider the sorts of sisters Jane has!'

Both women broke into peals of laughter. 'Oh, can you imagine?' Caroline asked. 'What if Miss Lydia was our sister and sitting here with us right now! The only conversation would be of officers.'

'Yes,' gasped Louisa, 'or Miss Mary. She would make certain that none of us, not even Mr Darcy, read anything other than sermons!'

They continued in this vein, and Caroline's sides were beginning to ache from laughing so hard, when the butler entered, carrying a silver tray with the day's mail.

'There is a packet for you, Miss Bingley,' he said with a bow, and held out the tray.

'Oh, it is from Eleanor!' Caroline cried upon seeing the familiar round hand on the envelope. 'But it is too thick to contain only her letter.'

'Well, do not keep me waiting,' Louisa said. 'Open it!'

Caroline fetched the letter knife from the writing desk and carefully slit the thick embossed paper. As well as Eleanor's usual thick letter, filled with news and gossip about London and their friends there, another letter tumbled out. It was in an envelope similar to Eleanor's writing paper, but was addressed in a firm but unfamiliar hand.

'Who could that be from?' Louisa asked.

Uncertain, Caroline opened it before Eleanor's letter. As soon as her eyes fell on the first few lines, she gasped and raised one hand to cover her mouth, but the other hand continued to hold the letter so she could read on.

'It—it is from Mr Tryphon,' she said. 'He says, oh, he says . . .' Her voice trailed off, but realising her sister was regarding her with great curiosity, she said, 'Louisa, you must forgive me.' She ran from the room.

She did not stop until she reached the security of her own chamber. Genney, her maid, was nowhere to be seen, but for once Caroline did not wonder if the girl was idle somewhere, no doubt flirting with a footman. Grateful to be alone, she took the letter from where it had been creased by her shaking hands, and read it again.

'*My darling,*' Mr Tryphon had written, '*please forgive me if this letter shocks you, but I can hold this in no longer. You must have realised, you who are so observant and caring of others cannot have failed to observe the joy I experience at every moment in your presence. You shine on me, dear Caroline, from above, and my life is only illuminated when I am with you. When we are not together, all is dark and dreary. I spend every waking moment thinking of you and treasuring every moment we have shared, and I dream only of you when I am asleep. These things are all that is keeping me from weeping for the lack of you. I long at every moment to fly to your side.*

Do not fear, dearest Caroline, if I may be permitted to call you this, that I am placing you in an uncomfortable situation, or that I will force any unwanted attentions. I cannot help myself though; my feelings for you will burst out through my very soul if I do not speak. I do not ask for any response from you. I will not burden you, the next time we meet, for there must be a next time or I will die. I wish only that you should know how very much I adore you, and hope that if any of your thoughts drift to me, they be happy ones.

Yours, with hope,
Stephen Tryphon'

Her hands shaking, so that the pages they held rustled like a living creature pushing its way through dense foliage, she sat on the edge of her bed.

What could this mean? Why had he written now, and not spoken earlier, when he could have expressed himself in person? But would she prefer that? Truly, it was out of kindness that he wrote now, so she could have time and privacy to absorb his words. If he had spoken to her directly, she did not know how she would have responded. She would have frozen, she presumed, or worse, run away. In either case, her reaction would have been rude and ungraceful.

How well he knew her, after so short an acquaintance. How thoughtful he was, to have spared her the mortification of hearing his words out loud. Still, despite his thoughtfulness, she was frozen, and indeed, had run away from Louisa. How her sister must be wondering. What could there be in a letter, Louisa must ask herself, that could send Caroline flying from a room? She would assume it must report a terrible accident that injured one of Caroline's friends, or even a death.

Caroline looked down at the pages, still fluttering, like a little bird trying to fly. She did not think she could discuss this matter with anyone at all. Well, maybe Eleanor, yes Eleanor would understand and she, with her wealth of experience, would know what Caroline should do. And she knew what Eleanor's first words would be. She would say, 'Caroline, what do you want to do?'

What did Caroline want to do? She was uncertain. She was to marry Mr Darcy, everyone knew that. But she recalled again the images of Mr Tryphon she'd thought of earlier, and of his touch, his scent, his voice, his breath on her hand, on her cheek. She wasn't sure what her response to those memories meant, but it was certainly different from her reaction to Mr Darcy. She'd held Mr Darcy's arm, and it was at least as firm as Mr Tryphon's, but she'd never become breathless at the mere thought of his touch.

She sat a time longer, her thoughts whirling until she began to develop a headache. *This is nonsense,* she told herself. *Put the letter aside. Burn it if you wish. Tell Louisa anything you choose about why you left her so precipitously.* But do not, another voice said, tell her what's in the letter. You must guard it, keep it safe, cradle it like a babe. Only then can it flourish.

Flourish? Did she want it to flourish? Of course not. Mr Tryphon's feelings for her could only end in disappointment. She must put them out of her head. She could be thankful to Mr Tryphon for showing her what a man's passion could be like, and she still wished to see him as a friend, but nothing could come of this. She must focus on Mr Darcy. She would replace any images of Mr Tryphon that came into her head with images of Mr Darcy. And she would work hard to experience the shortness of breath and pain in the chest that did describe what she'd felt earlier when thinking of Mr Tryphon, only when she thought of Mr Darcy.

She stood, determined to cast the letter into the fire. Her hands had another idea. With bemusement, she watched them find the key for her jewel box, open it, and slide the letter beneath the padded velvet that rested at the bottom of the box. Only when the letter disappeared from sight and the box was once again locked, did her hands return to her control.

* * *

Caroline returned to Louisa, surprised to discover that only a matter of minutes had elapsed since her quick departure from the morning room. Louisa was still alone, the gentlemen having decided to go out shooting even if the fog interfered with their sport. Louisa looked up, her expression merely a little curious, and Caroline was proud of her own composure as she re-seated herself and picked up the slipper she was embroidering.

'Please accept my apologies,' Caroline said, 'for my sudden departure. Something from breakfast must have disagreed with me.' Her voice did not waver once.

Louisa nodded. 'Of course. I suggest you speak to the cook and ensure this does not happen again.'

Caroline selected a piece of violet silk. Threading her needle was difficult, as despite her outward composure, her hands still shook a little, but at last the silk strand went through the needle's eye, and she began to embroider a tiny flower. And if her hands continued to tremble, and if Louisa noticed, not a word was said by either sister.

The next day Charles would not sit still, not for a moment, and at last declared he was determined to ride to Longbourn to inquire after Miss Bennet. Mr Darcy agreed to go with his friend, and Caroline and Louisa decided to accompany the gentlemen, in the carriage, as far as Meryton, since they wished to see if any new colours of embroidery thread had arrived.

Once in the village, Louisa entered the shop and Caroline, as she was about go through the doorway, glanced back to observe Mr Darcy. He sat a horse very well, his back erect, his head held proudly, his hands firm yet gentle on the reins. She hoped the sight of him would bring on at least a spark of the fire that had filled her when she'd thought about Mr Tryphon. Last evening she'd been pulled towards her jewel box, her traitorous hands itching to retrieve the letter and read it again. Somehow she'd resisted the urge, but last night her dreams had been filled with images that caused her to become overheated, so that she slept but poorly and had awoken to sheets dampened with perspiration.

Before she could find out if the sight of Mr Darcy on his horse did cause her chest to hurt or her breathing to become laboured, she caught sight of the two youngest Bennets hurrying across the street to meet up with one of the officers. Accompanying him was a young man who Caroline at first didn't notice, because the officer's red coat was so bright. Once she'd recovered from the glare of colour, she looked to the other man, and instantly her chest was filled, not with heat but with the dull cold of horror.

George Wickham! What was he doing here? Four Bennet sisters had now joined the two men, and her horror increased, for Mr Darcy and Charles had observed the women and were even now turning their horses to join the group.

Before Caroline could so much as call out to her brother to warn him, or to beseech Mr Darcy to come to her so he might avoid seeing the group, Charles was lifting his hat and saluting Jane, his smile wide and warm. Although Mr Darcy's back was facing her, Caroline could tell the exact moment he observed and recognised Wickham, for his shoulders stiffened. She walked a few steps along the street to where she could see both men's faces.

Darcy had gone white, and his jaw was clenched in his effort to retain his composure. Wickham's face showed a ruddiness that had not been there before, but his smile was easy and his eyes betrayed a mocking light. His bow was perfectly proper. Wickham had always been blessed with easy manners.

Caroline remained on the pavement, unable to look away, even when Louisa, who had finally noticed her sister had not followed her into the shop, came outside and called to her. When Caroline did not respond, Louisa followed her gaze, and her countenance, also, froze in shock.

The observed interaction was soon over, and Charles and Darcy turned their horses' heads and returned to Caroline and Louisa. Charles was all smiles, for he had just seen Jane, who was clearly much recovered, since she'd been able to walk to Meryton from Longbourn, and had suffered no ill effects. Darcy's face, though, was grim.

'We no longer plan to go to Longbourn,' Charles said, 'since the object of our visit has already been accomplished.' He turned to Darcy. 'Shall we accompany the ladies back to Netherfield?'

Darcy did not look at his friend, instead choosing to look away, down the street towards the edge of town. 'If you don't mind, I feel the need for some vigorous exercise, and would like to continue our ride and cover some ground. If you prefer to stay with your sisters, I am perfectly content to do so alone.'

Charles, in his happiness over Jane's state of good health, positively bubbled with energy, and quickly agreed that a good hard ride was exactly what he wished to do. The men trotted off, urging their horses into a canter as they left the last buildings of Meryton behind them.

'Oh my!' said Louisa, staring at Caroline, her eyes wide. 'What a dreadful thing to happen.'

Caroline nodded, too overcome to speak. 'What a dreadful thing for Mr Darcy,' she said at last.

Louisa nodded. 'I cannot think how he will bear up after this terrible blow.'

'He is strong!' Caroline said, and was astonished at the fierceness in her voice.

Louisa looked at her a moment, then said, 'He is. But I cannot forget how he suffered last year, because of that odious man. And I cannot forgive Wickham for dear Georgiana's sake, for her suffering was piteous indeed.'

Caroline swallowed in a throat gone dry. 'Please, can we delay our shopping a little while? I am in great need of something to drink and there is a tea shop down the way.'

Louisa agreed and, despite the small size and shabby décor of the shop, the tea it served was surprisingly acceptable. The two sisters said little, both lost in their memories of the previous summer, some fifteen months ago.

Mr Wickham was the son of the late Mr Darcy's steward. Wickham had been greatly favoured by the elder Mr Darcy, and when boys, Darcy and Wickham had been often in each other's company. They'd even attended Oxford at the same time, taking rooms together, but their natures had diverged greatly. Mr Darcy had applied himself to his studies and had led an exemplary life. It was at university he'd met Charles, and a strong friendship beneficial to both had developed. Darcy had tutored Charles in what he needed to know to take his place among the other wealthy young men, and Charles had encouraged Darcy to get out more among people, to relax at times and enjoy all that life could offer a young man in his position.

All of both Charles' and Darcy's encouragement, however, was wasted upon George Wickham. That young man had chosen a life of debauchery and personal pleasure, and so had wasted his chance to become educated and secure a respectable way of supporting himself. At last came a point when even Darcy, who out of loyalty to his deceased father had kept trying to help Wickham long past the time anyone else would have, could no longer turn a blind eye to the worst of Wickham's excesses. The elder Mr Darcy had hoped George Wickham would take orders and had requested that his son turn over one of Pemberley's richest livings to him. Wickham, however, when given a choice, had chosen to take a cash amount of money instead of working to become a clergyman. He took the generous amount of three thousand pounds offered by Darcy, and vanished.

Little had been heard of him since, until the disastrous time last summer. Caroline and Louisa did not know all the details but knew it had been shocking and terrible, for there was still a shadow in Georgiana's eyes, at times, when she thought no one could see her.

The ladies finished their tea, and went in search of silken thread.

*   *   *

Mr Darcy was very quiet that evening, even more so than usual, refusing to join a table for cards with Mr and Mrs Hurst, or to sit and converse with Caroline or Charles. The latter, of course, could speak only of Miss Bennet, and of how well she looked. Darcy spent the first part of the evening after dinner gazing out of the window or into the fire, but Caroline noticed that he turned his attention more and more often to Charles, not to speak with him but to observe. As the night grew darker, the shadows were reflected on Darcy's countenance.

Over the next few days, he continued to be taciturn. He went into Meryton not at all, no doubt to avoid having to see Wickham who, Caroline had learned, had joined the local militia.

'No doubt,' Caroline said to Louisa, 'he will be eagerly sought after by legions of Bennet sisters.'

Mr Wickham was the subject of much conversation in the neighbourhood, and Caroline learned a number of interesting details when receiving or making calls. 'George Wickham,' she said to Louisa, when they were both returning home in the carriage after visiting Lady Lucas, 'has become quite the favourite among the Bennets, just as I thought.'

'Although,' Louisa said thoughtfully, 'it appears that he prefers Elizabeth over her sisters.'

Caroline laughed. 'Miss Lydia's nose must be quite out of joint. I confess that I am not unhappy to see Miss Eliza occupying her time elsewhere.'

'She can mean nothing to Mr Darcy,' said Louisa, shocked. 'Surely you must know that.'

'Of course.'

Caroline gazed out the carriage. Outwardly, no one had cause to think that she feared Mr Darcy was showing too much attention to Miss Elizabeth Bennet. She recalled the smiles, his body leaning towards Eliza, the animation in his voice during conversation with her.

When she felt the most concerned about these silly trifles, she took out Mr Tryphon's letter. She had begun doing so regularly, and even though each time she read it again, she resolved to toss it in the fire, somehow it always ended up back in her jewel case. Reading it reassured her. If Mr Tryphon felt so strongly about her then surely Mr Darcy, with his superior taste and discernment, could feel no less.

She still had no idea how she would behave towards Mr Tryphon when next they met. His stay in town was apparently for an indefinite time, and Eleanor's letters continued to mention him in the most flattering light. Stephen had won a race in the park, or escorted her to the theatre and had the most interesting things to say about the play. Caroline missed her friends, both of them, for when she was with Mr Tryphon she felt she was the most beautiful, accomplished, and elegant woman in whatever room they happened to be in. Thinking this way, though, tended to bring on a repeat of the warmth inside her body and a flushed face, and despite how hard she was trying to experience these things when she was with Mr Darcy, she was unsuccessful. Surely that meant that Mr Darcy was the one for her. Her feelings for him were of long duration and had become stable. The strange things that happened when she was around Mr Tryphon occurred only because he was new to her. Plus, she associated him with Eleanor, and being around Eleanor was always dizzyingly exciting. That was the logical explanation for her unusual feelings, and she resolved now, as the carriage drew to a halt in front of Netherfield's imposing front doors, that the next time she saw Mr Tryphon she would be coolly correct, polite, perhaps show a bit of happiness at seeing him, her friend, but nothing more.

The day of the Netherfield ball was fast approaching, and a few days later Charles and his sisters drove out to deliver some invitations personally. As they approached Longbourn, Jane and Elizabeth, who had apparently been out walking, appeared from the shrubbery.

'Look,' Caroline whispered to Louisa so Charles wouldn't hear, 'there is a leaf caught in Eliza's hair.'

Charles wouldn't have heard even if Caroline had shouted, for all his attention rested on Jane. He leapt from the carriage before it had completely stopped moving, and hastened to her side. 'How well you look!' he exclaimed, and then seemed content to stand and beam at her.

'Jane!' Caroline cried, descending somewhat less precipitously from the carriage than had her brother. 'It has been an absolute age since we last met. Whatever have you been doing that has led you to so neglect your dear friends?'

Jane began to stammer something, but whatever she had to say was interrupted by Mrs Bennet, who hurried out of the house. 'Come in, come in,' she called. 'There is no need to stand about when there is comfort and refreshments ready for you.'

Caroline glanced at Louisa. They'd hoped they could simply stop by, hand over the invitation, and leave before they had to see Mrs Bennet, but this was not to be. Charles already had Jane's hand tucked into his arm, and he was walking beside Mrs Bennet towards the house, complimenting her on something or other about the garden.

'Really,' Louisa groused. 'Why must he do that? This garden is unbearably plain.' Jane glanced back, and instantly Louisa was all smiles. Hurrying to catch up, she said, 'It does my heart good to see you once again in the best of health. You can have no idea of the time I have spent pining for you, hoping you were fully recovered.'

'Thank you,' Jane said, as Louisa slipped her hand through Jane's arm on the other side from where Charles appeared to have taken up permanent possession, and they continued towards the house, talking of the lovely weather and the lovely garden.

Caroline, following them, glanced back to see Elizabeth hesitating before moving towards the house. Her attention was on Charles and her sister, and a small smile played on her lips. When she saw Caroline watching her, she came up beside her.

'I am,' Elizabeth said, 'very glad to see your affection for my sister. She still speaks warmly about the kindnesses you showed her while she was ill and in your house.'

'Of course,' Caroline said heartily. 'We could do no less for our dear friend.'

They both fell silent then, Caroline wondering if Elizabeth spent much time thinking about Mr Darcy. Of course she did; what girl in her position would not, when he held out the promise of great wealth and luxury?

They reached the house and entered the sitting room. Mrs Bennet called for tea and cake, and prattled on about something or other. Caroline and Louisa chose to spend their energy speaking to Jane, assuring her of their joy in seeing her today and how much, every day since she'd left Netherfield, they'd missed her. Meanwhile Charles, also, was trying to speak to Jane, and she attended him most assiduously, although she still showed her good manners and smiled and nodded at Caroline and Louisa whenever they paused for a moment without speaking.

'My other daughters,' Mrs Bennet said, so loudly that everyone in the room looked up in surprise, 'will be most sorry to have missed you, Mr Bingley. Kitty and Lydia went into Meryton.'

'And Miss Mary?' Charles asked.

Mrs Bennet waved a hand dismissively. 'Oh, she is somewhere about. I have not time to ensure I know where every one is, not with five daughters. Kitty and Lydia, though, for they are great favourites with the officers. And the new man, I think, has his eyes set on Lizzy.' She glared at Eliza. 'Although why she wouldn't accompany her sisters, when she knows there is a good chance of seeing him. Such a gentleman, Mr Wick—'

At this point, Caroline hastily stood up, set aside her untasted tea, and said, 'Thank you for your hospitality, Mrs Bennet. I am so sorry we have to rush off, but we have many calls to make today, to give out the invitations for the ball.'

'The ball!' Mrs Bennet clapped her hands. 'Oh, how wonderful. How much we are all looking forward to it, aren't we, girls?' She glanced at Jane and Eliza. Jane glanced at Charles and blushed before nodding, while Eliza, too, smiled and gazed into the distance.

Charles, surprised by his sister's abrupt end to the little party, stood also, and bowed in farewell. Jane and Mrs Bennet accompanied the Bingleys out to their carriage. As they left the house a young man appeared, wearing the wide-brimmed hat of a clergyman. He approached the group, clearly assured of a welcome. He looked as if he thought very well of himself, although Caroline could perceive no reason for his self-assurance, for he reminded her of nothing so much as a bantam rooster, strutting about a hen yard.

He reached them and made a low bow, even before looking to Mrs Bennet for an introduction. 'My dear friends,' she said to the Bingleys, 'please may I introduce our cousin, Mr Collins. Mr Collins, Mr Bingley, Miss Bingley, and Mrs Hurst.'

Mr Collins bowed again, so low this time that he wobbled a bit upon standing up, apparently experiencing some difficulty in realigning his body in a vertical position. 'It is my very great pleasure,' he said, 'to become acquainted with those of whom I have heard so much. And may I say that your persons are even more impressive than I was led to believe. I am certain that once I have the opportunity to converse with all of you, I shall form an even higher opinion.' He laughed, no doubt intending it to be charming but to Caroline he sounded somewhat like a donkey braying.

'And may I,' he continued, 'assure you that my patroness, the Honourable Lady Catherine de Bourgh, would be as equally delighted to meet you, if she were to deign to visit this part of the country.'

He blathered on, but at the name of Lady de Bourgh, Caroline and Louisa had exchanged a glance. How had this silly man the right to even mention the name of one of Mr Darcy's relatives? Turning her back on the group, even though Mr Collins was still speaking, Caroline waved to the coachman to assist her to enter the carriage. Louisa quickly followed her, and so Charles had no choice but to bow to Jane and Mrs Bennet, and depart. As the carriage began to move, Caroline looked back, and saw Mr Collins once again bowing, no doubt saluting the Bingleys' retreat.

'What an odd little man,' Louisa said, as a turn in the road removed Mr Collins from sight. 'Have the Bennets no end of strange relatives?'

Caroline laughed. 'Presumably not. But I did not think Mr Collins unduly strange. Risible, perhaps, but he was very polite.'

'Too polite, if you ask me. There can be such a thing as too many compliments.'

'What a strange thing to say.' Caroline personally thought that she could never tire of compliments. Louisa looked surprised at her comment, so she laughed to show it was a joke. 'Forgive me, it was a foolish jest. It is true, there are compliments and then there are compliments.'

Louisa laughed, too, to show she had known it was a joke. 'I understand completely. I think that what you speak of is the difference between a true compliment, and flattery.'

'That's it exactly.' Caroline leaned forward in her seat. 'It's as if you read my mind. A true lady is always conscious of when a compliment paid her is from the heart, deeply felt, or when it is given merely to curry favour.'

'Yes. And Mr Collins, despite the outward show of good manners, wished to present himself in the best light, when meeting us.'

'Although,' Caroline said thoughtfully, 'he is discerning, for he recognised us as people superior to himself and so worthy of his attentions.'

'I don't know how discerning he is. I suspect that the Bennets have spent much time speaking of us, telling him about our wealth.'

Caroline nodded. 'No doubt they seek to portray themselves in greater light through association with us. How I detest subterfuge of any sort.'

'I also.' The sisters smiled at each other.

The carriage slowed and Caroline looked out to see the Lucas home.

'Here we go again,' she said. 'Put your best smile on, Louisa, for we must once more become the happiest of all people when we issue these invitations.'

Louisa sighed. 'Oh yes, I am transported by joy.' She widened her eyes to appear tragic, and as they both laughed, they descended the carriage, filled with delight to see their dear friends, Sir William and his family.

* * *

Caroline was kept very busy during the days leading up to the ball, overseeing the servants to ensure that every detail was carried out exactly according to her requirements. Floors were cleaned and cleaned again. Furniture was polished until each wooden armrest and back glistened and the air was filled with the scent of lemon oil. In the kitchen, the cook's face shone also, from her exertions and from the heat, as hordes of footmen and maids carried huge platters from the pantry to the larder to the cold room. Outside, an army of gardeners pruned and trimmed and plucked and raked. Uniforms were washed and pressed, and donned for inspection, while the family's clothing was tended even more carefully, to prepare it for the special night. 'The house must be perfect,' Caroline was fond of saying, 'but the family must be resplendent.'

By the afternoon of the ball, she was exhausted. Sitting at her dressing table, she surveyed her reflection in the mirror. 'Puffy eyelids!' she pointed out to her maid. 'Genney, go to the kitchen and fetch me some cucumber slices.' She placed her hands flat on her cheeks, and exclaimed in horror, 'And my skin!'

Genney, who had just about gone out the door on her errand, returned to her side. 'Miss Bingley?'

'Look,' Caroline cried. 'Look at how the skin along my jaw, just here, and here, is sagging! I look hideous!'

'Do not speak so, mademoiselle,' Genney said. 'You are beautiful as always. I can see not a single detail that is unlike how it has always been. You merely require a time to lie down and rest, for you have been working very hard.'

Caroline stared even harder into the mirror, hoping to see this truth. Genney placed a hand beneath Caroline's elbow, and she allowed the maid to help her to her bed.

'I will be back,' Genney said, 'with your cucumber. And perhaps you would enjoy a refreshment, to bring the colour back into your cheeks.'

'I am pale?' Caroline started up from where she'd been about to lie back. 'You said nothing was changed.'

'Nothing is different,' Genney said soothingly. 'Poor mademoiselle, you work too hard, looking after all the others, and there is only Genney to look after you.'

'It's true; I do work hard—too hard.' Caroline lay back against the maroon velvet cushions, and let out a deep sigh. She waved a hand in Genney's general direction. 'Be quick. Fetch those cucumbers.'

She must have fallen asleep then, for she woke some time later. She couldn't see, and something cold and clammy rested over her eyes. She sat bolt upright with a frightened shriek, but as soon as she was up, her eyes began to work, and she looked down to see two rather shrivelled slices of cucumber sitting on her lap. Picking them up, she flung them away, uncaring where they went, for Genney or one of the housemaids would clear them away.

Looking at the window, she saw to her horror from the shadows that it was now late afternoon. 'Genney,' she shouted. 'Why was I permitted to sleep so long?' Genney came rushing in, looking frightened.

Caroline made an attempt to soften her tone, for the maid, being French, was very emotional. Still, she could not stop herself from saying, 'There is no time for your tears, unless you can use them to fill my bath.'

Genney pouted, and her lower lip trembled, but obediently she did not cry, and called a footman to fetch Miss Bingley's hot water. Caroline sometimes found it exhausting to be around her maid because of the exaggerated emotions, but only the most fashionable ladies in London had French maids. As they were difficult to find, Caroline wanted to keep hers. Typical French, she thought, think they are too good to work for just anybody. Before Genney, she'd interviewed two other French maids, and had offered each of them the job, but both had refused her. She'd been affronted, until she discovered that each had ended up in a titled household. Genney, however, had accepted the offer, and her performance, while a little rustic at first, had steadily improved under Caroline's tutelage.

Due in no small part to Genney's quick hands, by the time the first guests arrived, Caroline stood in the front hall with Charles. Her hair was swept up on her head, with tresses laced with diamonds tumbling down over her shoulders. Her gown, a pale yellow with brown lace trim, fit perfectly, emphasising her small waist and upright posture. Its décolletage was perhaps overly daring for outside London, but Caroline wanted everyone to recognise that she wore only the latest fashion.

The Bennets were one of the first families to arrive. 'Of course,' Caroline said over her shoulder to Louisa, who stood a little behind her, before pasting on her finest welcoming smile.

When there was a time no new guests were announced, Caroline turned to survey the room, to ensure those who had arrived were well looked after by the servants, and she noticed Elizabeth, who moved from place to place in the large room, her head turning back and forth. Clearly, she was looking for someone; and Caroline thought she knew who that someone was.

'I told you,' Louisa said. 'I saw Maria Lucas in the village today, and she said that Wickham had been to dine three times at Longbourn during the past fortnight alone, and that once, during a larger party, she saw Elizabeth and he walking together in the garden.'

Caroline raised an eyebrow. Apparently, this new gossip was too recent for her to have heard it.

'Maria said,' Louisa continued, 'that their heads were very close together as they conversed, and that at one point Elizabeth laughed very loudly.'

'That last,' Caroline said, 'is no news to me, for Eliza laughs far too often and too loudly, for my taste. I am distressed though, for I would not wish to inflict George Wickham on any young lady.'

'With the possible exception,' Louisa said slyly, 'of Miss Lydia Bennet!'

Caroline laughed, almost as loudly as she knew would be considered too loud if it came from Miss Eliza. 'Oh, that is marvellous, Louisa. What a pretty couple they would make.'

The butler appeared in the wide entry to the ballroom and took in a deep breath, clearly in preparation for announcing some new arrivals. Caroline stepped back beside Charles, and nudged him to turn around, as he'd been facing the room—no doubt following Jane's every move.

The rest of the guests arrived in good time, and Caroline was then free to circulate through the room. She corrected one servant who wasn't carrying his tray of canapés at the proper height, and another who had paused to put down a tray of glasses so as to wipe his forehead with a grimy handkerchief. He was sent to the kitchen, to assist the cook, and she found another footman to replace him, keeping the first man in mind in case she decided to release him from her service.

As she moved about, she saw Elizabeth speaking with one of the officers. The man was clearly giving her news that was most unwelcome, for she looked pleadingly at him, then grimaced. And then, and Caroline was shocked, Eliza looked about the room until she saw Mr Darcy, and she sent him a look so filled with venom that Caroline was sure, had Eliza had the power, Mr Darcy would right now be writhing on the floor, his body flooded with poison.

Caroline's attention was caught by Lady Lucas, who wished to compliment her on the wonderful party. And so it went for a little while, as she chatted and laughed with one guest after another, all the time keeping a firm eye on the servants.

She sat for a time with Charles and Jane, mentioning how delighted she was to have this time with her dear friend, but Jane was more interested in discussing George Wickham, of all things. Caroline and Charles did their best to answer Jane's questions, although they must have appeared puzzled, for Jane explained that Elizabeth had been enjoying his company and was disappointed not to find him present this evening.

'He appears,' Jane said, 'a very good sort of young man, one who would be well-suited for almost any profession. I understand that at one point he was keen to go into the clergy.'

Neither Charles nor Caroline said anything.

'Was there not,' Jane asked, 'a living destined for him by the present Mr Darcy's father?'

Clearly, despite the subject matter, Charles was unable to resist the open and innocent manner in which she asked her question, for he said, 'There was, but I understand it was only left conditionally to Mr Wickham, and so was at the discretion of the present Mr Darcy, who, although I cannot go into all the details, acted entirely properly. It was not Mr Darcy's doing that led to Wickham being denied the living.'

'But surely,' Jane said, 'since Mr Darcy is so honourable, and Mr Wickham has every appearance of all that is best in a young man, there can have been no blame on either side.'

Caroline and Charles looked at one another, and Charles said, with great delicacy, 'Wickham and Darcy have a long history, but I am not aware of all the details.' He then, with equal tact, changed the subject.

Caroline continued moving among her guests, smiling and sometimes stopping to speak. She noted when the musicians began tuning their instruments in preparation for the dancing that was to come, but she didn't think much about it, not expecting to dance the first dances herself, until the first set began and she heard laughter. At first it was circumspect, but gradually it grew until Caroline just had to look to see what had so enthralled her guests that they would behave in such a rude manner.

Turning, she realised that the laughter was well merited, and indeed, she had to work very hard to control her own mirth. For there was the Bennets' cousin, Mr Collins, moving in quite the wrong direction for the dance, bumping into one gentleman, stopping to bow and apologise, which put him even more out of step.

Oh, and it got even better! For who was the unfortunate young woman who stood up with this caricature? Why, none other than Miss Elizabeth Bennet. Caroline did snicker at that point, even though she tried to hide it behind her hand. Eliza appeared absolutely miserable, as well she might, and such shame could have descended on no more worthy a person.

Caroline moved away, knowing her duties meant she could spend no more time enjoying Miss Eliza's plight. Shortly thereafter, one of the officers approached—she never could bother to remember their names—and requested the next two dances. He appeared to be a personable fellow, and he was fairly high up in rank, so she accepted, although she did wonder why Mr Darcy had not yet asked her to stand up with him. It was only once the set began, and she stood facing her officer that she saw why. He stood not far away, only three down the line of dancers, and opposite him stood—Miss Elizabeth!

Surely, no, not even Miss Eliza would be so bold as to ask a gentleman to dance with her, so he must have asked her! Caroline was frozen in shock, so much so that she missed the musical introduction and was a moment late in taking her first step. A vision of Mr Collins filled her mind, and she determined to think no more about Mr Darcy, lest she appear as clumsy as the Bennets' cousin.

Once her feet took her through the well-known first steps, and appeared to be able to continue without too much attention, her mind wandered back to Mr Darcy, and she glanced down the line to where he held up his hand, Eliza's gloved fingers resting on top of it, as they turned about each other.

As she watched, Miss Elizabeth said something and Mr Darcy smiled before replying. Eliza looked rather disapproving, but Mr Darcy appeared to be enjoying himself.

Caroline had to get close enough to hear what they were saying. It was impossible that the two of them were dancing, especially after his comment at that awful ball in the Meryton assembly room. What had he said? Oh yes, that Elizabeth was not handsome enough to tempt him, and that he couldn't give consequence to young ladies who were slighted by other men. Yet, here he was, dancing with Miss Eliza, and he'd even said that he thought she had fine eyes. What was he thinking as he gazed into those fine eyes now?

It took some doing to get closer. At first she tried leaning forward whenever the dance step had her facing them, and then she stepped further back than the rest of the line, hoping to move a tiny bit closer so as to hear without appearing out of place in the dance. Neither of those tactics was successful, though. At last, out of desperation and to the surprise of her partner, as she and he moved down the line of dancers, instead of moving to the end, she ducked into a position just one couple away from Mr Darcy and Elizabeth. The officer stumbled as he hastily stopped his forward motion, and he at first ended up right next to Mr Darcy, being unable to move into place as quickly as Caroline did. Caroline took this as a sign that somebody favoured her and, apologising to the lady next to her, scurried around her until she stood right next to Elizabeth.

Now she could listen to her heart's content, although between the noise of the conversations held by non-dancers, and the orchestra, which surely was playing much too loudly—she'd have to speak to them about it—she was unable to catch every word. Still, she could hear enough to follow the conversation.

'. . . new acquaintance,' Eliza was just saying, and by Mr Darcy's raised chin and the colour which rose to his cheeks, Caroline was certain Eliza was speaking of Mr Wickham. She soon learned she was correct, and she glared at Elizabeth. How dared that young woman cause unnecessary pain to Mr Darcy!

He seemed to struggle for a moment, but at least replied in a reasonably measured tone. 'Mr Wickham is blessed with such happy manners as may ensure his making friends—whether he may be equally capable of retaining them is less certain.'

'He has been so unlucky as to lose your friendship,' replied Elizabeth with emphasis, 'and in a manner which he is likely to suffer from all his life.'

Caroline sucked in her breath, knowing, just knowing, that no matter how rude it might appear, she had to grab Eliza by the hair and toss her out of the house and out of Mr Darcy's life. Poor man, she could witness his suffering no longer. Just as she was about to reach out to grasp a handful of Eliza's dark curly tresses, a new step in the dance was announced by the music, and the officer grabbed her hand and turned her about.

By the time she was once again in position to show Miss Eliza just what sort of people she was dealing with, she saw that Sir William had paused near to Mr Darcy and was addressing him.

'Such very superior dancing is not often seen,' Sir William was saying. Caroline lost the next words as she had to step diagonally away from him towards her partner. She swivelled her head as she danced, trying to hear all she could.

'. . . your fair partner does not disgrace you,' the pompous fool was saying. 'I must hope to have this pleasure often repeated, especially when a certain desired event, my dear Miss Eliza,' and here he turned to gaze suggestively at Charles and Jane, 'shall take place.'

Eliza's eyes, and Mr Darcy's also, followed Sir William's. Eliza's countenance softened when she saw her sister, but Mr Darcy's lips thinned, and his brows lowered.

Caroline turned back to the dance, in time to hear Sir William say something about how Mr Darcy would not thank him for taking his attention away from his bewitching partner, before he finally moved away.

Darcy and Elizabeth continued speaking, but Caroline was no longer interested in hearing what they might have to say. Her mind was filled with an image of her brother, and the warm, gentle, and, yes, loving, smile she had just seen him bestow on Jane. Could Sir William be correct? Did everyone here count it as certain that her brother, Charles Bingley, would marry a woman with such low connections?

The second dance drew to a close, to Caroline's relief, for she had much to consider. Darcy and Eliza were still conversing, and the final dance steps once again took her near enough to hear.

'Merely to the illustration of your character,' Eliza said. 'I am trying to make it out.'

'And what is your success?' he asked, with interest.

She shook her head. 'I do not get on at all. I hear such different accounts of you as puzzle me exceedingly.'

'I can readily believe,' he said, and Caroline was once again impressed with the man's self-control, for despite the impudence in her words, he replied as if what she said had merit, 'that reports may vary greatly with respect to me; and I could wish, Miss Elizabeth, that you not sketch my character at the present moment, as there is reason to fear that the performance would reflect no credit on either.'

'But if I do not take your likeness now, I may never have another opportunity.'

Caroline relaxed at that, and she gave her partner such a warm smile that he involuntarily took a step closer to her, but she ignored him. At least Eliza realised she would not be spending much time with Mr Darcy in the future. Caroline smiled again, and upbraided herself for her silly fears that Mr Darcy could ever feel an attraction towards such a creature.

He apparently shared her feelings, for he coldly said to Elizabeth,

'I would by no means suspend any pleasure of yours.' They moved down the dance, then, and parted in silence.

Caroline was so well satisfied by her eavesdropping on this conversation, something Eleanor had shown her was not rude at all if done circumspectly, and could often be most entertaining, that she actually felt a moment's pity for Elizabeth. If that lady continued in her pursuit of George Wickham, sorry her lot would be.

Spying Eliza standing alone, Caroline hesitated a moment. Really, did she deserve this kindness? Caroline thought of herself as a kind person, one who gave something back to the world.

Torn between satisfaction over the good she was capable of doing and her disdain for the receiver of the charity, she spoke. 'So, Miss Eliza, I hear you are quite delighted with George Wickham! Your sister has been talking to me about him, and asking me a thousand questions; and I find that the young man has forgotten to tell you, among his other communications, that he was the son of old Wickham, the late Mr Darcy's steward. Let me recommend you, however, as a friend, not to give implicit confidence to all his assertions; for as to Mr Darcy's using him ill, it is perfectly false, for, on the contrary, he has always been remarkably kind to him, though George Wickham has treated Mr Darcy in a most infamous manner.'

Elizabeth's countenance did not reveal the least trace of what she thought, but at least she was listening, and Caroline hoped that some good would indeed come from her kindness to this young woman. Eliza, impudent and unfashionable though she was, still deserved to find happiness in whatever type of life her place in society could give her.

Continuing, she said, 'I do not know the particulars, but I know very well that Mr Darcy is not in the least to blame, that he cannot bear to hear George Wickham mentioned, and that though my brother thought he could not well avoid including him in his invitations to the officers, he was excessively glad to find that he had taken himself out of the way. His coming into the country at all is a most insolent thing, indeed, and I wonder how he could presume to do it.'

Elizabeth's face had changed, almost imperceptibly, but her brow was definitely lower than it had been, and her lips were pressed more tightly together. Nonetheless, Caroline was determined to complete what she had begun. 'I pity you, Miss Eliza, for this discovery of your favourite's guilt; but really, considering his descent, one could not expect much better.'

Elizabeth stood unmoving for a moment, her lips pressed so hard together now that they almost disappeared. Caroline fancied she heard the gnashing of teeth, when Eliza suddenly burst out, 'His guilt and his descent appear by your account to be the same.' Her anger was so palpable that Caroline took a step back. 'For I have heard you,' she continued, 'accuse him of nothing worse than of being the son of Mr Darcy's steward, and of that, I can assure you, he informed me himself.'

Really! Caroline thought. *The nerve of some people. They only hear what they want to hear, and so my efforts have gone to waste. None the less, I can rest easy, knowing that I tried.* 'I beg your pardon,' she said, proud of the icy calm in her voice. 'Excuse my interference; it was kindly meant.'

And it had been, she thought. Here she was, looking out for everyone's welfare, so the ball would be a success, and this chit had so little manners she had returned a kindness with rudeness. Glancing back at Eliza as she moved away, she couldn't keep a sneer off her face. If the girl was too ignorant to recognise good advice when it came her way, then she deserved a man like George Wickham.

A while later there was a pause in the dancing, while the musicians took a well-deserved break, and Caroline oversaw the tables set up and food laid out for the late-night supper. People gathered around eagerly, and Caroline sank into a chair to catch her breath. She spied Mr Darcy, standing by one of the tables.

Most people had selected tables and sat down to eat. Mr Darcy placed himself at one of the few that still held empty seats, and Caroline's heart sank when she saw Mrs Bennet sink into the chair almost exactly opposite to him. Her heart sank further when she noticed Eliza was also part of that table, and that she had been there before Mr Darcy joined them

Had he deliberately chosen to sit by her? Surely not, for he must have known that proximity to the daughter meant a greater chance of proximity to the mother. She seated herself at the nearest table to his, positioned to she could observe the proceedings and interfere if necessary.

Mrs Bennet wasted no time in fulfilling Caroline's expectations. She turned to Lady Lucas, who sat at a little distance but at the same table. 'I am so happy!' she said in her usual ear-piercing voice. 'I declare I must be the happiest mother in all of England.' She leaned across the unfortunate elderly gentleman who sat between the two ladies. 'Do you know why?' Before Lady Lucas could reply, she sat back, looking very satisfied with herself indeed. The elderly gentleman was also satisfied, for his hand, holding a fork, had been groping blindly for his plate, since Mrs Bennet, when leaning across in front of him, had blocked his vision of the table. Now, with a smile, he stabbed a large piece of fish with his fork and happily consumed it.

'I'll tell you why,' Mrs Bennet said, although Lady Lucas had not asked. 'It's because my Jane will soon be married to Mr Bingley!' Her voice rose in volume as she said this, and she clapped her hands. 'Just think of it: my Jane, mistress of Netherfield Park.' Her face frozen in horror, Caroline glanced to where Charles and Jane sat at another table. The two of them conversed, totally ignoring everyone else around them. She moved her gaze to Mr Darcy. He acted as if he had heard nothing of interest, but his head was bowed, his eyes studying his plate.

'I must say,' Mrs Bennet continued, 'I always knew Jane was so beautiful for a reason, but even I hardly dared imagine a match such as this! So many advantages! Mr Bingley is so charming, of course, and so handsome, but he is rich!'

Elizabeth at this point placed a hand on her mother's arm. Caroline had vaguely been aware of Eliza trying to hush her mother, but now she noticed that the fingers around Mrs Bennet's arm were white at the knuckles. 'Mamma, please, we can all hear you, there is no need to speak quite so loudly.'

Mrs Bennet glared at Eliza before continuing. 'And Mr Bingley's sisters are so fond of Jane. I am sure they must desire this match as much as anyone.'

'Mamma!' Eliza said again. Mrs Bennet attempted to shake off her daughter's hand and when she was unsuccessful, she turned to her daughter. 'Hush!' she said crossly. 'You know that you will benefit from Jane's marrying Mr Bingley.' Leaning once again towards Lady Lucas, and again disrupting the elderly gentleman's supper, she said in a loud whisper, 'You see it, do you not? Jane's marrying so greatly will throw my younger daughters in the way of other rich men! Oh, I just knew it, when first I saw Mr Bingley lay eyes on my Jane. I just knew it. And it is thanks to me that this match will happen, for I do everything in my power to ensure the two lovebirds have time together!'

Mr Darcy by now was glaring straight at Mrs Bennet, and his dark eyes were filled with fire. Elizabeth apparently observed this also, for she pleaded with her mother, in a soft yet firm tone. 'Mamma, please! Lower your voice.'

Mr Darcy kept eating, seemingly paying Mrs Bennet no notice, but his expression changed gradually from indignant contempt to a composed and steady gravity.

At long last, Mrs Bennet ran out of new things to say about the advantages of an alliance between the Bennet and Bingley families. By then Caroline had eaten next to nothing, but the food on her plate, now congealed, held no enticement. The hum of conversation in the room seemed like blessed silence, but before Mrs Bennet could think of something new to shout out to the world, Caroline rose, gestured to the servants to clear away the tables, and suggested that some music would be most pleasant.

Before she and Louisa could make their way to the pianoforte, though, another person rushed to take possession of the instrument. 'Oh no,' Caroline muttered to Louisa, who'd come up beside her. 'Not another Bennet.'

Caroline had had the misfortune of hearing Miss Mary during a party at the Lucas's. She still got headaches just at the thought of it. Slowly, she and Louisa made their way towards the piano, but before they reached it, Mary finished her song. Instead of leaving, she took the tepid applause her performance had merited, and started another piece. 'Handel,' Caroline said to Louisa, 'would never recognise this as his own music.'

Louisa nodded grimly. 'I am certain he never intended a rhythm such as hers to come anywhere near to one of his compositions.'

As Mary neared the end of the piece, crashing her fingers down on the keyboard with great energy, Mr Bennet appeared beside his daughter. He clapped politely along with the others, once she was done, and said, 'That will do extremely well, child. You have delighted us long enough. Let the other young ladies have time to exhibit.'

Mary's smile at her audience froze on her face, and then her mouth drooped. Without looking at her father, or at anyone else, she stood, back straight, and marched away from the piano. Caroline would almost have felt sorry for her, if she wasn't so glad that she would not have to listen to Mary perform another song. Moving as quickly as possible and yet retaining an air of elegance, Caroline sat at the instrument and began playing a popular tune by Mozart.

The evening dragged on, although the guests appeared to be having a good time. As different people performed at the piano, Caroline took a moment to sit down and take in a deep breath. This brief respite did her no good, for everywhere she looked, she was assailed by the sight of Bennets. How it was possible for only seven people to be in every part of the room, she did not know, but no matter where she was, Bennets were all about her.

There, in a corner, Miss Kitty looked coquettishly at an officer. Over by the windows, Miss Lydia's loud laugh drew her attention. Mary sat in a chair by the wall, her arms crossed across her chest, her lower lip thrust out into a pout. Sitting together on a sofa by the fireplace, Charles and Jane conversed, both leaning towards each other, their heads very close. Mrs Bennet sat by Mrs Long, her smug self-satisfied smile seeming to mock Caroline. A flash of movement caught her eye—Lydia again, this time running, looking over her shoulder with amusement at the officers in pursuit.

One comfort came to Caroline, at least, for Mr Darcy and Elizabeth were never to be found in the same area. Mr Collins was always in attendance on Eliza, and her pained smiles gave Caroline the only pleasure she found during the last hours of the ball.

The Bennets, of course, were the last to leave, and Caroline and Louisa resorted to yawns and frequent complaints of fatigue. Mr Collins professed his gratitude at being included in the invitation until he was out the door and his voice disappeared into the night. Mrs Bennet lingered, smirking at Charles, repeating several times her fondest hope that the entire Bingley party would soon join the family at Longbourn for an intimate dinner. Stevens practically had to push her outside with the heavy doors, before she moved enough out of the way for him to slam them closed.

Caroline and Louisa sank into chairs, their arms hanging limply at their sides. Darcy glowered at the front doors, as if thinking dark thoughts about those who could still be heard outside, until the crunch of gravel announced their departure. Mr Hurst lay stretched out on one of the sofas, snoring. Only Charles appeared as energetic as ever, a glow on his face.

Darcy turned away from the front door, and his eyes met Caroline's. Within them she read the message as clearly as if it had been spoken aloud. She nodded, in perfect agreement. *Yes,* she thought, *we have much to discuss.*

Chapter Seven

As planned, Charles left for London the day following the ball, to attend to business. Caroline knew that while her income kept arriving in her account according to its schedule, arranging this pleasant life for her took up a great deal of Charles' time. She had not the slightest idea what he did when he was attending to business. Sometimes she thought of asking what was needed to handle her financial affairs, as she knew she would be able to understand it. She'd always had a good head for figures, better than her brother, in fact, at least during the years they'd been tutored together in the nursery. She was probably quite capable of handling her own affairs, but finance was an area ladies never dealt with, as gentlemen felt it would be too much trouble for them. Caroline knew many women would be capable in areas that would surprise the men, but she also knew she owed Charles a great deal, especially her obedience and loyalty. It was this debt, and, of course, her love for him, that had determined her on this present course.

Charles had stayed abed longer than usual, following the exertions of the ball and the late hour the household had finally been able to retire. Caroline would once have thought it scandalous to sleep so late, but spending time with Lady Eleanor Amesbury had shown her that there was no need to force oneself to conform to outdated notions of when to eat and when to sleep. In town, Caroline had often returned from an evening at Eleanor's home well after midnight, and she knew that it was not uncommon for many of Eleanor's guests to stay up to greet the rising sun. That had always appeared a little extreme to Caroline, but now she decided, once she returned to town, which she expected would be very soon, she, too, would learn to dance until dawn.

Once Charles had departed on horseback, his sisters returned to the house from where they'd stood outside to wave goodbye. Mr Darcy had originally planned to accompany him, but due to the gravity of the situation, had decided to stay to discuss what could be done. Caroline didn't know what excuse he'd made to Charles for his change in plans, but Charles had apparently accepted it with his usual good humour.

Caroline, Louisa, and Mr Darcy assembled in the smallest sitting room, for Caroline believed it would be best if they were not too comfortable while they spoke. 'It would not do,' she said, 'for us to become relaxed and well-disposed towards the rest of the world, for we must not allow ourselves to soften in any way. We know what must be done.' Louisa nodded, and Mr Darcy, showing no expression, led the way to the room.

'We are all agreed, then,' Caroline said, since no one else wished to open the discussion. 'I have never seen Charles as smitten, or smitten with a woman so utterly unsuitable, as he is now.'

'I agree,' Louisa said. 'Jane is certainly lovely in appearance, but really, her conversation is very dull. I am going to summon some tea and cake, for I feel in need of fortification already.' She looked to Caroline for permission, and then rang the bell, before continuing. 'I cannot help, in fact, feeling that Jane has used some feminine wiles that we did not perceive in her, in order to secure Charles. Surely that is the only way Charles could ignore her unfortunate connections?' She laughed. 'Did you see, last night, Miss Lydia and Miss Catherine teasing the officers? I thought my eyes would pop out of my head, seeing how Lydia snatched Captain Denny's sword right out of his sash, and pranced about in front of him, not letting him take it back, even though he kept sending frightened looks at Colonel Forster, lest his superior witness him behaving in such a manner.'

Caroline laughed, too, at the memory, but then winced. 'And Lydia's laugh, so loud and piercing. Truly, she is the daughter most like her mother.'

The sisters discussed some more of the shocking behaviour displayed by all the Bennets. The tea arrived, and once everyone had been served, Caroline noticed that not only had Mr Darcy refused any refreshment, he'd also not once contributed to the discussion of this solemn matter.

'What think you?' she asked him. 'If I cannot give you so much as a slice of this lovely lemon cake, can you give us your thoughts?'

He'd been sitting very still, his long legs stretched out before him, his chin propped on his fisted hand, but now he stirred and moved himself further back in the chair so as to sit up straight. 'I am torn,' he confessed. 'I have known Charles many years now, and have witnessed his frequent attachments. He, as I am sure you know, experiences everything more strongly and freely than do other men. This occasion is different. His apparent affection is steadier than usual. At other times, his moods have swung from despair to ecstasy. Frequently.'

Caroline laughed. 'I quite understand what you are saying, Mr Darcy. I have many recollections of Charles in the nursery. One toy would be his favourite, clutched fiercely to his chest if Louisa or I so much as glanced at it, and then the next moment it would be overthrown and another one snatched up. Charles has never known his own mind, and he is fortunate, indeed, to have had two loving sisters to look after him when he was younger, and such a good friend as you during his university days.'

'And,' Louisa put in, 'how fortunate he is, indeed, to have all three of us to deal with this now. Many a man might find himself cast adrift once he attains his majority, but we, his family and friend, are loyal.'

'Fortunate, indeed.' Mr Darcy regarded both sisters for a moment with no expression, and then continued. 'I believe that Charles' regard for Miss Bennet is a stronger, more abiding, sort of affection. I think he truly is in love.'

Both sisters burst out talking at the same time. 'Nonsense. It is completely impossible,' Louisa said. Caroline's contribution was, 'He could not be so stupid. He has too much good sense to inflict such connections on his family.'

When both had fallen silent, Mr Darcy said, in a measured tone, 'One cannot always choose to whom one's affections fly.' He fell silent and gazed out of the window, and something in his countenance sent a flutter of fear through Caroline. He looked sad, no doubt at the thought of hurting his friend by separating him from a woman he appeared to genuinely love, but he also looked infinitely lonely.

'Are you,' she asked, more sharply than she'd intended, 'thinking of a pair of fine eyes?'

His head jerked at her words, but he continued to look out of the window as he spoke. 'I believe Charles thinks himself in love, and perhaps he truly is. If love is strong, and equal on both sides, the matter of unfortunate relations can be dealt with.'

'Nonsense,' Caroline said. 'Can you picture us dining with Mrs Bennet every evening? Entertaining her at your house in London?'

'Obstacles can be overcome,' he said calmly. 'However, in what I just said, the fact that the affection must be equal on both sides is imperative.' He leaned forward and for the first time appeared to notice the presence of tea and cake. Caroline hastily poured him a cup. 'I am not,' he continued, 'convinced that Jane's regard for him is true. It is strong, that much is obvious, but how much of her mother does she have in her? Are her feelings for him perhaps strengthened by her recognition of all such an advantageous marriage would offer, not only to her, but to her entire family?'

'I am convinced that this is the case,' Caroline said.

'I, too,' Louisa added. 'Jane has always been very pleasant with us, no doubt in order to gain our support of such a marriage. Mrs Bennet, last night, practically said this was the case, for she said that Charles' sisters wish the match to take place. Mrs Bennet, of course, is a very foolish woman and so I disregard anything she says, but this might have been taken as a command by her daughter. Jane is no fool, despite her parentage, and she would know that if she could win us over to her side, the match would be as good as done.'

'Her winning us over,' Caroline said, 'is, of course, impossible, for we know there is much more to marriage than material advantages.'

'Exactly.' Mr Darcy sat up straight so precipitously that his tea slopped over onto the saucer. 'I have no problem with Jane benefiting from a match, and I imagine that, if Charles is as smitten as he appears to be, he will view the connections as no more than a minor inconvenience.'

'Minor inconvenience?' Caroline snorted, a ladylike snort, of course, but still a snort, as there was no other way to show her opinion. 'Mrs Bennet is adept at making herself a major inconvenience in every situation in which she finds herself.'

'Charles has not been bothered by any of Jane's relations during any of the occasions we have been together,' Mr Darcy said. 'He is well able to focus on what he wishes to perceive, and his good nature means the difficulties offered by Jane's mother, and by her three younger sisters, do not overly upset him.'

He said, Caroline thought with alarm, *Jane's three younger sisters. He did not include Elizabeth as one of those who present difficulties.*

'However,' Mr Darcy continued, 'as I have already stated, I am not convinced of the equal strength of Miss Bennet's affection for Charles. Her countenance so rarely demonstrates any strength of feeling that I just cannot tell. But I am uncomfortable parting him from what may indeed be a true lifelong love based just on uneasy feelings and not on stronger evidence.'

Caroline had no trouble at all parting Charles from Jane, based on no evidence whatsoever. Charles, in her mind, was to marry Georgiana Darcy. This was even more necessary than it had been, for when Mr Darcy became involved in planning his sister's wedding, with Caroline's help, of course, he would no longer have time to think about fine eyes. Plus, once one marriage was planned, it would make perfect sense to plan a second one as well, that of Mr Darcy and Caroline Bingley. The two families would indeed become one, something she knew was greatly desired by everyone. The families were affectionate with each other, and they knew each other so well, that the joining had in fact already occurred. All that was needed now were the marriages, to show before God and the nobility, that the Bingleys and Darcys were one.

Mr Darcy still appeared uncertain, so Caroline quickly picked up on the one area she knew she could use. 'I, also,' she said, putting reluctance into her voice, 'wondered about Jane's motivations in spending so much time with Charles. I haven't wanted to voice my concerns, because I did believe Jane truly was a friend to me and Louisa. Now that you mention it, though, I wonder if perhaps her supposed friendship with us was no more valid than her apparently growing feelings for Charles.' Under the side table, where Mr Darcy could not see, she nudged Louisa's leg with her foot.

Louisa glanced over, surprised, but quickly caught on. 'Oh! Yes, I am so happy to hear you say that out loud, Mr Darcy and dear sister, for I, too, have had my doubts. Jane spends a lot of time gazing into space, or working on her sewing, when in our company. Surely if she were a true friend, she would give all her attention to us.'

Caroline winced, wondering if Mr Darcy would inquire if she and Louisa did not also spend time with their needlework when Jane was present, but fortunately he did not. 'Jane does give Charles all of her attention,' she said quickly, 'when she is with him, but I, too, have noticed that her countenance, while always appearing pleasant, lacks that true strength of character that comes from spending time with a person one truly loves.'

'I think, in fact,' Louisa said slowly, 'I am almost convinced that Jane cannot feel for Charles what he apparently feels for her. But how do we know the strength of Charles' regard?' She tilted her head to one side, almost as perkily as a bird, 'Charles, as we know, does nothing by half-measures. When he is happy, the whole world delights him, and when he is sad, there is nothing, and never will be anything, that can make him smile. Does it not follow, then, that when he loves, it is the greatest passion ever to exist in this world? Perhaps, once he spends time in town, with its many other entertainments, he will cease to think of Jane at all.'

'I suspect not,' Mr Darcy said grimly. 'But if this thing is to be done, if you also,' and he looked searchingly at first Louisa and then at Caroline, where his glance lingered, 'believe as I do that she does not return his affection, how are we to go about it?'

'Clearly,' said Caroline, 'we must close up this house and return to town.' She was surprised to hear herself say this, but it was a pleasant surprise, for the whole plan unfolded inside her mind as if she'd been thinking about this very thing for some time. 'Once there, we will convince Charles that we could not bear to be without his company for the days he spends on his business. We shall see, then, if his affection dissipates over time. If not, we will gently tell him of exactly what has been discussed here, today. It will not be difficult to convince him that Miss Bennet's regard was more in his head than it existed in actuality.' She smiled triumphantly, knowing Mr Darcy would be impressed with her organisational abilities

He still looked unhappy. 'Are we truly doing this for Charles' sake?'

'Of course.' Caroline blinked. 'What other reason could there be?'

He gazed at her for some time, his face, as usual, revealing nothing of his thoughts. Then he slapped his hands on his knees and sat on the edge of his chair. 'Very well. But I insist on being present when you speak to Charles.'

'Of course. I expected nothing else. You are his closest friend.' Caroline smiled, a creamy sensation of well-being flowing into her chest. 'And we can also tell him that one of our reasons for quitting Netherfield is your haste to once again join your sister. Dear Georgiana!' She looked back at him, an inquiring brow raised. 'I assume that you do, indeed, wish the reunion to come sooner rather than later?'

He nodded. 'Of course. I always miss her company when we are not together.'

'Although,' Caroline added with a coquettish smile, 'I know not how you will fill your time, without the writing of constant letters to her to occupy you.'

He smiled, too, but then abruptly turned sober. 'And what of Miss Bennet? Surely she deserves more than this sudden abandonment. We must ask Charles to return once more, to say goodbye.'

'Nonsense,' Caroline said. 'He can write to her from London.' When he still looked unhappy, she said briskly, 'Or better still, I will write to her myself, explaining matters. Oh, you needn't concern yourself,' she held up a hand when he began to speak. 'The letter will be kind and friendly. And gentle. I know precisely how to phrase it.'

He looked at her, clearly still concerned, but at length he nodded and stood up. 'Very well. I leave matters in your capable hands. And now I shall go for a ride, for this discussion has left me with a feeling that the walls are closing in on me.' With a quick bow, he left them.

Caroline relaxed her erect spine against the back of her chair and sighed. 'Why,' she asked Louisa, 'is it so terribly exhausting doing what is right for people?'

Louisa allowed her body, too, to sag out of its usual correct feminine posture. 'I do not know. But I am glad we have done it.'

Caroline nodded. 'I shall write the letter this instant, although I think it must not be sent until after we have departed. Oh, I must set the servants to packing.'

'I also,' said Louisa wearily. 'Plus I must find a way to convince Mr Hurst that he must leave this place which has comfortable beds, good shooting, and a considerable wine cellar. He will not be happy.'

Caroline sent her sister a sympathetic glance. 'Remind him that in town there are comfortable beds and good wine cellars aplenty. And he has killed plenty of birds, so he must dwell on the memories and not mourn the loss of opportunity to kill more.'

She stood. 'I shall return here shortly after dinner, to write the letter. I would appreciate your input, if you can spare the time.'

'I shall endeavour to be here,' Louisa said. 'Although, dealing with a husband can make scheduling difficult.'

Nonsense, Caroline thought. *Just look at how easily, and productively, I have just dealt with Mr Darcy. And he is not even my husband, yet.* To Louisa, though, she said, 'I quite understand. If you are not there, I shall write it myself, and show it to you before it is sent.'

Exchanging mutually satisfied smiles, the sisters left to prepare for the removal.

* * *

'Thank goodness,' Caroline sighed as she sank into the chair at the writing table, 'most of our things can be sent after.' No one had joined her yet, and so she was speaking to an empty room, but this was the first moment she'd had to herself all day.

Now, however, there was nothing more to do or say, except write the letter to Jane, and that wouldn't take long. She could no longer delay the realisation that had resided in the back of her mind ever since she'd determined what had to be done for Charles.

She was returning to London tomorrow. That meant that as soon as the day after, she could once again see him. Stephen Tryphon. She'd done her best not to think about him. After all, Mr Darcy was the only man she could ever want. Mr Tryphon's letter, though, had not been consigned to the fire. It still resided in her jewel box, hidden away, but the creases in the paper had sharpened due to constant unfolding and refolding, until they threatened to split open, leaving her nothing more than tatters of paper instead of those beautiful words—beautiful and frightening.

Caroline had never felt so out of control. Why had she not burned the letter? Why did she find herself, night after night, bringing it out to read again? There was no sense in burning it now, for she had its contents committed to memory. And each night, after she'd taken it out and opened it, and gazed at his strong, firm handwriting, she'd told herself, when she slid it beneath the velvet that lined the bottom of the jewel box, that in hiding it away she was likewise hiding him away—hiding his words and his presence that could send her senses, her skin, her heart, tingling until she could scarcely lie still in bed. Sleep was often long in arriving.

She'd struggled to not think of him, but now she could avoid the thoughts no longer. When she returned, one of her first acts would be to send her card to her dear friend Eleanor, announcing her return. She knew from Eleanor's letters that Mr Tryphon was still in town

Eleanor would no doubt share the news of Caroline's return with him, as soon as she received it. What would he do then? Would he feel as she did, impatient and yet a little frightened, knowing he would soon be in her presence? Would his breath come a little more quickly, would his heart seem to grow within his chest until there was barely enough room for his lungs?

Caroline switched her train of thought at this point, wondering if the heart actually did grow when one had feelings for someone, and if so, if that was the reason why the breath quickened, since there was less room for the lungs to expand. Her anatomical musings were interrupted when Louisa and Mr Darcy entered the room, both asking if she had yet completed the letter to Jane.

Unwilling to admit she had yet to begin, and resolutely pushing Mr Tryphon to the back of her mind, she said that she had been collecting her thoughts and wanted to ask their opinion of a couple of her ideas.

'We need,' she said, 'to make it clear that none of us will be returning to Netherfield this winter.' She looked a question at the others, and they nodded.

'All right, then,' she continued, 'and also that while Louisa and I are sad to not be able to say goodbye in person, I shall say nothing about Charles having any regrets.'

Mr Darcy had been fidgeting in his seat since he'd sat down, crossing his legs, uncrossing them, looking towards the window ands resolutely back at Caroline, crossing his arms, placing his hands flat on his knees. At this point, he stood, and said, 'It appears you have this well in hand. I must leave you now, to, um, speak to my valet about the packing of certain of my jackets.' He left the room.

'Well, that is odd,' Louisa said, looking at the door he'd just passed through.

'It's fine,' Caroline said, firmly. 'I plan to hint that Charles and Georgiana will soon be married, but was unwilling to say so in his presence. I will begin the letter, now, and read sections to you, so as to gain your thoughts. Is this agreeable to you?'

Louisa appearing amenable to this plan, Caroline picked up a quill, inspected it for sharpness, and began writing. *My Dear Friend, By the time you receive this, we shall have quit Netherfield and be well on the road to London, there to join Charles, who departed, as you know, to deal with some business affairs. He left in good time, so as to be able to dine at Mr Hurst's house in Grosvenor St.'* Reading this aloud, she looked to Louisa for her opinion.

'A trifle abrupt, do you not think?'

'Perhaps,' Caroline said, looking over the lines she had written. 'There is, however, no sense in being vague. Still, I shall attempt to assuage any hurt feelings that may result.' She resumed writing. *'I do not pretend to regret anything I shall leave in Hertfordshire, except your society, my dearest friend;'* There, Louisa, how is that?'

Louisa nodded. 'It suits the purpose very well.'

'Good. I shall continue. *'but we will hope, at some future period, to enjoy many returns of that delightful intercourse we have known, and in the meanwhile may lessen the pain of separation by a very frequent and most unreserved correspondence. I depend on you for that.'*

'Brilliant,' Louisa said of this, but there was a touch of doubt in her voice. 'Do you intend to take up a correspondence with her?'

'What matters that?' Caroline asked. 'What matters is that I am a good writer now. And the words I've just penned are intended to do as Mr Darcy wishes. We must not be cruel, of course, and so I cannot pretend to a coldness I do not feel. But now I must attend to the heart of the matter.' She laughed. 'Oh! I did not intend that pun, but it is a very good one, is it not?'

Louisa clapped her hands. 'It is indeed. I shall have to remember it, to relate to Mr Hurst.'

Caroline returned to the letter. '*When my brother left us yesterday, he imagined that the business which took him to London might be concluded in three or four days; but as we are certain it cannot be so, and convinced that when Charles gets to town he will be in no hurry to leave it again, we have determined on following him thither, that he may not be obliged to spend his vacant hours in a comfortless hotel.*' There,' she said, 'now that is a stroke of brilliance. Jane will be unable to disagree with our charitable reasons for leaving here, and she will appreciate any actions that tend to Charles' comfort.'

She continued, '*Many of our acquaintances are already there for the winter; I wish that I could hear that you, my dearest friend, had any intention of making one in the crowd—but of that I despair. I sincerely hope that your Christmas in Hertfordshire may abound in the gaieties which that season generally brings, and that your beaux will be so numerous as to prevent your feeling the loss of the three friends of whom we shall deprive you.*'

'Now that,' Louisa said upon hearing this last, 'is brilliant.'

'Yes,' Caroline crowed. 'By wishing her many beaux, I truly show that as far as we are concerned, there is not the slightest thought among us of her forming a match with Charles. But I must continue, and speak of Mr Darcy and his sister, so she sees that Charles was merely being his usual affable self, and not showing Jane any particular favour.'

'*Mr Darcy is impatient to see his sister; and, to confess the truth, we are hardly less eager to meet her again. I really do not think Georgiana Darcy has her equal for beauty, elegance, and accomplishment; and the affection she inspires in Louisa and myself is heightened into something still more interesting, from the hope we dare to entertain of her being hereafter our sister.*'

'There,' Caroline said with satisfaction. 'I wish I could be present to see Mrs Bennet's face when she hears that last. How dare she think that we would condone, much less wish, a match between our brother and one of her daughters?' She paused to sharpen the quill, before resuming.

'*I do not know whether I have before mentioned to you my feelings on this subject; but I will not leave the country without confiding them, and I trust you will not esteem then unreasonable. My brother admires her greatly already; he will have frequent opportunity now of seeing her on the most intimate footing; her relations all wish the connection as much as his own; and a sister's partiality is not misleading me, I think, when I call Charles most capable of engaging any woman's heart.'*

'That,' Louisa said, 'is well put, and is actually most kind of you, Caroline.'

'Yes, well,' Caroline said, and was astonished to find a wetness well up in her eyes. She knew, after all, what it was to meet a man who could engage a woman's heart, even if she knew she could not return his affection. Why, then, did she reread his letter every night? 'I do not wish to be cruel, but simply to make her understand that if she expected anything more of Charles, it was an honest mistake.'

Without waiting for Louisa to respond, she returned to writing. *'With all these circumstances to favour an attachment; and nothing to prevent it, am I wrong, my dearest Jane, in indulging the hope of an event which will secure the happiness of so many?'*

Caroline ended the letter with many best wishes for Jane's health and wellbeing.

Louisa took it up and read the whole out loud. 'It is perfect,' she said. 'I am in awe of your literary skill.'

Caroline smiled, without modesty. 'I thank you. I have sometimes thought of penning a novel, but who has time for such a frivolous pursuit?'

The letter was given to a servant who was to stay behind in the house, with strict instructions that it not be delivered until two hours after the family had departed. Then, well satisfied, the sisters went upstairs. They both slept well that night, even though thoughts of Mr Tryphon intruded into Caroline's dreams.

*   *   *

The closer they got to London, the higher Caroline's spirits rose. The removal had actually gone very smoothly. There were three carriages in their procession, one for Louisa, Mr Hurst, and Caroline, one for the servants, and one for the luggage that needed to come along right away. The rest of the servants, other than those who would remain in Hertfordshire to attend to the house, would follow later, with the rest of the luggage.

Mr Darcy had chosen to ride his horse rather than sit in the carriage on such a lovely day. Looking out of her window, Caroline could see the horse's shoulder and, just behind it, Mr Darcy's leg in its beautifully polished black riding boot. At first he'd ridden his horse hard, moving ahead with great speed and then returning, but for now he seemed content to let the animal walk at the carriage's pace.

'Mr Darcy,' she called to him, leaning her head out of the window and looking up to see him, 'can you see the city yet?'

'I'm afraid not, Miss Bingley. It will be another hour or so before it will come into view.'

'He is remarkably patient,' Louisa said.

Caroline pulled her head back inside, in part because leaning out and looking up always gave her a sore neck, but also to glare at Louisa. Louisa did not travel well. She always complained of a headache and sore bones from all the bouncing. Even this carriage, with its lush padded seats and the latest in springs and suspension, did not ease her journey. She also tended to become cranky when travelling, and while Mr Hurst could sometimes cheer her up, he was currently leaning back against the squabs, asleep with his mouth open. 'There is no point,' Louisa continued, 'in expecting Mr Darcy's response to change unless you wait longer than five minutes before repeating the question.'

'That,' Caroline said, 'is unfair. It's been at least half an hour since I last asked. And of course I know we are not close to the city yet, as not enough time has elapsed. I merely asked Mr Darcy so he could know that even if he is not with us in the carriage, we have not forgotten his presence.'

Louisa rolled her eyes upwards, as if asking for patience. 'Why, then, bother asking such an inane question, and even repeating it? I am certain he would rather be forgotten than have to deal with you, today.'

'What do you mean?' Caroline asked. She was genuinely curious, but she was also trying not to allow Louisa's foul mood to provoke her into a show of temper.

'You haven't noticed?' Louisa said with a smirk. 'He has been icily distant ever since we all breakfasted together this morning. I am surprised that you, who are such the expert observer of Mr Darcy, failed to see that he preferred to ride today because he had not the slightest interest in our company. When in company, after all, he might actually have to converse.'

'Your cruelty is uncalled for,' Caroline said sharply. 'He is a vigorous man who needs a great deal of exercise.'

'Oh, really? And what would you know of his vigour? Or that of any man?'

Caroline sighed. She really did not want to argue with her sister. She knew that Louisa's pique stemmed from an aching head and not from any personal animosity. She knew, also, that once arrived at the destination, Louisa would be extremely apologetic, so much so, in fact, that her beseeching pleas for forgiveness would become almost as irritating as her difficult temper during the journey. 'Obviously, I do not have your expertise in many areas relating to men. But I do know, and this stems from my detailed observations of this one man in particular, that while he often presents a cool, unruffled image to the world, beneath that lies much strength, both of mind and of body, and deeply felt passions.'

'Passions?' Louisa was clearly enthralled. 'Do tell.'

Caroline smiled, happy to hear her sister speak without the sharp edge to her voice. 'Have you never thought about how it is that two men of such seemingly different temperaments as Charles and Mr Darcy can be such close friends? Mr Darcy appears calm and controlled, never doing anything without having given it much thought. Charles on the other hand, almost never thinks ahead. His thoughts and interests change moment by moment. He is impulsive, and Mr Darcy appears to be the very opposite.'

Louisa started nodding as Caroline spoke. 'That is very well put. I understand completely. I am all agog, now, to learn why two such different men are friends.'

'It is because beneath his calm exterior, Mr Darcy's emotions are very strong indeed, but revealing them is something he believes would be ungentlemanly.'

'Charles reveals them,' Louisa said, the testy bite back in her voice.

'Mr Darcy thinks that it is well and good for Charles, because he is a very different sort of person. Mr Darcy has a very definite idea of what it is to be a gentleman in his position, for a man like himself. But since both he and Charles are passionate men, they share a strong bond of friendship.'

'And perhaps,' Louisa said, 'they are friends because they each have much to offer the other.'

'Exactly. Charles helps Mr Darcy enjoy himself a little more, while I have observed definite improvements in Charles since their friendship began. Charles is much more polished now, and is learning about business matters.'

'And to think before he makes major decisions.'

'Which I wish,' Caroline said with a sigh, 'he had done before taking Netherfield Park.' The two sisters smiled, fully at ease with each other and in accord for the first time that day. 'He should have known,' Caroline said, 'that only a house in a more fashionable county would work out.'

'In Derbyshire, for example?' Louisa had a mischievous glint in her eyes.

'Certainly,' Caroline said with great dignity. 'Derbyshire is very desirable.' She held up a hand. 'And before you say anything more, the fact that Pemberley is in that county only adds to its allure. An estate as grand as that can only add prestige to others in its area.'

Mr Hurst snorted, and began to choke. He coughed and woke up, looking bewildered. He glanced about for a moment, seemingly uncertain as to where he was. 'No wonder,' he said, once comprehension showed on his countenance, 'I was dreaming about being one of a pair of dice in a shaker, being rolled and thrown.'

'Have you been very uncomfortable?' Louisa asked, patting his cheek.

'I am quite comfortable, my dear,' he said, placing his hand over hers where it rested on his face. 'You know me, never one to complain.'

Caroline leaned her head back, and glanced out of the window. Mr Darcy was not in sight; he must again have galloped ahead. She closed her eyes for what seemed like only a moment, but when she opened them, the black horse once again moved alongside the window.

Peering out, she smiled up at him. 'I am so glad you are enjoying your ride.'

He looked down. 'I rode ahead only to ascertain how far we were from the point at which we will be able to first see the city.'

A warm glow rose up inside her. 'Why, Mr Darcy, that is uncommonly kind of you.'

He shrugged. 'It is uncommonly lovely today. The sun is shining, the foliage is very colourful for the time of year. And soon I shall be with my sister.'

'I long to see her, as well. Such an accomplished young woman, I would almost find myself envious when in her presence, were she not such a loving, generous person.'

He smiled at that, an open smile that made him suddenly look young and carefree. 'She is a very special girl. I am glad that you appreciate her so, Miss Bingley.'

The sun's rays that he was so enjoying seemed suddenly to shine within her chest. *You no longer think of fine eyes,* she thought. She kept her mouth shut, though, for she did not want to break the mood. *Surely, this is what love feels like. And Mr Tryphon's letter? That is no more than a minor flirtation, too insubstantial to even think about. When we reach town, I shall burn his letter.*

When they reached town, somehow it stayed where it was, inside her jewel box.

* * *

It took a couple of days for Caroline to fully recover from the stress of the journey, but once she felt fully resettled into life in the city, she sent her card around to a few select friends. She was not surprised to find that Lady Amesbury was the first to respond.

'Darling,' Eleanor said, entering the sitting room at Mr Darcy's house, which was where Charles and Caroline had chosen to stay. She held her arms out, and pulled Caroline into a hug. 'Let me look at you.' Taking both of Caroline's hands, she stepped back. 'You look marvellous. I am indeed happy to see you again!'

'And I, you,' Caroline said warmly. 'You look wonderful.' And indeed, Eleanor's skin glowed and her eyes shone.

'Country life obviously agrees with you,' Eleanor said, sitting beside Caroline on a settee.

'What nonsense you speak!' Caroline felt suddenly carefree, as if she was as relaxed as a bird soaring high above the world. 'Oh, Eleanor, I have missed you. The company in the country is very dull.'

'I am glad to hear you say that,' Eleanor said. 'I have arranged a number of entertainments especially for you.'

Caroline wondered for a moment how Eleanor had found the time to arrange even one entertainment, since she had only just learned of her return to town, but Eleanor was still speaking, outlining trips to the theatre, balls, a concert at which 'the best violinist I have ever heard' was to play.

'It all sounds marvellous,' Caroline said. 'Oh! I know not how I could leave all of this life behind!'

'I do not know either. Although, I confess the time we spent with you in the country was very pleasant.'

'I suppose there was the odd moment when I was content, although I cannot think of one at present!' Both women laughed merrily.

'There is,' Eleanor said, 'someone else who has missed you very much. And Caroline,' she held up a reproving finger, 'you were not nearly as good a correspondent with him as you were with me.'

Caroline was awkwardly silent. How could she explain that she thought of Mr Tryphon far more often than she should, and it was precisely because of this excess that she had to pretend she thought of him very little?

She was saved from having to reply by the entry into the room of Georgiana Darcy. Eleanor leapt to her feet. 'Why, who is this simply stunning young lady?'

Georgiana looked to Caroline, unsure of how to respond to this effusive greeting. Caroline stood too and said, 'Lady Amesbury, please permit me to introduce my very dear friend who is as a sister to me. Miss Darcy, Lady Amesbury.'

The two made their curtseys to each other. Truly, the child had matured since she had last seen her. Georgiana was taller now but more than in height, she had grown in manners and poise. Her posture, always elegant, now befit a young lady of consequence.

'Come,' Eleanor said to Georgiana, pulling her to where they could sit side by side, 'You must tell me all about you. I have, of course, heard much about you from your adoring brother, but his praise falls far short of the actuality.'

Georgiana blushed, but allowed herself to be pulled away from Caroline into the more intimate area Eleanor had selected. Caroline was left to sit across from them, separated from their couch by a large table, but she did not mind. She was content to sit back and gaze upon two of the people who were most dear to her.

Responding to Eleanor's eloquently enthusiastic questions and frequent laughter, Georgiana blossomed, turning from a shy young woman to an eager speaker, anxious to share the details of her life that Eleanor clearly found so fascinating.

'You must be very happy,' Eleanor said, 'to have more of a crowd in the house.'

Georgiana nodded. 'I am. My companion, Mrs Annesley, is very good company, but I am truly happiest when I am with my brother.' Then, glancing at Caroline, she quickly added, 'and our friends, of course, the Bingleys.'

'It's quite all right,' Caroline said. 'I understand that your brother has the premiere place in your heart.'

'Of course he does,' Eleanor said. 'And he will, until you meet that certain someone.'

Caroline knew that Mr Darcy would not approve of someone making that statement to his sister, but Georgiana merely blushed and looked down at where her hands were interlinked in her lap.

'Ah! Innocence,' Eleanor said with a fond look at Georgiana. Turning to Caroline, she added, 'How rare it is.' She picked up her cup of tea and drained it. 'I am having a little soirée Friday week. I hope you will be one of the party.'

Caroline nodded. 'I'd be delighted.'

'And you,' Eleanor said to Georgiana. 'It would make me very happy if you could be there, also. I would love to spend some time getting to know you better. I am certain we will be the best of friends.'

Georgiana looked up, interest warring with fear on her countenance. 'I am not certain—'

'Regrettably,' a masculine voice cut in, 'Georgiana is yet too young to be out in society.' Mr Darcy held out his hand to his sister, who took it and rose to her feet.

'Such a pity,' Eleanor said. She stood, also, and smiled at him. Something in that smile sent a frisson of cold up Caroline's spine, although she could not imagine why. Sometimes, she reflected, there was a touch of the predator in Eleanor, but surely her friend knew that Mr Darcy was intended for her. Eleanor would never flirt with him. The smile must simply reflect Eleanor's disappointment in not being able to spend more time with Georgiana.

'Dearest,' Eleanor said to Caroline, 'I must be off. It is lovely beyond measure having you back in town.' Caroline rose, and the two kissed each other's cheeks. With a swirl of skirts and a faint hint of perfume lingering in the air, Eleanor departed.

Caroline turned to see Mr Darcy looking with some concern at her. 'I would not presume,' he said, 'to say anything unfavourable about any of your acquaintances. I would prefer, however, that Georgiana not be included in any of Lady Amesbury's, er, entertainments.'

Caroline gazed at him in surprise, then shifted to where Georgiana stood, looking down. 'As you wish, of course,' she said, unable to keep a touch of frostiness out of her voice. 'I was not aware, however, that my friend is so objectionable to you.' She caught his eye and stared full on at him, unflinching.

'As you well know,' he said, icily polite, 'the friend of one's friend may not be viewed with equal affection. I intended no offence.'

'None taken,' Caroline murmured automatically. Once they were married, would Mr Darcy take this autocratic attitude towards his wife as well as his sister?

Mr Darcy bowed and led his sister out of the room, leaving Caroline to sink back into her seat and pour, with shaking hands, another cup of tea.

*　*　*

Charles was absent the next couple of days, tending to his business, and there had been no opportunity to speak to him, other than a quick explanation that they wished to keep him company while he was in town. This evening, however, all were quite at leisure, except Georgiana, who attended a concert with Mrs Annesley. It was time, Caroline knew, to discuss matters with her brother.

She had received a short note from Jane, in response to the letter she'd sent upon leaving Hertfordshire. It had merely expressed regret at the loss of her friends, and the hope that they would soon be returning to Nether-field. Caroline had wondered if Mrs Bennet had been so flouting of con-vention as to convince Jane to write to Charles. She assumed that not even that horrible woman would suggest such a thing, but just in case, she had asked Mr Darcy to instruct his butler that all mail arriving at the house for either of the Bingleys be given to her.

Charles took a chair by the fire, after he and Mr Darcy joined Caro-line in the sitting room after dinner. Stretching out his legs, he held up his tumbler of brandy, enjoying the way the fire glinted gold in its depths. 'It is very pleasant,' he said, 'to be here with my friends and family. I look forward, however, to returning to our country retreat.'

Caroline and Mr Darcy looked at one another, any previous disagree-ments forgotten in the face of this shared challenge.

'I am,' Caroline said, 'rather enjoying being here. The country is wet and dreary during the winter. Why do we not stay here, where our friends are and there are so many entertainments? I hear that Madame Irina Costanza will be performing at the opera hall next month.'

Charles looked surprised. 'I did not realise you are so fond of the opera.'

Caroline smiled at him, and then looked meaningfully at Mr Darcy. 'There are many things about me you do not realise, Charles. If a woman cannot maintain some mystery within her own family, she is in trouble, indeed.' She forced a laugh.

Mr Darcy took up his share of the responsibility. 'Charles, we believe that it would not be in your best interests to return to Netherfield. We fear only disappointment awaits you there.'

'What?' Charles shot to his feet. 'Whatever are you speaking of?'

Caroline held out her hand to Charles and he took it, as if seeking a lifeline thrown to a drowning man.

'You speak of Jane,' he said, and a hint of anger began to grow in his voice. 'I know you do not approve of her mother, but of Jane herself there can be no objection. She is the sweetest, gentlest, loveliest—'

'She is all that,' Mr Darcy said firmly. 'And while her connections are regrettable, I would have no objection to your attachment—'

Charles dropped Caroline's hand and brightened at this, but Mr Darcy continued, 'if I were convinced that her feelings for you were as strong as yours.'

Charles gaped at him, then sank limply back into his chair. 'I do not understand.' He rubbed his hand over his face.

'Charles,' Caroline said gently. 'You are a man of strong passions. You know this, I have heard you admit it.'

He lowered his hand to uncover his eyes and stared at her.

'And I well understand Jane's many attractions. Who could know better than I, her dear friend? But I have seen in her an indifference rather than a strength of feelings. She regards the world with great calm, no doubt in an effort to protect herself from the upheavals caused by her mother and younger sisters. I am unsure if she is capable of returning your affections in the way that you deserve.'

Charles turned to Darcy, fear in his eyes.

'I must concur,' Darcy said firmly. 'Out of my affection for you, I spent a great deal of time observing her, both in your company and without. She appeared content enough to spend time with you, but she also appeared equally content to be with her sister Miss Elizabeth.' He paused a moment at the mention of this name, and Caroline shot him a sharp glance. 'I did not,' he continued, 'witness anything that suggested to me a deeper regard for you.'

Charles closed his eyes. 'I cannot believe this. And I cannot believe that you two, the dearest people in my life, can so cruelly work to deprive me of the woman whom I intend to make my wife.'

Caroline and Mr Darcy once again locked gazes, deep concern on both their countenances.

'Charles,' Caroline said. 'We understand how disappointing this must be for you. Please understand we have only your happiness at heart. Can you not give it some time? Let us stay here for the winter. See if your feelings for Jane stay the same. If time and distance do not lessen them, then we can reconsider in the spring.'

'And,' Mr Darcy added, 'the lady's affection may also be affected by the same factors.'

Charles perked up a little at that. 'Yes,' he said eagerly. 'Caroline, you shall write to her and she will write back. I know she will and you both might mention me from time to time. Many an affection has been strengthened through regular correspondence.'

'I do not think,' Caroline said, putting reluctance into her voice, 'that we should contact her at all. You see, we, Mr Darcy and I, fear that Mrs Bennet, since she so clearly wishes the match only for the financial advantages it will bring her family, may be pushing her daughter into pretending an affection she does not feel.'

Charles gasped and put a hand to his chest, as if a spear had been thrust into his heart. He sagged back into his chair, suddenly drained.

'I am sorry,' Mr Darcy said, 'but it is best that this be halted now, rather than once it advances too far to be stopped.'

Charles drew in a shuddering breath. 'I cannot begin to believe this, but as always, I shall be guided by your superior understanding of the world.' He stood, and stared at Mr Darcy, who affected a casual air. 'You have never done me a disservice in all the time we have known one another, and I cannot think that you would do me one now.' He stared unseeing at his friend for a moment, his eyes unfocused, and then rushed from the room.

Mr Darcy sagged suddenly, his chin resting on his chest. 'We have done the right thing,' Caroline said, frightened by the pain she saw in his eyes. 'We have.'

He lifted his head slowly, as if raising an unbearable weight. 'We have. It is right, but now both of us must suffer.'

Caroline smiled. 'I thank you for your consideration of my feelings in this, as well as your own.'

He stared at her for a moment, his dark eyes revealing nothing, no pain, no understanding. 'Yes,' he said at last. 'Of course.' Without a further word he stood, bowed, and departed. The room, despite its cheery fire and the welcome familiarity of his house, was suddenly cold and empty.

A few days later, Caroline returned calls to several of her friends. She'd been remiss, not feeling much like going out while Charles wandered about the house, pale and wraithlike. He didn't eat, he didn't join the others when the Hursts came for dinner and cards in the evenings. He didn't go out, either, merely drifted from room to room, gazing at nothing, lifting a book or touching a glass of strong drink if one was placed in his hand, without reading a single page or taking a sip.

Enough time had passed since her friends' cards had been delivered that she would appear impolite. And perhaps if she resumed her usual round of activities, Charles would, also.

She chose to visit Eleanor last of all, in part because she wished to have a little more time to spend there, if Eleanor was in, and because there was a good chance Mr Tryphon would be there, also. She was not at all sure how she felt about seeing him again. She'd had no contact with him since receiving his letter that, tattered now, still resided in her jewel box. The letter had been quite outrageous, really, and she should be insulted and offended by it. She'd told herself that many times, especially since returning to town and realising that a distance of less than a mile separated him from her, but she could not muster any outrage. The thought of seeing him again brought only excitement tinged with fear.

Now, as she was shown into Eleanor's sitting room, her heart leapt into her throat when he rose to greet her and she realised that the two of them were quite alone.

'Eleanor begs your forgiveness,' he said, 'she is busy at the moment but wished you to come in so she will not miss this opportunity to see you. She will join us shortly.'

He smiled, and Caroline wondered how she could have forgotten how his smile warmed his eyes so she felt she was the only person in the world he wished to gaze upon, and how his voice warmed her and sent a sort of tickle into her heart. She curtseyed and, no words coming into her head, sank into the nearest chair.

His smile widened, and she swallowed in a throat suddenly gone dry. 'It is good to see you,' he said, sitting across from her and reaching to take her hand. Her eyes widened at his touch but he merely raised her hand to his lips and then released it.

'You did not respond to my letter,' he continued, but raised a hand before she could respond. 'It is of no matter. The letter was unforgivably forward of me, and I apologise. I am grateful that you are willing to see me again, after such a breach of propriety.'

He looked at her with such hope in his eyes that she could not help but say, 'The letter was unforgivable, as you say.' She laughed, to show that she was a woman of the world. 'I do forgive you, though, as the sentiments expressed were very well written and it is not in me to despise any manner of literature.'

He gazed at her, adoration now in those dark eyes. 'You are truly an angel. I had to pen those sentiments, for I could hold them within no longer. Caroline, you can be in no doubt about how I feel. Dare I hope that you return my affections?'

She blushed, and gazed down at her lap. In truth, now that she saw him again, her mind, and body, if she was honest with herself, were filled with confusion. No man had ever spoken to her as he did, no man gazed at her with such passion in his eyes. By comparison, Mr Darcy's behaviour, while utterly proper, was cold and distant, even though they were to be married. Her breath caught in her throat as she looked up again, and saw his face. 'I have to confess, Mr Tryphon,' oh, why did saying his name cause her heart to pound so hard; she was certain he could hear it, 'that you have become very dear to me as a friend of my friend Eleanor's—'

He bowed his head for a moment, and held up a hand. 'You need say no more. I understand. May I hope that we can continue to spend time together, as friends? It is too soon, but please, you must allow me to hope that with time, I will become more than just your friend's friend.'

'Of course.' She smiled, feeling on safer ground. It was exciting to have a man make love to her in this way. It had never happened before and, given Mr Darcy's sober nature, might never happen again. Why should she not enjoy it? It was harmless, after all. 'I enjoy your company, Mr Tryphon.'

He seized her hand again, and held it tightly. 'Thank you, Miss Bingley. Thank you.' They stared at each other, smiling, and then, releasing her hand, he said, 'Please tell me of the delights you experienced in the country after my departure.'

They spoke for some little time, she relating the more humorous of her experiences in Hertfordshire, he laughing heartily at all the right moments. At length, Eleanor joined them, full of apologies for not being there to greet Caroline when she first arrived. 'I trust,' she said, 'that Stephen has been entertaining you?'

'Quite the opposite,' Mr Tryphon said, rising at her entry. 'Miss Bingley has been entertaining me. She is quite the raconteur.'

'You are too kind,' Caroline said. 'Besides, the stories from Netherfield supply their own entertainment. They are simply too, too, droll.'

'I insist, then,' Eleanor said, 'on hearing every one of them. If they are so very funny, I am sure Stephen will not object to hearing them again.' She glanced at him and he nodded with a smile.

The rest of the afternoon passed quickly, with Caroline's tales interspersed with stories from Eleanor about who had left with whom after one of her parties, and who was not speaking to whom as a result. Mr Tryphon added the occasional observation but for the most part was content to observe. When Caroline left to return to Mr Darcy's house, she was not permitted to depart before promising to accompany her two friends to the theatre the very next evening, and she assured them she looked forward to the engagement very much.

Mr Tryphon, she decided, was merely a young man in the throes of passion, and she could not fault him for that. She was beautiful and accomplished, after all, and he was newly arrived in town. She must represent to him all that a woman of the highest social circles could offer, elegance and wit which, coupled with her sensitivity and kind nature, would be irresistible to a man with his naiveté and lack of understanding. She would enjoy his company until he cast his attentions on someone else, someone capable of returning his feelings.

She smiled at this, well satisfied with her handling of the situation, and firmly repressing the little shard of ice that pierced her heart at the thought of him bestowing that warm smile on any woman other than herself.

* * *

When Caroline entered the sitting room the next evening before her theatre engagement, she clutched a letter in her hand. 'I am all agog,' she announced to the assembled company, 'to share with you the news I have just received from Hertfordshire. I simply cannot wait another minute!'

'Well,' Charles said, leaning back in his chair, his hands behind his head, 'wait no longer. What is this news?'

He was attempting, Caroline knew, to appear as if news from Hertfordshire was of little consequence to him but the fact he had not mentioned Jane led her to suspect he still suffered from his mistaken hopes.

'It is from Lady Lucas,' she said quickly, to disabuse him of any such thoughts. 'Apparently Mr Collins has been most assiduous in seeking a wife, urged on by your aunt, Mr Darcy.'

He raised an eyebrow. 'I am well acquainted with how forceful her urgings can be,' he said with a rueful laugh.

'Mr Collins first turned his attentions on someone we are well acquainted with,' she said. 'Can you guess who?'

Louisa and Mr Hurst had joined them that evening, planning to console Charles, Mr Darcy, and Georgiana for the loss of Caroline while she was at the theatre. 'Miss Lydia Bennet!' Louisa said with a laugh.

Caroline shook her head, smiling. 'No, I am afraid not, although you are close! Anyone else?'

No other guesses were forthcoming, and so she announced, 'Why, none other than Miss Elizabeth Bennet!'

She'd been observing Mr Darcy out of the corner of her eye, and noted his reaction. It was small, too small to be seen by anyone who knew him less well than she did, but his shoulders had risen a tiny bit, and his lips had thinned. *So,* she thought, *no matter how he tries to hide it, he still has feelings for her.* Even though his objections to Charles' match with Jane would apply to himself. Mrs Bennet as a mother-in-law was simply beyond the realms of possibility. Still, she should take action to get him to declare himself as soon as possible. Once he was engaged to her, he would no longer waste any time with thoughts of Miss Eliza.

The reactions of everyone else to her news were as gratifying as she'd hoped. Louisa exclaimed with great glee how well suited the two were, one unduly dull, the other unduly impertinent. 'The balance,' she said, 'will be perfect.' Charles appeared somewhat concerned, but Mr Hurst laughed heartily.

'Only wait,' Caroline said, 'there is yet more.'

Louisa and Mr Hurst fell silent, gazing at her with great attention. 'Miss Elizabeth,' Caroline announced, 'turned him down!'

'She shows great sense,' Mr Darcy said, but his words were almost drowned out by Louisa, who stated, 'What a foolish girl! I always said she had pretensions far above her station. Marriage to a clergyman is beyond what she can hope for.'

Caroline glanced fully at Mr Darcy, but he said nothing more, merely returned her gaze with equanimity. 'And so,' he said, 'what became of Mr Collins' matrimonial expectations? I am sure you can enlighten us.'

'Indeed I can.' Caroline paused before giving the next piece of news. 'Three days later he proposed to Charlotte Lucas.' At their exclamations, she curtseyed, as if on a stage, before adding, 'And was accepted!'

'Mr Collins is fortunate, indeed,' Charles said, essaying a smile. It looked pinched on his thin face, for he had lost weight during the past few days, but it was the first smile Caroline had seen, and she was glad of it. 'Miss Lucas will make him an admirable wife.'

'But will he make an admirable husband?' Louisa asked. 'She will never get a word in edgewise.'

'It is a good match for her,' Mr Darcy said quietly, but such was his gravity that everyone fell silent. 'At the age of twenty-seven, she cannot have held out hopes for a husband at all, especially since her father, despite his knighthood, has very little to offer in the way of dowries for his daughters.'

Charles gave him a look that contained more anger than admiration. 'You are very concerned,' he said, 'about the happiness of most of the women in Hertfordshire. I marvel at your kindness.'

Mr Darcy returned the gaze serenely. 'I admired Miss Lucas, as I admired many of our acquaintance there. I can see no harm in wishing her, and others, happiness and as secure a situation in life as they can find, given the drawbacks their parentage has forced on them.'

Charles clamped his teeth together, but turned away without saying anything.

Happy with the reaction Lady Lucas' letter had received, Caroline left them to continue discussing it while she accompanied her friends to the theatre.

Chapter Eight

As the days passed, Caroline spent much of her time with Eleanor and Mr Tryphon. True to his word, Mr Tryphon was a perfect gentleman, saying nothing that could not be said in polite company. They dined at Eleanor's home and at Mr Hurst's, attended the theatre, a piano concert, and many parties. The only way he showed his continuing emotions was in the heat of his glance sometimes, when Caroline caught him looking at her when he thought her attention elsewhere, and his usual kissing of her hand when bidding her goodbye. Every time, his lips burned against her skin, even when she wore gloves, and his eyes looked up at her, revealing his heart.

Upon receiving Jane's letter professing her hope that her friends would return to Netherfield after Christmas, Caroline thought it best to end all such hopes. She began by stating, as bluntly as propriety would allow, that the family was well settled in London for the entire winter, softening the tone only by adding her brother's regret that he had left Hertfordshire too precipitously to pay his respects to all his friends there.

She continued by singing the praises of Miss Darcy, and mentioned how happy Charles was to be staying in Mr Darcy's house. '*I, too, am happy to be here, as I so enjoy the company of both Darcys, brother and sister, but my contentment is nothing compared to Charles'. He enjoys listening to Miss Darcy play the piano, and if I might be excused a sister's fond bias, I think she is becoming partial to him, also. She often chooses to sit by him when we are all together in the evenings; even if she spends the time reading without conversing, his proximity appears to give her much contentment.*'

Deciding that she had made her point, and that it would be cruel to continue along these lines, she noted that she had not yet filled a page, and so wrote about her admiration of Mr Darcy's good taste, as demonstrated by some furniture he was considering purchasing for one of the sitting rooms. Closing with many professions of affection for her dear friend, Caroline sealed the letter and sent it off, at last able to put Hertfordshire and all of its Bennets out of her mind.

After a fortnight, Caroline moved to Grosvenor Street, for Louisa claimed that with only her husband for company, her days were very dull. Even once Charles was the only Bingley to stay on in Mr Darcy's home, most evenings were spent at one or the other residence, for the entire company enjoyed the entertainments possible with a larger complement of people.

Christmas was a truly joyous season that year, for Charles and Georgiana appeared, to Caroline's fond eyes, to be forming a stronger attachment. Georgiana, like her brother, had a more serious nature, but Charles could get her laughing as he told stories about her brother during his university days.

One evening, spent at Mr Hurst's home even though he and Louisa had been invited out after dinner, the others remained in the comfortable sitting room.

Caroline admired the facility with which Charles spoke of his university days, because George Wickham had been there with Mr Darcy, and so had been included in some of the escapades. Charles was able to pull out of his memory only those stories that did not involve Wickham or, if that man had been present, he could leave out any detail concerning him, without giving the impression that anything was missing from the tale. Charles also, of course, had to select stories that were suitable for the ears of a young lady, but fortunately he and Mr Darcy had been well mannered even during their youth, and so there was not much to tell of risqué adventures.

Or, and Caroline paused in her thoughts, perhaps she too had been kept from learning some of the things that young men at university could get up to. Intensely curious now, she listened to what Charles was saying.

'How we first met?' he inquired of Georgiana. 'Surely your brother has told you that story many times.'

Georgiana laughed. 'Yes, he has, but I have observed that sometimes the details of an event differ depending on who is relating them.'

'I, too,' said Mr Darcy, lowering the book he had been reading, 'would like to hear your version.'

Charles smiled at his friend. 'Are you so much more elderly than I that you cannot remember?'

'No, what I fear is that you will forget that my advanced age requires you to treat me with respect. I fear I will not be portrayed in such a manner as I deserve.' He stated this with utmost seriousness.

Charles and Georgiana were not fooled, though, and they both broke into laughter. Mr Darcy laughed also. Caroline joined them, even though she had not been a part of the conversation, simply because it made her happy to see Mr Darcy laugh.

Her embroidery held no allurement this evening, and the book she'd selected to read because Mr Darcy had recently finished it, was very dull indeed. 'I will offer my support to Miss Darcy,' she said, 'and join my voice to hers so that we may hear your story, Charles.'

Looking about, Charles shrugged. 'How can I refuse, when I am surrounded by so many eager faces? But are you all so certain you wish to hear such a dull tale?'

'It is not dull at all,' Caroline said. 'Nor is it so long as to be wearisome. We have spent more time discussing whether you should tell it than the telling will take.'

He held up his hands in good-natured surrender. 'Very well!' Taking a sip from his tumbler of brandy, he began. 'Once upon a time, dear ones, there was a university and at the university there were two young men.'

'Only two?' Georgiana asked in a pretended wondering tone. 'They must have received a great deal of attention, indeed, from all the professors.'

Charles frowned at her. 'How can I proceed if there are all these interruptions?'

'There has been only one interruption, so far,' Mr Darcy pointed out, helpfully.

'I am merely preparing for those that are to come.' With great dignity, Charles looked from one face to another, until everyone assumed his desired mien of attentiveness.

'There were other young men there also, but as they do not figure largely in this story, for brevity's sake I have chosen to ignore them.' He paused, as if expecting another interruption, but no one said anything.

'We will,' he continued, 'refer to one young man as Charles, and the other as Darcy.'

'That is something I don't understand,' Georgiana said. 'Why, Mr Bingley, are you referred to by your Christian name by your family and friends, while my brother is called by our last name by almost all of our intimate acquaintances?' Turning to her brother, she added, 'Our cousin, Colonel Fitzwilliam, calls you Fitz, does he not?'

'He does,' Mr Darcy said, 'but for most people, Fitzwilliam is too much of a mouthful. And since our mother's family was the Fitzwilliam family, it confuses some people, who don't know whether my appellation as Fitzwilliam refers to my first or last name. Our cousin uses the short-ened name Fitz in part because of this confusion.'

Charles, who had sat through this conversation with admirable patience, now interjected, 'It is because he is Darcy. Look at him.' They all did. 'His name suits him and he suits the name.'

The others continued to study Mr Darcy, and Caroline thought she could understand what Charles meant. The name Darcy was elegant, handsome, refined, just as the man was.

'May I continue?' Charles asked. 'The young man hitherto referred to as Charles, had a very good impression of himself. He was the first in his family to receive higher education, and since he had done well during all levels of his schooling, he assumed university would be no different. He spent his first few days in a confused daze for there were a great many students there—'

'The young men who shall not be mentioned?' Caroline asked.

He ignored her. 'There were also a great many rooms, most of which were intended for different purposes, and Charles found it difficult to find the correct room for the correct purpose at the correct time. He muddled through, with increasing success, but he still had no opportunity to shine.'

'And he wanted to shine?' Georgiana asked.

He nodded. 'Charles wanted to show the entire world that even though he did not stem from a family of scholars, he was worthy of being a member of the university. One day, perhaps a little under a fortnight of his arrival, he arrived in a room at the correct time but discovered it was the wrong room for his purpose. Instead of a seminar on the ancient philosophers, there was something entirely different going on.' He paused, for suspense, and his audience did not disappoint him, for they remained silent, awaiting his next words.

'At the front of the room two men stood, facing an audience of perhaps a dozen others. One man was speaking, without a single interruption, I might add. He talked about the war with France and Napoleon.' He turned to the women present. 'I shall leave out the details, because no doubt they deal more thoroughly with the issue of war and how it is carried out than you would wish to hear. Suffice it to say that his argument for the way Britain had treated Napoleon was compelling. By the time this man finished speaking, I was convinced that everything Great Britain had done for the past many years was exactly what had been required, and that our leadership was inspired and infallible.

'The event was not over then, even though the audience, with me joining in, had applauded enthusiastically. I discovered it was then the turn of the other man standing at the front to speak. He was a tall fellow, with dark wavy hair. He appeared relaxed, and I assumed he would comment on the brilliance of the other fellow's talk. When he began I took a chair at the back of the room, instead of leaving to find my seminar. I would have been unpardonably late, in any case.'

'The other man was my brother!' Georgiana exclaimed.

'He was indeed.' Charles smiled. 'He spoke on the opposite side of the issue, on how wrongheaded Britain's treatment of Napoleon had been and how events might have differed, and lives been spared, had we taken a different tack.'

He turned again to the two women. 'As I discovered at the end of the session, the people present were members of the debating club. I had never heard of this form of discussion, formal and yet wide-ranging. It works thus: an issue that has more than one side is selected, and two people are assigned at random, one to argue for, and the other, against. They each have an opportunity to speak, uninterrupted, for a set amount of time. There is a scoring system which deals with the number of clear points made by each.'

Georgiana clapped her hands. 'It sounds fascinating. I would so like to attend a debate.' She looked pleadingly at her brother. 'Can you arrange it?'

He frowned. 'Debates are not usually suitable for young ladies. Tempers sometimes rise, and the language, while it must be gentlemanly, can become rough.'

Upon seeing her disappointment at her brother's disapproving tone, Caroline quickly said, 'Perhaps we can arrange a debate for ladies. Women, after all, have brains also, and when we are informed of the facts of an issue, are quite capable of developing a coherent argument.'

Charles burst out laughing. 'I am indeed well aware of ladies' ability to argue. And you truly can be single-minded when you wish to be. Debate requires much more self-discipline than women have.' He turned to Mr Darcy. 'Do you not agree?'

Mr Darcy thought for a moment. 'I do agree, in principle, and a few months ago I would have agreed without hesitation. I have, though, encountered a female who can more than hold her own in any discussion.'

Caroline froze. Goosebumps arose on her skin and she folded her arms across her chest, grateful for the current fashion of long sleeves. There was only one woman he could mean. Elizabeth Bennet. 'Surely,' she said quickly, 'you cannot admire such a trait in a woman. What man could possibly wish to be challenged during every conversation, or on each decision he makes?'

Mr Darcy raised an eyebrow. 'Forgive me if I gave the wrong impression. I did not mean to state that the person in question is argumentative, just that she has a lively mind, and is well able to discuss all manner of issues in an interesting and stimulating manner.'

Caroline did not respond, for she was uncertain what to say. Before much time in silence had passed, Charles cleared his throat. 'Shall I continue the story, or would we prefer to discuss how to hold a discussion?'

'Oh! continue, of course,' Georgiana cried. 'We had only just reached the point where my brother spoke. I long to know more about his performance.'

'There is little to say of his performance,' Charles said wryly. 'It was magnificent. By the end of his allotted time, I was convinced Great Britain had the most foolish leadership of any country in the entire world, and that, had we only asked this man how best to handle Napoleon, the war could have been entirely averted.'

Mr Darcy laughed. 'Come now, Charles. Are you so easily swayed as that?'

'I was on that occasion!' Charles cried. 'I rushed out of the room in a frenzy; my mind swirling with all that I had heard and observed.

'Once my fevered thoughts had ebbed somewhat, I found my way back to my rooms. By then I had begun to realise that I had, in the space of less than an hour, believed with all my heart two entirely opposing views. I knew I had to learn how to speak as those men had. At my first opportunity, I signed up for the Debate Club.'

'So that is when you first met my brother?' Georgiana said. 'When he told me the story, he described a slightly different occasion.'

Mr Darcy smiled reminiscently. 'My first memory of Charles is of the event he is about to relate. He first saw me as he has described, but I was much too wrapped up in myself and in my performance to notice a late-comer. This may come as a shock, dear sister, but I was rather conceited at that time in my life.'

Georgiana rolled her eyes. 'Dear brother, I am not as naïve as you choose to believe. Knowing your faults, though, only helps me love you better.'

Mr Darcy was speechless for a moment, then a tender smile grew on his face. Caroline watched, unable to look away even though this was clearly an intimate moment between brother and sister. If only she could draw such a look of adoration from him. Perhaps she should try letting him know how she felt about him, and speak of love, just as Georgiana had done. She wasn't sure of what to say or how to voice it. She'd ask Eleanor for advice.

'The story,' Charles said, 'is quickly done. I joined the club, was assigned an issue, and debated it. Over the next weeks, I participated in two practice debates, and then my first in actual competition. Much to my delight, although not to my own conceit's surprise, I was declared the winner. The following event, however, was much different.'

'You debated against Mr Darcy,' Caroline said with a smile. 'And lost.'

'You are correct,' Charles said. 'I prepared for the debate, thoroughly researching the area, and practising the points I wished to make on any fellow student unfortunate enough to fall into my clutches. I spoke, as I thought, brilliantly, not so quickly as to be hard to understand, yet efficiently to make the best use of my time. I modulated my voice, raising it when I approached an important point, hushing it when I wished to create a moment of suspense. It was all for naught.'

'You lost,' Georgiana said sadly. 'Please forgive me for asking you to relive an unpleasant experience.'

'Nonsense,' Charles said cheerfully. 'It is through our mistakes that we learn.'

'And it was not all for naught,' Mr Darcy said. 'For after the event was over, Charles came to congratulate me, and as I had been impressed by his speech, especially from a man so recently come to debating, we spoke at some length.'

'Both of you complimenting each other!' Georgiana said.

'Indeed.' Mr Darcy smiled at Charles. 'The compliments created an atmosphere in which we were both kindly disposed to one another, and when we parted, I invited Charles to join me for dinner at my rooms the following day. We continued to seek out each other's company often. We soon found enough to admire in each other that the friendship grew rapidly.'

'Thank you,' Georgiana said to Charles. 'It is a lovely story, and you told it very well. In fact,' and here she sent a mischievous look at her brother, 'based on your telling today and my brother's recital of the story some little time ago, I declare you, Charles, the winner of this debate.'

Mr Darcy stood and applauded, and Caroline followed suit. 'Very well done, indeed,' she said to Charles. 'Although,' and she looked sidelong at Mr Darcy, 'your friend is no mean storyteller himself. I so enjoy listening to him. Everything you have to say, sir,' and she turned to face him, 'is fascinating and provides me with food for thought.'

Mr Darcy bowed in response to this. Taking out his pocket watch, he held out a hand to help Georgiana rise to her feet. 'It is growing late,' he said, 'and so we must end this gathering and head home.'

Charles rose, also, and bowed to his sister. 'Good night, Caroline. Please tell the Hursts that I hope they spent as delightful an evening with their friends, as we did here.'

'I shall.' Caroline summoned the butler to show them out and then, not quite ready to prepare for sleep, returned to the sitting room. She sat in the chair Mr Darcy had used, and tried to sense any remaining warmth from his body, but there was none.

She didn't know what to do. Why had he not yet proposed? She'd been reluctant to return from his house to this one because it meant they were less often in each other's company. And yet he'd had plenty of opportunities to speak, since the two households spent much time together. And surely he could have arranged for a moment alone with her, simply by inviting her to take a walk in the gardens, or taking her aside when they were at the theatre or another place where the proximity of crowds somewhat oddly made it easier to speak privately.

Mr Tryphon had certainly taken advantage of those sorts of opportunities. While he had not let one word about his feelings for her pass his lips, he still enjoyed spending time with her, and she found no objections. They spoke of many things, fashion, music, the latest plays, who had been seen with whom at which party or ball. There were no awkward silences with him, unlike when she was with Mr Darcy. Mr Darcy so often seemed disapproving of her, or refused to reply to some innocent comment she made. With Mr Tryphon, there was always something to say, and he listened with his entire being, often laughing or appearing thoughtful at something she said. Sometimes he paused a moment before replying, but she knew this was so he could frame the most apt response. There was no disapproval from him, no frowns, no picking up a book and losing himself within it while she still spoke.

Mr Tryphon, she realised now, found her fascinating. Mr Darcy, well, she was not sure what he thought. She enjoyed being fascinating. Feeling disloyal, she remembered that at times Mr Darcy did enjoy her company. He always put down his book whenever she played or sang at the piano. He admired her needlework and had said he was very happy with the slippers she'd embroidered and given to him for Christmas. He'd given her a charming vase, and had promised to see it filled with flowers. She kept the vase in the smaller parlour of Mr Hurst's house, where she and Louisa often sat, for the winter weather had become very cold, and the fire did a better job of heating the smaller room.

Every time she saw the vase and flowers, they reminded her of

Mr Darcy. Surely his constancy in sending the flowers corresponded to the constancy of his feelings for her. Why, then, did he not speak?

Perhaps it was due to that horrible aunt of his, Lady Catherine de Bourgh. She, Caroline knew, wanted Mr Darcy for her daughter, Anne, a miserable sickly creature. Mr Darcy would not marry Anne. She knew him well enough to understand that he would not allow his life to be dictated by another, not even his mother's sister.

No, Caroline would have to take matters into her own hands. If words of love were what he liked to hear, she would find a way to give them to him. Perhaps he was unsure of how she felt about him. She knew that a woman of accomplishment and intelligence could seem self-contained to a man. She would show him her vulnerable side, and how much she needed his strength.

Yes, that was a good plan. She'd discuss it with Eleanor, of course, but she knew her friend would approve, and would be impressed with Caroline's ability to be assertive and go after what she wanted.

Later, as she lay in bed awaiting her slumber, she ran through some things she could say to Mr Darcy. She could comment on his firm forearm and how secure she felt when he escorted her to dinner. She could pluck a piece of lint, real or imagined, from his sleeve, and tell him how much she enjoyed performing the little task for him. She could pretend fear while at the theatre, appearing overcome by a sword fight or by the sorrow of two lovers cruelly separated from each other.

But why, when she thought of firm muscles, a protective presence, a person for whom to perform little tasks, did a different man monopolise her thoughts? It was Mr Darcy she loved, was it not? And if she did not love him now, she would after they were married, just as he would come to adore her. There was no reason to be thinking of Mr Tryphon. None at all.

To prove that he meant nothing at all to her, she took out his letter, the one that had spoken of love, and read it through, determined to discover not the slightest warm feeling in response to it. She read it slowly, repeating each word inside her head, and was pleased to discover that when she finished it and put it back in her jewel box, she felt nothing at all. Her heart rate was as steady as always, her breathing soft and smooth.

Mr Darcy was the man who quickened her pulse, and if that reaction did not happen naturally, well, she would simply find a way to make it happen. Practice, she reminded herself, makes perfect. For a moment she brought the image to mind of Mr Darcy's forearm and increased the rate of her breathing, but after a few breaths she began to develop a headache.

Tomorrow, she promised herself. Tomorrow she would practice, even though there were no engagements planned for the day that would bring her and Mr Darcy together. Practice on her own would be even more effective, so that the next time she saw him, she would be perfect in her loving responses to him.

When she fell asleep, though, it was not Mr Darcy who entered her dreams and quickened her pulse.

* * *

On New Year's Day, Caroline received a call and an invitation from Eleanor, who was planning a grand ball for the evening of January 7th. Many of the finest entertainers would be there: Bettina Squires, a much admired soprano; Daniel Scott Allen, a famous pianist, and because Eleanor was Eleanor, and so her parties always had to be slightly risqué so as to be spoken of with envy by those who had not been invited, a troupe of jugglers and acrobats who were known as much for the living sculptures they made with their bodies as for their ability to juggle with flaming torches.

'Why did you select January 7th?' Caroline asked her friend. 'Why not have such a ball on New Year's Eve?' She felt somewhat put out, for her family's New Year's celebration, held at the Hurst's home, had involved too much food and too much time spent playing cards. Caroline had not heard a single word from Eleanor during the week between Christmas and New Year, and was certain that her friend had been running from party to entertainment, from dinner to breakfast served at an event that involved people dancing all night. 'Were you,' she continued, 'too busy with all your other invitations to have this ball on New Year's Eve?'

Eleanor waved a hand vaguely. 'And why should the eve of January 1st get all the attention? Consider the feelings of all the other dates. How left out they must feel!'

She laughed and Caroline, still vexed but unable to resist Eleanor when she was at her most charming, smiled in turn. She couldn't resist repeating her last question. 'How did you spend New Year's Eve?'

Eleanor looked away for a moment, so that the light streaming in the window to one side cast her face in shadow. 'Oh, it was very dull. I was out of town, if you must know.' She turned back to Caroline and stuck her lower lip out in a pout. 'But why speak of a time already past, when it is so much more amusing to discuss what is yet to happen!' She clapped her hands. 'Let me tell you about my ball!'

For a while she regaled Caroline with details of the food her cook would prepare, the musicians she'd hired for the dancing, the décor and lighting she planned to use to create the proper atmosphere, and the people who would be in attendance.

Despite her bad mood, Caroline was impressed. 'You have surpassed yourself, dear friend. It will be a most delightful ball.'

Eleanor smiled, clearly pleased with herself. 'There is only one thing required for it to be the perfect event.'

'What might that be?' Caroline was genuinely curious, for she could not think of a single detail that Eleanor had not already perfected.

'It lies in your power, my dear.' Eleanor took both Caroline's hands in hers.

'Anything,' Caroline said. 'You know that I would do anything for you, because you have given me so much with no thought of recompense.'

'What nonsense you speak,' Eleanor said lightly. 'You are my friend, it pleases me to please you. I ask nothing more, and wonder now if I should feel insulted that you would even mention such a thing.'

She made as if to withdraw her hands from Caroline's, but the latter immediately tightened her grip and said, 'Please, you must know me well enough to understand I meant no offence. None at all!'

Eleanor relaxed her hands. 'Of course. You are such a sweet creature you could never intend harm to anyone. I was merely having a little joke with you.'

Caroline laughed, as if enjoying the joke, although she still did not understand what had just happened. 'Please. Tell me what it is I can do for you.'

'For me?' Eleanor laughed. 'No, it is for the ball, so that everyone present may secure even greater enjoyment. What I wish is a mere trifle.'

She paused, and Caroline leaned closer, awaiting the knowledge she required to make her friend happy.

'A trifle,' Eleanor said again, looking away from Caroline. 'As you can see, the invitation includes everyone of your family, and Mr and Miss Darcy as well. It would make me very happy if you could persuade the Darcys to attend.'

'Both of them?' Caroline struggled to hide her surprise. Since returning to town, Mr Darcy had attended only two of Eleanor's entertainments, and those, he'd said, he'd gone to only because he wished to meet the guest of honour. Caroline had been surprised at that, as the guests he'd been interested in had been an elderly violinist who barely had the strength to hold up his instrument, and the author of one of the books Mr Darcy enjoyed. Caroline had picked it up after that engagement, but found nothing of interest, so it was a mystery to her why Mr Darcy not only wanted to meet the writer, but had spent much of the evening in conversation with him.

Despite his interest in some of Eleanor's guests, he had refused Georgiana's requests to accompany him to Eleanor's house, so that she too, might meet these people who so impressed her brother.

'I am afraid,' Caroline said haltingly, 'Mr Darcy is of the opinion that his sister is yet too young to go out much into society.'

Eleanor stood up, her back rigid. 'Is this how little you care for me, that you cannot perform this one little favour?' She turned to face Caroline, who was alarmed to see her friend's eyes fill with tears. 'Have I asked so much of you in the past that you are weary of my demands?'

'No!' Caroline shot to her feet and attempted to put her arms around Eleanor. 'You have asked nothing, nothing of me. I would do anything for you, you must know that.'

Eleanor pulled away from the embrace. 'And yet, despite your pretty words, you refuse me the one thing I ask.'

'I will do it,' Caroline said desperately. 'I will explain to Mr Darcy that your ball will be the epitome of propriety, that his sister will be exposed to nothing that could upset her.'

Eleanor seized Caroline's hands and danced her around in a circle. 'Oh, I knew your affection for me was true. I knew I could trust you. How dear a friend you are!'

Caroline smiled, and allowed herself to be pulled into Eleanor's arms. Even as she relaxed into the warmth of her friend, she wondered how on earth she could convince Mr Darcy that it would be appropriate for Georgiana to attend this ball. He had, after all, been at some of Eleanor's other parties and while their unexpectedness and different sort of entertainments were much of the appeal to Caroline and Eleanor's other friends, she could see why Mr Darcy would disapprove of men who were accompanied by their mistresses, and of some of what went on in the darker corners of the rooms.

She squared her shoulders; she would find a way. In fact, Eleanor's making this request was fortuitous, for it would allow Caroline an opportunity to practise showing her love to Mr Darcy. She hugged Eleanor more tightly, and smiled. Killing two birds with one stone was always an efficient use of one's time.

* * *

Three days after Eleanor had made her request, Caroline's continuing attention to the post paid off. Among the usual pile of envelopes delivered to the Hursts' house was one whose address had been written by a familiar hand: Jane's.

Once she'd reached the privacy of her own chamber, Caroline began to read.

'My dear friend,
Words cannot express how lonely we are without your presence nearby.
The holidays have passed happily enough, though, for our relatives, the
Gardiners, who live in town, were here to raise our spirits. I trust that
you and your family also spent a merry Christmas, surrounded by the
lights and gaiety of town.

Oh! I have just reread what I wrote, and I see that the above
could be taken to insinuate that I am jealous of you, or petulant
that you have left us. This is not at all what I meant, but instead of

wasting this paper and ink, I shall merely explain that I wish for nothing more than your happiness. I am glad that you are in the place where you are happiest.

I do have a specific reason for writing, one that I hope will increase your happiness as I know it will increase my own. We can soon be reunited, for my Aunt and Uncle Gardiner invited me to accompany them to their home on Gracechurch Street, and there I shall reside for some weeks. I so look forward to seeing you, dear friend.'

The letter rambled on for several more lines, something about Charlotte Lucas's wedding to Mr Collins. This last would likely have afforded Caroline much amusement, but her mind swirled with a medley of fears.

Jane, in town! Once she was here, she was likely to expect a call from Caroline, and to make calls here to Grosvenor Street. More than that, she would expect that Caroline would pass on the news of her presence in the city to Charles.

Caroline went to her dressing table and checked her appearance, and was relieved to see that she had suffered no obvious effects from the shock of that letter. Turning her face from side to side, she decided she looked very well indeed. Well enough to speak to Mr Darcy. The letter had arrived at the right time, in a sense, for she had had no opportunity to show her affection to Mr Darcy or to convince him to attend Eleanor's party with Georgiana. He and Charles had been otherwise engaged ever since Eleanor's visit, away on business during the day, meeting friends at their club during the evenings. Tonight, however, everyone was to gather at Grosvenor Street. Tonight, she could put her plan into motion.

* * *

'Mr Darcy,' Caroline said to Louisa the next evening, as they left the gentlemen, 'will discover that no woman can make him as good a wife as I. If he doesn't propose, it will be due to his own stupidity, for it certainly won't occur because of any lack of effort on my part.'

Louisa, overseeing the servant who had just wheeled in the tea cart, said, 'And he is not a stupid man.'

'No.' Caroline arranged herself so as to present the perfect image to anyone entering the drawing room. She chose a settee set at an angle to the door, and sat at a slight angle on the cushions, to best present her elegant posture. Beside her, her gown was artfully arranged to cover much of the settee, so that another person wishing to join her on it would be forced to sit in the smaller area at its other end.

'You did obtain Mr Hurst's cooperation?' she asked Louisa, who was still fiddling with the tea things.

'There is no need to worry, Caroline, all will ensue as you planned.'

Caroline looked about the room, moving her head carefully so as to not ruin so much as a single carefully arranged curl on her head. She and Louisa had had several of the chairs removed, while others were arranged around the table for cards. Caroline and Louisa had decided that the game would be played by the two Hursts, Charles, and Georgiana, leaving Mr Darcy with nowhere to sit other than on the settee with Caroline. Mr Hurst was not a gentleman skilled in keeping secrets, but his participation had been necessary for the plan to succeed. And if Mr Darcy did learn at some point in the future of how much effort Caroline had exerted on his behalf, surely he would be flattered. Perhaps she could even tell him herself, sometime, with great humour, of course, but also showing him how much she loved him.

Her exertions had begun when he and Georgiana had first arrived at Grosvenor Street, earlier that day. Caroline herself had personally taken Mr Darcy's coat and hat. True, this had involved something of a tug of war, because he expected the servants to take his things, but she prevailed in the end.

Then, over dinner, where of course she sat next to him, she had entertained him with tales of what she had learned about ongoing life in Hertfordshire, and speculations about the Collins' marriage and the possible offspring who might result from such a union. She could tell he appreciated her wit and incisive views of the lives of those people they'd known but, thankfully, no longer had to see socially.

She had refrained from mentioning any of the Bennets, not wanting to upset Charles, even though she knew he had completely recovered from his foolish infatuation. And there was no reason to mention Miss Elizabeth, not when the other inhabitants of the area provided such fodder for amusement.

She had also ensured that Mr Darcy received the fullest bowl of soup, the very choicest cut of lamb, the freshest-looking boiled potatoes. At one point, as the footman lifted a slice of fish, Caroline had been forced to 'accidentally' bump his elbow, so that the slice fell to the floor, and she herself pointed out the one she thought suitable for Mr Darcy. The footman apologised profusely, and Caroline knew Mr Darcy had been impressed by how graciously she accepted his apology.

Now, as she completed her preparations for when he entered the room, she felt confident her pleas to allow Georgiana to accompany them when they went to Eleanor's soirée would succeed. Surely, now that he realised how much she could do for him, he would grant her this small favour. Plus, her efforts to show him how much she had to offer had only just begun.

Georgiana, who had gone to the retiring room a few minutes earlier, returned to the drawing room. She approached Caroline, clearly intending to join her on the settee, as there was nowhere else to sit, but Louisa quickly requested her help in setting out the tea things and so the space beside Caroline remained empty.

By the time the gentlemen finally appeared, Caroline had readjusted every fold in her gown several times, and her neck hurt from holding her head at the angle she and Louisa had decided, that morning, provided the most advantageous view of her features from the room's door.

All for naught, as it turned out, for as he entered, Mr Darcy was looking back over his shoulder, laughing at something Charles, who was just behind him, had said. Fortunately, Mr Hurst played his role to perfection, moving straight to the card table, and calling to Charles and Georgiana to join him.

Caroline quickly snatched up a book she had brought just for this moment, and so her head was bent studiously when Mr Darcy, after spending some moments walking about the room, presumably looking for somewhere to sit, joined her on the settee.

It took a little effort for him to sit without messing up her gown, but he did accomplish this feat, something observed by Caroline out of the side of her eyes as she continued to look at her book. After some moments of silence, Caroline put down the book, closed her eyes and sighed, as if in rapture from what she'd just read.

Opening them, she said with surprise, 'Why, Mr Darcy! I had not realised the gentlemen had joined us. As I'm sure you know, reading can be so involving that one does not notice a single thing going on in the room where one sits. Why, it's a good thing there hasn't been a flood, for I'm sure I would not have noticed until the water was up to my neck!'

He regarded her for a moment. 'I do indeed know how easy it is to lose oneself in a book.' He took one out of his pocket and opened it.

'Georgiana,' Caroline said, 'also loves to read, does she not?'

'She does.'

'I am so pleased to hear that.' Caroline shifted slightly on the settee, moving back from the front edge, on which she'd been perched, and also closer to Mr Darcy. 'One can learn so much from books.'

Mr Darcy shifted, also, possibly trying to move away from her so as not to crowd her, a gentlemanly thing to do. His efforts were unsuccessful, as Caroline knew they would be, for directly on his other side was the settee's arm. She smiled. Her plans had been perfectly designed.

He apparently took her smile to mean she was happy about the educational value of books, for he said, 'I was not aware that you were so interested in the improvement of Georgiana's mind.'

Good. He is becoming more and more aware of my qualities. 'I adore Georgiana. Why, I have long thought of her as my own sister.'

He raised a brow. 'Indeed.' He turned his attention to his book.

'While books are of inestimable value,' she said quickly, 'no education can be complete without experiencing the world.'

He turned again to face her. 'I agree.'

'And yet,' Caroline said, and was unable to keep a slight tremor out of her voice. Now came the most difficult part of her plan. 'Georgiana has been very much sheltered.' She held up a hand as Mr Darcy began to speak. 'I understand why, of course I do. She is yet very young, and she has required time to learn and practice the womanly arts.'

He again started to say something, and she rushed on. 'Her musical education alone has taken much of her time, for I know how conscientious she has been about her piano practice. And the time has truly been well spent, for she is a most accomplished young lady.'

His book now lay forgotten on his lap. *Truly,* she thought, *his eyes are now fully opened.*

'She is,' he said slowly. 'And I am well aware of your admiration and affection for her. I am glad of it, for lacking the presence of a mother, and having no sister of her own, her relationships with women are a great comfort to me.'

'Dear Mr Darcy,' she said daringly, laying a hand on his sleeve. 'You have been both brother and father to her. And she is a glowing testament to your efforts on her behalf.'

He flicked his eyes down to where her hand rested, most of it on his cuff, but her little finger rested against the skin on the back of his hand. *Just think,* she wanted to say, *what a wonderful father you will be to our children.* Something like that, though, no one in her right mind would dare to say. Well, maybe Eleanor, who seemed to thrive on being outrageous. But while she could be excused, and even admired for her audacity, Caroline had to be more circumspect.

'I was thinking,' Caroline said carelessly, as if what she thought did not matter in the slightest, 'that she might benefit from joining me at Lady Amesbury's evening of entertainment.'

'Certainly not,' he said, so quickly it was as if he had known what she was about to say and had begun his protest before she finished speaking.

'Please hear me out,' she said, thinking that if Elizabeth Bennet could dare to contradict him, she certainly could. 'There will be two musicians of the finest quality present. Just think of how much she would love to listen to a musician who is even more accomplished than her piano teacher. And the soprano—perhaps Miss Darcy will be inspired to learn to sing. I am certain she would have a lovely singing voice.'

Mr Darcy's brows were lowered, and he stared at her with an unblinking gaze, but at least he hadn't said 'certainly not' again.

'You, of course,' she hurried on, 'are invited as well, as you always are.' She allowed a little flattery to seep into her tone, to show how impressive it was that he was always invited to every event hosted by Eleanor. As far as she could tell, he was the only man not within Eleanor's most intimate circle of friends to be so honoured. 'I understand that you have concerns about the nature of some of Eleanor's entertainments, but she has assured me this will be a simple evening of music.' And it would be, for Eleanor had, at Caroline's urging, cancelled the jugglers and acrobats so there would be nothing Mr Darcy could object to. Caroline did wonder why Eleanor so badly wanted both Darcys in attendance, but had not had an opportunity to ask. 'She simply wants to bring pleasure to all her guests, and she knows how much Miss Darcy loves music.'

'Pleasure, indeed,' he said, but the hard edge had gone out of his voice, and she thought she saw the corners of his lips quirk into the tiniest of smiles.

'Eleanor heard Miss Darcy play the pianoforte,' Caroline said, hoping to bring the deal to a close, 'the last time she dined with us. She was very impressed, both with the quality of the music and the joy Miss Darcy brought to all who heard her. Can Eleanor not be permitted to bring equal joy to your sister?'

Mr Darcy regarded her for a moment. 'What you say is certainly plausible. What I cannot understand, however, is what motive Lady Amesbury has in wanting to secure Georgiana's presence at her house.'

'Motive?' Caroline was flabbergasted. 'What other motive can there be than to bring pleasure to the friend of her friend?'

'I do not know,' he replied, 'and that is what makes me uneasy.'

So close, Caroline thought. *He was on the point of agreeing. What has made him pull back?* Ideas for how to handle this newest obstruction swirled in her head. Selecting one, she forged ahead. 'I do not understand, Mr Darcy, why you have this unreasonable concern about Lady Amesbury. She is my dearest friend.' She allowed her eyes to grow shiny, by blinking furiously to build up tears. 'If you doubt my dear friend, does that mean you also doubt me? After all, if I have chosen to become intimate with a person who is apparently so dangerous, so scheming, that you cannot permit your sister to set foot inside her home, then you must believe I am a very poor judge of character, indeed.' The tear built up until it teetered at the edge of her lower eyelid. She let it rest there, and saw his gaze drawn to it.

'I meant no—' he began. 'I intended only—' He sighed, squared his shoulders and, placing his hands on his knees, stood up. 'I mean no disrespect to either yourself or your friend. Georgiana will accompany us for some little time. I will bring her home once the musical portion of the evening is over.' Giving her a small bow, he left the room leaving Caroline to sit alone, her eyes still damp, to savour her triumph.

* * *

The evening of Lady Amesbury's 'Tardy New Year's Eve Party,' as the invitation named it, Caroline dressed with unusual haste, surprising her maid. As soon as she was ready, she hurried downstairs to the waiting carriage. She had arranged to go to Mr Darcy's home and proceed to Eleanor's with them. Mr Hurst's carriage would return here to convey Mr Hurst and Louisa.

She wanted to be early. Not impolitely early, just early enough to have an excuse to go upstairs to where Georgiana would be getting ready. Georgiana was a lovely young woman and her maids, under the guidance of Mr Darcy's taste, always clothed her beautifully, but Caroline wanted to ensure that her soon-to-be sister did not merely blend in among the many beautiful young women who would be present. No, she wanted Georgiana to shine like a red ruby or a green emerald among all the transparent diamonds who made up much of Eleanor's guest list. Then, when Mr Darcy saw how much everyone admired his sister, and how gracious she could be even among such august company, he would no longer have any concerns about either his sister or his future wife being friends with Eleanor. Indeed, he'd probably encourage Georgiana's attendance at future entertainments, for many of the people present this evening would be very useful acquaintances to have. Through Eleanor, Georgiana, and Charles, would meet many statesmen as well as people close to the royal family. The connection with Eleanor would aid Charles, as well, and once he and Georgiana were married, the Darcys and the Bingleys could well become regulars at court.

What lovely couples they would make. Caroline settled herself in the carriage for the short ride to Mr Darcy's house. She and Mr Darcy, both so tall, so dark. Charles and Georgiana, both blond, although Charles' hair tended to appear reddish in a certain light, both of slighter builds than their siblings. Perhaps there could be a double wedding. All society would be agog for days, if not weeks, over an event such as that.

Caroline arrived at the Darcy home, as she had planned, at just the right time. 'The master has come down,' the maid who greeted her at the door reported, 'and he is in his study. Miss Georgiana is not yet down.'

Caroline handed her coat to the footman and asked to be shown to Miss Darcy's rooms. As an intimate of the family, no servant in this house would have denied this request, and the maid quickly took Caroline upstairs.

Georgiana stood before her full-length mirror, and turned to Caroline without surprise when she knocked and entered. 'You must tell me,' she cried, 'does this dress make me appear to be . . . young?'

'You are young,' Caroline said fondly, 'but the dress makes you appear to be a beautiful young . . . lady.'

And it did. The blue silk, sprigged with tiny flowers embroidered in grey, was perfect for Georgiana, bringing out the flush of youth in her perfect skin, heightening the dark blue of her eyes. The bodice was the perfect shape, rounded as it moved from neck to shoulder, with a small vee in the centre to produce just the suggestion of a décolletage.

The gown flowed out over Georgiana's hips, giving the suggestion of a slightly fuller figure than the girl had. Fine-boned and slim, Georgiana had not the current fashionable figure, which tended towards Caroline's rounder curves, but she moved with such grace that no one would dare criticise.

'That blue,' Caroline said, 'is brighter than any colour I've seen you wear before, but it suits you very well, my dear. Did you select this gown, or did your brother offer his suggestion?'

Georgiana looked down shyly. 'It was my own choice, Miss Bingley.'

'You have chosen well.' Caroline smiled, pleased. The girl obviously had a good instinct, one which would serve her well in the higher circles she'd soon move amongst. Her hairstyle, too, was the slightest bit daring, displaying her long neck and her small ears. In the lobe of each rested a single pearl.

Georgiana picked up her long gloves, and turned to Caroline with an impish smile. 'Well? Do I pass muster?'

Caroline smiled, although she was surprised. 'Why you should suppose I have come here to inspect you is beyond me! I would never interfere in something so important as one's own selection of clothing.'

Georgiana gave her a smile Caroline could not interpret, and led the way downstairs. *Really,* Caroline thought, *she grows more like her brother every day. I will have to ensure that she remains feminine, with none of what is so present in characters such as Eliza Bennet.*

Mr Darcy appeared at his study door as they reached the front hall. He gave both of them a cursory glance and, as he showed little if any enthusiasm for the evening's entertainment to begin, Caroline said brightly, 'Is the carriage ready?'

'Yes, madam,' the footman said, and produced everyone's coats and Mr Darcy's hat.

Caroline could not help but wonder why Mr Darcy did not swell with pride when he entered Eleanor's house with the two ladies, one on each arm. Instead, he put on the cold, haughty look that Caroline remembered so well from Hertfordshire. But what had been amusing during an assembly in Meryton was not at all funny here. She tightened her grip on his arm and beamed widely enough, as she saw Eleanor approach, to make up for his dour expression.

'Welcome, friends,' Eleanor said warmly. If she saw anything amiss in Mr Darcy's less-than-effusive greeting, she showed no sign.

'My dear,' she said, taking Georgiana's hands in hers. 'I am so happy to see you.'

'Thank you, Lady Amesbury,' Georgiana said shyly, curtseying.

'I am very much looking forward,' Eleanor continued, 'to hearing your opinions of the musicians who will perform tonight. I knew when I heard you play that you have a discerning ear, and I suspect there is a discerning mind to go with it.'

Mr Darcy sent Eleanor a sharp glance, as Georgiana blushed and looked down.

'There is a little time before the concert will begin,' Eleanor said. 'Please.' She swept her arm towards the room and the people gathered there, sitting or standing in little groups, conversing.

Mr Darcy took his sister ahead into the large room, while Eleanor indicated, with a hand on Caroline's arm, that she wished her friend to linger a moment.

'She,' Eleanor whispered, 'is lovelier than I remember, and I recall being very impressed the last time I saw her.'

Caroline saw with satisfaction that Georgiana, in her restrained gown, did indeed stand out among the crowd. Most women wore either pastel or dark colours, but even among the colourful crowd, it was Georgiana, with her excellent posture, who caught the eye.

Speaking of catching the eye, she saw a familiar figure making his way over to the Darcys, apparently wishing for an introduction to Georgiana: Mr Tryphon. For a moment Caroline felt poised, like a bird extending its neck in preparation to take flight; held back by Eleanor, pulled by Mr Tryphon.

She took a step closer, as he bowed to Mr Darcy and then turned glowing eyes on Georgiana. Mr Darcy made the introduction, and while Caroline could not hear what he said, she observed he seemed to have no reservations about this one of her friends, for his manner was easy, his features relaxed.

Caroline only discovered she'd taken another step towards the little group when Eleanor's hand, still on her arm, brought her to a standstill. She wouldn't have progressed much further, for what she saw next froze her limbs into immobility. Mr Tryphon kissed Georgiana's hand, bowing low as he did so, his gaze slanting up to her face, his eyes warm.

'I am so glad,' Eleanor said, seemingly unaware of Caroline's shock, 'that you were able to persuade Mr Darcy to bring his sister. She will meet ever so many people who will be of great benefit to her.'

Caroline turned to her friend. 'Indeed,' she said faintly, before looking back at the little tableau. Mr Tryphon was standing upright again, conversing with Mr Darcy. Georgiana stood by the two men, Mr Darcy holding her arm protectively in his. Her eyes were fixed on Mr Tryphon. She smiled again as both men turned to her shorter form for a moment, and then Mr Tryphon bowed and left them. He headed towards Eleanor and Caroline, and the latter inhaled, her first air in some time, she suspected, although she had not been aware of holding her breath.

Mr Tryphon beamed at Eleanor. 'She accepted!' he said. 'The first two dances!'

'I was sure she would,' Eleanor said warmly. 'For who indeed can resist you, Stephen?'

Their gazes locked for a moment, and Caroline suddenly felt like a small child whose parents have just alluded to a world they alone share, a world that cannot be comprehended by a mere child. But then Stephen turned to her, seemingly noticing her for the first time.

'Caroline! How lovely to see you.' He raised her hand to his lips instead of bowing low over it, and his lips brushed her skin with only the briefest, lightest touch.

'Mr Tryphon,' she said, and curtseyed. Her calm, almost bored tone, did nothing, she was pleased to hear, to reveal the tumult of thoughts in her head. He had asked Georgiana for the first two dances? That meant Mr Darcy must have agreed to remain at the party after the concert was over. Earlier, Mr Darcy had adamantly refused to even consider delaying his sister's departure from this house for a single moment after the last note of the concert had ceased to ring in the room. And, Mr Tryphon always danced with Caroline for the first two dances.

Caroline stood in a daze as Eleanor and Mr Tryphon spoke. She knew not what they discussed, and if they attempted to include her in the conversation, she was unaware. Eventually, Eleanor took Caroline's arm, and she came out of her daze to observe that Mr Tryphon had moved away and was once again in the Darcys' company.

'Come, my dear,' Eleanor said. 'The concert is about to begin, and I know you will wish for a good seat, so that you can observe all that is going on as well as hear it.'

Although her friend's tone was gentle, was that a malicious light in Eleanor's eyes? But why would there be? Still, as Eleanor guided Caroline to a chair resting just behind where the Darcys and Mr Tryphon sat in the front row, Caroline couldn't help but believe that, for some reason, Eleanor felt a sort of triumphant glee at Caroline's expense.

The concert began with Maestro Daniel Scott Allen, the pianist, playing a concerto, accompanied by a string quartet. At any other time, Caroline would have been ecstatic to have the opportunity to observe the technique of a musician of this level of expertise. Certainly Georgiana was not wasting the opportunity, for she leaned forward to better see his hands, not turning away even when Mr Tryphon pointed out particularly difficult passages or the fancy flourishes the pianist appeared to enjoy. Georgiana nodded in response to each comment, and when the man completed the concerto, she cast a beaming smile on Mr Tryphon as if he, and he alone, had made this musical experience possible for her.

Caroline could not recall a single note, or even who the composer had been, for she'd been too intent on watching Mr Tryphon as he leaned towards Georgiana's slight form. She'd been able to hear practically every word he'd whispered in her ear, and was glad that each comment had been focused solely on the music and the pianist. Why, then, did Georgiana glow as she smiled at him now? If anyone was to be thanked for her presence here, it should be Caroline, for without her efforts to convince Mr Darcy to bring his sister, both Darcys would even now be sitting at home, spending a dull evening together.

Eleanor rose from where she sat on Mr Darcy's other side, to thank the pianist and introduce Bettina Squires, the soprano, who came out to enthusiastic applause. Caroline automatically patted her palms together, her attention momentarily removed from those who sat in front of her. Eleanor was such a gracious hostess, and she thanked her guests very prettily. Caroline tried to catch her friend's eye as she resumed her seat and the soprano prepared to sing, but Eleanor's gaze rested fondly on Georgiana and Stephen. Caroline felt very small all of a sudden, as if she existed inside a tiny soap bubble, its fragile walls keeping her isolated from everyone else in the room. Even the soprano's voice, a powerful one, appeared wispy and distant, so that Caroline could hardly hear the song.

After an eternity, the concert ended. The chairs for the audience were removed, and the quartet began tuning their violins and other instruments in preparation for the dancing.

'Was that not truly sublime?' Eleanor asked.

Caroline blinked, and discovered that she, and her chair, rested in solitary splendour in the middle of the room. She hastily stood so a footman could take the chair, and turned to her friend.

'Which song was your favourite?' Eleanor continued.

Caroline made some reply but she knew not what she said, as she watched Mr Tryphon tuck Georgiana's hand through his arm to lead her to their places for the dance.

'I am surprised,' Eleanor said, 'to hear you say you preferred the lieder, for there was not one on the programme.'

Caroline wrenched her eyes away from Mr Tryphon and gaped at her friend.

'I had thought you better educated in music,' Eleanor said, and now there was no mistaking the malice in her eyes.

'Why,' Caroline gasped, 'would you speak so to me? I can see no motivation other than a wish to make me appear foolish.'

Eleanor smiled nastily, and opened her mouth to say something, but at that moment Mr Darcy appeared at Caroline's side. Eleanor's unpleasant expression vanished so quickly and completely that Caroline had to wonder if it truly had been on her friend's face, and Eleanor gave a little laugh. 'Forgive me,' she said, taking Caroline's hand, 'my words were sharper than I intended, no doubt due to the fatigue that overwhelms me now, after all the effort of preparing for this evening's entertainment.' She swayed a little on her feet, looking to Mr Darcy, who placed a hand on her elbow to steady her.

'Oh, thank you, sir,' Eleanor said in a faint voice, and as he led her to a chair at the side of the room, she looked back at Caroline. 'We will speak later,' she said, her voice somehow stronger. 'I long to have one of our intimate little chats, dear one.'

Caroline stood, unable to move, until she saw Mr Darcy leave Eleanor after asking one of the servants to bring her something to drink. He then returned to Caroline. 'May I have the honour of your hand for these two dances?' he asked.

Caroline let out a sobbing breath, and with it came all the fears and confusions she'd experienced since entering this house that evening. She let them fall away, imagining them flowing down her person and across the floor, to vanish in the shadows away from the lamps. Smiling at Mr Darcy, her spirits animated, she said, 'I'd be delighted.' Resting her gloved hand on his, she followed him to the end of the lines of men and women, taking her place across from him.

As the dance progressed, Caroline was glad she knew the steps well enough that she didn't need to concentrate on where her feet took her. Ignoring her feet meant she had almost enough concentration to keep both Mr Darcy and Mr Tryphon in view. Almost enough, though, meant that she quickly grew breathless and dizzy, as she turned her head in ways current fashion in dancing did not approve of at all. Mr Darcy, she thought, was looking at her with concern, so she flashed him a brilliant smile, and then, as she moved between him and the next gentleman in the line, she glanced over to where Georgiana and Mr Tryphon were. Georgiana, like all the women, was moving diagonally between gentlemen, while the men stood still, one arm outstretched, the hand ready to provide the pivot point for the turn the ladies would make in the next part of the dance. Georgiana, as always, moved gracefully, her head held elegantly atop her long neck. She'd passed Mr Tryphon and bestowed a smile on the gentleman beside him. Caroline had been introduced to that particular man, one who was well known for his fondness for the ladies and the ability of his wife to ignore his dalliances. He, jaded though he was, could not resist the innocent beauty of Georgiana's smile, and as Caroline watched, his cheeks reddened and he smiled back without any sign of the usual hunger his eyes revealed when he looked at most women. Mr Tryphon, Caroline noted, had also seen the gentleman's reaction to Georgiana, but instead of frowning, he looked almost proud, as if her smile somehow reflected well on him. Caroline was certain he had never looked so proud when he was with her, and so, as she made the turn and returned to the place across from Mr Darcy, she smiled even more brilliantly and said to him, 'Your sister dances beautifully, Mr Darcy. I am surprised that you were willing to permit her to dance with a man you have known for such a brief time as Mr Tryphon.'

He raised a brow. 'He is a particular friend of yours, is he not, Miss Bingley? Surely I could seek no better reference than that!'

She stared at him a moment, wondering if there could possibly be a touch of sarcasm in his voice, but his countenance showed only the polite interest used by all couples when they conversed during a dance. Glancing back at Mr Tryphon, she saw him say something that won him a laugh from Georgiana. His response to that revealed far more than polite interest, his eyes fixed on that lovely young face, and Caroline had to swallow suddenly to keep an acidic burn arising from her stomach.

Resolved to look no more down the line of dancers, she fixed her eyes on Mr Darcy, admiring his erect carriage, the noble tilt of his head as he turned, the way he stood at least half a head taller than almost all the other gentlemen. There was no gathering, not in any court in the whole world, in which he would be out of place. A surge of pride welled up inside her, as she pictured herself on his arm, equally at home in those royal palaces.

At the end of the dance, Caroline took his arm, and instead of returning her to a chair, Mr Darcy permitted her to accompany him as he walked to where his sister stood. As they approached, Mr Tryphon bent his head to whisper something into Georgiana's ear, his lips close enough that Caroline could see a wisp of her hair dance from the movement of his breath. Mr Darcy must have observed this also, for she felt his forearm tighten under her fingertips.

As Mr Tryphon moved back from Georgiana, she turned and spotted her brother. Instantly her face lit up, and Caroline wondered how she could have thought her earlier smiles revealed any joy at all compared to this one. 'Brother,' Georgiana cried, 'I am so happy to be here. Thank you again for permitting me to attend.'

He smiled in turn, never able to be severe when in her presence. 'I am glad you enjoyed the concert so much, my dearest, but it is time we returned home.'

Instantly her expression clouded. 'Must we leave so soon? Lady Amesbury told me that Mr Scott Allen specifically requested that I play for him.' She clasped her hands in front of her breast. 'It is too great an honour, I know I shall play very ill indeed, but I cannot refuse such a great musician.'

As if the sound of her name had drawn her close, Eleanor stepped to Mr Darcy's other side. Taking his arm, she looked beseechingly at him. 'Please, it is yet early. And the maestro truly does wish to hear Georgiana.'

'Really? And how did his request come about? He cannot have known about Georgiana before this evening, and the concert was for him to play for us, not for his audience to play for him.'

Eleanor looked down, seemingly a little embarrassed. 'It is my doing, I confess.' She lifted her head, darting a saucy smile at him. 'But you cannot fault me, for he asked me who would be in attendance this evening, and I could not resist singing Miss Darcy's praises. Indeed, no one who has heard her play could possibly resist speaking in glowing terms about her delicate touch on the keys and the emotion she can draw from them.'

Georgiana rested a hand on her brother's chest, clutching the lapel of his forest green jacket. 'Please, the maestro is the best musician I have ever heard, it would mean so much to me to hear his suggestions on how I can improve.'

Mr Darcy frowned at Eleanor. 'I am not in the habit of being blind-sided. In the future, you will be certain to speak with me in any matter affecting Miss Darcy.'

Looking abashed, she nodded.

'And when is this command performance to take place?' he asked.

Eleanor truly did seem subdued. 'It can be now, if that is your wish,' she said, her voice flat, without any of the merriment it usually held.

'Very well.' Ignoring Mr Tryphon, Mr Darcy took Georgiana's hand, practically pushing Eleanor away as he slipped it through his arm. Turning to Caroline, who still clutched his other arm, he nodded. 'Miss Bingley.'

Recognising her cue, she released his arm and curtseyed. 'Mr Darcy.' Eleanor and the Darcys moved through the crowd towards a room Caroline knew held another pianoforte, leaving Caroline alone with Mr Tryphon.

They regarded one another for a moment. Their former easy camaraderie appeared to have evaporated, and the silence became awkward, but Caroline was determined to not be the first to speak. It appeared that he also had made the same resolution, but he was no match for her.

At length his resolve, as she knew it would, crumbled. 'I trust you enjoyed the performances?' he said, looking in her direction but not meeting her eyes. She chose not to respond and rather than dealing with further silence, he hurried on. 'This is yet another of Eleanor's most successful parties, but I thought the concert was a high point that even she will be hard pressed to top in the future.'

Realising that if she ignored him any longer she would be opening herself to accusations of impolite behaviour, she raised her chin. 'I very much enjoyed the performances.' Then, fixing him with an unblinking regard, she added, 'Some more than others.'

He coloured slightly, and she knew her barb had hit home. With the total lack of dissembling that she so admired in him, because it meant he could be open about his feelings for her instead of hiding everything under a society-imposed façade, his expression changed to one of shame. 'I deserve that. I have behaved abominably towards you, and you had every reason to expect more from me. Can you forgive me?'

'I don't know,' she said, looking abruptly away, as if something to the side was far more interesting than anything he might have to say. She did, however, permit a small trace of thaw to enter into her voice.

'I acted as I did at Eleanor's request,' he said, and at that her attention returned to him. 'Oh no,' he added when he saw her horrified expression, 'she did not ask me to do anything at all that could hurt you, dearest Miss Bingley. She merely wished me to ensure that Miss Darcy felt welcomed in her house, and that I act in such a way as to ensure her comfort and enjoyment during the evening. Any fault is mine alone, for I fear I went beyond what was required, and in ensuring Miss Darcy's happiness I ignorantly trampled upon your own.' He held out a hand.

She drew in a breath, and the action raised her bosom so that it filled her décolletage before the exhalation let it retreat to its usual position. His long hair was worn loose as usual, and errant curls framed his face, giving him the appearance of a mischievous boy who has been caught out but knows his charm will prevent any real punishment. Part of her wanted to let him see that he was an adult, and so his actions did have true consequences, but his smile widened, he tilted his head to the side, and he permitted his outstretched hand to just barely brush her forearm. Even through her glove, a jolt of heat ran up into her throat. Unable for a moment to breathe, she sighed, taking in an even deeper breath before letting the air out, enjoying how his eyes strayed below her neck before quickly returning to her face.

'Please,' he said, 'my future happiness rests in your hands.'

She lifted her chin again, revelling in the moment. She'd always known of the power a woman could hold over a man, but never before had she used it so blatantly. At the same time a small flicker of disappointment flared in her mind, and she realised she was disappointed that even Mr Tryphon could fall prey to such tactics. Still, he was her friend and the only man who, even though she loved Mr Darcy, had helped her understand the sensations some books had described.

Mr Tryphon cleared his throat, and Caroline realised he'd been waiting for some time to learn if she would bestow forgiveness on him. She stared at him for another moment, gratified to see his face lose colour, for he could only fear that she could not accept what he had done. She smiled then, and said, 'You are my friend. I cannot despise you.'

He seized her hand and raised it to his lips, and if his touch on her arm had seemed warm, it was nothing compared to the fire that surged through her from the heat of his lips and the moisture of his breath. He then turned her hand and pressed his mouth to her palm, and she came the closest she had ever come to fainting.

Caroline prided herself on never having fainted, scorning those who were so fragile they lost consciousness instead of facing what life chose to throw at them. She gritted her teeth and stared firmly off into the distance until the dizziness passed and she was able to smile at Mr Tryphon as he reluctantly released her hand.

As they stood together, chatting as amiably as they ever had, Caroline heard a surge in the conversation at the far end of the room, and looked over to see the Darcys, Eleanor, and the maestro leaving the room where they'd been closeted while Georgiana played for the maestro.

Mr Tryphon hurried away from her, without even bowing, and she stood frozen, bewildered by the sudden change. What was going on? She had forgiven him, even though he had treated her very badly. Did that mean he felt it was all right to continue to treat her badly?

She resolved that her friendship with him was no longer important, but at the thought a cold wind arose in her chest, and it dissipated only when she recalled the heat of his mouth on her palm. Never before had she encountered a contact that so completely joined another person's body to hers. Suddenly all that had happened, her dismay at seeing his attentions to Georgiana made sense. She was jealous!

But how could that be, when it was Mr Darcy she loved? She thought again of what the books had said about love, about the shortness of breath and dizziness it could cause. Those sensations came over her in the presence of only one man, and he was not Mr Darcy.

Caroline moved to where an empty settee stood by the side of the room, and sank into it, heedless that her gown was twisted beneath her and so would wrinkle. How could she be in love with Mr Tryphon?

She realised she was sitting with her shoulders slumped, and resolutely raised herself into the proper posture. Standing, she smoothed her gown over her hips. This did not matter. Loving Mr Tryphon could change nothing. She would still marry Mr Darcy. Most women, she knew, loved men other than their husbands. And, if Eleanor's parties were anything to judge by, plenty of men loved women other than their wives. Caroline and Mr Darcy, of course, would learn to love each other and so would not be tempted by other people. Somehow, Caroline suspected she would never be able to stop loving Mr Tryphon. It didn't matter. Caroline would never be unfaithful to Mr Darcy, just as he would never be unfaithful to her.

She looked across the room, to where Georgiana was speaking in an animated fashion, closely attended by her brother and Mr Tryphon. Just the sight of him tightened her throat. He was not so tall as Mr Darcy, nor were his shoulders as broad, but his figure was manly and elegant, and it drew her eyes in a way Mr Darcy's form never had. She would, Caroline decided, permit herself to enjoy his company, but not one sign of her feelings would show. She would continue as she had, prodding Mr Darcy to propose. Nothing could stand in the way of that marriage, for it represented the only way Caroline could improve her standing in life, and that was the only ambition she could affect. All her education, all her intelligence and other accomplishments were powerless to do anything but assist her in making the most advantageous marriage. Mr Tryphon, despite his fine manners and costly clothing, had never mentioned an estate, a club membership, or any of the trappings that went with being a wealthy young man about town. Even if he did have an estate, it could be nothing compared to Pemberley. No, no matter how much her heart urged her towards him, it was with Mr Darcy that her future lay, and nothing could be permitted to prevent her from taking that path.

Chapter Nine

⤬

The next evening, when the Bingleys and the Darcys gathered for dinner, Georgiana could speak of nothing but the maestro. Indeed, Caroline had never heard the girl speak so many words in one evening. She leaned over to Louisa, who sat nearby, and said, 'Miss Darcy needs to be reminded that a young person does not monopolise the conversation in this manner.'

Louisa appeared surprised, but said only, 'The maestro's compliments offer a taste of what life has in store for her. A young woman as lovely as she, and with the fortune she possesses, will never lack the acclaim of society. She will learn, and no doubt will become as jaded as any of us.'

'I am not jaded!' Caroline said, seemingly in an overly loud voice, for everyone turned to look at her. She concentrated on her food, until they returned to their own meals and conversations. 'Whatever do you mean?' she asked Louisa, more decorously.

'I think it would be wearisome to be always in the spotlight.' Louisa stabbed a forkful of duck. 'I would not exchange my position in the world for any amount of titles or honours.' She raised the duck, dripping with orange sauce, to her lips.

'I am speechless,' Caroline said. 'How can you say that, you who married for wealth and position? How can you deny that a larger estate or richer purse would not tempt you if you were not yet wed?'

Louisa raised her napkin to her mouth. 'I can deny it. I married as I had to, for the family and for myself. I did well. But I am not going to spend the rest of my life always wanting more than I have. I am not going to spend one second wishing for what I do not have. I have Mr Hurst and I prefer to focus on all that I have achieved instead of on what I have not.'

Caroline thought for a moment, covering her tangled thoughts by taking a bite of duck herself. *Self-sacrifice—that is, after all, the role of a woman. That is what I am doing also. By denying my feelings for Mr Tryphon and resolving to accept Mr Darcy, for whom I feel deep affection, certainly.* Her thoughts wandered for a moment, as she realised how pale her feelings for Mr Darcy were compared to what she felt for Mr Tryphon. *However, by accepting Mr Darcy, I am doing what is best for the family. A link to the foremost family in Derbyshire will greatly benefit the Bingleys. And when the link is two-fold, when Charles marries Georgiana, there will be nothing to stand in our way. Soon, the Bingleys will be spoken of with as much respect and envy as are the Darcys.*

'I am happy for you,' she said at last to Louisa. 'I envy your ability to attain happiness, and admire what you have done for the family.'

Louisa scraped up the last orange sauce with her last piece of meat. 'You will find happiness too.' Dropping her fork, she turned to Caroline and took both her hands. Looking sidelong down the table to where Mr Darcy sat, she added, 'I suspect it will not be so very difficult for you to find.'

The sisters laughed, and suddenly Caroline was happy. Why would anyone be sorry to lose Mr Tryphon when a man such as Darcy was to be hers? No, happiness was not so very difficult to find at all.

Later, when the ladies retired to the parlour, Georgiana shyly told Caroline and Louisa that the maestro had offered to give her some lessons on the pianoforte. 'He is to be in London some weeks longer, staying with Lady Amesbury. He told me that if I come to her home every other day at five o'clock, accompanied by my brother, he will teach me.' She clasped her hands together in joy. 'Oh, just think how much I shall learn. And, how honoured I am that such a man would take notice of one such as me.'

'Nonsense,' Caroline said, although she was surprised to hear of this offer. Why had Eleanor not mentioned it? 'You are a very good musician, and a good teacher is always delighted to find a student worthy of his efforts.'

The gentlemen joined them at that point, and Caroline studied Mr Darcy curiously. Had he truly agreed to his sister returning to Eleanor's house on a regular basis? And why did the lessons have to take place there? The Darcys' pianoforte was a very fine instrument. If the lessons were held in the Darcy house, Mr Darcy would not have to be inconvenienced by the necessity of escorting his sister to Eleanor's home.

She was called by Mr Hurst to make up a table for cards, and it was not until later, when she and the Hursts returned to Grosvenor Street, that she had further time for reflection.

Surely, Eleanor knew having the lessons take place in her house would be inconvenient. There would be the sounds caused by the musicians on the piano, and Mr Darcy could not be left entirely to his own devices while he waited to take Georgiana home again.

Mr Darcy, his own devices—slowly a thought grew. He would need to be entertained. Perhaps that was why Eleanor was so interested in the younger sister of one of her less-frequent guests. Eleanor was at present unmarried, enjoying the scandal of hosting so many entertainments all on her own. Could she be thinking of the benefits of taking another husband?—A wealthy husband?

Surely that could not be true. Eleanor had plenty of her own money, it showed in every facet of her home, in every meticulously planned detail of her parties. She had no need for a man in her life, as she had often told Caroline. A man would only tie her down, prevent her from partaking in all the enjoyments she could grasp in her own two hands.

Caroline got ready for bed, calling Genney to brush out her hair. The seed, once planted, would not go away. Did Eleanor have designs on Mr Darcy? The more she considered this, the more convinced, and the angrier, she became.

What a conniving minx Eleanor was! How dare she set her cap at a man such as Mr Darcy? True, she was titled, even though the title wasn't hers by birth, but only by marriage. Caroline wasn't exactly sure how many times her friend had been married, but she knew there were at least two husbands who had died, leaving the lovely young widow alone with her grief. And her title. *But that isn't enough, not for Lady Amesbury. She has to claim a new man, and not only that, he is the man she knows is her friend's intended!* How many times, Caroline wondered now, had she spoken of her long-awaited marriage? And how many times had Eleanor reassured her that Mr Darcy would speak, that he was only awaiting the right moment? Did Eleanor now think that because Caroline had not yet secured the engagement, that Mr Darcy was free to be pursued?

'Leave off,' she snapped at Genney, who was tidying the dressing table. Genney's eyes grew moist and Caroline, knowing how easily the maid could become sulky, quickly said, 'I am sorry, I did not mean to speak so harshly. It is only that I am very tired and wish to be alone now.'

Genney nodded, curtseyed without looking at Caroline, and scurried out of the room. Caroline wondered for a moment if Genney's services were truly worth having to deal with such a temperamental creature, but then, remembering that all the French were overly emotional, put the matter out of her mind.

* * *

Thinking about conniving minxes reminded Caroline of Elizabeth Bennet, and that reminded her Jane was in town, and she hadn't yet told Louisa and Mr Darcy. The next afternoon she requested their presence in the smaller breakfast room, knowing Charles was otherwise occupied.

'I realise,' Caroline said, after having shown them Jane's letter, 'that the chance of Charles meeting her unexpectedly is extremely small, given the part of town she is in, but I believe we still need a plan of action.'

Mr Darcy's countenance had gone completely still when he first heard mention of Jane Bennet. No doubt he was remembering the danger that lady presented to his good friend but why didn't he immediately speak up to denounce this new tactic in what was obviously a Bennet ploy to entrap Charles?

'Mr Darcy,' she said loudly, 'I can see that this news has greatly distressed you. Do you have any suggestions for what we ought to do?'

His head jerked up and he stared at her without comprehension for a moment. Her disquiet grew. Clearly the woman he had been thinking of had not been Jane Bennet. Was he reliving memories of her sister?

With a small shake of his head, as if to push aside any thoughts that were consuming him, he said, 'Surely there is no need for concern. Miss Bennet and Charles will not move in the same social circles. It is highly unlikely that their paths will cross.'

Caroline and Louisa looked at each other. 'You are correct,' Louisa said. 'People who live in Cheapside are not often to be found in our section of the city!'

'Although,' Mr Darcy added, 'I suppose you must call on her, Miss Bingley, since she has written to you.' His eyes, dark and unreadable, focused on Caroline.

She sighed. 'Yes, I must. A person in my position can do no less, although I do not relish the prospect.'

'I suppose I must accompany you,' Louisa said with an even bigger sigh.

'Perhaps not.' Caroline knew how brave she must appear to be. 'I will not ask you, sister, to share in this burden. It was I, after all, whom Jane thought of as her particular friend.'

'I thought you enjoyed her company,' Mr Darcy said. 'Was your behaviour in her presence all an artifice?'

She thought she heard disapproval in his voice. 'No, of course not.' Then, thinking that sounded too sharp, she added, 'Jane truly is a sweet creature. But after a time I discovered there was little of substance in her mind. A woman raised without the benefit of an education and all the experiences that my upbringing gave to me has much less to offer in the way of conversation.'

'I am surprised.' He rose to his feet and wandered over to the window, which looked out into a grey fog that revealed only the occasional glimpse of the trees that stood not far from this side of the house. 'I found that both the elder Miss Bennets had much of interest to say, and that their conversation ranged over a most impressive range of topics.'

Caroline glanced at Louisa, unsure of what to say. Fortunately, Louisa spoke up. 'Fascinating conversation or not, I am certain we are all in agreement that Charles must not learn that she is in town.'

'Yes,' Caroline said, glad that the focus was no longer on fine minds, to go with fine eyes.

Mr Darcy turned back to face the room again. 'Is that truly necessary? I confess I am uncomfortable with a falsehood of that magnitude.'

Caroline waved her hand dismissively. 'Nonsense. It is not a falsehood unless he asks if Jane is in town, and we say she is not. All we will be doing is not passing on a piece of information, and in her letter Jane did not request that I inform Charles of her presence here. Your conscience, Mr Darcy, need suffer no qualms.'

He still appeared uncertain, and before she could stop herself, she burst out, 'Why you are spending even the smallest moment in concern for people like the Bennets is beyond me. They are nothing to those of our standing.'

His eyes hardened, but having begun, she had to finish it. 'Fine eyes notwithstanding, you know their situation in life is beneath ours. You have said so yourself. I cannot believe you would risk my brother's future happiness out of some misguided concern for people who are not worthy of a moment's consideration from any of us.'

He seemed, for a moment, to look back into his own head instead of at her and Louisa. At length he returned to his chair and sank down into it. 'You are right,' he said, his voice now firm. 'We will say nothing of Miss Bennet's presence in town to anyone. In fact, it would be wise if the three of us did not speak of this again.' Placing his hands on his knees, he stood up. Bowing to the two women, he left the room.

*   *   *

During the next week Georgiana attended her piano lessons with the maestro, accompanied by her brother. Eleanor arranged another soirée at which the maestro would perform, and Georgiana pleaded to attend. Mr Darcy agreed, although Caroline could tell he was not happy.

Caroline had not seen nor communicated with Eleanor since her real-isation that her friend was after Mr Darcy. Caroline observed him when he returned from each lesson and saw no signs that he was becoming smitten. Feeling somewhat better, and wondering if she had perhaps done her friend a disservice, she decided to attend Eleanor's concert and act as if nothing had changed.

When she arrived, in company with her brother and the Darcys, Elea-nor's greeting was as effusive as always. Her own must have been a little chilly despite her efforts, for Eleanor stepped back and gave her a search-ing look before turning to greet Mr Darcy and Georgiana.

During the evening, Eleanor stuck to Mr Darcy's side until Caroline felt she must rescue him. She moved across the crowded room, without knowing what she would say or do, until she approached them and heard him speaking about Georgiana's lessons.

'I am sorry,' he was saying, 'but I will be unable to accompany my sister in the future. I have business to complete in town before I depart for Pemberley. If the lessons are to continue, Mr Scott Allen will need to attend Georgiana in my house. I will inform him that I will place a carriage at his disposal, so that this will not inconvenience him overly much. I thank you, again, for your generosity in offering your home and your pianoforte for my sister's use.' He bowed and before Eleanor could respond in any way, stalked away.

Caroline's anger had been building, at Eleanor for making Mr Darcy miserable with her constant attention, and for attempting to steal a man she knew was the intended of her supposedly dear friend. Fortunately Mr Darcy was much too intelligent to be misled by Eleanor's wiles.

Her anger withered and died when she looked back from watching Mr Darcy walk away, and saw her friend. Eleanor stood completely still, her small form revealing none of the vivacity and gay spirits that usually caused her to be seen as a person taller than she actually was. Her shoulders sagged, her head was bowed, but her eyes still rested on Mr Darcy's back as he made his way through the throngs of people. Her eyes were moist and Caroline wondered, with shock, if she was about to weep.

She took a step towards Eleanor, torn by the need to comfort and the need to confront. Her long-term affection won the battle. 'My dear,' she said, taking a step closer and holding out a hand.

Eleanor looked up and saw her. For a moment, Caroline felt a shadow overcome her at the fear she saw in her friend's eyes. 'Caroline!' Eleanor cried and took her friend's hand. 'Isn't this just the loveliest party I have ever given? Everyone is so jovial, and so appreciative of my efforts to provide entertainment for my friends. And Mrs Deaverson has outdone herself; truly she is a marvel of a cook, even if I did select the menu myself. And the music,' Eleanor clasped her hands at her breast and looked up at the ceiling in a paroxysm of elation, 'Mr Scott Allen is a gem, is he not? So talented, and so willing to share it with the few friends I invite to hear him play.'

'He is,' Caroline said. She was still uncertain of what to say or of how to react to this friend who, even though she appeared much as she always did, was apparently adept at hiding her true feelings. Caroline was certain she had seen fear in Eleanor's eyes, and a great sorrow in the stillness of her body for those few moments. If Eleanor could hide that so successfully, did that mean that her affection for Caroline was also just another of the many roles Eleanor could play?

Eleanor tucked Caroline's hand through her arm and they walked together towards the supper tables. 'Ah,' she said. 'I see Stephen is once again at Miss Darcy's side. Such a dear boy, that one, and so conscientious whenever I ask him to carry out some little request. Look at how Georgiana has blossomed since she first came to my little soirée. She looks like quite a different person, no longer the shy, unopened bud.'

Caroline sent a sharp glance at Eleanor's choice of words, but her friend seemed oblivious of saying anything out of the ordinary. Not for the first time, Caroline wondered how Charles felt at seeing another man so monopolise Georgiana's time during a social engagement. Searching the room for him, she saw him sitting in a small group of younger people, seemingly quite relaxed and happy to be conversing with them. Charles was so good-natured and it wasn't in him to be jealous. Still, Georgiana, once she was out, would be a most sought-after prize by many young men and some not so young, too. With her lovely figure and elegant manners, and her fortune, she would not long remain unmarried. *I had better speak to Charles and urge him to make his intentions known. If he does not speak soon, he may risk losing his future happiness.*

Mr Darcy, who had apparently waited until Caroline was no longer in Eleanor's presence, appeared at her side as soon as Eleanor was called away by a servant to deal with some crisis in the kitchen. He announced he was taking Georgiana home. Now that she knew he was true to her, Caroline relaxed in his presence and she even dared to rest her hand on his chest for a moment, as she moved closer to him, looking up into his face with a lively smile. 'I will see you tomorrow?' she asked.

He stepped back a little, and shook his head. 'Unfortunately, I will not have that pleasure. I have a number of matters which require my attention.'

'I am sorry.' Caroline remembered her goal of showing her affection more fully. 'I shall miss you terribly.' She smiled again, and fluttered her eyelashes, just a little, nothing that could be construed as flirtatious, but enough that he cocked his head and gazed at her with rapt attention.

'Do you have something in your eye?' he said. 'Do you require assistance?'

She laughed, even though she felt a blush coming on, and swatted him lightly on his shoulder. 'No, of course not. I cannot think why you would ask such a thing.'

He stared at her a long moment longer, and then bowed and left to collect his sister. Caroline stood in the same spot, feeling the overly wide smile still stretching her lips, as she watched him speak briefly to Mr Tryphon before hustling Georgiana away. Mr Tryphon turned and caught sight of Caroline. He apparently thought the smile was for him, because he quickly made his way to her side.

'At last,' he said. 'I am freed from my responsibility and can spend my time as I wish.'

For a moment, a dark thought entered her mind. If Eleanor was brazen enough to chase after Mr Darcy for his money, could Mr Tryphon not have equally base motives for spending time with Miss Darcy? 'You did not seem overly burdened by your responsibility.'

He raised his eyebrows in surprise. 'My dear Miss Bingley! Surely you cannot think I enjoy spending time away from you? Please, you must not think so unkindly of me.'

She looked into his warm brown eyes, and saw only the open countenance of a young man newly come to town and not yet acquainted with the convoluted relationships that sometimes existed between people. She envied his innocence. What was wrong with her, that she could think so unkindly about not one but two of her dearest friends? 'I could never think unkindly of you.'

His face brightened, and he took her hand to kiss it, but she pulled it away. A woman about to become engaged to Mr Darcy could not be so free with other men. 'I think, though,' she continued, 'that you will no longer be burdened by that particular responsibility. I suspect Mr Darcy will not allow his sister to attend any more concerts held at private homes.'

Mr Tryphon said nothing, and Caroline was shocked to see something of Eleanor's fear in his eyes. But how could that be? Why would either of them fear the loss of either or both Darcys at a party? Mr Darcy had rarely accepted the invitations in the past, so nothing would change. Could her suspicions have some basis in fact after all? 'Why,' she asked, realising Mr Tryphon was less adept than his hostess at hiding his emotions, 'are you so dismayed that you will not have to dance attendance on Miss Darcy? I thought,' and despite herself, her voice sharpened, 'you disliked the duty.'

'I do. I did,' he said, but the words seemed to have appeared automatically, without anything behind them. He stared into the distance, his eyes unfocused. Suddenly he snapped his attention back to her. 'I am delighted, of course, for it means I can spend more time with you.'

She looked at him with scepticism.

'Truly,' he said. 'I know I have appeared distant towards you, but I know also that you are too kind a person to punish me now by pretending a harshness your gentle heart cannot feel.' Suddenly, he fell to his knees in front of her. 'You know how I feel,' he said, reaching a hand up towards her face. 'I have told you, I have even committed my love on paper. Tell me, you must tell me, you read that letter, and you know the truth of my affection for you. Please, Caroline, I cannot hold myself back any longer. Say you return my love. Say you will become my wife.'

All throughout the room, the buzz of conversation faded, and heads turned to regard this spectacle. Caroline had never felt so mortified in her life. Nor had she felt as alive. *I do love you,* she wanted to say. But the words that came out of her mouth were different. 'Mr Tryphon, I am greatly honoured by your proposal, and by the affection you profess to feel for me.'

'I do not profess it!' he cried, ignoring the attention that now focused on him. 'I do not "feel" it. I am it, it is impossible to separate it from my very being!'

'I understand,' Caroline said, looking about, grateful that the Darcys, at least, had already left and so were not here to witness this. 'I am honoured, as I said, and I do not underestimate the strength of your emotion.' *I don't, and if I stand here much longer, I shall fall to the floor, unable to keep myself from being in your arms.* 'I must tell you, however, that I have an understanding with another man, and so I can never be yours.'

He closed his eyes, and the pain inside her resonated from the pain she saw on his face, but then he rose to his feet and his face grew stony as he regained control over his emotions. 'I did not know,' he said tightly, each word clipped. 'I would have thought our friendship was such that you would have confided something so important as an engagement.'

'We are not engaged,' Caroline said, suddenly miserable. 'It is simply the knowledge that we will become so, and I am sorry I did not think to mention it to you.' She hadn't mentioned it, she realised now, because she had been falling in love with Mr Tryphon, ever since they first met, and she had enjoyed his growing love for her too much to want to say anything that might put a stop to it.

He looked at her, standing very close, and in his dark eyes she saw fear. There was no mistaking it, even though in the tight press of his lips and the lowering of his brows she saw that the fear was becoming overshadowed by anger. Unintentionally, she took a step back.

Charles appeared at her side, and she had never been so grateful to have been granted a brother as well as a sister. 'Is everything quite all right?' he asked, placing an arm around her shoulders.

A few other men, she noticed, had moved closer, and while she disliked appearing weak, she was grateful for their concern. Clearly, since everything in Mr Tryphon's posture and expression demonstrated anger, they were prepared to defend her.

At Charles' words, though, Mr Tryphon seemed suddenly to realise everyone else was interested in the little drama he had caused. 'All is well,' he said to Charles, 'and I would hope that we are well enough acquainted, Mr Bingley, to know I would never allow distress or harm to come to your sister.' He bowed. 'I have made a fool of myself, for which I apologise, but I can feel no regret, for she is a prize worth any amount of embarrassment.' With that, he left. Caroline was unable to keep her eyes from following him as he moved through the clusters of people, his head held high, until he disappeared through a doorway that she knew led to the private areas of the house.

Charles also watched him go. 'I thought that was very well spoken,' he said to Caroline. 'You could do much worse than him.' He squeezed her shoulder, and removed his arm, so he could turn her to face him. 'I assume you refused him?'

'I did,' Caroline said with a sigh. 'Perhaps it was a mistake.' Then, suddenly she came to her senses. She was going to marry Darcy and become mistress of Pemberley. It had not been a mistake and she was grateful for the inner strength that had enabled her to do what was right. If she'd been close to weakening, it was only because the proposal had been so unexpected, giving her no time to decide how to handle the situation. When Mr Darcy proposed, she would know what to say.

She did love Mr Darcy, how could she not? Her feelings for Mr Tryphon, while strong, were nothing more than an infatuation, just like Charles' affection for Jane Bennet. She would think no more of Mr Tryphon, and continue with her plan to convince Mr Darcy she was ready for his proposal.

She smiled warmly at her brother, and looked about the room, rising to her full elegant height. Already most people had looked away, tired of what was only a small and unimportant occurrence during one of Eleanor's parties. After all, many dramas were played out here, most of them much more interesting than this one.

Caroline glared at the few people who still dared to look at her, and they too returned to their previous entertainments, conversing with other guests, or eating and drinking while they observed the flow of life around them.

'Do you wish to depart now?' Charles asked. 'You must be fatigued.'

Caroline turned to him. 'Not at all. I am always energized by Eleanor's parties. There are so many interesting people among her circle.' *And I cannot leave now, or people will think I'm distressed by what has happened and am running away. No, I must act as if I turn down a man's proposal every other week.* She gave Charles her warmest smile. 'I am not ready to leave yet. Would it be all right if we remained a small while longer?'

He, as she well knew, could refuse her nothing when she smiled at him like that. And so she moved among the crowds, some of whose whispering stopped suddenly as she neared, making witty remarks and expressing her satisfaction with the concert and the fascinating conversations she always had with Eleanor's friends. Only after she had spoken to everyone at least once, and they all seemed to have forgotten what had so interested them before, did she realise suddenly that she was very tired. Seeking out her brother, she told him she was ready to return home. Only then, as she looked for Eleanor so she could take her leave, did she realise that her friend was nowhere to be seen, in fact, she had left the room shortly after Mr Tryphon did, and had not returned.

*   *   *

The next day brought a dreaded visit. She was tired, for she had passed a restless night. The few moments of sleep she had found were filled with images of Stephen, holding her hand, pressing his lips against hers. When at last morning arrived and she could get up, her lips felt warm and full. Staring at her face in the mirror, she was horrified to see dark shadows under her eyes. And was that a wrinkle running from the edge of her mouth up to her nose?

She rang for Genney, determined to ignore her mirror all day. She was just tired, that was all. She'd spend a quiet day at home, perhaps read a little, even though Mr Darcy wouldn't be there to see it. That suited her well, though, for she was in no mood to deal with anyone or anything.

And then Jane arrived.

The butler showed her in, without first inquiring if Miss Bingley was at home to callers. Stevens had been with the family at Netherfield Park, so no doubt he recognised Jane as a family friend, but Caroline would have to speak to him.

Jane held out her hands as she advanced across the room to where Caroline sat by the fire, her sewing on her lap and her mind filled with thoughts of Mr Tryphon. Caroline was so shocked by Jane's appearance that at first she thought Jane was an image from her head, just as Mr Tryphon was. Realising this was indeed a nightmare become flesh and blood, she rose to her feet, so busy wondering where Charles was at that moment that she barely said two words to her unwanted visitor. Thank goodness Charles was living in a different house!

Jane sat down across from Caroline, and held her hands towards the warmth of the fire. She appeared a trifle bewildered and Caroline, to buy herself a little time before she had to speak to Jane, rang for a servant to bring some refreshments.

'How lovely to see you,' she said at last, finding her good manners.

'But, I am so surprised to see you.' She was, even though she had known this could happen when she didn't respond to Jane's letter announcing her presence in town. Realising that her lack of response could be seen to indicate poor manners on her part, Caroline continued, 'How long have you been in London? You naughty girl, why did you not let me know you were here?'

'I sent you a letter.' Jane appeared somewhat surprised for a moment, but then her expression softened. 'I did suspect it must have gone astray. I hope you will forgive me for simply appearing in this manner. I should have sent another letter, when you did not respond to the first, for I know you could not be so cruel as to deliberately ignore me.'

Caroline experienced the smallest of twinge of guilt at this, but quickly pushed it away. She had acted in the best interests of her brother, indeed of the entire family. 'How are you, my dear friend?' she asked.

She barely listened as Jane prattled on about her parents and sisters. Their health was no concern of hers, neither were tales of Lydia's most recent escapade or what Charlotte had written to Lizzy about her new life in Hunsford, married to that clergyman whose name Caroline could not recall. She poured tea and handed over a plate with a slice of cake, and nodded sometimes and smiled when Jane's expression seemed to expect it.

Her full attention was pulled into focus when Jane paused and then asked, 'And how are you and your family? Your brother, is he well?'

Caroline uttered a little laugh that even to her ears sounded false. 'Oh, Charles is very well. He is busy, dashing hither and yon with Mr Darcy, and I barely see him.'

They both sat in silence for a little time, and then Caroline, her fatigue washing over her so strongly that she feared she might collapse, leaned forward and said, 'My dear, while it is delightful to see you, I am expected with my sister as we have an outing planned. I am sorry you cannot see the others, but they are not present at this time. Charles, in fact, will not even be present for dinner, which is a shame, for Miss Darcy will be joining us. He was most upset when he learned he would miss seeing her, for the two of them enjoy each other's company very much. Still, no doubt they will see one another tomorrow, and sometimes a little absence

will make the heart grow fonder. Is that not so?' She laughed and rose to her feet.

Jane rose too. 'I truly am happy to see you,' she said, although her voice sounded somewhat uncertain.

Caroline took her cue. 'I am happy, also. It is delightful to know you are where I can easily see you, whenever I wish.'

She walked Jane to the front door, offered a carriage to take her home, and was relieved when Jane told her that her aunt, and her aunt's carriage, were only a short walk away. Jane thanked Caroline so profusely for see-ing her, even with no notice of the call, that Caroline wondered if she'd have to summon a maid with a broom to sweep Jane outside. She did depart at last, and Caroline closed the door behind her and leaned her back against it, too tired and overwhelmed to move.

* * *

Caroline told Louisa about Jane's visit later that day, but was not able to inform Mr Darcy until several days had passed. Louisa was suitably hor-rified on Caroline's behalf, and sufficiently sympathetic that Caroline felt much better. Mr Darcy's reactions were another matter.

She saw her chance to speak to him alone one evening, when everyone had gathered at his house. He'd left the card room and was about to slip into his study, when, from further down the hall, she called to him. He looked annoyed at first, but settled his features into a patient expression when she reached him.

'I apologise for disrupting your escape from the card tables,' she said with a smile.

'I am found out.' His smile was very small and of very short duration. When she did not immediately speak again, he added, 'Since your apol-ogy indicates you have not chased me in order to drag me back, I presume there is another matter you wish to discuss.' He took a step towards his open study door.

'There is,' she said quickly. 'I wanted to tell you that Miss Jane Bennet is continuing in her plans to ensnare my brother. She was in Mr Hurst's house, walked boldly in as if she had every right, only four days ago.'

Mr Darcy flinched when she uttered the name 'Bennet', and she was glad to see he took this matter as seriously as she did. He even clenched his hands, which were by his sides, into fists and closed his eyes for a moment. 'How is Miss Bennet?' he asked.

This was not what she had expected him to say, and she stared at him, unable to speak.

His expression grew very still, and he said, 'I trust that your silence does not mean you have some terrible news to impart, and are considering how best to soften the blow.'

She wanted to smile, to assume what he said was a joke, but he gazed at her with such calm, yet such deep emotion, that all she could say was, 'Miss Bennet appears very well, and had no terrible news to tell.'

He closed his eyes again, and when he opened them, he appeared the same as usual, dignified and elegant. 'I assume you have not mentioned her call to your brother?'

She shook her head, still staring at him.

He moved to enter his study, but just before he passed inside and turned to close the door behind him, he asked, without looking back, 'Did Miss Bennet mention if her family is in good health?'

'She did,' Caroline said faintly. 'They are all well.'

He nodded, still with his back to her, and closed the door.

* * *

For the next few weeks, Caroline did her best to put all thoughts of Bennets out of her mind. She knew it was unpardonably rude for her to not return Jane's call, or even to send a line or two explaining why she had not been by, but the thought of having to go to Cheapside was, as Louisa agreed, simply too repugnant.

She also saw nothing of Eleanor or Mr Tryphon during that time. She'd wondered if she should turn down any invitations she received from Eleanor, but was saved from having to decide by not receiving any. While she was deeply wounded by her supposed friend's silence, she knew that most of her pain came from not seeing Mr Tryphon. Why had he gone and spoiled everything by proposing? How she wished they could continue the easy friendship they'd had during the past many months. She

missed it. Missed him. And she missed Eleanor, too; her vivacity and playful attitude towards life.

No one else noticed that invitations from Lady Amesbury had ceased. The maestro did not come to Mr Darcy's house to teach Georgiana but the young lady, after an initial disappointment, seemed perfectly content to continue studying with her regular teacher.

Caroline sewed, and tried to spend at least a few minutes each day reading. She went for carriage rides, and walks on the finer days, made calls and received them. She helped Louisa select new wall coverings for the small drawing room. Mr Darcy still did not propose.

Instead he continued preparations for himself and Georgiana to return to Pemberly. Caroline tried her very best to show him how bereft she would be once he was gone, but other than an invitation to come and stay later in the spring, he showed no signs that he would miss her.

Then, a few days before the date set for his removal, Mr Darcy sought her out. They were in the Grosvenor Street house, late afternoon. She had hardly seen him for many days, since he was so occupied with settling business affairs here in town so he could return to Pemberley with his mind at ease.

She was in the corridor just outside the dining room, for Louisa was feeling unwell and Caroline had offered to oversee the servants' preparation for the meal. When Mr Darcy appeared, he looked much the same as always, wearing his dark blue coat with beige breeches. She observed some differences from his usual demeanour. There was a slight shine to his forehead, almost as if he was perspiring, but surely that was impossible, for she'd never seen him appear dishevelled in any way other than at Netherfield, when he'd just returned from a horseback ride. His shoulders looked tense, and he was opening and closing the fingers of both hands as he came to a stop in front of her.

She stifled a gasp. Clearly he was preparing to speak. At last! She thought about what she could say in a gentle reprove for his waiting until the last minute before his departure, and how unkind he'd been to leave her in suspense all this time. It would have to be voiced in the gentlest, most loving of tones, of course, but surely he would understand he deserved it.

And was he truly going to propose just outside the dining room of her sister's house? It was strange, but no doubt his passion meant he could not wait for a more romantic site.

He took in a deep breath, let it out, took in another, all without saying anything. His fingers continued to clench and unclench until, as if he noticed them, he thrust his hands into his pockets.

Caroline thought of touching him, of placing her hand on his arm or chest, to show him he need not fear being refused. She didn't want to appear forward, though, and settled for simply saying, 'Mr Darcy? Is there something you wish to say to me?'

He took in another breath, as if mustering his strength, and said, 'I am sorry to disturb you, Miss Bingley. I merely wanted to inquire if you have had the pleasure of seeing Miss Bennet again.'

Caroline's jaw dropped and she gaped at him for what must have been a full minute before she could adequately control herself enough to close her mouth. 'Miss Bennet?' she said faintly.

'Yes,' he said, and his words came faster and faster. 'I am returning to Derbyshire, as you know, well, of course you know, to Pemberley, and since I am returning to the country it made me think of my last sojourn in the country; in Hertfordshire, but of course you know that also.' He appeared to run out of steam for a moment, but then continued, looking over her head as if what he had to say was of no moment. 'I simply wondered if you had word of any of our friends in Meryton, if they are well.'

Caroline found she was opening and closing her mouth now, gasping for breath, and even though she knew it made her look like a fish, she was unable to stop. Calling upon all her strength, she composed herself and said, 'I am afraid I have not had that pleasure.'

His gaze returned to her face, and she thought she saw accusation in his dark eyes. Quickly, she added, 'I have been terribly busy, and I know how very rude it is of me to not have returned Miss Bennet's call. In fact, I was planning to do so tomorrow, so I should be able to answer all your questions after that time.' Now she saw a terrible fear and hope on his countenance and, unable to be in his presence a moment longer without bursting into tears, she dropped a quick curtsey and hurried away.

How she sat through the dinner and the card games that followed, she did not know. She knew she was pale, for even Charles noticed and asked if she felt unwell. She answered him, as she did all comments directed at her, in a commendably steady voice. Louisa, whose headache had abated enough for her to preside during dinner, kept sending concerned looks at her sister during the evening, but it wasn't until the guests had departed, and Caroline had just enough energy left to feel proud of her performance that evening, that the two sisters were able to speak in private.

They were in Caroline's bedchamber. Caroline sat at her dressing table, removing her jewels. Her face stared at her from the polished surface, looking like a caricature from one of the newspapers, an image of a witch or other spirit from the world beyond. Her eyes were dull, the skin around them appeared bruised, and the skin beneath her high cheek bones seemed to have wasted away, so that her whole face looked haggard.

'What has happened?' Louisa asked.

Caroline was not sure how to put what had happened into words, but then Louisa rested a hand on her shoulder. That gentle touch was all it took to reduce Caroline's defences to crumbling dust. 'It's Mr Darcy,' she said in a trembling voice. 'I think he has feelings for Elizabeth Bennet!' And then she could hold back her tears no longer.

For a while, Caroline sobbed in her sister's arms, paced about her room, wailed while lying face down on her bed, and pounded her poor innocent pillows until one burst, filling the air with feathers. At length, once again held tenderly by Louisa, who appeared uncaring of the stains Caroline's tears made on her gown, Caroline grew quiet.

'There, there,' Louisa murmured, stroking Caroline's unbound hair, for it had come unpinned. 'It doesn't matter, everything will be all right.'

'How can you say that?' Caroline asked, raising her tear-streaked face from the comfort of her sister's shoulder.

'He is much too sensible a man to throw away everything he has, his position in society, the esteem in which he is held by all who encounter him and, even more importantly, his sister's reputation as a Darcy, to ever consider marrying someone like Lizzy Bennet.'

When she heard that name, a fresh wave of tears overcame Caroline. Once she'd recovered, she said haltingly, for crying had given her hiccups, 'That makes sense, truly it does, and I thank you for reminding me.'

'Of course it does.' Louisa fetched a small towel and dampened it in the basin.

Caroline lay back and closed her eyes as the cool moist towel soothed her brow and temples. 'But,' she said as the puffiness left her face and she began to relax, 'Do I want to marry a man who has feelings for a woman who is so unsuitable?' She straightened her spine.

'You mean a man who loves another woman?' Louisa picked up a hairbrush and tended Caroline's hair.

Caroline flinched at her sister's blunt words. 'Do you truly think he loves her?'

'That matters not.' The hairbrush caught in a tangled curl and Louisa tugged harder to work it through. 'You love another man, and yet you would marry Mr Darcy.'

Caroline bowed her head as Louisa's brush strokes tugged on her scalp. 'Is it so very obvious?'

'Obvious?' Louisa ceased brushing while she considered the question. 'To me, yes, because I know you so well. To others? I don't think so. Although,' and she laughed and began brushing again, 'his proposal in the middle of a crowded room did draw attention to the two of you!'

Caroline grimaced. 'I wonder if Mr Tryphon truly does love me.'

Louisa placed her hand on Caroline's shoulder and leaned around so she could see her sister's face. 'He does. Of that there can be not the slightest doubt at all.'

'Why? Because he proposed in such dramatic fashion?' Tears pricked against her eyes and she stood, moving away from the bed where Louisa still sat, hairbrush in hand.

'It has been obvious since he first met you.' Louisa moved to where Caroline stood by her dressing table, and brandished the brush in her face. 'It is there to be seen by anyone who has eyes.'

Caroline swallowed down a throat that still felt raw from her weeping. 'Mr Darcy? Do you think he has seen it?'

'I know not. Mr Darcy plays his cards very close to his chest.'

A laugh bubbled up inside of Caroline, at the thought of Mr Darcy sitting at a poker table, his cards pressed against his perfectly cut jacket, his eyes moving from side to side as he looked suspiciously at the other players, all of whom wore filthy clothing and sported several days stubble on their faces. The laugh burst out, and she couldn't stop it. Laughing so hard she found it impossible to stand, she staggered over to her bed, and collapsed onto it.

'What?' Louisa asked, beginning to laugh also.

'Nothing,' Caroline gasped. 'It's nothing; it's not even very funny.' She struggled to stop laughing, for she could tell that if she didn't, she would begin to cry again. She took in a deep breath and held it, forcing her shoulders to relax, and gradually regained control. She stood and smoothed out the bed's coverlet, for it had become badly wrinkled. The tears were difficult to vanquish, as she asked, 'Why has Mr Darcy not yet spoken?'

Louisa sighed, and put the brush back on Caroline's dressing table. 'I don't know. He may think it has all been arranged, and that an understanding is all that is needed for the moment.'

Caroline finished with the coverlet, and began to pick up feathers from the rug that lay beside the bed. 'No. Look at the attention and care he devotes to all business matters. What is marriage, but another contract? He would expect that also to be properly drawn up and signed, even if it is no more than a verbal agreement at first.'

'Leave that for the servants.' Louisa pulled Caroline to her feet. 'If Mr Darcy has not spoken, then he cannot have realised the depth of Mr Tryphon's affection for you. Perhaps it would be a good thing if you continue that friendship.'

'I don't know.' Caroline looked for something else that needed her attention, but there was nothing. 'I have not seen him for some weeks. It seemed better that way. I did not wish to further wound him.'

'And you were afraid that being in his presence would further wound you.'

'Yes.' Caroline sighed. 'But I truly do not wish to cause him any more pain. It would be too unkind.' She paused and looked up in surprise. 'I suppose I must love him, since I think that.'

Louisa smiled. 'There is nothing wrong with thinking of his needs ahead of your own. But he is a man, after all. Men toy with the emotions of women all the time. If speaking with Mr Tryphon, laughing with him, in front of Mr Darcy can help you gain what you want, then I see no difficulty.'

Caroline stood very still. Although the thought of spending time with Mr Tryphon again brought a glow into the vicinity of her heart, she was not sure it was fair to use him in this manner.

'Let me guess,' Louisa said, cocking her head to one side and studying Caroline. 'Your head says it's wrong but your heart says "yes, yes!"'

'You know me too well.' Caroline looked at her bed but knew she'd be getting precious little sleep that night. 'I don't know what I will do.'

'Give it time,' said Louisa, preparing to leave. 'What is meant to be will happen, you will see.'

The next morning Caroline arose and dressed, even though her eyelids felt as if they were coated with sandpaper and her temples throbbed from fatigue. There was one thing that was meant to be, and she could put it off no longer. She summoned the carriage and directed the coachman to be ready to take her to Gracechurch Street.

Just the thought of seeing a Bennet curdled her stomach, and she found herself unable to eat her usual breakfast. A sip of tea and a bite of dry toast was all she could manage. How could she look at Jane, speak politely to her, while the knowledge that Mr Darcy would want to hear word of Elizabeth pounded inside her head?

Caroline had never been to Cheapside and, as the carriage took her from fashionable, to less fashionable, to unfashionable, she had to bite the inside of her lip to keep from screaming at the coachman to turn around and whip the horses so she could return, as quickly as possible, to where she belonged.

Why, the area was positively filthy. No one had scrubbed these stone walls for a very long time. And why had the servants not cleaned the windows? The houses were all crammed in together. And the people on the street, well, it would be better not to think about them now and not speak of them to anyone once she'd returned home.

She lifted her skirts as the coachman handed her out, and didn't let them fall as she walked to the front door of the Gardiner's house on Gracechurch Street. The bronze door knocker had at least been polished some time during the past year, but she summoned the coachman, who lifted it for her, so that she didn't have to touch it.

When the door was opened by a saucy looking maid, Caroline hoped with all her heart that Jane was not at home, and so she could leave her card and depart this place at once. Alas, her hopes were not realised. The girl bobbed a hasty curtsey and asked Caroline to follow her. Trying to hold her breath, for Cheapside air must surely be unwholesome, Caroline walked across the tiled floor and through a door held open by the maid.

Beyond the door was a sitting room and despite herself, Caroline had to admit it was a lovely room, with large French doors that in pleasant weather would be open to the garden at the back of the house. The room was well-proportioned, and not overly full of furniture and knick-knacks, nor was it woefully bare of anything that could provide comfort to both family and visitors.

Jane was seated in a chair by a window, with a shawl over her shoulders, her head bent studiously over a scrap of linen. At Caroline's entrance she looked up, startled, and then leapt to her feet, a glad smile upon her face. Caroline ignored her outstretched hands and seated herself on a settee close to the fireplace.

Jane's smile faltered for a moment when Caroline did not take her hands, but she quickly recovered and took a seat across from her. 'My dear friend,' she said. 'It is very pleasant to see you.'

'I am very sorry,' Caroline said, 'to have taken this long to return your call.' There, that was enough said. Caroline would not make excuses for refusing to come to this place.

Jane blinked, looked at her hands as if she wished she had her embroidery or something to focus on, but she had left it on the chair by the window. Looking up again, she said, 'How is your family? Is Mrs Hurst well?'

'Thank you,' Caroline said. 'My sister is in the best of health, as is her husband.'

'And your brother?' Jane asked, speaking as if he meant nothing to her, but Caroline noticed that her shoulders tensed up and she pressed her lips together tightly after she asked the question.

Clearly, Caroline thought, *we did the right thing in concealing Jane's presence in town from Charles.* 'My brother is well,' she said, 'but terribly busy, unfortunately much too busy to visit any old acquaintances who might chance to be in town.'

Jane blinked again, and Caroline was certain she saw a shadow come over those large blue eyes, and so knew her dart had found its target. 'Oh yes,' she continued, 'so busy, and any free time he might discover, he makes certain to spend it with Miss Darcy.'

'Miss Darcy,' Jane echoed.

'Yes. I am very excited about the growing bond between them, and the joy they take in one another's company.' Caroline smiled, hoping it appeared she had nothing to think about other than planning her brother's wedding. She had a feeling that her nose was still pinched from trying to breathe as shallowly as possible. So, instead of smiling some more, she continued speaking. 'I have never observed Charles to be so taken with anyone, not in all my born days—or his, for that matter.' She laughed. 'After all, it is his days that are important, would you not agree, Miss Bennet? My brother has led a charmed life, with so many events that have fallen into place to provide him with the utmost happiness and satisfaction. His friendship with Mr Darcy, for example. Without that friendship, which has brought him and his family much joy, he would not have met Miss Darcy. So you see how a life can be neatly assembled, with all its pieces fitting together perfectly.' She stopped, because she was beginning to feel dizzy. Perhaps she should try taking in a slightly deeper breath.

'I am happy for him,' Jane said, and even though her voice was faint, Caroline detected a true emotion beneath the words.

'You are truly a sweet girl,' Caroline said without thinking and then, afraid that if she appeared to enjoy Jane's presence in any way, Jane would make another call on her which would necessitate Caroline returning to Cheapside, she put on her haughtiest expression. 'And how are your family?' She rose and wandered over to the window, as if she had no interest in Jane's response, which was the truth.

Jane prattled on for a time, about her assorted sisters, and then segued to her parents. Caroline watched a spider, which was busily spinning a web just outside the window. Then, bored with watching such industry, she turned back to the room. 'I am glad that all is well,' she said, cutting into Jane's stream of words.

Tea and cakes had arrived, brought by the same maid who'd answered the front door. Jane held out a plate for Caroline and she realised that once again her good manners meant she could not, as she'd planned, take her leave right away. She ate the cake and gulped the tea as quickly as she could, longing to bring this visit to an end.

'And what of Netherfield Park?' Jane asked. 'Will we have the pleasure of seeing you there?'

Caroline took too large a bite of cake in her haste, and choked for a moment while forcing it down. It wasn't bad cake, actually, moist and redolent with cinnamon; it was a pity she was forced to eat it so quickly. When she stopped coughing, she took a sip of tea. Her eyes were watering a bit, but she gamely ignored her discomfort. 'Oh, I doubt that Charles has any intention of returning to Hertfordshire. I should not be at all surprised if he decides to give up the house.' Without pause, she rose smoothly to her feet. 'And now, I must take my leave. Thank you for the tea and cake. No, no.' She held up a hand, for Jane, too, had risen. 'There is no need to see me out. It is very easy to find one's way about this house.' And with that she left.

Once in the coach again, with the houses she passed growing larger and sitting in their own gardens, she could finally breathe again. As her dizziness abated, she settled herself more comfortably in her seat. Overall, despite its discomforts, she could be pleased with the visit. She was certain Jane now knew there was no likelihood of any attachment between herself and Charles. No doubt she'd now return to where she belonged, to Hertfordshire, and its little entertainments and woeful lack of interesting and refined society. And now Caroline could look forward to all of her plans and desires falling into place, exactly as she'd planned.

*   *   *

Alas, the Darcys departed for Pemberley, and Mr Darcy had not yet proposed. Caroline knew, however, how busy he had been, and added to his business affairs was concern over the health of some of his older tenants.

She had faith that his intentions towards her were unchanged, and determined to offer him all the support she could by not pestering him about matters of the heart while he was otherwise occupied.

Charles moved to the Hursts' home. He was morose at first, missing his friend and, Caroline thought, the pleasure of his friend's sister's company as well. His sorrow had a benefit, though, for Charles was more often at home and so was at leisure to escort his sister to all the entertainments that London had to offer. February and March passed quickly, amid a whirl of parties, the theatre, intimate suppers, and concerts. Her days were filled with receiving and making calls, fittings for new gowns, and spending time with Louisa.

She received no invitations or notes from Eleanor, nor did she see her friend at any other engagements. At first she decided this was for the best, for her emotions were still tumultuous, torn between belief that the friendship was true and that Eleanor had indeed been hunting Mr Darcy. After a time, she became concerned, wondering if her friend had become ill or if some other calamity had befallen her.

Plus, Caroline missed seeing Mr Tryphon, his smile, the warmth in his eyes, the way they could converse and never notice how quickly the time passed while they were together. At length, she sent a note to Eleanor's house and, when it was not answered, began to make inquiries among her acquaintances.

Most of the people whose homes she visited did not know Eleanor. One evening, at the theatre, Caroline saw a member of parliament who had been seen frequently at Eleanor's soirées. Since he had been introduced to both herself and her brother, she asked Charles, during the intermission, to escort her to his box to pay their respects.

'Mr Thewlis,' she said, after the pleasantries were completed, 'it is a pleasure to see you again. I have read in the newspaper about your speeches in parliament.'

'Thank you,' he responded. A portly man, he spoke slowly, breathing heavily between phrases. 'I am honoured that my small contributions to the governing of this fair kingdom have come to your attention. And, if I may be so bold,' he added with a glance at Charles, 'I am impressed that a lady such as yourself not only reads a newspaper but absorbs the details of what it includes.'

She stifled her annoyance, knowing he intended a compliment. Her brother, as always, was oblivious to the things she was forced to bear, simply because of her gender, but he glowed in reflected pride and beamed at her. 'I thank you,' she said to Mr Thewlis, 'as I thank all men who toil on our behalf in parliament.' She allowed him a moment to preen in her admiration, then pressed on with the true purpose of her coming to see him.

'I trust that amid all your labours on our behalf, you have some time left over for personal enjoyment.' She smiled up at him. 'Such as attending this play. Do you also permit yourself to seek the company of friends, such as our mutual acquaintance, Lady Amesbury?'

He gazed upwards, as if in transports of joy. 'Ah, the dear Lady Amesbury.'

Caroline suspected he was indeed recalling moments of joy, although the moments he recalled were not spent with Eleanor but with a young lady to whom he had been introduced at one of Eleanor's parties. Mr Thewlis was unmarried, and while this particular friend of Eleanor's had probably hoped her interactions with him would eventually end in a proposal, Eleanor had told Caroline, with a laugh, that the lady needed to be much stingier with her affections if she wished to find a husband among the better class of London's bachelors. Caroline had laughed then, with Eleanor, and she smiled now, remembering how ridiculous Mr Thewlis had appeared, bustling about the room to fetch his new friend drinks and food to tempt her as she rested, half-reclining on a settee in one of the more shadowed alcoves of the room. His face had grown increasingly red from his exertions, but he'd hardly noticed his increasing difficulties in drawing breath, as the young lady had smoothed the hair from his brow and rested her small fingers on his plump lips and tickled him under his many chins. His expression then, as it was now, had been one of true bliss.

'Dear Lady Amesbury,' Caroline said now, to recall him from his memories, 'I have not seen her in some time. I trust she is well?'

He blinked at her for a moment, then said, 'She is very well, although I, too, have not had the pleasure of seeing her, either. I know she is in good health, though, because I recently received word of her from one of my colleagues in parliament. She is spending time in the country, at a house not far from his estate, and he has had the good fortune to be introduced to her at a ball held by one of his many friends in the area.'

'I am glad to hear it,' she said automatically. *Was Mr Tryphon with Eleanor?* she wondered, but could see no reason to ask that would not raise questions in Mr Thewlis' mind.

She glanced at Charles and he, ever sensitive, bowed to Mr Thewlis, saying that he and his sister must return to their box now, for the next act of the play. Once she and Charles were again seated, and the curtain rose, she turned her head towards the stage, and stared unseeing as people on stage fell in and out of love.

Chapter Ten

～

Caroline picked listlessly at her toast, poking it with one finger until it rested, teetering, on the edge of her plate, then lifting it and taking a small bite. Even slathered with butter and marmalade, it felt dry in her mouth, and she glanced about the table, feeling certain that everyone could hear her chewing. None of the servants, or her brother, seemed to be paying her any attention, even though each time her jaws came together it sounded to her ears as if she was hitting gravel with metal hammers instead of simply eating with her small, even teeth.

She poked at the toast again, and then noticed that her finger had become sticky. She sat up straight and wiped it on her napkin, then sighed and settled back in her chair, letting her head fall back, wondering why she felt so out of sorts today. True, it was raining heavily, as it had been for three days now, but that was only to be expected during spring in London. Her calendar for the day held few enticements. She could expect a couple of calls, neither of which held the promise of entertainment or even lively conversation, but they would at least help the time pass.

Across the table from her, Charles let out a strangled cough. He'd been sorting through the morning post, but once he'd told her it contained nothing for her, she'd left him to it and had allowed her bleak mood to overcome her. Looking at him now, however, she saw his fingers turning white under the pressure they exerted as he held a few thin pages. His eyes wide, he feverishly flipped through the letter, clearly reading it through more than once.

'Charles,' she said, a sisterly concern tightening her chest, 'whatever is the matter? What can have you so upset?'

'It's a letter from Darcy,' he told her, his voice quiet.

'Oh, do not tell me,' she said, her hand going to her heart, 'that something terrible has happened to dear Georgiana.'

'No, no.' He put down the letter and tried to smile reassuringly at her.

'Is it Darcy, then, who has you in such a state?'

'Both of our friends are in good health. There is no need to be concerned.'

'Darcy is visiting his aunt, Lady Catherine, is that not true?' Caroline said. 'And Miss Darcy is at Pemberley.'

'You have a good memory,' Charles said.

'The Darcys are our dearest friends.' Caroline picked up her toast. 'They are often in my thoughts.'

'You are a good friend to them.' Charles slid the assorted envelopes and papers strewn across the table in front of him into a pile, and stood.

'Charles,' Caroline said, her voice sharp with sisterly disapproval, 'surely you cannot think of leaving before you have told me what was in Mr Darcy's letter that so disconcerted you.'

'I was not disconcerted.' He clutched the untidy pile of opened letters to his chest.

She stood, also, realising that she had no appetite for toast or anything else. 'Charles, I have known you far too long, and your countenance is far too open and expressive for you to fool me. What is in that letter?'

'What letter?' He took a sideways step towards the doorway.

'The letter from Mr Darcy,' she said, trying not to grit her teeth.

'There is nothing in it to concern you, my dear sister. Just news and tales of doings that would only interest his male friends.'

His eyes were open, seemingly guileless, but Caroline saw the brief motion as they flicked towards the doorway.

'Surely,' she said, 'there can be no secrets between Mr Darcy and myself? I am his intended, after all.'

Something that sounded like a laugh that was being strangled escaped his lips and he immediately looked away, his gaze now resting on the crumbs lying on the table's white tablecloth. 'Mr Darcy has proposed, then?' he said to a particularly large crumb.

Caroline hesitated, and he picked up the crumb between thumb and forefinger, rolling it between them, before putting it back on the table next to another one that was nearly its equal in size.

'No,' Caroline said at last, knowing she must answer.

He made no response, and continued to place crumbs in a row, ordered by size.

'But we both know we are meant for each other,' she said. When he didn't look up, she added, making her voice as firm as possible, 'We will marry, he simply has not spoken yet.'

'Are you so certain?' Now he did look up, his face filled with gentle concern. 'If you were to ask his aunt, she would tell you he was intended for her daughter.'

Caroline waved a hand dismissively. 'He will never marry such a sickly creature as Anne de Bourgh. He needs a woman in the peak of health, someone with an elegant disposition and all of the accomplishments a young woman can hope to attain.'

His expression did not change, but she sensed there was something he was keeping from her, something in that letter.

'If you refuse to show me that letter,' she said lightly, 'I will think it contains either grave news indeed, which you have denied, or that it shows that Mr Darcy has lost his mind. What has he done?' She laughed. 'Ask Miss Eliza Bennet to marry him?'

Charles stared at her, his face suddenly very red. He began to choke, coughing in an alarming manner. Caroline hurried around the table, to pound him on the back, but as soon as she reached him, he shook his head and, clutching the day's post even more firmly than before, he raced out of the room.

* * *

'I followed him, of course,' Caroline told Louisa later that same day. 'He went into his study and despite my knocking, refused to grant me entry.'

Louisa shook her head, making sympathetic noises.

'I could hear him continuing to cough, and so I left to find a servant to fetch him a glass of water.' Caroline paused to recall the state of mind she'd been in during that time, confused, angry, and afraid all at the same time. 'By the time I returned to his study with the water, he was no longer coughing and when I knocked, calling out to him, he opened the door.'

'And what happened then?' Louisa clasped her hands in her lap to keep them still, for they had been twisting in each other's clasp.

'He appeared quite himself, his face no longer flushed, his breathing as easy as ever. He did accept the glass of water and sipped it with every appearance of enjoyment.'

'Do you think,' Louisa asked, her hands once again twisting, 'that he had some sort of fit? Did he appear overly in need of water or did he merely sip it to be polite, since you had gone to the trouble of bringing it to him?'

Caroline thought, until she realised her brow was furrowed. Hastily she relaxed it before unsightly lines could appear on her smooth skin. 'I think,' she said slowly, 'that he was thirsty. He took the glass in both hands, even though it was one of the smaller ones, you know, the ones with the floral engraving just below the rim?'

Louisa nodded, her eyes clinging to Caroline's. 'Please go on.'

'Such a glass can be held quite comfortably with one hand by some-one whose hands are large, as are Charles'.' Caroline pictured her brother drinking in her mind, so as to furnish Louisa with every possible detail. 'And yet he raised it to his lips with both hands. I don't think he lowered one hand from it until he had taken several sips and was moving to place the glass on his desk.'

'Ah! He did not finish all the water.' Louisa's brow was furrowed now, as she tried to make sense of her brother's strange actions.

Caroline smoothed the lines from her sister's forehead. Yes, Louisa had already found a husband, but that was no reason to let herself go. 'He may have finished it later,' she said. 'I cannot remember, exactly. My mind, now my concern for his immediate health was gone, was occupied with wondering where he had put Mr Darcy's letter.'

Louisa nodded. 'Of course. You are very good in a crisis, Caroline; I have often noted it. You keep a cool head while others around you are close to panic.'

Caroline smiled to acknowledge the compliment, although she didn't think she'd been involved in very many crises. She'd always endeavoured to ensure that her life, and the environments in which she found herself, were arranged to forestall anything unexpected or surprising. Still, she had handled herself very well this morning, and she supposed that Charles' dangerous coughing could have become a crisis, if she had not been there to help him.

'Did you find the letter?' Louisa asked, after both sisters had had enough time to think about what could have happened to their brother if he had continued to choke, and to be grateful it hadn't.

'No. I am most perplexed. It was not on his desk, and while some papers had fallen to the floor, I assume as he was fighting whatever it was that had lodged in his throat, I did not see it there either.'

'Could it have been underneath one of the other papers?'

Caroline shook her head. 'The surface of his desk, while somewhat untidy, was not cluttered enough to completely cover the letter. And, while he drank, I quickly pushed some of the paper on the floor aside, with my toe, and so revealed what lay beneath them. The letter was not there.'

Louisa's hands were now clasped at her breast, and she gazed at her sister with admiration. 'You truly have a mind unsurpassed by anyone else I know. Who else would have thought to search in that manner, even as she assisted Charles?'

'It was nothing.' Caroline stood, unable to sit as her frustration about the letter arose once again. 'I cannot think where he could have put it but, even more, I cannot think what could have been in it that led to him denying me the joy of hearing Mr Darcy's words.' She paced back and forth in the Grosvenor Street house's sitting room. It was not as large as the room the family had used in Netherfield Park, but there was no comparison, for the room here was in town while the other room was in, and here she shuddered, Hertfordshire, where Bennets had sat on its furniture and walked about on its carpets.

'Alas, I cannot help you.' Louisa rang the bell to summon a servant to bring refreshments. 'I cannot think of a single thing it would be necessary to hide from you. Perhaps I should ask Charles myself about—'

'No!' Caroline whirled from where she stood by the fireplace. 'I thank you,' she said more quietly, in response to Louisa's shocked countenance, 'but surely this matter is but a trifle.' She seated herself again beside her sister and patted her hand. 'Just as there are matters that women do not discuss with men, there must be some things that men prefer to keep to themselves. I am certain that Mr Darcy's letter contained nothing more mysterious than a reference to an incompetent barber or a poorly brushed suit.'

'Or,' Louisa said, laughing, 'a badly tied cravat.'

Caroline joined in the laughter and looked with appreciation at the tea and fruit-covered tarts that were being set out on the table. Despite her seeming relaxation and willingness to forget the morning's occurrences, she could not put the letter entirely out of her mind. Somehow, she would find a way to discover its contents.

* * *

Caroline could not stop thinking about Mr Darcy's letter. She'd managed to convince Louisa that she'd put the matter out of her mind, because she didn't want her sister to become concerned. Unfortunately, this meant she could not speak to Louisa about it, and as there was no one else she could trust, her thoughts about its whereabouts and what it could contain were left entrapped inside her own head, swirling around and around with nowhere to go.

Over the next several days Caroline found reasons to enter Charles' study. She needed to ensure that the servants were doing an adequate job of cleaning it, or that the fire had been built up enough to ensure that he was warm and so would suffer no further coughing spells. She even ventured into his bed chamber, one evening when he had decided to forego the usual card game and practice billiards instead.

'Darcy,' he'd said, 'is the victor far too often during our games. I must endeavour to give him at least a little competition, or he will become weary of playing with me.'

'Nonsense,' Caroline had said, more sharply than she'd intended, but her tension over her inability to find the letter infused everything she did or said. 'Mr Darcy's affection for you will not permit him to forego the pleasure of playing with you.'

'The pleasure of soundly beating me, you mean,' Charles said with a smile.

She'd thought of convincing him that he did not need to acquire better skills at billiards in order to ensure his friend would spend time with him, until she realised that if he was occupied in the billiard room, he would not know if she told the Hursts that she had a headache and would retire.

No, that wouldn't work, for Louisa, out of sisterly concern, would follow her to see if she could apply a cool cloth to Caroline's forehead. No, instead she would say she felt a headache coming on, and so needed to run upstairs just for a moment, to fetch a powder Charles' physician had concocted for exactly this situation. This excuse would provide less time for a search, but at least she could be certain of being alone for a few minutes. She'd have to keep watch for servants, but there should be no reason for Charles' valet to be in his rooms at this time.

As she'd expected, there were no servants around. At any other time, this fact would have caused concern that Louisa was not strict enough with her household staff, but for now Caroline was relieved.

His sitting room held a small writing desk. Its drawers were unlocked, and she quickly searched through the papers. She found old letters there, from several of his friends, including Mr Darcy, but the one she sought was not there. The other furniture in the room, the chaise, the armchair, and the small tables scattered about in convenient locations, were bare of anything, ornaments or papers. A shelf between the two windows held the trophies he'd won at school, but no papers were concealed beneath or within any of the cups.

She stuck her head into his bedroom, overcome with a sudden and most atypical shyness. The room was very masculine, with its wood-panelled walls and dark burgundy rug that matched the bed's coverlet. Paintings of favourite hunting dogs and horses he'd owned over the years covered the walls. Even his pony Spot, the first equine he'd been permitted to ride, had a portrait hanging where he could see it when he sat up against his pillows.

She smiled, seeing the picture, her mission forgotten for a brief moment. How Charles had loved that pony. He'd insisted on calling it Spot, even though its coat was a uniform chestnut brown, without a single marking anywhere. He'd spent every moment he could with it, and while Caroline felt her parents should have insisted that he spend more time in the schoolroom and less in the stables, she'd understood that there was a genuine bond between her brother and the beast.

He'd spent long afternoons talking to it while it stood in its stall or was let out into the pasture. Spot came to him whenever he called. He'd stand beside it, leaning against its shoulder, speaking in a soft voice, and its ears flicked, making Caroline think that the pony was listening to every word. She wondered, sometimes, what Charles was telling it, for even though he was never a quiet child, she got the sense he confided things to Spot that no other ears heard.

She smiled now, leaning against the doorway between Charles' rooms, her body relaxing for the first time in days as she remembered her brother, Louisa, and herself, as young children. How carefree they'd been, running among the trees that stood about their family house, playing endless games in the nursery with puppets and blocks, looking forward to those evenings when their parents would join them for a cup of hot cocoa before the children were sent to bed.

Suddenly, she snapped back to the present, her hand going to her mouth in shock. What nonsense she'd been thinking. Look at everything she'd attained during the years between childhood and now. Why on earth she'd thought, even when lost in memory, that anything could be better than her life now was beyond her. Wealth, position in society, all the accomplishments a young woman today could gain were hers. The only thing lacking, an advantageous marriage, was within her grasp. If having those things meant less time to gambol in flowery fields, so be it.

She took a step into Charles bedroom, glancing about quickly. There were many places in which a small number of pages could be hidden, the drawers and cupboards that held his clothing, the drawers in the tables that stood on each side of the bed.

She had no idea how long she'd been standing here, lost in nostalgia, but she feared that it had been long enough that Mr Hurst would send Louisa to find her. No doubt he was impatient to start the game. And, her strange reluctance to enter the room, the sense that this was an invasion and not something a gentlewoman should do, was strong enough that she turned and quickly left to return downstairs. She'd just have to think of another way to learn if the letter was there.

Her chance came the very next day, for she encountered Charles'
valet, Byrnside, in the hall outside her own rooms. No one else was about.

'Byrnside,' she said.

He turned and inclined his head in respect. 'Miss Bingley?'

'I wonder if you could help me with a trifling but troubling matter.'
She lifted her chin, wanting to appear businesslike.

'Of course,' he said, clasping his hands in front of his waist-coated
stomach. 'I am at your service.'

She nodded. 'Charles wanted to show me a letter from Mr Darcy, but
he is unable to produce it. It is possible that these pages became mixed
among some of Charles' other letters. You know how careless he can be,
scooping up everything in his path into one untidy pile.'

She smiled, and as expected, Byrnside smiled back, a rueful but fond
expression on his countenance.

'Charles,' she continued, 'could have brought the papers into his rooms,
and left them lying about his sitting room. Or, if he was particularly distracted that day, he could have thrust them into a pocket or pushed them
into a drawer which usually would not contain such a thing. I know that
you do an excellent job of looking after Charles' clothing and other personal items. Have you seen handwritten pages anywhere among his things?'

She waited with baited breath as he cocked his head and took a
moment to consider her question. Was he merely running through the
past few days and listing any items he found among Charles clothing? Or,
was he thinking what a strange thing this was for his master's sister to be
asking? Would he mention it to her brother?

After a moment, he merely looked back at her and said, 'I am sorry,
Miss Bingley, but I cannot recall seeing any letters at all. I regret being
unable to offer you assistance in this matter.'

'I thank you for taking the time to answer my question,' she said, 'and
there is no reason for you to regret anything, for this is only a trifling
thing. In fact, I'd appreciate it if you do not mention it to my brother.' She
laughed in a girlish manner. 'I would not wish him to know I am unhappy
with his personal habits.'

Byrnside inclined his head. 'Of course,' he said. 'You can always rely
on my discretion.' He left her and continued down the corridor.

She went back into her sitting room and sat down, resting her head in her hands. She had looked everywhere she could think of for that letter. Instead of the frustration making her wish to forget about the source of such annoyance, she was more determined than ever to find it.

She sat up and squared her shoulders. She knew Charles would never burn or otherwise dispose of a letter from his friend. This meant that it had to be somewhere. And if it wasn't in all the places she'd thought of, she would just have to look in the places that had not come to mind.

Where did Charles spend his time? His club. If the letter was there, she had no hope of finding it, for women were not permitted to enter the building.

Therefore, she must hope it was somewhere else.

She knew the letter had become an obsession. Probably it contained nothing more than something relating to the male body that was thought, by men, to be too distressing for a female to know about. She felt powerless to do anything about this obsession, even though it was driving her to do things that were insane. Searching her brother's rooms! She knew how incensed she'd be if anyone, even Louisa, were to search through her rooms. She'd feel hurt and betrayed. Violated. She had treated her brother, whom she loved with a strong sisterly affection, abominably. And yet, she could not stop searching.

She'd been ignoring her friends, not returning calls, not receiving them either, even when she was at home. It was difficult to sit still, to speak of banalities, when her mind burned and twisted, desperate to know what the letter contained.

Her need to know was understandable, surely. She would soon become engaged to Mr Darcy, she had a right to know what was happening in his life. It was beginning to affect her life in other ways. She wasn't eating much. She couldn't sit with the others over a meal and pretend that everything was fine, when every fibre of her being wanted to grab Charles by the shoulders and shake him until he gave her the letter. She had trays sent to her room, sometimes, but had little appetite. But just yesterday, Louisa had mentioned that Caroline looked peaked, and wondered if she should call a physician.

She didn't require a doctor. All she needed was to find the letter. But she'd searched every place she knew that Charles kept important papers.

Two days after venturing into his bedroom, Caroline was sitting at the dining table. It was mid-afternoon, long past luncheon, and too early for tea to be served, and so the room was a quiet haven.

A sheet of paper lay on the table. She'd already got a blot of ink on the white linen tablecloth, but she didn't care. She was going through the house, in her mind, and methodically making a list of every place she hadn't already looked that Charles could have used as a hiding place.

She heard the door from the front hall into the dining room open, and looked up with annoyance, for there was no reason for a servant to be passing that way at this time of day. Instead, Charles and Louisa entered, both appearing most solemn. Caroline's eyes were drawn to the pages clutched in Charles' hand.

Louisa and Charles sat across the table from her. For several moments, no one spoke. They both regarded her with affection, but Caroline was convinced she also saw pity in their eyes. Charles' glance dropped to the table, and aware that he could read upside-down, Caroline snatched up her list.

'I know what you are doing,' Charles said.

'It's nothing.' Caroline attempted a laugh. 'Just a household list.' She waved her page in the air, then crumpled it in her lap.

'Louisa and I have spoken.' Charles continued. 'We are agreed upon this course of action, although it fills us with concern for you.'

'What is there to be concerned about? And I have duties I must be about.' Caroline leaned forward to stand up, but before she could complete the action, Charles raised a hand, and she stayed in her chair.

'I told you,' he said, his voice low and gentle, 'that I could not share the contents of Darcy's letter. I said this out of concern for your feelings.'

He paused, as if waiting for her to argue. When she did not respond, he glanced at Louisa, took in a deep breath, and continued, 'The matter, however, has gone too far. You are not eating, and probably not sleeping well either. And, you are going into parts of the house where you should not.'

Caroline felt her cheeks grow red, and she held her breath to try to stop the blush. He knew! What must he think of her? Surely he was here now to discipline her in some way. What if he sent her to live alone at

Netherfield? No one but the servants and people like the Bennets to speak to. No, that would be too cruel.

But surely Louisa understood and would not support him. She waited for his next pronouncement. When it came, to her relief, his voice was mild.

'Louisa and I are concerned for your health.' They both gazed sadly at her. 'We have decided to let you know the contents of Darcy's letter. We both think that doing so will not make you happy; in fact it may well upset you greatly. We cannot go on watching you destroy your health and beauty in this manner.'

Caroline let the aspersion he cast on her appearance pass her by. At last! She would learn the contents of the letter!

'Did you hear me?' Charles leaned forward. 'You will, in all probability, be very much distressed by what you will learn.'

Caroline hesitated, glanced at Louisa. Her sister nodded slowly, then said, 'I agree. It would be best, Caroline, for you to put this matter entirely out of your head. The contents of the letter do not concern you, and I fear for you. Can you not simply forget this foolishness?'

'You have read the letter?' Caroline glared at Charles. 'So you believe the contents fit for one sister and not the other? How dare you be so judgmental?'

'Caroline, enough!' Charles' voice was sharp.

'He only just showed it to me,' Louisa said, holding out a hand imploringly. 'He wanted to know if I thought it the only thing that would stop your physical decline.'

'I want to read it.' Caroline clasped both hands on the table, to stop their trembling. 'Surely there is nothing that can be so terrible it needs to be hidden from me? Charles assured me that Mr Darcy and his sister are in good health. What else would upset me more than discovering that I, alone in this family, am not fit to learn what my intended has communicated?'

'I am not so sure he does intend to marry you,' Charles said heavily. 'Has he ever said anything that would lead you to assume he did intend to propose? Has he, God forbid, done anything that a man who is nothing more than a family friend should have done?'

'No, of course not. Mr Darcy is a perfect gentleman.'

'Then what,' Louisa asked, 'makes you so certain he will ask you to marry him?'

'It has long been understood,' Caroline said impatiently, 'that there are many advantages to linking our two families with bonds that are even stronger than the friendship we share. I know he feels the same.' She reached out for the letter. 'But why are we speaking of this? Give me the letter.'

Charles laid the pages on the table and smoothed them carefully. 'I think it best that you hear the words in my voice, instead of reading them in Darcy's hand.'

'What nonsense—' Caroline began, but then Charles spoke again, and she fell silent.

'Mr Darcy writes,' he said, almost apologetically, 'to tell me that he asked Miss Elizabeth Bennet for her hand in marriage.'

A sudden rush of sound filled Caroline's head. It surrounded her with the scent of salt, for it sounded like the vast ocean had, the one time she'd been to Brighton. 'Miss Elizabeth Bennet?' she said, as if she'd never pronounced such words before.

'Asked,' Charles continued, 'and was refused.'

Charles' words made no sense. They passed over and through Caroline like the enormous waves at the shoreside.

'The only thing more,' Charles continued, 'about this subject is as follows.' He cleared his throat, lifted the pages, and read,

> *'In the normal state of affairs, I would not burden you with such a confidence, but the effect of what transpired has turned my disposition decidedly for the worse, and I cannot put the image of her, saying to me "if you'd behaved in a more gentlemanly fashion" out of my mind. It consumes me, and sadly my feelings for her are, as yet, unchanged.*
>
> *It is my hope that by unburdening myself, and in so doing asking you, my good friend, to share my pain, I will at last be able to, if not find peace, at least pass a few moments in which I do not think of her.'*

Charles let the pages fall to the table. Both he and Louisa looked across the table at Caroline, who was sitting very still.

'I don't see why you were at all concerned,' Caroline said, pleased that her voice did not tremble. 'He has asked her, fortunately for him she refused. Now that he has this, this . . . infatuation out of his head, he will naturally propose to me.' She smiled at her brother and sister, as the ocean sound grew louder and louder in her head. Black grew from a single point in her vision, grew rapidly until it filled the room and the space inside her head, and she fainted.

*   *   *

When she awoke, she was lying on the settee in the larger drawing room. Something wet dripped down her face. It felt almost like tears, but surely there was no reason for her to cry and besides, tears were hot and this moisture was cool. She looked around, but everything was a blur. Then her sister's face swam into focus, as she bent close over Caroline, and applied a damp cloth to her forehead.

When Louisa saw her sister's eyes were open, she lightly ran another, dry, cloth over Caroline's face, cleaning away any dripping water, and then put it away. 'There you are,' Louisa said, trying to sound stern but her smile gave away her relief. 'We told you that learning what was in Mr Darcy's letter would only distress you. I hope this will teach you to listen to Charles.'

Caroline pushed herself to a semi-recumbent position, and waited while a surge of dizziness rose in her head and then subsided. 'I remember when Charles wore short pants, as do you. It is most difficult to take anything he says seriously when I have that image of him in my mind.'

Louisa's smile grew. 'I agree, if one's sisters remember a brother as a little boy running around with a mop of reddish curls and grass stains all over his clothing, it is difficult for him to gain respect from them. But Charles is a man, and so has a much greater understanding of the ways of the world. You would do well to remember he has only your best interests at heart.'

Caroline sighed, and sat up all the way. 'I know he does. But surely we women can also have a say in what is best for us?'

'Perhaps there are times when that is true.' Louisa paused, her eyes looking into a place far distant. She then stood, and busied herself clearing away the bowl of water and cloths. 'This series of events does not support your argument. Charles was very worried that you might faint, and that is exactly what has occurred.'

'Some women faint all the time. I am made of stronger stock than that.'

Louisa studied her for a moment. 'You are still very pale. But I must go and tell Charles that you have awoken. He will be much relieved.'

Caroline attempted to sit up straighter, and when she succeeded, to rise to her feet, but at that her body rebelled. Her legs began to shake and she quickly sat back, resting her head on a cushion.

Mr Darcy asked Eliza Bennett to be his wife. Caroline tried to make sense of this statement, these words strung together, but she couldn't. And there was the other statement, one that made even less sense. *She refused him.* How was this possible? Perhaps Caroline was ill and her memory of what the letter had contained was a fever-driven hallucination.

She did remember, though. Her fears of Eliza's wiles had been well-founded, and the minx had somehow beguiled poor Mr Darcy. No doubt her refusal had brought him back to his senses, and to Caroline.

But that made no sense either. If Eliza had wanted to entrap Mr Darcy, a wealthy and handsome man of considerable position in society, why then had she refused his proposal? Caroline's head began to throb, and when her brother rushed into the room and knelt beside where she rested, she could barely lift it to smile at him.

He took her hand. 'Caroline, you look very ill indeed. You must go upstairs and lie down. I insist.' He turned to Louisa. 'Please fetch her maid. I will assist her up the stairs myself.'

Caroline raised herself somewhat on the settee. 'Charles, I am perfectly fine. I just need a few moments more to rest, and perhaps a cup of strong tea. There is no need for all this fuss.'

He acted as if she had not said a thing, and wrapping his arm about her, helped her to her feet, through the hallway, and up the stairs, his body pressed to her side providing warmth as well as strength, until he delivered her to Genney, who stood just outside Caroline's rooms. From there, Caroline was taken by Genney and Louisa into her bedchamber, where her gown was loosened and she was made to lie down.

She felt dizzier than ever after the exertion of climbing the stairs, and thought to protest that she would have much better remained on the settee, but realised she didn't have the energy to speak above a whisper. 'Please,' she said, so softly she feared she would not be heard, 'bring me some tea.'

Genney, after a glance at Louisa, left the room and returned a few minutes later bearing a tray with a cup and saucer, a pot of tea, and a plate of small dry biscuits.

'I think it best,' Louisa said, 'if you remain here for the evening. If you eat the biscuits, we will consider then whether more food will be brought.'

Caroline's stomach rebelled at the thought of eating even a biscuit, but she held out her hands eagerly for the cup of tea Louisa poured for her.

'I have put two sugars in,' Louisa said sternly, 'instead of your usual one, and there is plenty of cream, as well. I know this is not your usual preference, but these additions will do you good.'

Caroline did not care. The aromatic scent of her favourite blend of Indian teas twined about her head and into her nostrils, that alone giving her the strength to sit up and hold the cup in hands that did not tremble. She took a sip of the liquid, hot enough to soothe the inside of her body as it flowed down through her. This gave her energy enough to smile at her sister. 'Thank you, Louisa. This is just what I need.'

Louisa looked worried. 'I am glad, but I think I shall stay by your side, in case you are taken ill again.'

'Please,' Caroline said, after drinking half the cup. 'I would prefer to be alone for a time. I think I shall sleep a while.'

Louisa still appeared uneasy. 'Very well, but I insist that you eat one biscuit before I go. And once I do, you can be assured I will check on you very often.'

'You are a good sister.' Caroline nibbled at a biscuit, managing to spill most of it as crumbs onto the lace doily that covered the tray without Louisa observing. 'There,' she said, when she'd finally washed the last dry morsel down with her second cup of tea. 'As you see, I am perfectly well now, and there is no need for concern.'

Louisa nodded, appearing somewhat less anxious, and she and Genney left the room. Caroline lay back with a sigh.

* * *

She did not rise from her bed that evening, and decided to rest the next day also. Although she scorned this weakness in herself, she could not find it in her to care overly much. Not enough to bestir herself, in any case. *When he arrives,* she thought, *there will be plenty of time for me to arise. And he will come soon, for it has been some days since his letter arrived, and it is likely that it was some days after his foolish proposal before he felt ready to confide in Charles. Even now, he must be on his way, riding to town, to me.*

But the following day passed, and the one after, and still Caroline did not attempt to leave her bed. Louisa spent a lot of time with her, sitting and reading aloud, working on sewing. When sewing, she asked frequently for advice from Caroline, showing her the embroidery, wondering aloud if she should use the light or darker green, or the silk thread or the cotton. Caroline knew Louisa thought this would get her interested enough in the work that she would wish to see her own hands busy with colour and texture. But Caroline had no interest in anything. She liked it best when Louisa read to her, for then she could ignore both tale and voice, and lose herself in her thoughts. *He is coming. He is on the road, even now. Perhaps he enters the outskirts of the city at this very moment.*

He did not come. Caroline wondered if he had been delayed by some dire event at Pemberley, and began to inquire at first once a day, but soon several times, if any letters had arrived from the Darcys. The answer was always in the negative.

'I can trust you, can I not?' Caroline asked Louisa one day. 'There can be none of this foolish thinking that I need to be protected. If a letter had arrived from Pemberley, you would tell me!'

'I would never lie to you,' Louisa said, 'and I am offended that you would think such a thing.'

'I'm sorry.' Caroline sighed and turned her head back and forth on her pillow. How was it possible to feel so restless, and so weak, both at the same time? 'You are being a good sister to me, and I repay you very ill.'

'Nonsense.' Louisa stood and did not look at Caroline. Instead, she wandered over to the window, and pulled the curtains back. 'It is a lovely day out. Winter is long passed, and spring has taken hold. Would you not enjoy a short ride in the carriage? I know how you love to see the new tender leaves.'

As far as she knew, Caroline had never given a single thought to leaves, tender or not, other than to dislike the way they cluttered the paths where she wished to walk in autumn. It was now spring, according to Louisa, and so the leaves were on the trees, where they belonged, and would not inconvenience her.

She let Louisa's comment pass her by, as she had ignored all attempts to draw her out of her room. Louisa had never reacted to this before, but today she left the window and came to stand by Caroline's bed.

'Caroline, this has gone on long enough. You cannot continue to lie here and grow thinner and paler by the moment. What are you waiting for?'

'You do not know?' Caroline was shocked enough to sit up. 'I wait for him, of course.'

The fierceness left Louisa's face, and she sank down on to the bed, uncaring that she sat on an edge of Caroline's nightdress so that Caroline was unable to move. 'He, I suppose, is Mr Darcy.'

'Of course.' Caroline placed her hands on either side of her and wriggled a little, to see if she could work the nightdress out from under her sister. It did not move at all.

'Caroline, while you have been lying here, apparently thinking of nothing other than Mr Darcy, the rest of us have lived our lives. We have not thought constantly of only one thing or of only one person. Charles has founded a debating team at his club. Mr Hurst went to his tailor and for the first time has permitted himself to be talked into ordering a yellow waistcoat. And I, I thought myself with child.' She paused, and raised one hand to cover her eyes. 'I was certain of it, but if there was a growing life inside me, I lost it.' Her shoulders trembled, and Caroline knew her sister wept.

'Louisa,' she whispered. 'Why did you not tell me of this sooner?'

Louisa dropped her hand and wrapped both arms around herself. Her cheeks were wet. 'I did not wish to burden you, when you clearly had enough to deal with on your own.' Slowly her expression changed, and her eyes sharpened. When she spoke again, anger tightened her words.

'How can you do this to us? We have been beside ourselves with worry. Charles even consulted a physician.' She raised a hand when Caroline began to protest. 'We did not allow him to see you. You stated you did not wish to see a doctor, and we acquiesced to your wishes. That does not mean we believed you healthy. Charles described your symptoms and the physician prescribed a tonic, which I gave to you in your evening cup of chocolate.'

Caroline, incensed, tried to pull herself away from her sister but was held fast by her traitorous nightdress. 'So! You have not been entirely forthcoming with me! How can I ever trust you?'

Louisa's shoulders slumped, but her voice was still sharp. 'You are behaving like a child. You are old enough to know one cannot always receive what one wishes for.'

Caroline bit off her angry retort. Something in the way Louisa sat, curled in on herself, and with eyes that gazed off into the distance, seeing something too far away to be fully recognised, stilled her tongue.

At length, Louisa stood. 'I have invited someone here. Someone who wishes very much to see you.'

'I wish to see no one!' Caroline cried, and lay back. 'Who is there to see if it is not Mr Darcy?' she said softly, so that Louisa bent closer in order to hear. 'What is there to live for if I am not to marry him? Who am I, if not mistress of Pemberley?'

Louisa sat back down on the bed. Caroline was careful, this time, to whisk her nightdress out of her sister's way. 'Is that truly what you think?' Louisa asked, and scorn sharpened her words. 'Do you think I wanted nothing more than to be Mrs Hurst, mistress of nothing more than an insignificant estate and of a house on the unfashionable side of Grosvenor Street?'

Caroline felt she was viewing her sister as if for the first time. She had never thought about what Louisa might have wanted, or if she would have preferred for her life to have taken a course different than the one it had followed. 'You appeared happy when Mr Hurst proposed.'

'Happy?' Louisa thought for a moment. 'I suppose I might have been, at times. I was to wed a landed gentleman, and that was good for the family. But there was another . . .' Her voice trailed off.

'Another?' Caroline took in only the smallest of breaths, afraid of distracting her sister.

Louisa was silent for a long time. Then she nodded. 'Another. Charles refused his permission. He felt the gentleman was unsuitable because he was younger than I.'

Caroline gasped. There was no need to be silent now. Sitting up, she wrapped her arms around her sister, pulling her back to rest against her breast. 'Oh, Louisa. I had no idea.'

'No one did. I felt too ashamed of where I had placed my affections to speak of it to anyone, even you, dearest sister.' Louisa tensed for a moment, trying to free herself from Caroline's embrace, but then relaxed into it.

'It must have been a difficult decision for Charles, to disappoint a beloved sister's hopes.'

'Oh, it saddened him, I know.' Louisa placed her hands on top of Caroline's, which were clasped at her waist. 'But he was newly come to the position of head of the family, and his responsibilities weighed heavily upon him. I think he regretted his decision later, but I had accepted Mr Hurst by then, and Charles agreed to that marriage.'

'Regretted it?' Caroline's head was spinning. After thinking of nothing but Mr Darcy, it was difficult to move outside herself and admit the world. Her sister needed her, though, and no matter what happened or did not happen, Caroline's love for Louisa and Charles could never be pushed aside.

'Charles told me once that I did not smile after I was married, the way I did before. He began to ask, then, if I thought that I would be smiling differently if—But then he broke off what he was about to say, and turned away from me. But I knew.' She pulled away, and this time Caroline let her go.

Louisa stood, straightening her gown. Then she turned back to Caroline. 'That is why,' she said, and her voice seemed to come from someone else, 'I felt torn when Charles appeared to be falling in love with Jane Bennett. If I had thought for one moment, if I had believed that he truly did love her, and she him, would I have acted differently?'

'You would not,' Caroline said stoutly.

'I might have.' There were again tears on Louisa's cheeks. 'I might have. I would not like to think I am a person who would deny him happiness simply because he denied me.'

'Charles would have had cause to regret it if we had let him marry Jane. Just as Mr Darcy will in time see how very fortunate he was that Eliza refused him.'

'Can you be so very sure?' Louisa wandered through the room, picking up objects, a hairbrush, a vase, a bracelet, and discarding them. 'Both Charles and Mr Darcy can afford to marry a woman with no fortune. And both of them are secure enough in their positions in society that such a wife would not greatly affect their standing.'

Caroline tried to laugh, but her heart was thumping in her chest. 'But those connections! Can you see Mrs Bennet and her younger daughters staying here in this house, and meeting your friends? Can you see them accompanying Mr Darcy and Elizabeth to court, when Georgiana is presented?'

Louisa dropped her head, and stared at her feet for a moment. 'No, I suppose not. You are right; it would have been a mistake for us to act in Charles' case any way other than we did.'

There came a tap at the door. 'Ah!' Louisa said. 'Your friend is come.' She left the bedchamber and returned shortly, followed by Genney and—Eleanor!

Eleanor swept into the room amid a rustle and flow of pink silk. The scent of lilacs rose from the fabric, and from her skin. The scent roused Caroline, so much a part of her friend that she knew she would never be able to smell that flower without an image of Eleanor, head thrown back in laughter, coming to mind.

'Dear one!' Eleanor bent at the bedside to brush her cheek against Caroline's. 'Why is it so musty in here?' She marched to the window and pulled the drapes even further apart. 'You!' she pointed at Genney. 'Open this window at once, and do the same for every one in these rooms.'

She turned back to Caroline and stood, one foot tapping, her hand cupping her chin. 'What am I to do with you? I thought that surely, if you were languishing, you were doing so in a rose-strewn boudoir with a gentle breeze wafting your unbound hair as you reclined on a chaise! And there would be a young man who looks like a Greek god playing the harp in a corner, as you wept copious tears that somehow, instead of making your face puffy and your eyes red, created a Caroline more beautiful than ever.' She sent a mischievous smile at Caroline.

Caroline, knowing well she did not appear beautiful, nonetheless could not help but respond to her friend's gaiety. 'I cannot think of one thing missing from the picture you paint. If only I could meet your expectations.' She sighed, and the momentary lifting of her mood vanished as she considered Miss Elizabeth's sparkling eyes and her own faded beauty.

'I can think of one thing more,' Eleanor said, and standing in the centre of the room, she spread her arms wide. 'The Greek god in the corner is clad in nothing more than a gauzy wisp of white fabric wrapped about his hips!'

Louisa gasped, and then pressed her hands to her mouth as she began to giggle. Caroline was shocked to see her always-proper sister overcome with mirth. Her eyes widened even more as Eleanor too, first stared at Louisa and then began to laugh herself. She held out her arms to Louisa, and the two collapsed into each other's embrace, laughing so hard they lost their balance and collapsed onto the thick Persian rug.

So ridiculous did they appear, half-reclining on the floor, still shaking with laughter, that Caroline could not help it. She sat up, swung her bare feet from her bed to the same soft rug, and said, 'I am all astonishment! How is it that a couple of little girls have taken over the bodies of my sister and my friend?'

The other two stared at her for a moment, then they looked at each other and laughed even more loudly.

With no conscious effort, Caroline felt her lips widen into a smile, and then part as a sound emerged from her mouth. It was more a croak than a laugh, but it quickly changed, becoming ever smoother and more energetic until she too laughed, and allowed the other two to pull her down until she sat on the floor, the three of them forming an untidy but mirthful heap. Their gowns and her nightdress, Caroline reflected, were no doubt wrinkled beyond help, and then she caught herself in surprise, realising that was the first thought about anything other than Darcy and Eliza she'd had in days.

As if her thought was a signal, Eleanor rose to her feet, offering Louisa and Caroline her hands. As she assisted them to rise, she said, 'Tell your maid, Caroline, to prepare a bath, and once you are dressed and have eaten, the three of us shall venture out.'

'And,' Louisa cried, 'let London beware, for the three laughing fools are about to set forth!'

Caroline, again surprised to see this side of her sister, but enjoying it immensely, clapped her hands, and called for Genney to come, at once.

* * *

After lunch, which lasted long and was filled with talk about trifles and humour found in the foibles of others, and ended with the largest straw-berry shortcake Caroline had ever seen, the three ladies walked arm-in-arm along the street, heedless of those who had to step into the gutter to get past them. 'Tonight,' Eleanor said, 'you must be my guests. I have planned an intimate supper and only my most favourite friends will be present.'

Caroline, who knew Eleanor had a great many favourite friends, was suddenly overcome with fear at the thought of appearing in society, even though she knew no one else could possibly know of Mr Darcy's foolish, and ultimately futile, proposal, and how it reflected on her. Louisa turned to her and said, 'Caroline, you cannot think how much it relieves my mind to see you once again with colour in your cheeks. Please, let your friends see you, so that they too can be assured there is no need for further concern.'

Caroline was touched at the thought that people, many of importance in society, were concerned about her. Really, what option did she have? She could not stay hidden in her bedchamber forever.

Arriving at Eleanor's home that evening, as Charles handed her and Louisa out of the carriage, Caroline felt she was the picture of serenity and confidence. She wore her newest gown, a confection of deep reddish-brown, its skirts overlaid with yellow lace, the bodice embroidered with tiny dark brown beads. Her hair was swept high atop her head, and Gen-ney had woven yellow flowers through the strands. She held her head high and swept up the steps and through the door.

Once inside and announced, she was delighted that several people approached her right away, saying how glad they were to see her and that she had recovered from her illness. One such person was in the House of Lords, and another was sister to one of the queen's ladies. It was only after the crowd of well-wishers drifted away to other conversations that Caro-line noticed that this gathering was, as Eleanor had said, intimate.

Instead of the usual throng filling the huge room, there were only about twenty people present. The space had an almost cathedral-like feel, for the voices of these few could not fill it, and even though the furniture was placed closer to the centre, this left an empty space about the walls. Eleanor, though, appeared as bright and energetic as ever, vivacious as she moved from guest to guest, ensuring that everyone was introduced to everyone else, and had someone to speak to and something to drink.

It was only after she finished her observations of the room that Caroline realised one frequent guest in particular was nowhere to be seen. She considered the indelicacy of inquiring after a man one has refused, but buoyed by the effusive greetings she'd received, and by being once again in society after spending so much time alone, she decided to be daring. 'I do not see,' she said to Eleanor, 'your friend Mr Tryphon. Is he no longer in town?'

Eleanor took her arm and drew her away from the other people. 'No, no, he is still here, and learning of your kindness in inquiring about him will do him much good.'

'Has he been ill?' Caroline asked, frightened, wondering if he had entered into a decline after her refusal.

'No.' Eleanor looked at Caroline with such intensity that Caroline moved a step back. 'He is here, in the house,' Eleanor continued. 'He is the kindest of gentlemen, as you well know, and did not wish to come into the room unless assured his presence would not cause you any distress.'

Caroline had not thought of Mr Tryphon during the days she'd hidden herself away. Darcy and Elizabeth had been the only faces haunting her. *Does that mean I do not love him after all?* she wondered. But as soon as she saw him now, hesitantly peering at her from a doorway, she realised how foolish that errant thought had been.

He wore the coat she'd always loved the best on him, made of ice-blue wool, its pale colour heightening the contrast his black hair and brows made against his skin.

She perceived nothing else. The din of conversation, clinking glasses, and laughter, faded away as if they did not exist. His gaze focused on only her. A tentative smile grew on his lips, as if he could not hide his joy at seeing her, even as he feared what her reaction would be. She knew what that smile meant, for her lips formed the same hopes and questions.

As he came near, without conscious thought she raised her arm, her hand reaching out to him. He mirrored the move, and in a moment, although it seemed an eternity, his fingers grasped hers, his warm hand the perfect size to hold hers, not so large that she felt he tried to control hers, but just large enough to make her feel connected and protected by his touch.

Her other hand began to reach out also, to cup his face, to caress his cheek, but then she remembered they were not alone, and that she had refused his proposal, in this very room.

'You are pale,' he said softly, and his other hand, the one not still grasping hers as if it were a lifeline he could never release, rose to cup her face, the thumb caressing her cheek. She swayed on her feet, and he put a hand beneath her elbow.

'You are unwell, Miss Bingley,' he said. 'Please, permit me to find you a seat.'

The room reappeared then, all at once, the noise and light overwhelming. A small distance away, Eleanor stood watching them, with an almost avaricious gleam in her eyes. *That could not be right,* Caroline thought. *Perhaps she is angry with me for hurting him when I refused him, or perhaps she is happy to see us happy. I cannot tell. But surely her interest in what is between Mr Tryphon and myself can be nothing more than that of a tender friend?*

'I thank you,' Caroline said faintly, unsure of what she was thankful for. 'I am better than perhaps I appear, and I do not need to sit down.'

'I think,' Eleanor said, and Caroline saw that she had come to stand with them, 'seeing you again, Stephen, is all the tonic Miss Bingley requires.'

There was a slight edge to her voice, and again Caroline wondered, but she was quickly distracted when Mr Tryphon said, 'Is that the case, Miss Bingley? I would be delighted if it were, for then I should be happy to ensure your constant health by permitting you to see me at all times.'

He smiled, his eyes still warm, and Caroline did not know what to say, or even if words could express what was in her heart.

Charles had apparently noticed when Mr Tryphon had entered the room, for he approached now, all smiles, happy to greet an acquaintance. If her brother had been angry at Mr Tryphon's presumption in proposing in such a dramatic manner, or if he'd been sorry Caroline had not accepted him, there was no sign of it. He greeted Mr Tryphon with the same easy manners he showed to every soul he encountered, and soon had everyone laughing as he recounted an amusing incident at his club.

Caroline watched the little group, taking advantage of her brother's arrival to observe her friends. If she had not thought of them during the previous days, she knew now it was a sign only of her distress over Mr Darcy's proposal to Eliza, and nothing to do with the affection she bore them. Even if Eleanor had truly been working to trap Mr Darcy into marriage, even if Mr Tryphon had thought of marrying Georgiana, Caroline knew she would forgive them.

Mr Tryphon did not leave her side the entire evening. He kept her laughing with his comments on mutual acquaintances, and shared news she had missed during her illness.

'Lady Torrance is in seclusion,' he whispered, his breath warm on her ear. 'It is a huge scandal, for no one thinks Lord Torrance, who is, as you know, much older than his wife, is capable of fathering a child.'

Caroline gasped at the indelicacy of what he told her, even as she thrilled to be in the circle of those who knew the intimate secrets of a family as highly placed as this one.

'Still,' Mr Tryphon continued, 'a new young wife could well represent a fountain of youth for an elderly husband.'

Caroline nodded. Lord Torrance had lost his first wife, a woman not much younger than he, and one possessed of a sour disposition. 'Or,' she said, filled with a spirit of adventure, 'the lady found her own fountain of youth, in the form of a young lover!'

Mr Tryphon feigned shock, opening his eyes comically wide and placing a hand before his mouth. 'Miss Bingley. Surely a sheltered young lady such as yourself could not possibly imagine such a thing!' She smiled, trying to appear enigmatic, and he leaned in even closer and said softly, 'Your imagination is one of the things I adore about you.' For a moment, before he moved away again, she thought that his lips brushed her cheek, but the touch was so fleeting she did not know if it was her much-valued imagination.

During supper, he encouraged her to take a little wine. 'For medicinal purposes,' he said, as he held out a morsel of beef on his fork for her to try.

Caroline shone all evening, she knew it because her heart was filled with such a glow it escaped the confines of her body. Other people were drawn to her light; never before had she been the object of so much attention. Everyone wanted to make her laugh; everyone wanted to hear her opinion on the latest fashions or the last play they'd seen at the theatre. Unaccustomed to having people cluster around her, she never felt overwhelmed, never worried that what she said might appear foolish to these sophisticated and powerful people. For Mr Tryphon stood at her side, a source of encouragement and support. When she was a woman of such beauty and accomplishment to him, how could she fail to be so to everyone else?

She was still glowing when Charles helped her and Louisa into the carriage for the trip home. Mr Tryphon and Eleanor stood in the doorway of Eleanor's house, the light behind them shining on to the stairs and the walkway beyond, glistening on the pavement, for it had rained earlier. Both raised a hand in farewell as Charles entered the carriage and pulled the door shut. Caroline leaned out the open window to wave her own goodbye.

'It is indeed very good,' Charles said, 'to see you are once again yourself.'

'Who else would I be?' she answered saucily, and then laughed at his surprised expression.

He grinned at her and said, 'I have only been waiting for this, to see you healthy again, before giving you some news.'

Beside her, Louisa leaned forward and said, 'Charles.'

'She is fine, as you can see,' he responded.

'I think we should wait.'

'She needs to know, and it is better coming from us. What if she runs into them on the street?'

'That seems highly unlikely,' Louisa said in a tight voice.

'Enough!' Caroline said. 'I will not sit here and permit the two of you to talk about me as if I am not here, or not in my right mind.' She glared at both of them. 'What is this news?'

Louisa sighed loudly and turned to look out of the window at the street. Charles sighed also, but more quietly, and then said to Caroline, 'The Darcys are back in town.'

'I see.' Caroline was not sure what she felt at hearing this. Joy, certainly, for it could only mean Mr Darcy was going to propose. Just as she'd thought; now that his foolish infatuation was over, he would turn to her. But thinking of Mr Darcy, even picturing him on bended knee, brought only a sense of disquiet. Instead, images of Mr Tryphon rushing in and pushing Mr Darcy to one side filled her mind. 'How long,' she said to Charles, 'have they been here without you letting me know?'

'Three days. And I am sorry if my withholding the knowledge of their returning to town has upset you. It was done out of the best of motivations, in case it sent you into a graver illness and extended the time during which we did not have the joy of your company.'

'Nicely put,' Caroline said, and indeed it was good to hear that her presence about the house had been missed. 'But you should know me better than that. The doings of anyone other than those in my immediate family can have no effect on me.'

Louisa gave Caroline a look of frank disbelief. Ignoring her sister, Caroline continued, 'I trust that this foolish, although well-meant, concern for me has not led you to snub the Darcys in any way.'

'Of course not,' Charles said. 'I have seen Darcy only at the club, for the intention of this trip to town is to order new clothing for both himself and his sister. And this is news that should please you—they plan to return to Pemberley in a few weeks and we are invited to accompany them.'

Pemberley. Of all places in England, it was her favourite—the expansive grounds, perfectly framed by every window in the great house; the refined elegance; the beautiful and expensive furniture and décor— although of course she had some changes in mind—the perfectly trained servants, all made the estate one of the most respected in the country. Travelling there as its soon-to-be mistress would be pleasant indeed. The image of Mr Tryphon receded a bit in her mind, but only a bit.

Neither Charles nor Louisa said anything more, but both studied Caroline with worried expressions. She determined to reveal nothing of the turmoil this news had brought, and smiled serenely during the rest of the trip home to Grosvenor Street.

Chapter Eleven

The Darcys came for dinner the next evening. Caroline knew she was unusually subdued when they all sat down at the table, and Louisa kept sending her concerned looks. Her mind was full, leaving no space for witty conversation.

From beneath her lashes, she studied Mr Darcy. While his gaze did pass over her from time to time, she could read no yearning, no sign of pent-up love. Of course, Mr Darcy rarely revealed his emotions, but she'd thought he'd want to show his feelings for her, because he regretted his foolishness in proposing to Elizabeth Bennett. He must be deeply ashamed of his behaviour, and she must be supportive of his feelings by never revealing that she knew of his folly.

Caroline was almost grateful he was waiting. Her thoughts were so roiled that the tossing and turning in her head was even worse than the tossing and turning she'd done in her bed last night. She'd barely slept at all, although she felt surprisingly well today. She could only assume all the resting she'd done over the last many days meant she did not need her usual eight hours of beauty sleep.

As she'd dressed for dinner, she'd studied herself in the mirror. She'd lost a bit of weight during her illness, and now her eyes appeared even larger and her cheekbones stood out more starkly, giving her a waifish yet refined appearance. While Genney had been able to cinch her waist more tightly, her bosom had lost none of its fullness, and swelled slightly above her décolletage with its usual smooth curves. Knowing she'd be seeing Mr Darcy tonight, she'd taken extra care with her appearance.

As she'd sat at her dressing table, examining herself as Genney worked on her hair, she couldn't help but think that before going out to Eleanor's home the previous evening, she'd been in a hurry and so had not been as immaculately coiffed. That had not seemed to matter to Mr Tryphon. To him, she was always beautiful.

As the evening progressed, Caroline did everything she could to facilitate Mr Darcy having some time alone with her. When the ladies left the gentlemen to their port and cigars, she lingered in the hallway instead of going straight to the drawing room with Louisa and Georgiana. She knew he could easily make an excuse to Charles and Mr Hurst, and follow her, but he did not.

When the gentlemen joined the ladies, she begged off the card game, and sat in the furthest corner, first ensuring there were two chairs there, and stuck her nose in a book, but he, seemingly quite willing, joined the game.

Later, when Georgiana sat down at the pianoforte, instead of turning pages Caroline retreated to the back of the room. She'd assumed Louisa would help with the pages and Mr Darcy could join Caroline while all eyes were on his sister. But though Louisa did step forward, ready to aid Georgiana, Mr Darcy moved quickly to offer his service to his sister.

Later still, when the Darcys, and Charles, for he was to move back into the Darcy house, were preparing to depart, Caroline lingered outside the front door, while those who were leaving called for their coats and hats, and waited for the carriage to be brought. Mr Darcy could easily have slung his coat over his arm instead of taking the time to put it on, and so he could have come outside, into the warm lilac-scented night air, but he did not. Caroline stood with Louisa and Mr Hurst on the top step and waved goodbye as the carriage rattled off.

The next weeks passed surprisingly quickly. Caroline said nothing of her frustration with Mr Darcy to her brother or even to Louisa, for she did not want to see the same concern on their countenances as had been there during her recent illness. She saw one or the other of her suitors most days, often seeing both at the same time. Being with Mr Tryphon now entailed even more pleasure than before; because since she had refused him, they both could relax into the joys of friendship. Mr Darcy still did not speak, and Caroline began to think that he was waiting for when all of them were at Pemberley. Of course he was, for there could be no setting more romantic, or more meaningful, a place to arrange an engagement that would bring joy to so many in both families.

Being in the same room as Mr Darcy and Mr Tryphon, was not without its difficulties. Propriety demanded that she treat both with the same distant politeness. She could only hope her sister was the sole person to take note of the burning glances Mr Tryphon sent her way, and that Louisa did not observe the equally burning, though more circumspect, glances she sent Mr Darcy's way.

Mr Tryphon appeared perfectly happy to spend time with her, and did not mention marriage or any other official change to their relationship. He often took her hand in his, when he could do so unobserved, and sometimes, if they stood at a distance from other people, would caress her cheek. Other than this, his behaviour was that of a perfect gentleman. Caroline found she welcomed his touch. He made her feel alive.

This last was a rather perplexing realisation. If the warmth of his finger on her lips made her feel alive, did that mean she had not felt alive before she met him? Did not feel alive when they were apart? And if she felt less alive when she was not with him, did that mean she was closer to being dead?

These thoughts caused her great confusion, and formed lines on her forehead, which Mr Tryphon could always erase by smoothing his hand across it. Caroline wished she could speak of these thoughts to Louisa or to Eleanor, but did not. Eleanor appeared entirely too interested in what Caroline thought of Mr Tryphon, whether she found him handsome, whether he was not the most elegant dancer in all of London, and whether she was aware of the very great compliment he was paying her in devoting so much of his time and attention to her. Caroline could not imagine why Eleanor so frequently asked questions like these. The only thing she could think of was that her friend was jealous, but surely that was ridiculous.

Fortunately, the muddle of thoughts receded somewhat as the time for the removal to Pemberley drew near. Details of packing and planning the journey served nicely as a distraction, and so Caroline took on even more of the preparations than she usually did.

The day before their departure, Caroline went to Mr Darcy's house to assist Georgiana. Pemberley was the girl's home, but she was still very young and could not always make the best choices of gowns or shoes or jewellery to be worn in the country.

Georgiana was delighted to see Caroline, of course, and led her up to her rooms, where the bed and seemingly every other horizontal surface was covered with clothes. The overall effect was like walking into a rainbow of colour and texture, the mixture somewhat disorienting, but Caroline was soon able to establish an organisation of sorts. Georgiana professed herself happy with the way this organisation would make her decisions easier, but while Caroline was engrossed with deciding whether gowns and overskirts should be arranged in pairs, so Georgiana could know which to wear together, or whether the two should be laid out separately, gowns on the bed, the others over the dressing table, the girl slipped out of the room, and so was not present to receive the benefits of Caroline's hard work.

Caroline waited for a while, thinking Georgiana had something of a personal matter of which to attend, but when she did not appear, even though Caroline spent some time rearranging the way she'd laid out Georgiana's shoes, choosing to move them from the back wall to placing them by gowns they best suited, she set out in search of her.

As she walked down the hallway towards the drawing room, she heard her brother's voice. It was quieter than his usual buoyant tone, but she could make out the words. 'I confess, and do not think poorly of me, I beg you, but I still think of her.'

Another voice responded, male. He must be standing further from the door, for she could not understand what he said, but it sounded to her like Mr Darcy.

She paused outside the door, which was pulled almost fully closed, curious to know of whom they spoke.

It appeared a third person was present in the room, for a young female spoke. 'They are sisters?' *Georgiana.*

The conversation continued, mostly between Charles and Mr Darcy, but her brother must have moved, or turned away from the door, for she could no longer hear either man well enough to know what he said. Her brother sounded melancholy, she thought, but then his mood must have changed, for his voice rose, finding more of its usual enthusiasm. 'Yes! I do recall that incident! It was a delightful day, was it not? The sky clear, the sun trying its best to warm us . . .'

Mr Darcy spoke again, and then Georgiana chimed in. 'Oh, I would so like to meet her!'

At this point Caroline, who still had no idea of what or whom they spoke, yet feeling a slight unease, opened the door. The three inside fell silent, all turning to look at this new arrival.

Mr Darcy, as she'd thought, stood at the far end of the room, near the double doors which stood open to the delights of spring; a soft breeze and the sounds of birds twittering as they went about their business. He was his usual reserved self, and yet Caroline thought she detected the slightest hint of a flush in his cheeks, as if he had been thinking of something that brought about a heightened emotion.

Her brother, to her surprise, looked very much as he had when the three Bingley children had been much younger, and Caroline had discovered him in the pantry, with traces of the pie he had been strictly forbidden to eat smeared on his face.

Before she could examine him further, Miss Darcy approached and said, 'Dear Miss Bingley, I am so sorry. You must have been awaiting my return for some time, and you are here only out of kindness. Can you forgive me for not returning at once?'

With her brother and Mr Darcy looking on, Caroline could not possibly continue her examination or ask questions to determine what they had been speaking of. She smiled at Georgiana and, taking the girl's hand, said, 'Do not distress yourself. I was able to make good use of the time, and so the final packing will be completed very quickly.'

Georgiana was effusive in her apologies and gratitude, and as she clearly wished to return to the task immediately, Caroline had no choice but to follow. As she left the room, she turned back and saw the two men gazing at each other, and each countenance showed an identical expression of mingled joy and loss that sent a shudder through her. It was only when Georgiana inquired if she felt a chill and wished for a shawl that Caroline was able to look away and close the door behind her.

* * *

There was one more obligation facing Caroline before she left town for Pemberley. She'd been invited to dine with Eleanor and Mr Tryphon that evening and, as she wished to bid them goodbye, she had accepted. She'd expected the occasion to be one of Eleanor's typical intimate suppers, with twenty or more guests, but when she was ushered in, she saw the large marble-topped table was covered with a cloth only at one end, and there were only three places set.

At Caroline's surprised look, Eleanor smiled. 'Surely you cannot think we'd waste any of our last precious minutes with you on other people?'

Mr Tryphon pulled out a chair for Caroline, and took his place beside her. 'I cannot believe you will so willingly leave us, your poor friends, to pine away during your absence.'

'If only,' Caroline said, 'I could have both the pleasure of your company and the pleasures of Pemberley at the same time.' To her surprise, she realised she meant this. She could picture Mr Tryphon in that grand house, walking its halls, playing billiards, dancing, sitting during a quiet time, contemplating the beautiful grounds.

Mr Tryphon would not be out of place, even in such an enormous house. Perhaps his own house was equally grand. 'I have described Pemberley to you in the past,' she said, 'but have not heard about your own estate. Surely you cannot insist on modesty with such a good friend as I.'

He glanced at her, opened his mouth, but then closed it again without saying anything.

'Dearest Caroline,' Eleanor said, 'you cannot seek to fill our last evening together by speaking of stone and stream. Please, do not deny us the pleasure of your conversation. You are such a witty speaker, your words filled with interesting observations. Stephen! I forbid you to say a word about anything other than Miss Bingley's beauty. In fact, I command you this minute, without taking time to think, to tell us ten things you most admire about her!'

'Ten things! How can you set me such a daunting task!' He pretended horror, but Caroline thought, for a moment, that she saw relief in his eyes. He laughed, to show that speaking of things he admired in her was not daunting at all, and took her hand.

'How shall I speak?' he asked, raising her hand to his lips. 'In what order can I list my admirations, for so many crowd my mind I cannot tell one from another?'

'You are procrastinating,' Eleanor said, waving a finger at him. 'You were told to begin at once.'

He sighed and looked meekly down. 'Very well. Miss Bingley, I admire your beauty, of course, and am sure that could go without saying; your elegance and your many accomplishments. Your musical ability is without peer, your voice out-sings the lark, and your embroidery is exquisite. I very much admire the cushion you sewed for Eleanor, and indeed, if it is not too risqué to admit, it rests on my bed, for I appropriated it, and I hug it every night before I go to sleep.'

As he had been speaking, he'd lifted his head to gaze directly into her eyes, and although the image of him, dressed for sleep, hugging the stitches she had made, one by one, brought a rush of warmth to her cheeks, she did not so much as blink, not wishing to look away even for the tiniest of moments.

'I admire your fashion sense,' he continued, 'for you are always dressed in the very latest of styles, and sometimes it appears you have a role in determining what is to be most fashionable, for I swear I have seen you in styles that only later appear at court. Your smile bewitches me, the touch of your hand warms my very soul, the colour of your eyes is as clear as the most precious of gems, and the colour of your lips,' and here he dropped his voice and moved so his mouth was only the slightest of whispers away from hers, 'shows me that you must taste like the very sweetest of strawberries.'

His breath tickled her lips, and almost without conscious effort, they parted. Time stopped then; she could feel the warmth of his skin, almost taste the softness of his lips, feel the roughness of the skin around them, for even though he was clean-shaven, he was one of those men whose beard grew more enthusiastically than that of others.

With an effort, he pulled back and, somewhat aghast at how close she'd come to wanton behaviour, and yet disappointed at the same time, Caroline withdrew her hand from his and raised it to smooth her hair.

'That is only seven,' Eleanor said, but her voice sounded as if she was a cat speaking of cream.

'It was ten,' Mr Tryphon protested, laughing.

'Well,' Eleanor said, 'I suppose if you count the three accomplishments you listed as separate items, but I would have thought such a ploy beneath you. I am certain you have gravely insulted Miss Bingley by finding such a paltry few items to praise.'

'Even if you count the accomplishments as only one,' he said, 'and I do not agree that you should, for each is a marvel in of itself, my list is short only two.'

'No, I shall not change my mind. You listed seven, for you said her beauty could go without saying, and so I assumed you did not include it in the list.'

'But he did say it.' Caroline laughed, wondering anew how she would survive away from these two friends.

'Very well.' Stephen turned back to Caroline. 'Far be it from me to skimp on my compliments to you, dear Miss Bingley.' He raised her hand to his mouth and, one at a time, kissed the tip of each finger. 'I admire this finger, and this one, this one also, and last but not least, the smallest one of all.' He lowered her hand to rest on his firm thigh and seemingly without noticing, he covered it with his own. 'There!' he said to Eleanor. 'Now my list contains more than the ten you asked for.'

Eleanor laughed and clapped her hands. 'Very good, sirrah! I confess you have carried out my command very well.' She waved at her footman and indicated that the first course should be brought.

Her hand still on his leg, for he had not thought to release it, Caroline was aware of every tensing of his muscles as he shifted in his chair. She should pull her hand away, but did not want to deal with his embarrassment when he realised what he'd done. No gentleman would allow a lady to touch him in such an intimate manner, even though no one else could possibly tell, unless they were beneath the table. Mr Tryphon would be mortified, once he realised. While she waited to work out what to do, she put her other hand on her own leg, and marvelled anew at the difference between men and women. Her own was curved, the muscles softer and smoother. His muscles made the top of his thigh almost flat, and very hard compared to her own.

Without conscious thought, she moved both thumbs in small circles, and then, suffused with her own mortification, froze, unable to so much as look over at him to see if he'd noticed. She knew her face was bright red, but fortunately at that moment the soup was served. He removed his hand from hers to reach for his serviette and she snatched hers away. Risking a quick peek at him, she was relieved to note that he appeared to be unaware anything unusual had occurred. Irrationally, she was suddenly annoyed that the physical contact had not affected him in the least, and she determined to ignore him for the rest of the meal. Smiling across the table at Eleanor, she said, 'What a delicious soup!'

Bidding her friends farewell at the end of the evening was more difficult than she'd expected, and she had to fight back sudden tears as she waited at the door for the carriage to be brought.

Caroline could not help but think this was probably the last time she would experience the easy company of these friends. When she returned from Pemberley, she'd be engaged to be married, and could no longer spend time in this manner.

Just before she took the footman's hand to climb into the carriage, she turned back to look at her friends. They stood on the top step, and both lifted a hand to wave. She tried to smile at them, but was suddenly blinking back tears and she turned away and stepped blindly into the carriage. She lowered one hand to her thigh and felt again the firm warmth of Mr Tryphon's muscle. Remembering all the times her fingers had rested lightly on his equally firm and warm forearm, she quickly covered her eyes with both hands and tried not to weep.

Why was she behaving so foolishly? Soon her every dream would come true and she would be mistress of Pemberley. It was what she'd planned would happen ever since Charles first brought his new friend, Fitzwilliam Darcy, home to meet his family. She could not permit anything, not even love, to defeat her now.

She drew a handkerchief out of her reticule and blew her nose, then sat up straight, making sure her posture was entirely correct. As the carriage moved down the street, she lifted her chin. She was Caroline Bingley, and her every move was elegant, every action entirely correct. Clinging to that thought, she returned to Grosvenor Street, ready to leave the next day for Pemberley and her future.

* * *

While the gentlemen often made the trip between Derbyshire and town relatively quickly compared to travelling in a carriage, they had determined to break the journey so as to not overly fatigue the ladies. When they stopped at an inn for luncheon, a letter was delivered to Mr Darcy. After a quick glance at it, he announced he would ride on ahead, for there were some matters he needed to discuss with his steward.

'There is no need for concern,' he added. 'I merely wish to get this business taken care of, so that when we are all together again my time and attention will be available to you, my guests.'

While Caroline was sorry to lose his company during the long journey, she suspected that the reason he wished to have no distractions while she was at Pemberley was so he could give her all the attentions a man pressing his suit could offer. And yet, as he bade them farewell, she wondered why she did not feel more pleasant anticipation at the thought she'd see him again at Pemberley.

The rest of the journey passed pleasantly enough. Louisa was in surprisingly good humour, and Georgiana chattered about the places the carriage passed. Charles preferred to ride his horse, even at the carriage's slower pace, but he sometimes sat with the ladies and Mr Hurst for a change, as he put it, in the scenery.

The inn they stopped at for the night was sufficiently clean and surprisingly comfortable. Georgiana grew quiet as the journey neared its end, and Caroline feared the travel had been too much for the girl, but she perked up and became animated as the carriage turned on to the long gravel drive that led to her home. 'I do so love it here,' she said. 'Especially when all my favourite people in the world are gathered together.'

Caroline smiled. Perhaps there was hope after all for Charles and Georgiana. She took the girl's hand. 'The bonds between our two families will only grow stronger as time progresses.'

'I do hope so,' Georgiana said and then turned to the window as the gracious house, so perfectly situated by the lake, came into view.

Once they had arrived, and the organised chaos of luggage being carried in and everyone being shown to their rooms was past, the party gathered in one of the afternoon drawing rooms. 'I trust, Darcy,' said Charles, taking his favourite chair by the fireplace, 'you have completed your business and so can join us as we strive mightily to be as idle as possible.'

'I shall do my utmost to please you,' Mr Darcy said.

Something in his tone of voice caught Caroline's attention, and she examined him for the first time since her arrival. He was smiling, and looked quite at ease as he settled himself into the wingchair on the other side of the fireplace from Charles. He often smiled, she thought, and was never so relaxed as when he was here, at Pemberley, but there was something more. Something she couldn't put her finger on. His smile was perhaps a trifle wider, his countenance showing a joy that went beyond his usual pleasures, but surely he was simply happy that his guests had arrived in good time and safely. His gaze became unfocused for a moment, as if he was thinking of something else, and his smile became a grin.

He was almost . . . glowing! He reminded her of nothing so much as a man in love. Her breath caught suddenly in her throat, and she had to reach for the cup of tea a servant had just handed her, to prevent a cough. This could mean only one thing. He was definitely going to propose.

'You look like a cat,' Charles said, 'who has just been given a pint of cream.'

Apparently, Caroline thought, *I am not the only person to notice the change in Mr Darcy.*

'Your business,' Charles continued, 'must have gone exceedingly well.'

Darcy blinked, as if he'd only just realised Charles was speaking to him. 'It did indeed. And upon my return, I discovered a friend of ours is in the area, staying no further away than the inn at Lambton.' He looked about at everyone. Did his eye rest longer on Caroline than on anyone else? She was not sure.

Mr Darcy stood up, as if filled with such an energy he could no longer stay still. 'Can you guess who it might be?' He paused, and Caroline was amazed to see his playful air. 'No? I shall tell, you, then. Miss Elizabeth Bennet! She is visiting the county with her aunt and uncle.'

Caroline felt as if he had thrown a bucket of cold water over her person. She looked over to Louisa, and saw the same horror reflected in her sister's eyes. 'Miss Eliza Bennet?' she asked slowly. 'Here in Derbyshire?'

Mr Darcy had now locked eyes with Charles, and it appeared a silent communication passed between them. It was interrupted only when Georgiana leapt up from the settee on which she'd been perched.

'Would it be too much for me to ask if I might seek an introduction? I very much would like to meet her.'

Mr Darcy turned to his sister, smiling. 'I well know it, and yes, I have arranged that we shall see them at their inn tomorrow.'

Georgiana clasped her hands together. 'Must we wait so long? I feel perfectly recovered from our journey, and I know I shall not sleep at all tonight if I must wait.'

Mr Darcy appeared delighted by Georgiana's enthusiasm, even as the unfolding scene filled Caroline's heart with ice.

'I see,' he said, 'I must take you immediately, for I would not wish to cause you ill health due to lack of rest.'

Georgiana beamed, but things became worse for Caroline, for now her brother spoke up. 'I would like to accompany you, also. It would be a great pleasure to be reacquainted with Miss Elizabeth Bennet. Although,' and his face fell, 'while an introduction to Miss Darcy can be nothing but pleasant for all, do you think Miss Elizabeth will wish to renew our acquaintance?'

'I am certain of it.' Mr Darcy clapped his friend on the shoulder. 'But if you have doubts, you can remain in another room and I will ask her.'

Chattering excitedly, the three left the room to call for the carriage. Mr Hurst had stayed in his room to rest, and so Caroline and Louisa were left alone.

'It appears,' Louisa said dryly, 'Mr Darcy did not wish us to accompany them on this visit.'

'Would you have wanted to go?' Caroline asked in surprise. 'I assumed Mr Darcy did not ask us if we wished to go because he already knew what our response would be.'

'I confess to a touch of curiosity,' Louisa said. 'I wish to ascertain if she is regretting her refusal of Mr Darcy's proposal, and so has come here in order to try to entice him again.'

'Judging from his apparent joy at introducing his sister, and the fact he has spent no more than a few minutes with us, his guests, before rushing off to see her, I would say her plan is working.' Caroline fought the urge to bury her face in her hands. Here she was inside Pemberley, the house she'd thought to oversee as mistress, and once again a Bennet was interfering with her plans. There was no sense in giving in to despair. She would simply have to speak to Mr Darcy, to make her expectations clear. Surely, if she spoke with logic and reminded him of all the disadvantages such a match would entail, disadvantages he had pointed out when Charles had been in danger of succumbing to Jane's wiles, he would remember who he was and what was important.

'I know that look,' Louisa said, and Caroline lifted her head to find her sister observing her closely. 'What are you planning to do?'

'Whatever can you mean?' Caroline asked, innocently.

'I know you are plotting something. And when I see that expression on your countenance, I am never sure if I should feel excited or appalled.'

Caroline opened her eyes wide, attempting to appear as innocent as a little kitten. She could only maintain the expression for a few moments before her eyes began to hurt, and so she sighed and said, 'I never can hide anything from you. But I am planning to do nothing more than speak to Mr Darcy, to see if I can discover his intentions.'

Louisa's eyes opened wide, but her expression, one of fright, appeared genuine. 'Caroline! You cannot tell him you know of his proposal to Elizabeth, for that would betray your brother. Charles should never have permitted you to see that letter.'

'He showed it to you.'

'Yes. There was no harm in showing it to me, however, since I would never say anything about it to anyone, and I most definitely would not tell Mr Darcy I saw it. Caroline, you know how greatly Charles values their friendship. You must not do anything to jeopardise it.'

Caroline sighed. 'I am insulted you could think such a thing of me. I had not the slightest intention of saying anything about his foolish proposal.'

Louisa began to apologise, but Caroline swept on. 'I am far cleverer than you appear to think. I know how to seek information from a gentleman in such a way that he will not realise our conversation was anything other than the usual discourse of people such as ourselves in society.'

'Of course you do,' Louisa said, her hands folded in her lap, 'and I am sorry I suggested otherwise.'

The sisters stood to leave the room. *Oh dear,* Caroline thought. *Now what am I going to do?*

*   *   *

When the moment for a private conversation with Mr Darcy presented itself, Caroline still had not the slightest idea of what she would say. She trusted her good sense to see her through what she knew would be a most painful discussion.

Mr Darcy, Charles, and Georgiana had returned to Pemberley, and all three appeared quite satisfied with their visit. Indeed, Georgiana could speak of nothing but Miss Elizabeth, her beauty, her warm smile, the kindness in her eyes. Even Charles appeared more animated than he had for some time, retelling a humorous story Miss Elizabeth had passed on about something Sir William Lucas had said. Caroline ate mechanically, uncaring of what she put into her mouth, and kept what she hoped was a polite smile, and not an ugly grimace, on her face.

Mr Darcy excused himself after the meal, saying he wished to check on the progress of his gardeners as they replanted a section of land by the stream. As the others began an animated conversation about the merits of Charles' favourite hunting dogs, Caroline slipped out of the room. Pausing only to send a maid for her blue shawl, she ventured outside and soon found Mr Darcy standing on a little rise that overlooked the lake.

Drawing in a deep breath, she approached him. 'It appears, Mr Darcy, the meeting of your sister with Miss Eliza went exceedingly well. Georgiana seems to have fallen madly in love with Miss Bennet. But what of your impressions? Are those famous eyes still as fine as ever?'

He turned to regard her, and she thought she saw disapproval in his eyes, so she hurried on. 'I do hope you are not going to invite her to Pemberley. I suspect that if she came here, she would be adding up the cost of every single thing she sees, just like that odious little cousin of hers did in talking about Rosings. What was his name? Collins! Yes that's it, Collins.'

He looked at her for a moment longer, and then said stiffly, 'As a matter of fact, Miss Darcy invited Miss Elizabeth, and her aunt and uncle, to dine with us. I also expect the ladies to make a call here, to see yourself, Louisa and my sister, in the near future.'

He squared his shoulders and set his jaw, and fearing that he was about walk away, Caroline had a sudden inspiration. Perhaps she was going about this the wrong way. He did not appear to like it when she insulted Eliza, and so perhaps she should take another tack. 'Good,' she said, heartily. 'I shall look forward to seeing her. Doing so will bring me many fond recollections of our time in Hertfordshire, and of her dear sister Jane.' *There*, she thought. *He shall see that I can be gracious to all classes of people, and so will not be concerned about how I might treat his tenants. And, by mentioning Jane, I have reminded him of his opposition to Charles' infatuation.*

He tipped his head slightly to the left, his eyes still studying her, but she thought now that they appeared a trifle warmer than before. 'I am glad to hear you say that,' he said, and there was a touch of thaw in his voice. 'I am fond of Miss Elizabeth and would not like to think that one of my guests would be rude to her while staying in my home.'

Caroline gasped, and struggled to quickly bring her countenance back under her control. 'I am never rude to anyone, and you can rest assured I will behave with proper decorum, as I always do.' How could he speak to her so unkindly? But then, remembering what she wished to learn, and since he was clearly annoyed with her, she decided she might as well be in for a pound as well as for a penny. 'Am I to assume, then, that wedding bells will soon ring out for you and Miss Eliza?'

It was his expression that changed now, and he had an even greater struggle to regain his control. What he could not hide, not from her and certainly not from himself, was a gaping sorrow. *He is in love with her. It was love that drove him to propose, and he clearly loves her still, even though she refused him.*

'I am afraid I cannot answer that inquiry.' He made her a stiff bow and stalked away.

It was a good thing, she reflected as she watched his broad-shouldered form recede, that he had left her when he did. For her mouth had already been forming words, wanting to ask if there was no hope of an alliance between their two families. Asking that would have been a shocking breach of propriety. She had been associating too much with Eleanor, for the people who attended her soirées often spoke openly of their friends and lovers. But it would not have done to speak in such a manner to Mr Darcy. Even if he could have supposed she spoke of her hopes for Charles and Georgiana, he would have known it was of herself she spoke, and her hoped-for marriage with him.

She wanted to weep. She wanted to sink down onto the flower-strewn grass and howl out her grief. She knew now how foolish she'd been. Probably he'd never had any intentions concerning her. He'd treated her with the distant politeness he'd show any sister of one of his closest friends. Thank goodness she'd always been circumspect, and so no one, other than Louisa and Eleanor, knew of her hopes.

She didn't weep. She squared her shoulders, lifted her chin, and walked with dignity along the laughing stream, hoping that the sights and sounds of Pemberley, its birds and flowers and the sweetly singing brook, would soothe her soul, and not simply remind her of all she had lost.

*　*　*

When she returned to the house, she encountered Louisa, who took one look at her and pulled her into the closest room. It happened to be one of the smaller morning rooms, and was blessedly unoccupied.

Louisa led Caroline to a settee and, when she didn't sit down, pushed her on the shoulder until she did. Then, dragging a chair over so she could sit facing Caroline, knees to knees, she said, 'Tell me.'

Caroline gazed at her sister's face, which was close enough to take up her entire vision. She knew that face so well, was familiar with every tone on the skin, every small line by the eyes. She saw only concern, and so said, in a voice so dull she wasn't sure it was her own, 'He is in love with Miss Elizabeth Bennet.'

'But she refused him.' Louisa sat back, appearing affronted.

'Yes, she did.' Caroline's lip trembled, and she struggled for a moment before she could continue speaking. 'And how dare he still have feelings for her!'

Louisa studied her for a moment, and then laughed. 'Oh, well done. I am most relieved to discover that disconsolate though you are, your sense of humour and your backbone are still present.'

Caroline thought about how she was sitting. It was a scandalous posture, really, her shoulders slumped, her back curved. She could not find the energy to sit up straight. 'While I hope you are correct about my ability to see the lighter side of some aspects of life, I confess I do not think my backbone is still present. The only thing holding me upright at all is my ingrained sense of propriety.'

Louisa smiled. 'There, see? You can still laugh, even at yourself. And as Mr Darcy was refused by Eliza, he will soon get over this unfortunate lapse on his part and his affections will return to you.'

I am convinced, Caroline thought, *he has never thought of me as a possible match,* but this was too horrible to share, even with Louisa. Saying it aloud would make it become too real, as if only by not speaking could Caroline cling to any sort of hope. And so she said nothing.

'You cannot give up,' Louisa said. 'Mr Darcy knows you are the most suitable match for a man of his standing. He cannot, he will not, consider one such as Elizabeth, not when he must realise how fortunate he was to be refused. Why, can you imagine her standing by his side, in the front foyer, ready to greet guests from court? She doesn't even know how to do a formal curtsey!'

Caroline thought about Eliza bobbing in front of the prince regent, and falling over as she attempted to greet him properly, but even this image could not make her smile.

'You cannot give up.' Louisa jumped up and paced about the room, her steps and bearing almost military in their precision. 'I will not permit it. This is not the Caroline I know. My Caroline would never give way to despair.'

'Perhaps it is time I recognise that reality is better than despair,' Caroline said slowly. 'And I suspect that you have always known that my hopes might well be dashed.'

Louisa opened her mouth, clearly to deny what Caroline had said, but then her shoulders slumped a little. 'Perhaps. But I have wanted to support you. You are my sister and I love you. All I have ever wanted is for you to be happy.'

Caroline thought about everything that had occurred recently, the buoyancy of confidence and hope, and the descents into despair, and realised that, despite what her sister might think, despair had become more familiar than she liked. The lassitude that had overcome her when she had first learned Darcy had proposed to Elizabeth had been overwhelming, so much so that she was unable to leave her bed, much less her rooms. And now? Would she again be overcome by that dreary weight, pinning her down?

As if she had read her mind, Louisa sat down again and, taking Caroline's limp hands, said, 'You cannot permit this to affect you so strongly. I do not think any of us, or you, can withstand another period like that of your recent illness.'

Louisa's dear face appeared so distressed that Caroline somehow discovered the strength to nod her head, and then to force herself to her feet. 'That will not happen. I promise you. Oh, but how shall I face him? Here we are, planning to stay for some weeks.' She lifted her chin. 'I think this is what I most cannot forgive Miss Eliza, that my time at Pemberley, so long awaited, should be tarnished by her tendrils wrapping still about Mr Darcy.'

'I, personally, shall never forgive her any part of it. She has behaved in a truly reprehensive manner. Just imagine, she somehow found out when Mr Darcy would be here, and she contrived to "accidentally" meet him here, in his own grounds!'

Caroline was overwhelmed by a surge of love for her sister. And then, like a sudden ray of sunshine pushing through a dark cloud, a thought blossomed in her mind. Mr Tryphon. If Mr Darcy was truly lost to her, then she was free to marry Mr Tryphon. Stephen—a man who did love her, and whom she loved in return.

She looked about her, at the thick rug beneath her feet, the fine furniture and the perfectly trained servants, the beautiful vista beyond the window. She thought about the stables, the many fine horses, and the large number of carriages, of all sizes, ready to take her wherever she might wish to go. Here she was, living at Pemberley, with all that it could offer. How, surrounded as she was by its luxury and beauty, could she even think of giving it up? Being mistress of Pemberley was all she'd dreamed of since she'd first met Mr Darcy. His person, his wealth, his estate, there was nothing more she could ever want.

She buried her face in her hands, ignoring Louisa's warm hand, placed out of concern on her shoulder. How much more of this could one body withstand before being torn literally into two pieces? Should she follow her heart or her head? She did not know.

*   *   *

'Clearly,' Louisa whispered to Caroline, the next morning, as they stood to receive their callers, 'Eliza was unable to wait a second longer to add up the value of everything in the house.'

Caroline would have smiled, if she had not been feeling so utterly wretched. As if to mock her, the sun was shining brightly outside, and the day was already pleasantly warm. Outside the windows of the saloon, the distant hills glowed with their joy of summer, and birds sang paeans to love from the leaves of the oak trees.

Georgiana stood a little ahead of the Bingley sisters, which was her place as hostess. But did the girl, Caroline thought, have to be so eager to greet her visitors? Why, she was positively fidgety, clasping and unclasping her hands, shifting her weight from foot to foot. Caroline supposed that, were she feeling more charitable, she would assume Georgiana was nervous, but in her current mood, the girl seemed to express only an unseemly desire to see Eliza and the aunt who lived in Cheapside as soon as possible.

The callers were shown in. Georgiana greeted them prettily enough, Caroline supposed, although she stammered once or twice, and said very few words. 'Perhaps,' Caroline whispered to Louisa, 'our dear Georgiana is more sensible than I feared, for her greeting is not very effusive.'

'I think,' Louisa murmured back, a fixed smile on her face directed at the visitors, 'she is merely shy. She has very little experience, after all, of playing hostess without her brother at her side.'

Caroline sighed, and without looking at the visitors, waited for

Georgiana to sit before sinking into a chair herself. An awkward silence ensued, but since Georgiana had wanted these callers to come to Pemberley, Caroline was determined not to help her out in any way. Everyone smiled at everyone else, until Mrs Annesley, Georgiana's companion, who'd been sitting quietly in a corner, spoke up.

'Is this your first visit to this part of the country?' she asked.

'Oh no,' the aunt said. 'Why, I spent many happy years of my youth no further from this site than Lambton!' This led to a conversation about the merits of Derbyshire and growing up in the country in which Caroline, thankfully, did not need to participate. The awkwardness vanished, for even Georgiana ventured to take part in the discussion now and then, and Caroline took advantage of being ignored at present to study Miss Elizabeth.

Despite Louisa's surmise that Eliza would be adding up the value of every piece of furniture in the room and each painting on the wall, she was giving all her attention to those participating in the conversation. She smiled at Georgiana a lot so presumably she was more interested in becoming friendly with Mr Darcy's sister. No doubt she thought that would best help her win him and thus the monetary value of her desired marriage could wait.

Caroline couldn't help drawing a huge sigh, although she perked up when she recalled Mr Darcy had already been refused by Eliza. A man of his standing, of his pride, would not belittle himself by risking a second refusal. Still, she remembered the tone of his voice and the look in his eyes when he'd spoken of Elizabeth the day before, and could not quiet her nerves.

Caroline had chosen to sit at a little distance from where Georgiana had placed her guests, which meant she could not easily speak to them, but at length she realised that despite her dislike of these callers and their existence in this area, her good breeding behooved her to at least inquire after the Bennet family's health. Fortunately Elizabeth seemed to realise Caroline's lack of interest in the subject, and replied with brevity.

Caroline was relieved of any other social burdens, although Georgiana required reminding of her obligations as hostess, once servants had appeared with refreshments. Fortunately, Mrs Annesley assisted the girl.

As everyone was engaged in partaking of the lovely fruits, cakes, and other delicacies, Mr Darcy entered the room. Caroline had just taken a large bite from a slice of poppy seed cake, and was forced to turn away, so he would not witness her in the unbecoming act of chewing. When she finally was able to swallow, which was difficult in a mouth suddenly gone dry, she saw he was speaking to Georgiana. 'Why don't you tell us, dear one, of your latest musical triumph?'

Georgiana, eyes downcast at first, spoke shyly of playing before some royal guests the week before, in town. Caroline had been present and had thought that Georgiana played very well for such a young person. Not as well as she herself would have, of course, but unfortunately she was not invited to take a turn at the pianoforte.

Caroline's eyes quickly moved to Elizabeth, to see if she was fawning over Mr Darcy, or otherwise flirting, behaviour which surely he would frown upon. To her surprise, and disappointment, Elizabeth appeared entirely at ease, smiling at Georgiana and asking questions to draw out more details of her performance. But wait, no, she did take a quick sidelong glance at Mr Darcy. No doubt about it, whatever reason she'd had for refusing him, and surely the only reason she could have had would have been to further inflame Mr Darcy's interest in her by appearing out of his grasp, she seemed quite receptive now.

Caroline ground her teeth, quietly, and had to restrain herself from stamping her foot. How dare this minx entertain hopes of winning Mr Darcy? Elizabeth had not spoken directly to him now, she was much too clever for that, but Caroline could tell her meek air was not doing her any harm in his eyes. Quickly, knowing she must remind him of the reasons he had refused to even entertain any thoughts of long-term connections with the Bennets, she asked, 'Pray, Miss Eliza, are not the—shire Militia removed from Meryton? They must be a great loss to your family.'

She wanted to mention Wickham, for she now regretted not encouraging Eliza's interest in that gentleman, but dared not do so in Mr Darcy's presence. Elizabeth, though, appeared to completely understand all that remained unsaid, for she flushed, but when she spoke, her tone was reasonably composed. 'It is of little matter, for we have many distractions in Hertfordshire.'

Elizabeth did glance at Mr Darcy while speaking, but he was looking, with concern, at his sister, whose countenance was also flushed, and somewhat distressed.

Elizabeth continued speaking, attempting to lift Georgiana's gaze from her hands which were twisting together on her lap, and at length the girl smiled at something Eliza said. Mr Darcy smiled warmly at Elizabeth, and Caroline's heart writhed within her chest and she began to experience strong sensations of nausea.

She could not leave the room while the visitors yet remained, but fortunately for her composure, the visit did not last more than a few minutes longer. As Mr Darcy left the room to see the callers out, Caroline took in some deep breaths of air, and her head cleared.

'I declare,' Louisa said, 'I thought they would never leave.'

Caroline was not yet ready to speak, but Georgiana, appearing confused, said, 'I did not think their visit overlong. The time passed most pleasantly.'

Caroline could not allow this remark to go unchallenged. She could not permit Elizabeth to use her wiles on Mr Darcy without at least trying to dissuade him. It was for his sake, after all, that she needed to be so harsh, for a marriage with one such as Eliza would surely ruin him.

'Ah,' she said, 'the innocent joys of youth. Time passes, I find, more heavily as one grows older and I, for one, am unwilling to waste any time with visitors such as Miss Elizabeth and her aunt.'

Georgiana now appeared distressed. 'You are not so very much older than I. And the call did not last more than a half hour, which is perfectly acceptable.'

'You are indeed a sweet girl,' Caroline said, 'unwilling to see anything other than good in any one. But you need to be careful not to be taken in by the appearance of goodness alone.'

Georgiana's lips trembled, and she was unable to speak, so Caroline turned to her sister. 'Did you not observe how very dowdy both of our visitors appeared? Indeed, speaking of age, I think Eliza risks ruining her skin with all her running about the countryside.'

'I thought,' Georgiana said, her voice little above a whisper, 'their appearance was perfectly lovely.'

Caroline shrugged and, enjoying herself now, continued to denigrate

Elizabeth's person and behaviour. Something inside her could not just give up and allow Eliza to be triumphant. She was now feeling much better than a few minutes earlier and so, when Mr Darcy appeared, she invited him to join in the game.

'How very ill Miss Eliza Bennet looks this morning, Mr Darcy,' she cried. 'I never in my life saw anyone so much altered as she is since the winter. She is grown so brown and coarse! Louisa and I were agreeing that we should not have known her again.'

He did not answer at first, choosing to sit by his sister and take her hand. Only once she had given him a tremulous smile did he say, 'I would have known her anywhere. I could discern no alteration other than that she is rather tanned, which is no miraculous consequence of travelling in the summer.'

'Indeed?' Caroline replied, a sense of desperation filling her heart. 'For my own part, I must confess that I never could see any beauty in her. Her face is too thin; her complexion has no brilliancy; and her features are not at all handsome. Her nose wants character—there is nothing marked in its lines. Her teeth are tolerable, but not out of the common way; and as for her eyes, which have sometimes been called fine,' she smiled at Mr Darcy, hoping he would respond with humour, but he did not. 'I could never see anything extraordinary in them,' she continued, determined to surge ahead. 'They have a sharp, shrewish look, which I do not like at all; and in her air altogether there is a self-sufficiency without fashion, which is intolerable.'

Mr Darcy had turned back to his sister while Caroline spoke, and he reached now to brush a thumb over her cheek, and to whisper something to her. She nodded resolutely in response, and so he turned back to Caroline. His brows were lowered and a small frown curved his lips downward. Taking heart, since this appeared to Caroline to show he was reconsidering his praise of Eliza, she swept on.

'I remember, when we first knew her in Hertfordshire, how amazed we all were to find she was a reputed beauty.' His brow lowered further, and Caroline knew she was succeeding in her aim, and that surely he could no longer think well of that minx. 'I particularly recollect your saying one night,' she said with a laugh, 'after they had been dining at

Netherfield, "She a beauty!—I should as soon call her mother a wit."' She burst out laughing, joined by Louisa, but Mr Darcy did not show by any word or expression what he was thinking. Worrying for the first time that perhaps she had gone too far, for Georgiana appeared on the verge of tears, Caroline added, 'But afterwards she seemed to improve on you, and I believe you thought her rather pretty at one time.'

'Yes,' Mr Darcy replied, standing up and tucking Georgiana's hand through his arm, 'but that was only when I first saw her, for it is many months since I have considered her as one of the handsomest women of my acquaintance.' He then escorted his sister from the room, leaving Caroline gaping at Louisa in shock.

'How very rude of him!' Louisa said. 'This behaviour can only be the result of the time he has spent with Miss Elizabeth and her aunt.'

Caroline attempted to smile at her sister's staunch support, but could not. 'Oh Louisa, what am I to do? Yes, I love Mr Tryphon more than I do Mr Darcy, but I know nothing about Stephen, where he lives, how large his estate, from whence he draws his income. And ever since I first met Mr Darcy and came to Pemberley, I have wished for nothing more than to become its mistress.'

'I know.' Louisa stood, her fists clenched at her sides, reminding Caroline of nothing so much as a bantam hen, prepared to defend its nest. 'I do not think Mr Darcy is going to rush off and wed Elizabeth, and so this means you have time. When we return to town you can speak more to Mr Tryphon. But if it is Pemberley you want, my dearest, then Pemberley you shall have.'

'But how?' Caroline asked, her voice rising into a wail.

'We shall think of something.' Louisa nodded, her face stern. 'I know that we shall think of something.'

*   *   *

Caroline spent a quiet evening. She'd thought about staying in her rooms, and thus not be required to act as if everything was fine, but was concerned that her brother might worry if she secluded herself so soon after her recent illness. She could not bear to be part of the evening's entertainment, a game of whist, and so sat in a corner with a book open on her lap.

Mr Darcy was part of the game, but she hoped he observed her sitting studiously, her head bent over the page. None of the words that rested on the page entered her mind, although she did think to turn a page once in a while. When at last the game ended, she pleaded fatigue and hurried upstairs.

The next morning she rose early, having slept little, and took extra care with her appearance, needing to chide Genney on two occasions; the first because her strokes while brushing Caroline's hair were not even, the second because the stupid girl could not find a gown that Caroline agreed to wear. The maroon was too dark, the blue too sad, the orange too lively. Finally settling on a pale brown with yellow trim, Caroline suffered Genney's efforts with ill-concealed impatience as the maid tied and buttoned.

When she at length came downstairs to the breakfast room, she discovered that Mr Darcy had already eaten and left the house. Louisa and Caroline ate little but Charles, seemingly unaware of their low spirits, spoke happily about the dinner for that evening, at which the Gardiners and Miss Elizabeth were expected. Caroline and Louisa glanced at each other and both heaved huge sighs.

Caroline's spirits were not raised when she discovered, upon asking a servant, that Mr Darcy had gone to Lambton. His return, not long after she'd finished her breakfast, further depressed her, for even as he was striding into the foyer, he announced he needed to go to London, and would leave as soon as he could be ready.

'London?' Caroline gasped. 'But we have just come from there!'

'I am aware of that, Miss Bingley.' He did not even break stride as he passed her.

His valet appeared, somehow knowing, even from upstairs, that he was required. Mr Darcy announced that he'd be leaving, for how long he did not know. The valet simply nodded, as if his master returned to Pemberley only to depart immediately on a regular basis.

Mr Darcy then paused and turned to Caroline, but it was only to ask if she knew where he could find his sister. Caroline shook her head, her bewilderment growing.

'Might I inquire as to the reason for this sudden journey?' she asked.

'Surely there is no business so urgent that it must tear you away from the pleasures of your home; and from the company of your friends and family.'

He shook his head slightly at that, almost as if coming to his senses, as if he'd been far away in his mind and only now recollected where he was. 'I do apologise,' he said, going so far as to take her hand. 'I realise that I am being a poor host, but this is a matter of some urgency that cannot wait.'

She was about in make further inquiries, but the hallway was suddenly filled with other questioning voices, as Charles and Louisa appeared.

'What is this I hear?' Charles demanded. 'Are you truly heading off to town, right this minute?'

Mr Darcy laughed. 'No, not this very minute. But I am afraid that I do have to leave you, and will possibly be away for several days. My sister, however, will be happy to serve as your hostess, and will be at least as able as I in ensuring your comfort and entertainment during your stay here.' He turned, as his sister appeared.

'Brother,' she said, her eyes wide. 'Is there trouble?'

The girl appeared positively frightened, and Caroline moved to her side and took her trembling hand.

Brother and sister looked at one another and Caroline was certain that something was communicated, even though no words were spoken. Whatever it was, it seemed to calm Georgiana, for she stopped trembling and, pulling her hand out of Caroline's, turned to the three Bingleys with a smile that, if not confident, at least did not waver. 'Please,' she said, waving a hand towards her favourite morning room. 'Make yourselves comfortable. I will join you shortly.'

Not knowing what else to do, the three Bingleys entered the sunlit room, while Georgiana and Mr Darcy walked along the hall towards the stairs. Caroline, the last to leave the hallway and enter the room, saw the two of them, heads bent towards each other, as they spoke softly. Mr Darcy rested a hand, gently, on his sister's shoulder, and then glanced back to where Caroline stood, half in and out of the room, watching him.

He nodded to her, and then turned a corner and was gone.

* * *

While she was relieved that Mr Darcy's absence meant there was no dinner with Elizabeth and her relations, the days he was gone passed slowly. Georgiana grew into her role as hostess and even appeared to grow physically, for with her increasing confidence she held her head higher, appearing ever more elegant. She held a supper party for some neighbours, and on a day when the weather was particularly fine, she ordered up a picnic lunch for herself and her guests.

During the supper party, Charles stepped easily into the role of host, his affability and relaxed nature acting as a natural counterpoint to Georgiana's somewhat tense poise. Caroline watched as the two of them greeted the guests as they arrived, thinking wistfully of what a fine couple they made. She had little energy for them, for her concerns over her own prospects rested too heavily in her mind.

Now, at the picnic, she sat on a blanket that had been set out on the grass for her by a servant, and nibbled a piece of bread and jam; she watched as Charles told a story of his and Mr Darcy's time at university, and Georgiana let her head fall back as she laughed. At a little distance, Mr Hurst held up a large strawberry so that Louisa could take a bite from it, an unusually demonstrative gesture for him, but an affectionate one all the same. In the air, birds chased one another, their songs taunting Caroline, who was seemingly the only creature alone on this beautiful warm day. All about her, Mr Darcy's property glowed in the sunlight, the lake sparkling as swans swam in pairs and swallows skimmed the surface as they dipped their beaks to drink. The hills shading to a greyer green as they receded into the distance, the trees growing denser as they climbed from grassy sward to the increasingly steep and rocky cliffs that ran by the river; they all appeared to have only one purpose in appearing so beautiful, and that was to taunt Miss Caroline Bingley with all she would never have.

Was Mr Darcy even now with Miss Elizabeth Bennet? Did they sit together in his fine house in town, laughing at the foolish pretensions of one Miss Bingley? Did Mr Darcy raise Eliza's hand to his lips, gazing into her eyes as his warm breath caressed her skin?

The thought of lips pressed to the back of a lady's hand brought Mr Tryphon to her mind. His image, with his dark eyes filled with warmth as he gazed up at her, was vivid enough to send Mr Darcy and Eliza into the background, although it didn't banish their derisive laughter completely.

Mr Tryphon. She hadn't heard from him since she'd come to Pemberley. No card, no letter, nor from Eleanor either. Did they also see her as an object of scorn, someone to be laughed at for her aspirations and self-importance?

But, she was important. Without conscious effort, she rose to her feet. She was Miss Caroline Bingley, and on her shoulders rested the aspirations and dreams of previous generations of Bingleys, all of whom had worked hard, not for personal gain but for the family name. She, Louisa, and Charles owed everything they had to them. Louisa had done the best she could, and while her marriage to Mr Hurst was a respectable one, it did little to increase the family's standing in society. Charles took his good fortune far too casually, as evidenced by his lack of action in securing Georgiana's affections. No, if anyone was going to continue the Bingley family's ascendance, it would be Caroline.

She took a few steps towards the lake, her head high, her shoulders resolute. Suddenly Georgiana and Louisa were on either side of her, each taking one of her arms, each prattling about something or other. Caroline tipped her head back so the sun could warm her face. The three women continued down the grassy slope to the lake, where they were greeted by swans hoping for bread crusts.

* * *

When Mr Darcy returned, late one evening, he slipped into the house quietly, during dinner, so no one was aware of his presence until after he'd been to his rooms and changed his dusty travelling clothes for something more respectable.

Caroline had been ignoring the conversation, which consisted of Charles and Mr Hurst each arguing that his particular favourite hunting dog was better than the other man's dog. They were apparently both convinced that if one dog's name was spoken more often than the other's, that dog would emerge victorious. The last time she'd dredged up enough energy to pay attention, she'd heard:

'Bullfinch!'

'No, no, Digger can run circles around old Bully.'

'He cannot! Bullfinch might be older, but that means he is wilier.'

'Being wily matters little when another dog gets to the bird first.'

'Bullfinch returns the birds in better condition, and more often.'

'Nonsense, Digger does.'

'No, Bullfinch does.'

'Digger!'

'Bullfinch!'

Judging from the inflections of the two speakers, nothing much had changed in the dialogue. Glancing about, Caroline saw Louisa was engaged in drawing little circles in her rapidly drying gravy with her fork, while Georgiana was attempting to be a good hostess, and so appeared to be paying attention to what the gentlemen were saying. Judging from the rapidity with which she turned her head towards each man as he spoke, the poor girl was likely to develop a violent headache.

Georgiana's body suddenly relaxed, and the change was enough to draw Caroline's attention. Following the younger woman's gaze towards the dining room door, she saw Mr Darcy, leaning against the side of the entry, a small smile playing about his lips as he observed the battle. The two men continued their fiery discussion, so involved in it they did not observe Darcy's appearance until Georgiana leapt up and ran lightly to greet him.

'Forgive me, gentlemen, but you're both in error,' he said as he made his way to the table, one hand clasping Georgiana's. 'There is no dog that can hold a candle to Trevor.'

'Trevor!' Charles howled the name in outrage. 'That piece of mange running about on four legs, and that's only on a good day, cannot be dignified with the term "dog"!' He leapt up, fists held before him as if to attack Mr Darcy, before breaking into a big grin and taking Mr Darcy's free hand in his. 'It is good to see you. You must be famished. Please sit!— And your business? Has it been concluded satisfactorily?'

Smiling, Mr Darcy clapped Charles on his shoulder and made his way to his chair, left empty at the head of the table.

'It has, indeed. Thank you for your inquiry.'

There was something in Mr Darcy's usual rich tone that made Caroline sit up and study him more carefully—a richer touch of velvet in his voice; his hair, slightly mussed as if he'd brushed it in haste, gave him a more relaxed mien; a depth in his eyes, not warmth exactly, but something of a cat who has been in the cream. Or, given the recent topic of conversation, a dog who has successfully retrieved its prey.

He was in particularly good spirits throughout the meal. Caroline, though, felt chilled, and even asked a servant to fetch her a wrap, for whenever Mr Darcy's gaze happened to pass over her, he looked through her as if she were a ghost. He didn't see her at all, sitting there in her pale green gown, but he did see something, a sight that from time to time curved his lips into a satisfied smile.

She was more invisible than she'd ever been in her whole life.

And so her conversation became ever more lively, her laugh louder, her expressions as vivacious as possible. Everyone else responded and appeared to enjoy her company, Charles adding several witty comments, Georgiana clapping her hands in delight. Even Mr Hurst threw back his head and laughed at one of her particularly humorous tales. Mr Darcy smiled only to his own agenda, his eyes gazing into the distance at sights to be seen only inside his head.

Chapter Twelve

❧

A few days later, at breakfast, Caroline picked up the *Courier*, one of the London newspapers. Conversation was non-existent, as everyone else appeared not yet fully awake, and so, bored, she flipped through the pages to the social news. 'Oh!' she cried, slapping a hand on the linen tablecloth, 'this is news that is too good not to be shared.'

Everyone looked up at her, sleep-blurred eyes coming into sharper focus.

'One of the Bennet sisters has been married!' Caroline said triumphantly. 'And you'll never guess which one and to whom!'

Charles and Mr Darcy's eyes sharpened further and, waiting before the revelation so that suspense could grow, Caroline thought she saw fear on both men's countenances. She let the silence drag even longer, thinking, *Serves you right, both of you, for entertaining such silly and clearly unsuitable hopes.*

When she could wait no longer, fearing she would literally explode if she didn't tell them right away, she announced, 'Miss Lydia Bennet! Can you believe such a thing! And to none other than our own Mr Wickham!' With a triumphant smile, she laid the paper down and looked about to drink in their shock and amazement. She was, however, cruelly disappointed.

While Louisa's face was a classic dropped jaw and widened eyes, Charles looked only a trifle surprised, his emotion conveying mostly relief. And Mr Darcy appeared completely unruffled, her news not affecting him in the least. She continued to watch him, assuming it would take a moment for her words to sink in, but he glanced towards the opposite end of the table, where his sister sat and his expression, when he returned it to Caroline, was one of muted fury.

Too late, Caroline recalled that all mention of Mr Wickham was forbidden in Georgiana's presence. She quickly hid her glee and said, 'The announcement is pitifully small, not worthy of anyone in society's notice. No surprise there; the Bennets have no chance of being so much as noticed by anyone we know.'

Georgiana, her lips trembling, stood up but at a gesture from her brother, sat down again and, squaring her shoulders, said, 'Would anyone like another cup of tea?' in a voice that while not strong, was at least spoken loudly enough to be heard by all at the table.

Mr Hurst wanted more toast, and so everyone sat, staring at their empty plates or, in Georgiana's case, pushing her scrambled eggs around and around the plate with her fork, until Mr Darcy stood to signal the end of the meal. As he had been staring at Caroline, after sending a proud look at his sister, Caroline was glad to leave the room. While she craved notice from Mr Darcy, the expression in his dark eyes had not been one of affection. Before she reached the door, he spoke to her brother. 'Charles, there is a matter I have long needed to confess to you. Will you do me the honour of joining me in my study?'

'Of course.' Charles looked a little surprised at the formality of the request but, affable as always, readily led the way to the room mentioned. Caroline and Louisa looked at each other, both wondering why Mr Darcy had used the word 'confession' and not 'business' or 'matter of mutual interest', but as neither had the slightest idea, they proceeded to the morning room, where they were both decorating new church bonnets. Invited to join them, Georgiana indicated that she would return to her rooms.

As they passed Mr Darcy's study, they heard a sudden shout from their brother, and both froze in place. The sound had been somewhat muffled by the study's thick door, and they couldn't tell if he'd been calling out in anger, surprise, or humour.

'Should we check to see if everything is quite all right?' Louisa asked in a whisper.

Even though Caroline was most eager to learn what was being said inside the room, she knew if the men were interrupted, they would cease speaking of anything of interest. Since she could now hear the low murmur of both men's voices, she said with a sigh, 'It does not appear that anything terrible has occurred, and it does not become us to eavesdrop. Let us continue on our way.'

Louisa looked at her with some surprise, no doubt because eavesdropping had, at times, been a useful pastime for Caroline, but she made no comment. Caroline did wish to learn what it was that Mr Darcy had found so urgent to say to Charles.

As it turned out, she did not have long to wonder. She and Louisa had barely had time to fetch their bonnets and ribbons, and seat themselves at the table the servants had covered with needles, threads, lace, and other necessities, when they heard the men's voices out in the hallway, and realised the conversation must have been concluded. Satisfactorily, it appeared, for both men sounded jovial.

After a short time of further talk, the gentlemen joined the ladies in the morning room. Before Caroline could open her mouth to ask if their business was of a nature that could be shared, they both fixed her with a cold stare. Mr Darcy's was like his usual hauteur, but Charles, instead of regarding her with brotherly affection, clenched his jaw in anger. She shrank back in her chair, and all thoughts of asking anything vanished from her head.

Mr Darcy sank into a chair and asked Charles, 'I forgot to ask while we were discussing the matter, but does your lease on Netherfield Park still have time on it?'

'Why, yes,' Charles said. He turned away from Caroline. 'There are several months remaining.'

'I suggest you send a message to have the house prepared for its master's return.'

'I shall do so at once,' Charles said with more than his usual show of enthusiasm.

'Return to Netherfield Park?' Caroline asked, rising to her feet. 'What on earth for?'

Charles glanced at Darcy before replying. 'I have a matter of the utmost importance which must be dealt with.'

'But can you not conclude your business from here? We are so comfortably situated at Pemberley.' She approached her brother where he stood by the window and laid a hand on his arm. To her surprise he moved away from her, so her hand fell through empty air to rest again by her side. The movement was so abrupt she almost thought he'd purposely avoided her touch.

'No, sister,' he said, moving to the fireplace. 'This business is of a personal nature, and can only be concluded in Hertfordshire.'

A terrible thought grew in Caroline's mind, and she reached behind her, groping to find the table and the back of her chair. She slowly sank down onto it, her eyes held by Louisa's, who clearly was thinking the same thing. Still, she determined to try once more to deter him from this course of action. 'You realise, of course, that to go to Netherfield is to find ourselves in the endless dreary company of Bennets. There are so many of them, after all, even with Lydia married, and all of them have no end of embarrassments to inflict on their betters. You must agree, Charles, that we will be much better off here, with the sort of company we prefer. Surely Hertfordshire has nothing to offer that cannot be found in Derbyshire.'

Charles looked at her in silence for a moment, and then sighed. 'Hertfordshire has many pleasant aspects that are found nowhere else, not even in the gracious home of our friend, Mr Darcy.' Mr Darcy inclined his head to acknowledge the compliment, but Charles continued to speak without looking at his friend.

'Caroline and Louisa, you have done me a great disservice, in hiding from me the knowledge that Miss Jane Bennet was in London while we also were there. How terribly rude she must have thought me, to not send her so much as a polite note.' He paused, clearly in the grip of some strong emotion. 'You could well have inflicted more damage on me than you could have imagined.' He heaved a huge sigh. 'Still, since Darcy was a part of this too, I cannot assign all the blame to you. And you know well my nature; I cannot long remain out of sorts. I have forgiven him and I will, in time, forgive you also. But please, if you wish to win back my affection in a timely fashion, desist from any talk that insults the Bennet family or the area they call home.'

Caroline's jaw dropped. Never before had her brother spoken so sternly to her. She was about to protest, to show him that, head of the family or not, he could not treat her like this, but she noticed that Mr Darcy's dark eyes were fixed on her. And so, she merely inclined her head respectfully. 'As you wish, Charles. Although, you must admit that some of the Bennet sisters' behaviour has at times been reprehensible. Still, why you think we would insult Miss Jane Bennet, when she is our dear friend, is beyond me.'

Charles held up a hand. 'You would be better off, Caroline, if you had ceased speaking after your first sentence. Do not add to the burden of anger I carry.'

Caroline turned to Louisa, whose countenance reflected the same hurt and astonishment Caroline felt, but neither tried to speak. They turned back to their bonnets, although as Caroline picked up a piece of pretty yellow ribbon to add to hers, she noticed it danced about in the air, because her hands were trembling.

The gentlemen left them in peace shortly after Charles had delivered his cruel words, and Caroline and Louisa worked in silence for a time. After a while, Caroline heard voices outside, and went to the window to see the two men with several servants carrying their guns, and a pack of dogs, all of whose tails were wagging. 'They have gone hunting,' she said. 'Now, Louisa, what do you make of this and what are we to do about it?'

'Do you seek my thoughts on the fact that Charles clearly seems determined to run after Miss Bennet again, or that he spoke so terribly to us? And as for what to do about either, I have not the slightest idea. Indeed, I am still in shock. Please, call for some tea and refreshments. Even though it is early, I fear I will faint if I do not receive some sustenance.'

Caroline rang for a servant, thinking hard. 'About Charles treating us so abominably, all we can do is let time pass. As he said, he never can remain angry for long, and he will soon approach, begging our forgiveness. As for the other matter, it is far more serious. Can you imagine us with Lydia Wickham as a sister-in-law?'

'Surely Charles would not allow that! Just think of how painful it would be for Mr Darcy to receive that man in his home!'

The mention of Mr Darcy brought an even worse thought into her head, one she would no doubt have discovered immediately if she hadn't been so shaken by Charles' treatment of her. 'Louisa,' she gasped. 'Did it not appear to you that Mr Darcy also intends to go to Netherfield Park? What if he sees Charles' continuing interest in Jane as indicating he should continue to pursue Miss Elizabeth?'

'Surely that cannot be!' Louisa's hands went to her mouth.

'I know she has refused him, but I am told that some gentlemen take a refusal to be nothing more than an attempt to increase his ardour by increasing the challenge.'

'Mr Darcy would not fall for such a ploy!'

'No,' Caroline said darkly, 'but I wouldn't put it past Eliza. Why else would she have refused him? A woman in her situation, turning down the position and wealth that would be hers if she became mistress of Pemberley? It is unthinkable.'

Louisa nodded, and then reached out eagerly as a tray of tea and cakes was brought to them. Caroline picked up her bonnet, but the item, the height of fashion in town, held little allure. 'I feel a headache coming on,' she told her sister. 'Please forgive me if I leave you, but I need to lie down.'

'Of course,' Louisa said, a cake already halfway to her mouth. 'I hope that you are soon recovered.'

'I hope so too,' Caroline said, but the thought of Mr Darcy in the same area as Miss Elizabeth did not permit the ache to depart.

* * *

Charles' pique had vanished by the time the evening meal was served, and he spoke as ever he did, enthusing over the hunt they'd had that day, and where he planned to fish on the morrow. While he did not beg her forgiveness, or so much as hint at an apology, Caroline decided to allow the matter to drop, for she had larger matters to occupy her mind.

Over the next several days, Mr Darcy continued to be the affable and gentlemanly host he always was but Caroline, after much close observation, became convinced that he was different. Although he appeared relaxed, there was something of a coiled spring about him. Even when he sat still, reading or listening as his sister played at the pianoforte, Caroline felt as if he was holding himself back from something. She had no idea what the thing might be, and did not mention her theory to Louisa or Charles, not wanting to appear foolish. She could not overcome the sense that Mr Darcy was longing to surge into action, but for some reason was holding himself back.

One afternoon Charles sought out his sisters as they sat in the music room, Louisa turning pages as Caroline played. Georgiana was with her music tutor and Mrs Annesley, using the smaller instrument in her rooms.

'Louisa, Caroline,' Charles said, waving a letter in the air. 'We have been invited by our friends the Restons in Scarborough to visit them for a few weeks. I have informed them that I will be unable to take advantage of their kind invitation, but that you and Mr Hurst will be happy to see them.'

'I beg your pardon?' Even as she spoke, Caroline's thoughts spun. *He wishes to ensure that I will not be in Hertfordshire to interfere with his plans. Oh! Foolish man. Never before has he so needed his sisters.*

'I believe I spoke clearly,' he said, sitting down and placing both hands flat on his knees, the letter dangling from one corner. 'It has been some time since you have seen your school friend, Emily Reston. Are you not happy to think of being with her again?'

'Of course I am,' Caroline answered automatically. 'But will you not need a hostess while you are in Hertfordshire?'

Charles raised an eyebrow, and for a moment looked uncannily like Mr Darcy. 'I would think that you'd welcome this opportunity to not have to be in the same county as the Bennet family. Has your attitude towards them changed for the better?'

Caroline hesitated, unsure of how to respond. She had no wish to again anger her brother, but she was incapable of lying. She chose to avoid the question. 'And what of Georgiana? Are we to leave her all alone? Or does she travel with you and Mr Darcy to Netherfield?'

Mr Darcy walked into the room at this point, and clearly had heard her question. 'Georgiana will remain here, as she has her companion, her lessons, and her work about the estate to occupy her. And I will be able to stay in Hertfordshire only long enough to see Charles settled, as I need to spend some days in town; Georgiana will, if she wishes, join me there. So you can see that your concern, while reflecting admirably upon your character, is not necessary.'

Had he just paid her a compliment? Caroline had no time to wonder.

The danger of allowing Charles, alone and undefended, to become prey to Miss Bennet was unthinkable. She must find a way to be with him, so she could protect him from making a disastrous decision. The fact that Mr Darcy would stay only briefly gave her some solace, for clearly he was not intending to renew his suit with Elizabeth, but Charles was the one she must consider now.

'My dear brother. Louisa and I cannot bear to think of being parted from you. If we must leave Pemberley, at least permit us to be all together.'

'Mr Hurst was delighted by the news, when I told him,' Charles said dryly. 'I assumed he spoke for Mrs Hurst also.' He turned a questioning gaze on Louisa. Caroline didn't bother turning to look at her sister. She knew she would never disagree with her husband so publicly. She realised, also, that if she protested too much, Charles' suspicions would be raised, and that might make him act in whatever manner he knew was least like what she wanted for him. Very well, she would go to Scarborough, but would plan to cut the visit short, and travel to Netherfield as soon as possible.

When the time came to leave, Caroline looked back at Pemberley, its warm pinkish-brown stone glowing in the early morning sunlight and wondered if the next time she saw it, she would arrive as its mistress. Somehow, that seemed a very forlorn hope. Sighing, she turned to face forward as the carriage crunched over the gravel drive, ignoring Georgiana, who stood on the front steps waving goodbye.

* * *

Delightful as it was to see her friend Emily, Caroline found the time in Scarborough moved forward so slowly that sometimes she wondered if she should do what she'd been told prisoners locked away in tiny cells tended to do, which was carve a mark into the wall to mark each passing day. At least if she did that, she would see actual proof that the days were passing by.

Good manners required that she stay at least some weeks, and indeed it was pleasant to see Emily again, but each day seemed the same, for her thoughts were the same—wondering what was happening in Hertfordshire. The only thing that changed was her increasing desperation. Finally, after more than three weeks had passed, the news she'd dreaded arrived in the form of a letter, announcing that Charles was engaged to Jane.

She read the letter through several more times, but found no mention of another engagement. Did that mean Mr Darcy was no longer interested in Elizabeth? Or, was it that they were engaged also, but Charles felt he should permit Mr Darcy to pass on the news?

It was only on the fifth perusal of the letter that she noticed Charles had said he had joined Mr Darcy in town and expected to remain there for a few more days before they both returned to Hertfordshire.

'We must return to London as quickly as possible,' she told Louisa after handing her the letter.

They went in search of their hostess, finding her in the nursery dandling her first child, a fat and rather ugly baby of eleven months, on her knee. Emily, although naturally disappointed her guests were leaving so soon, understood completely that of course they needed to be in town so as to help arrange the wedding.

Three days later they were in town, and were invited to dine with the Darcys that evening. Mr Darcy, Caroline thought, had seemed surprised to learn they had left Scarborough, but not displeased. Georgiana, who'd arrived from Pemberley only the previous day, was her usual shy yet gracious self.

If Charles was effervescent during most of his life, now he was positively bouncy. 'While it does my heart good,' Caroline whispered to Louisa, 'to see our brother so happy, I wish his engagement brought joy to the rest of us.' Louisa had no opportunity to respond, for Charles seized her by her waist and waltzed her around the room.

During the meal and the card game that followed, Caroline studied Mr Darcy carefully, yet circumspectly. He showed no sign of unrequited love. Perhaps her hopes were realised, and he truly had no further interest in Elizabeth.

She was still concerned, though, and voiced her misgivings to her sister once they had arrived back at the Hurst's house on Grosvenor Street. Louisa listened sympathetically, but had nothing particularly useful to say.

The next morning, Louisa entered Caroline's bedchamber. Caroline, still fatigued from the journey, lingered in her bed, sipping a cup of tea, and she languidly raised an eyebrow at her sister.

'It's perfect!' Louisa declared. 'It's the only way to bring him to his senses!'

Caroline watched her sister pace the room, seemingly too excited to stay still. She nibbled the toast Genney had brought, and drank more tea, content for now to wait to learn what Louisa was on about.

Louisa spun away from the window and practically threw herself down on Caroline's bed. Caroline winced as her teacup was violently shaken in her hand, causing the liquid inside to slosh onto its saucer.

'How can you sit so calmly?' Louisa demanded.

'For one thing,' Caroline said, somewhat impatiently, 'you are displaying enough energy for both of us. And there is one other thing—I have not the faintest idea of what you speak.'

Louisa laughed and then, taking the cup and putting it on the breakfast tray, took Caroline's hands in her own. 'I told you we would find a way to bring Mr Darcy to his senses, show him he cannot possibly think of making Eliza Bennett mistress of Pemberley.'

Despite herself, Caroline felt a small frisson of excitement shiver down her spine. 'And how, might I ask, will we bring about this miracle?'

Louisa smiled, mischief flashing in her eyes the way it had when they had still been in the nursery and she was planning some new escapade that would be fun for herself and her sister, and could be blamed on Charles. 'It's very simple. We write a letter.'

Caroline's impatience grew, but she decided to play along, since Louisa was so clearly enjoying herself. 'To whom?'

'His aunt,' Louisa said, putting a space between each word. 'Lady Catherine de Bourgh.'

Caroline sat back against the pillows Genney had arranged, as the true genius of this idea soaked into her head. 'Louisa,' she breathed, 'you have outdone yourself. Lady Catherine is determined that he marry her daughter, Anne. She will not for one second permit him to so much as think about a person such as Eliza.'

Louisa nodded. 'And he is equally determined not to marry his cousin. But Lady Catherine will do a thorough job of pointing out all the reasons an alliance with Miss Bennet would be a disaster. Once he is again rational, he will forget about Eliza. When he considers Anne, he will realise there is a much more palatable choice for him to make. Who better than the sister of his closest friend?'

Caroline clapped her hands, and then wrapped her arms about Louisa. Louisa melted for a moment into the hug, but then pulled free, her cheeks a trifle pink, for the Bingleys were not much given to such displays of affection. Caroline pushed her bedclothes away, and stood, calling for Genney. 'I will dress immediately, and we shall compose this letter at once!'

* * *

They did not have long to wait to discover the results of their letter for, as luck would have it, they were spending the afternoon, a few days after it had been sent, at Darcy's house.

Caroline was sitting in one of the sitting rooms that faced the front of the house. A carriage arrived, and Lady Catherine descended, her head held high, her blue eyes glinting in the sunshine with an icy glare sharper than the point of an icicle.

She swept into the house the moment the door was opened, ignoring Davenport's polite offer to take her cloak, pushing Molly aside with a swipe of her arm when the parlour maid asked her to wait until she'd been announced to the master.

Without needing to be shown the way, like a predator on the scent of her prey, she went straight to the study, where Mr Darcy, Caroline knew, was currently ensconced with Charles and the owner of the bank with whom Mr Darcy did business.

Lady Catherine flung the door open wide with a resounding crash. 'Fitzwilliam.' Her voice was not unduly raised, but the word seemed to echo into the sudden stillness. 'I will speak to you at once. Alone.' She waved her hand as if shooing away a fly, and the banker, all dignity lost, scuttled out of the room behind Charles. Lady Catherine closed the door practically on his heels.

He gave a quick nod to Caroline and Louisa who had left the sitting room in hopes of discovering more about the result of their letter and rushed away to the safety of the outdoors. Charles remained in the hall with his sisters. 'Caroline,' he said affably. 'You are staring at that door so keenly I would be astonished if you could not see right through its stout oaken planks.'

'Would that I could,' she said, her ears seemingly moving outwards from her head in the effort to hear what passed within.

'I am all astonishment,' Charles said. 'Are you truly going to stand out here and eavesdrop on a private conversation?'

Neither sister answered him, both moving closer to the door so they could press their ears against it. Charles grasped Louisa's shoulder and pulled her back. 'What would the servants think to see you acting in this unseemly manner?'

Caroline couldn't hear anything other than a rumble of voices, one shrill, the other moderated and low. She cursed Mr Darcy for installing such thick doors.

'Our presence here,' she said, 'will prevent the servants from listening, as they are wont to do. Far better that we hear what passes, so we can console Mr Darcy, than a housemaid or footman become privy to his private life. Servants do gossip so, you know.'

'Console?' Charles examined Caroline carefully, his face only inches from hers. 'How is it you know he will require sympathy? Can it be that Lady Catherine's unheralded arrival here was not so unexpected by you?'

Caroline and Louisa looked at each other.

'Aha!' Charles said. 'You have been up to something. You never could hide anything from me, not even when we were innocent children. Although given your current proclivities, I have to wonder if you ever were inno—'

'Oh do be quiet, Charles,' Caroline said crossly. His voice was drowning out any words she might have been able to hear from the study. Just as she was about to press her ear against the door again, it suddenly opened.

Without deigning to notice the three in the hall, Lady Catherine moved majestically past them. She was followed by Mr Darcy who, surprisingly, was smiling. 'I thank you, Aunt,' he said. 'What you have told me has greatly cleared my mind.'

'I knew you were capable of seeing the right path,' she said. 'Although, you should be ashamed of yourself for falling for that minx's wiles.'

'Oh, there are many things I have done and said recently,' he said, holding out his arm to escort her down the hall, 'of which I am deeply ashamed. I intend to rectify the matter immediately.'

'You are a dear boy.' Lady Catherine patted his arm. 'Now I must return to Rosings.'

'You do not wish to stay and take some refreshment before your journey?'

'I thank you for your hospitality, nephew, but I have travelled too many roads during the past days. I wish to return home at once, now that my mind is set at ease.'

'I am glad I could be of assistance.' Mr Darcy's smile was now a broad grin.

*　*　*

The entire house seemed to be holding its breath during the hours after Lady Catherine's departure. Caroline felt lightheaded, as if she too, was refraining from taking air into her lungs. When Georgiana returned from an outing with Mrs Annesley, she seemed to sense the strain, for she quickly retired to her rooms.

Even though Mr Darcy must have realised he was the subject of everyone's gaze, that everyone was bursting with the need to know what effects his aunt's visit had caused and what he planned to do now, he remained frustratingly the same as usual.

He spent some time in his study, sitting at his desk and going through some papers. He'd kindly left the door open so Caroline, who discovered a frequent need to pass through the hallway, could see he was apparently completely absorbed by his work. He then moved to the library, and sat down with a book.

Caroline joined him, picking up the first book she saw and sitting across from him, dropping her head as if engrossed in her book while she sent glances through her eyelashes to try to ascertain exactly which book it was that held his complete attention. Alas, she could not quite read the gilt letters on the book's spine, and so had to lean forward to see more closely.

She came close to losing her balance and tumbling from her chair onto the floor, at which point Mr Darcy looked up, eyebrow raised, and asked if she was quite all right. Raising her book to hide her flushed cheeks from him, she discovered she had selected a volume that discussed the merits of raising rabbits to put meat on the table, which included graphic diagrams of how best to kill and butcher them. Closing her eyes tightly in mortification, she heard Mr Darcy rise, pause for a moment before her, and then his footsteps grew softer as he left the room.

Dropping her book with relief, she hastened over to where he had been sitting, hoping he'd left his book on the table by his chair. She was in luck and reached to snatch it up. It was a treatise on the merits of the British parliamentary system. She dropped it into the chair he'd been using, surprised beyond words.

Where were the ardent poems about love she'd assumed he'd want to absorb? Why was he not, even now, kneeling before her, having realised that she was the only true choice he had for a wife?

When she finally bestirred herself, it was time to dress for dinner. At table, Mr Darcy appeared exactly the same as always, sitting with perfect posture, cutting his meat with deliberate strokes, responding occasionally to Charles' conversation about his new boots. Caroline knew she was unusually silent during the meal, but no one appeared to notice except Louisa, who was also captured by the heavy atmosphere inside the house, the sense that everything was in abeyance, waiting to learn what would happen.

It finally did. Rising from his chair as the ladies left the dining room to leave the gentlemen to their port and cigars, Darcy said to Charles, 'I think we should ride to Netherfield Park first thing tomorrow morning.'

And at that moment, Caroline realised she'd lost. She would never be the mistress of Pemberley. She'd known this before, but a tendril of hope had always remained. Now though, there was no hope at all.

In the parlour, she and Louisa sat in silence, both too overcome to find the energy to speak. At last, Louisa sighed and said, 'I suppose we must inform the maids to pack this evening.'

Caroline had been feeling as if she was surrounded by a heavy damp fog, too thick to permit her to so much as think, never mind move. Suddenly, while the fog did not lift, a dim light shone off in the distance, showing her the path. 'I,' she said, 'will not be leaving London.'

'Stay here?' Louisa asked, astonished.

'Do you think,' Caroline asked bitterly, 'that I wish to be in Hertford-shire to congratulate Miss Eliza on her engagement to be married?'

Louisa was even more astonished. 'You think that after his aunt's visit he will propose to Elizabeth and not to his cousin Anne?'

'I am certain of it. I know him well, and he is still in love with Eliza. Her ploy has worked, his love is more passionate than it was before she refused him, and she will not turn him down this time.'

'Oh, Caroline,' Louisa began, but Caroline stood and went to the window. Against the backdrop of street lamps and houses with glowing windows, listening to the clops of horses drawing carriages up and down the fashionable street, she studied her reflection in the glass. Her eyes appeared enormous; her hair rose much higher over her face than it did in the proper mirror in her bedchamber, and down one side of her face, a ripple in the glass made it appear that her cheek sagged down, pulled by the inexorable force of gravity.

'I know now,' she said to her flawed reflection, 'what I must do. Just as Mr Darcy returns to the one who refused him, so too shall I go to the one I have refused.' Squaring her shoulders, she turned away from the almost-frightening image in the window. 'I will wed Stephen. I love him, although I was willing to put that emotion aside for the sake of advancing our family. Stephen is a gentleman with an estate, and while it cannot possibly be as grand as Pemberley—'

'No estate can be as grand as Pemberley,' Louisa interjected.

'Exactly,' Caroline nodded. 'Still, he is a good match, any man with Eleanor's patronage must be. And I shall be happy with him. Oh! Louisa, I have never been, nor will be, as happy as I am in his presence!'

And just like that, with no particular effort on her part or, she suspected, any outward change, the burden she'd carried during the past many months dropped away, leaving her feeling as light as air. She even danced a little pirouette, which caused Louisa to burst into laughter.

At that point the gentlemen joined them, eager to discover the joke, but Caroline merely poured tea for them and sat, her eyes dancing now instead of her feet.

* * *

Caroline had last received a letter from Eleanor while she was in Scarborough, and that letter had been forwarded from Pemberley. In it, Eleanor said that she was living very quietly, preferring peace from the constant social whirl. This surprised Caroline, but in truth she hadn't thought much about her friend while her mind had been so filled with fears about Mr Darcy.

Now her mind was clear, and she sent a note to Eleanor, announcing her arrival in town and mentioning her hope to see her dear friend as soon as possible.

Eleanor sent a letter back the very next day, inviting Caroline to dine that evening. Caroline accepted with alacrity, and spent much effort ensuring she would look her best.

When she arrived, Eleanor ran lightly to greet her, giving her a kiss on each cheek. 'Let me look at you,' Eleanor cried, standing back. 'I declare, it has been ages. You must promise me this very moment that we shall never be parted again!'

Caroline smiled, and studied her friend in turn. Eleanor looked tired. The skin beneath her eyes was puffy, and there was a crease on her forehead that had not been present before.

The house seemed tired too, as Eleanor led her through different rooms to a small sitting room Caroline had not seen before. The larger rooms were dark, lit only with one or two lamps, and it appeared that some of the furniture was no longer in place. Perhaps Eleanor had moved it to different rooms, wanting to leave more space for dancing when she entertained.

When Caroline mentioned this, Eleanor seemed a trifle embarrassed, and then laughed. 'Oh no,' she said. 'I have no need for dancing these days. I much prefer to see only my very closest friends, and I now send out invitations very sparingly. I am so fatigued with great crowds and the noise they create. How much better it is to be able to speak intimately with those one most values. Would you not agree, my dearest?'

Caroline hid her surprise, and nodded, unsure of what to say. She was unable to visualise her friend living a quiet life. In the past Eleanor had been most fully alive when in society, surrounded by hordes of men to flirt with, and women about whom to gossip.

The small sitting room looked, Caroline thought, like a room one might have given over to the housekeeper. The furniture was well-used, upholstered in fabric that had been so long out of fashion Caroline could not recall having ever seen it before. There was only one window, and it was small and gave a view on to a back alley where Caroline could see a driver in his cart filled with barrels of ale. Why on earth would Eleanor choose to sit in a room where she could see only servants, Eleanor who had always prided herself on knowing everything that happened in society?

It would be impolite to ask though, and so Caroline turned her mind to the thought that was foremost in her visit here. 'Will Mr Tryphon be joining us?'

'Oh!' Eleanor broke into a wide smile. 'He will be so happy to hear that you have asked about him!'

'Has he gone away, then?' Caroline asked, her heart jumping into her throat. Had she missed her opportunity?

'Oh no,' Eleanor said quickly. 'He is here, keeping me company. But he was unsure of how you feel about him, and did not wish to cause you any distress with his presence.'

'Foolish man,' Caroline said indulgently. 'I could never be anything but delighted to be in his company.'

Eleanor studied Caroline for a moment, in silence, and Caroline wondered at the hope she saw suddenly flare into her friend's eyes. Then Eleanor leapt to her feet. 'I shall fetch him at once!' she cried and ran from the room.

Why did she go herself and not send a servant? Caroline wondered, but all thoughts then vanished when she realised she would soon see Stephen. She stood and sat again, ensuring her gown was draped in the most attractive way. She raised a hand to her hair, but found no errant strand to concern her. Thrusting her shoulders back, raising her head to show off her elegant, long neck, she endeavoured to appear completely unconcerned.

She did not have long to wait. Within moments she heard the sound of footsteps approaching, and Stephen burst through the door, followed closely by Eleanor.

'My dear Miss Bingley,' he cried. 'Words fail me. Let me say only how very beautiful you are, and how happy I am to see you.' He fell to his knees before where she sat and seized her hand, bringing it to his lips. She realised suddenly how much she'd missed seeing his brown eyes gazing so hotly up into her face. She put her other hand over the one that still clasped hers, and smiled, foolishly, she knew, like a little child when given a sweet, but it did not matter, nothing mattered, other than she was with Stephen once again.

The evening passed quickly. Eleanor spoke but little, her eyes never leaving the two who had so much to say to one another that they scarcely noticed her lack of conversation. Over the next several days, Caroline saw them often. They came to dine at the Hurst's home twice, and once she took them to the theatre, where they sat in Mr Darcy's box, empty since he was out of town. They went for rides in Mr Hurst's carriage, and sometimes she and Mr Tryphon walked together, her hand resting on his hard-muscled forearm.

Although Eleanor had left them alone a couple of times, he did not renew his proposals. Caroline wondered at this, for she knew he was even more in love with her than he had been. She knew from the times he spent gazing at her in silence, a small smile playing on his lips, and how he touched her often, little caresses that were not improper, but full of heated promises. He was fascinated by everything about her and everything she said, and she in turn never tired of learning more about him.

She therefore gave him all the encouragement she could, caressing his cheek when no one could see, giving him her full attention when he spoke, and letting her eyes linger on his broad shoulders, his deep eyes, and thick wavy hair. Indeed, it was no hardship for her to do these things, for she loved looking at him. At times she even caught herself looking, out of the corner of her eyes, of course, at the ripple of muscles that showed on his thighs through his tight breeches. At these times her breath grew tight and hot in her throat and, dragging her eyes towards the more respectable parts of his person, she wondered how it would feel to run her hands over those wide shoulders, or to have that broad chest pressed against her softness.

At last, there came the day when she realised he was ready to speak. Eleanor had left them alone in the small sitting room. Caroline hardly noticed the shabbiness any longer, all her senses filled with Stephen whenever and wherever she was with him. He sat across from her, looking down at his hands in his lap, his fingers twisting and untwisting. Twice he raised his eyes to her, opening his mouth as if to speak. She smiled encouragingly, but each time he looked down again. Finally, when she was wondering if she should encourage him in some way, perhaps even ask if he had something particular to say to her, he rose and squeezed onto the small settee beside her. It was small enough that the side of his leg pressed against her own, and he had to raise his arm, laying it across the back of the settee just above her shoulders, in order to fit his broad frame into the available space. She did not draw away and closed her eyes to let the heat of the contact between their thighs, even through his breeches, and her petticoats and gown, wash up through her body.

She opened her eyes to find him smiling at her. 'Is my proximity,' he asked, 'so wearisome to you that you feel the need to drop off to sleep?'

'No,' she gasped, 'in fact, your nearness has quite the opposite effect.' She paused, amazed at how forward she was being, yet knowing nothing could stop her from showing him all that was in her heart. 'When I am with you, my breath comes faster, as if I have been running, but any running I have been doing is towards you, my dear, dear Mr Tryphon.'

He seized her hand. 'You do not know how much it means to me to hear you say that,' he whispered. 'I, too, am not myself when I am with you. Or perhaps I should say, I am more fully myself only in your presence. I love you, Caroline, I have since the day we met, and I cannot hide from you any longer.'

'I love you too,' she said, and had to look down from the sudden blaze in his eyes.

'My darling,' he cried, and touched her lips with his.

Caroline had never imagined there could be a sensation this exquisite, and she parted her lips to gasp. At her tiny movement, he deepened the kiss, but so tenderly, she hardly realised it when her mouth opened to his.

Just when she thought she would faint, her head whirling, her body seemingly about to catch fire, he pulled back, leaving her breathless.

'My dear,' he said, pulling away, and she almost cried out at the sudden loss. He moved to his knees and rested one forearm on her lap, holding her hand in both of his. 'Will you do me the great honour of becoming my wife?'

She smiled, knowing that never before in her entire life had she been this happy. 'I will.' She hoped he would rise then, and kiss her again, this time taking her in his arms, but he remained gazing up at her, his gaze suddenly troubled.

'What is it?' she asked, suddenly afraid. 'Does my acceptance not make you happy?'

'It does,' he said. 'You cannot imagine how much. But as I said earlier, I cannot hide a single thing from you. You love me, and so I must be true to myself, so that I can be true to you.'

She laughed, her happiness pushing away all negative emotions. 'I love every aspect of you, Stephen,' oh, how saying his name out loud was the most beautiful sound in the world, 'and there can be nothing that will change that.'

'I know,' he said. 'A woman as beautiful as you, on the inside as well as the aspect you show the world, could love no less fully. And yet, for my own sake, I must speak.'

'Very well,' she said. 'Speak, if you must. But promise me that when you are finished, you will kiss me again.'

The fire returned to his gaze and standing, he pulled her up and into his arms. It was as wonderful as she'd thought. His body was so warm, his arms hard and yet tender about her. She opened her mouth eagerly this time to his, feeling her head tip back with the force of his passion. Never had she felt so loved, and so safe, as here, with him, pressed close to his breast.

Too soon, he pulled away. 'That is a promise of what shall be yours,' he said, sounding as breathless as she. 'But I must speak or I shall forget myself, and I could never forgive myself for being false to you.'

They sat together on the settee, and he turned to her, his expression serious. 'As I said before, I loved you the moment we met. That was not the plan, although it was not an unwelcome occurrence from my point of view.'

Caroline pulled back a bit, although there was no space. 'I don't understand. Do you mean you did not wish to fall in love at this point in your life? Do you not feel ready to marry?'

'No,' he said fiercely. 'I wanted to marry you from the start. But I would have proposed even if I had not fallen in love.'

A small shiver ran down her spine, but she did not speak.

'If we had not met that time at the theatre, we would have soon met elsewhere. Eleanor cultivated your friendship so as to bring us together.'

'Eleanor?' She knew not what to think or say. 'Why are you telling me such strange things?'

'Oh,' he said, rising to his feet. 'I fear you will hate me. But I must tell you, before we are wed. I could not bear to see the disappointment on your lovely face once we are truly man and wife.'

'I could never be disappointed in you,' she whispered. 'Please, stop speaking, you are frightening me.'

'I must speak,' he cried, anguish in every word. He tugged at his coat's lapels. 'You see these clothes?'

'Yes,' she said, now totally bewildered. 'I have long admired your good taste and sense of fashion.

He laughed, sounding almost angry. 'My sense of fashion! All of my clothing has been purchased for me by Eleanor. It was at her bidding that I met you in the guise of a wealthy young gentleman. She has long been spending the last of her money, and she wished me to wed a wealthy woman so I could share that wealth with her.'

Caroline gasped, and curled into herself around the sudden pain in her heart. 'Why would she think you would give her money, unless—' She paused, the thought too terrible to put into words.

'Yes,' he said bitterly, 'she and I were more than just friends for a long time.' He fell to the floor before her, burying his face in his hands. 'All that stopped once I met you. You must believe me, it's true. From the moment I first saw you, you were all I wanted out of life.'

'Eleanor has betrayed me, made use of what I thought was genuine affection to help improve her own situation.' That thought was so painful she could scarcely draw breath. Quickly she turned to something else, also horrible, but slightly less devastating. 'You are not wealthy, then?'

'Alas, no,' he said, looking up. 'I come from a good merchant family, as I was given to know you do, also. My father was not as successful in business as yours, and so while we are comfortable, we are no more than that.'

'Your estate?' she said faintly.

He hung his head. 'There is none. But surely, Caroline, dear Caroline, if we are together, we shall be happy. Is that not true?'

'I had thought so,' she said slowly.

He knelt up and wrapped his arms around her waist, laying his head in her lap. Against her conscious will, her fingers twined into his hair, the other hand caressing his shoulder. 'You have enough money for both of us,' he said, his voice muffled, his breath warming the soft space at the top of her thighs. 'Eleanor will have nothing, I promise you that. Her behaviour has been despicable, and I regret the very day I first took up with her.' He lifted his head then, and looked up at her. Through his eyes, she knew, she could see into his very soul, and all that was there was a true and strong love for her.

'We will live on my fortune?' she asked. 'You will bring no land to the family?'

'No,' he said. 'But surely none of that matters. I love you and you love me. I know you love me, I could tell from your kisses, even if I hadn't known already from everything else you have said and shown me.'

'I do love you,' she cried in despair. 'Oh, Stephen, I do.' She leaned forward and down, this time initiating the kiss herself. 'But,' she said, pulling herself away and rising to her feet, 'I cannot marry you.'

'Do not say that,' he cried, holding out his arms to her.

'I have my responsibilities,' she said, feeling her shoulders square as she spoke, 'to my family. While the Bingley wealth did originate in trade, we have moved well away from that status. A marriage to you will not better our position in society; in fact, it will take us back, closer to our shameful start.'

'But,' he cried, 'your brother is to marry a woman of no fortune and land. I heard the news. Everyone has been speaking of it.'

She closed her eyes for a moment, trying to push away her shame. 'Exactly,' she said. 'That is why I must marry well.'

'Or not at all?' he asked. He rose to his feet, his face shuttered now. 'You would prefer a possible marriage in the future, one that might well bring you no joy even if it did bring land and perhaps a title, over the happiness and passion you know will be yours if you wed me?'

She wrapped her arms about herself, in part to control the trembling that had overcome her, and in part to keep those traitorous arms from reaching out to him. 'I must,' she said. 'Alas, I must.'

She turned away from him, then, and it was the most difficult thing she'd ever done. She turned her back on him and left the room, making her way through the shabby rooms, empty now of their fashionable furniture and beautiful works of art, empty also of the sounds of laughter and gay conversation; but nothing to match the emptiness inside her.

She did not encounter Eleanor as she left the house—the only blessing in the darkness that surrounded her. In a daze, she found herself in the carriage, making her way home.

Home? The house in which she currently resided was Louisa and Mr Hurst's home. And her brother's current home, Netherfield Park, could never be a place where Caroline would feel at home, not with Jane as its mistress.

When she reached the house on Grosvenor Street, she found a letter from her brother, announcing Mr Darcy's engagement to Elizabeth Bennet. The darkness that enveloped her was so thick that this new blow had little effect.

'It does not matter,' she said aloud to the empty house. She lifted her chin and pulled herself to her full height, looking down at the world from over her nose. 'I am Miss Caroline Bingley. I am wealthy and well-educated. I am elegant and accomplished. While I have all these things, I will be at home no matter where I find myself.'

Why, she wondered, when all these things were true, when all these things had brought her the enviable position in society she now held, did she feel so alone? She sank down onto a chair, upholstered in the latest fashion and, uncaring that her shoulders slumped, buried her face in her hands.

* * *

'Miss Bingley requests the honour of your presence . . .'

She paused to read over the words. Were they the right ones? Yes, she decided, they were, and picked up her pen again. '. . . at a ball to celebrate the engagements of Mr Fitzwilliam Darcy to Miss Elizabeth Bennet, and Mr Charles Bingley to Miss Jane Bennett.'

The sound of laughter caught her attention, and she glanced out of the open window to where Charles and Jane, Darcy and Elizabeth, played croquet on Netherfield's grassy lawn. Darcy had his head thrown back, his laugh rising to the sky. Caroline had heard him laugh more during the past weeks than during her entire acquaintance with him before his engagement.

She forced a smile, almost convincing herself that the sight of such joy in people she cared for provided her with, if not happiness, a sense of lightness. Sometimes a woman in her position could not attain the life she sought. Sometimes she had to continue to do what was proper, best for herself and her family.

If joy did not grace her with its presence, she would find contentment in the presence of family and friends. Who knew, perhaps someday a fitting marriage for her would present itself.

She looked again out of the window. Darcy's arms were about Elizabeth as he guided her through a stroke with her mallet. Caroline had not thought her heart could break into even smaller pieces, but each time she saw them thus, the pain inside her rose up anew.

She stood, determined to push these thoughts away. *I must look not to what I do not have, but to what I do. I am fortunate in so very many ways.* She pressed her hands against the burning in her eyes until she was once again in control, the perfectly elegant and accomplished woman.

Seating herself again at the writing desk, she continued the invitations for Netherfield's next ball.